新理念大学英语 710 分四级
备考全攻方略

王新博　陈效新　刘艳芹　杨　芳　主编

东华大学出版社

图书在版编目（CIP）数据

新理念大学英语710分四级备考全攻方略/王新博
等主编.—上海：东华大学出版社，2008.10
ISBN 978-7-81111-447-8

Ⅰ.新... Ⅱ.王... Ⅲ.英语–高等学校–水平考试–习
题 Ⅳ.H310.42

中国版本图书馆CIP数据核字（2008）第150558号

新理念大学英语710分四级备考全攻方略

王新博　陈效新　刘艳芹　杨芳　主编

东华大学出版社出版　　　　　　　上海市延安西路1882号
新华书店上海发行所发行　　　　　苏州望电印刷有限公司印刷
开本：787×1092　1/16　印张：14　字数：470千字
2008年10月第1版　　2008年10月第1次印刷
印数：0 001～6 000 册

ISBN 978-7-81111-447-8/H·193　　　定价：28.00元（含mp3光盘）

编 委 会 名 单

主　审　栾述文　孙秀丽　武学锋

主　编　王新博　陈效新　刘艳芹　杨　芳

副主编　张青华　王　芳　赵　宁　牛力维
　　　　王新福

前　言

大学英语四级考试从其诞生至今已走过了二十多个年头,对推动我国大学英语教学,提高大学英语教学质量,甚至从促进一个学校的软环境建设方面,可谓是功不可没,对教学的贡献是有目共睹的。但随着我国改革开放的深入及市场对外语人才要求的提高,大学英语教学也面临着极大的挑战。在目前形势下,大学英语教学的目的可概括为:培养能力,提高素质,全面发展。与之相伴的大学英语四级考试也应重新定位,更好地发挥其指挥棒的作用,真正成为衡量大学生英语基本技能的一把公平的尺子,而非"沦落"成应试教育的助推器。诚然,有教学就应有检验教学的测试手段。如何设计出效度、信度和区分度都适宜的试题决非是件容易的事。所幸的事,经过多年酝酿,新的大学英语教学改革已经得到了稳步的推进和实施。全面实施新的大学英语教学要求,培养学生的英语综合应用能力,特别是听说能力已经成为新的教学目标和外语界同仁的共同心声。作为检验新教学要求的大学英语四、六级考试也伴随着新教学要求的颁布实施,进入了实质的操作阶段。自2006年12月份大学英语四级新题型的开考,标志着新大学英语四级测试改革经多年的酝酿、试用,已正式投入使用。经过近两年的运行,它对教学改革的推动作用已初见端倪。除了口语暂时因某些客观条件所限,未能大规模实施测试外,旨在提高英语应用能力的其他各类题型已在新四级测试中得以运用,这吻合了我国目前对外改革开放的形势,也体现了社会对大学毕业生外语技能的迫切要求。

根据《全国大学英语四、六级考试改革方案(试行)》,新的全国大学英语四、六级考试由以下四个部分构成:①听力理解;②阅读理解;③完型填空或改错;④写作和翻译。听力理解部分分值比例为35%;其中听力对话15%,听力短文20%。听力对话部分包括短对话和长对话的听力理解;听力短文部分包括选择题型的短文理解和复合式听写。阅读理解部分分值比例为35%;其中仔细阅读部分(Reading in Depth)25%,快速阅读部分(Skimming and Scanning)10%。仔细阅读部分分为:①选择题型的篇章阅读理解;②篇章层次的词汇理解(Banked Cloze)或短句问答(Short Answer Questions)。快速阅读理解部分测试的是浏览阅读和查读能力。完型填空或改错部分分值比例为10%。完型填空部分采用多项选择题型,改错部分的要求是辨认错误并改正。写作和翻译部分分值比例为20%;其中写作部分(Writing)15%,翻译部分(Translation)5%。写作的体裁包括议论文、说明文、应用文。在成绩报道上,新四级测试改革了以百分制的报道方式,改为总分710分。学生成绩的报道共由四个部分组成,即:听力249分,阅读249分,完型填空或改错70分,作文与翻译142分。

看得出来,新大学英语四级测试大大加大了对听力的检测力度,把听力和阅读放在了同等重要的位置上。这也恰恰吻合了新的大学英语教学要求。我们有理由相信,这一考试改革的意义将伴随着大学英语教学改革的不断深入而更加凸现和明确,因为检验学生综合应用语言的能力应成为新大学英语四级考试的最终目标和归宿。

本书在前期第一版的基础上,结合新四级测试的形势发展,进行了大规模的修订、补充和完善。因而,和第一版相比,该书内容更加翔实丰富,是全新指导大学英语新四级的必备"考典"。本书共分三章,第一章全面收录了截止目前已经考过的新四级测试真题五套。第二章编写了"高保真"仿真模拟试题五套作为考前冲刺演练和预测。所有考题均严格按照教学大纲,以考核实际语言应用能力为目标进行设计,以期能在短期内,快速掌握新四级题型,熟悉各题型的解题方法,从而达到提高技能、培养能力的目的。第三章是对新四级各单项进行考前强化训练和实战演练。本书内容翔实,资料新颖,是我们多年教学和对测试探索的结晶。该书在第一版使用时,曾获得良好的口碑。我们有理由相信,经过这次全面升级修订,它还会成为全程指导新四级的一部力作。考试不是大学英语教学的最终目的(end),只是检测学习效果的手段(means)。我们期盼,通过本书的考前强化训练,读者可以真实地检测到自己的语言水平和有待提高之处,并通过本书的"细嚼慢咽",启迪心智,从而达到提高英语技能的目的。

本书的编著者们都是多年从事大学英语教学工作,具有丰富教学经验,且教学效果优良的一线教师。他们最了解学生的苦衷和语言学习中的困难和障碍,因而使该书更具有针对性。全书由王新博主持策划和编写,王新博、陈效新、刘艳芹、杨芳担任主编,副主编有张青华、王芳、赵宁、牛力维、王新福。本书在成书的过程中还得到了中国石油大学(华东)大学英语一系全体教师的大力支持和帮助,他们在使用过程中提出了许多中肯的建议。

本书在成书的过程还参阅了大量的国内外公开出版的各类教学资料,在此我们无法一一列出,谨向这些书的作者们一并表示衷心的感谢。

由于我们学识水平有限,编写工作浩繁,难免挂一漏万,出现疏漏,敬请广大读者及外语界同仁批评指正。

编　者

目　录

第一章 全真试题篇

本章收录了自 2006 年 6 月新四级试考以来迄今已用过的国家新四级全真试卷共 5 套(截至到 2008 年 6 月),旨在帮助考生了解国家新四级的考试题型、难易度及考试动向等,是全方位了解新四级最权威的资料来源。试做全真试卷可以帮助考生全面衡量自己的应试能力,把握各部分的时间分配,知己知彼,为复习备考提供最有效的依据。建议考生"化整为零",先试做某一套,然后总结得失,找出差距,复习一段时间后,再做下一套,作为检测自己复习效果的手段。

2006 年 6 月全国大学英语四级考试试卷

Part I Writing(30 minutes)

注意:此部分试题在答题卡 1 上作答。

Directions: *For this part, you are allowed 30 minutes to write a short essay on the topic of students selecting their lectures. You should write at least 120 words following the outline given below:*

1. 有些大学允许学生自由选择某些课程的任课教师
2. 学生选择教师时所考虑的主要因素
3. 学生自选任课教师的益处和可能产生的问题

On Students Selecting Lecturers

Part II Reading Comprehension(Skimming and Scanning)(15 minutes)

Directions: *In this part, you will have 15 minutes to go over the passage quickly and answer the questions on Answer Sheet 1.*

For questions 1-7, mark

Y(*for YES*)　　　　　*if the statement agrees with the information given in the passage;*

N(*for NO*)　　　　　*if the statement contradicts the information given in the passage;*

NG(*for NOT GIVEN*)*if the information is not given in the passage.*

For question 8-10, complete the sentences with the information given in the passage.

Highway

Early in the 20th century, most of the streets and roads in the U. S. were made of dirt, brick, and cedar wood blocks. Built for horse, carriage, and foot traffic, they were usually poorly cared for and too narrow to *accommodate*(容纳) automobiles.

With the increase in auto production, private *turnpike*(收费公路) companies under local authorities began to spring up, and by 1921 there were 387,000 miles of paved roads. Many were built using specifications of 19th century Scottish engineers Thomas Telford and John MacAdam (for whom the macadam surface is named), whose specifications stressed the importance of adequate drainage. Beyond that, there were no national standards for size, weight restrictions, or commercial signs. During World War I. roads throughout the country were nearly destroyed by the weight of trucks. When General Eisenhower returned from Germany in 1919, after serving in the U. S. Army's first transcontinental motor convoy (车队), he noted: "The old convoy had started me thinking about good, two-lane highways, but Germany's Autobahn or motorway had made me see the wisdom of broader ribbons across the land."

It would take another war before the federal government would act on a national highway system. During World War II, a tremendous increase in trucks and new roads were required. The war demonstrated how critical highways were to the defense effort. Thirteen percent of defense plants received all their supplies by truck and almost all other plants shipped more than half of their products by vehicle. The war also revealed that local control of highways had led to a confusing variety of design standards. Even federal and state highways did not follow basic standards. Some states allowed trucks up to 36,000 pounds, while others restricted anything over 7,000 pounds. A government study recommended a national highway system of 33,920 miles, and Congress passed the Federal-Aid Highway Act of 1944, which called for strict, centrally controlled design criteria.

The interstate highway system was finally launched in 1956 and has been hailed as one of the greatest public works projects of the century. To build its 44,000-mile web of highways, bridges and tunnels, hundreds of unique engineering designs and solutions had to be worked out. Consider the many geographic features of the country: mountains, steep grades, wetlands, rivers, deserts and plains. Variables included the slope of the land, the ability of the pavement to support the load, the intensity of road use, and the nature of the underlying soil. Urban areas were another problem. Innovative designs of roadways, tunnels, bridges, overpasses, and interchanges that could run through or bypass urban areas soon began to weave their way across the country, forever altering the face of America.

Long-span, segmented-concrete, cable-stayed bridges such as Hale Boggs in Louisiana and the Sunshine Skyway in Florida, and remarkable tunnels like Fort McHenry in Maryland and Mt. Baker in Washington, met many of the nation's physical challenges. Traffic control systems and methods of construction developed under the interstate program soon influenced highway construction around the world, and were invaluable in improving the condition of urban streets and traffic patterns.

Today, the interstate system links every major city in the U. S., and the U. S. with Canada and Mexico. Built with safety in mind the highways have wide lanes and shoulders, dividing medians, or barriers, long entry and exit lanes, curves engineered for safe turns, and limited access. The death rate on highways is half that of all other U. S. roads (0. 86 deaths per 100 million passenger miles compared to 1. 99 deaths per 100 million on all other roads)

By opening the North American continent, highways have enabled consumer goods and services to reach people in remote and rural areas of the country, spurred the growth of suburbs, and provided people with greater options in terms of jobs, access to cultural programs, health care, and other benefits. Above all, the interstate system provides individuals with what they cherish most: personal freedom of mobility.

The interstate system has been an essential element of the nation's economic growth in terms of shipping and job creation: more than 75 percent of the nation's freight deliveries arrive by truck; and most products that arrive by rail or air use interstates for the last leg of the journey by vehicle. Not only has the highway system affected the American economy by providing shipping routes, it has led to the growth of spin-off industries like service stations, motels, restaurants, and shopping centres. It has allowed the relocation of manufacturing plants and other industries from urban areas to rural.

By the end of the century there was an immense network of paved roads, residential streets, expressways, and freeways built to support millions of vehicles. The highway system was officially renamed for Eisenhower to honor his vision and leadership. The year construction began he said: "Together, the united forces of our communication and transportation systems are dynamic elements in the very name we bear-United States. Without them, we would be a mere alliance of many separate parts."

注意:此部分试题请在答题卡 1 上作答。

1. National standards for paved roads were in place by 1921.

2. General Eisenhower felt that the broad German motorways made more sense than the two-lane highways of America.

3. It was in the 1950s that the American government finally took action to build a national highway system.

4. Many of the problems presented by the country's geographical features found solutions in innovative engineering projects.

5. In spite of safety considerations, the death rate on interstate highways is still higher than that of other American roads.

6. The interstate highway system provides access between major military installations in America.

7. Services stations, motels and restaurants promoted the development of the interstate highway system.

8. The greatest benefit brought about by the interstate system was _____.

9. Trucks using the interstate highways deliver more than _____.

10. The interstate system was renamed after Eisenhower in recognition of _____.

Part III *Listening comprehension* (*35 minutes*)

ection A

Directions: *In this section, you will hear 8 short conversations and 2 long conversations. At the end of each conversation, one or more questions will be asked about what was said. Both the conversation and the questions will be spoken only once. After each question there will be a pause. During the pause, you must read the four choices marked A), B), C) and D), and decide which is the best answer. Then mark the corresponding letter on **Answer Sheet 2** with a single line through the center.*

注意:此部分试题请在答题卡 2 上作答。

11. A) The girls got on well with each other.
    B) It's understandable that girls don't get along.
    C) She was angry with the other young stars.
    D) The girls lacked the courage to fight.

12. A) The woman does her own housework.
    B) The woman needs a housekeeper.
    C) The woman's house is in a mess.
    D) The woman works as a housekeeper.

13. A) The Edwards are quite well-off.
    B) The Edwards should cut down on their living expenses.
    C) It'll be unwise for the Edwards to buy another house.
    D) It's too expensive for the Edwards to live in their present house.

14. A) The woman didn't expect it to be so warm at noon.
    B) The woman is sensitive to weather changes.
    C) The weather forecast was unreliable
    D) The weather turned cold all of a sudden.

15. A) At a clinic.
    B) At a restaurant.

C) In a supermarket.   D) In an ice cream shop.

16. A) The woman did not feel any danger growing up in the Bronx.

     B) The man thinks it was quite safe living in the Bronx district.

     C) The woman started working at an early age to support her family.

     D) The man doesn't think it safe to send an 8-year-old to buy things.

17. A) The man has never seen the woman before.   B) The two speakers work for the same company.

     C) The two speakers work on the same floor.   D) The woman is interested in market research.

18. A) The woman can't tolerate any noise.   B) The man is looking for an apartment.

     C) The man has missed his appointment.   D) The woman is going to take a train trip.

Questions 19 to 21 are based on the conversation you have just heard.

19. A) To make a business report to the woman.

     B) To be interviewed for a job in the woman's company.

     C) To resign from his position in the woman's company.

     D) To exchange stock market information with the woman.

20. A) He is head of a small trading company.

     B) He works in an international insurance company.

     C) He leads a team of brokers in a big company.

     D) He is a public relations officer in a small company.

21. A) The woman thinks Mr. Saunders is asking for more than they can offer.

     B) Mr. Saunders will share one third of the woman's responsibilities.

     C) Mr. Saunders believes that he deserves more paid vacations.

     D) The woman seems to be satisfied with Mr. Saunders' past experience.

Questions 22 to 25 are based on the conversation you have just heard.

22. A) She's worried about the seminar.   B) The man keeps interrupting her.

     C) She finds it too hard.   D) She lacks interest in it.

23. A) The lecturers are boring.   B) The course is poorly designed.

     C) She prefers Philosophy to English.   D) She enjoys literature more.

24. A) Karen's friend.   B) Karen's parents.

     C) Karen's lecturers.   D) Karen herself.

25. A) Changing her major.

     B) Spending less of her parents' money.

     C) Getting transferred to the English Department.

     D) Leaving the university.

Section B

Directions: *In this section, you will hear 3 short passages. At the end of each passage, you will hear some questions. Both the passage and the questions will be spoken only once. After you hear a question, you must choose the best answer from the four choices marked A), B), C) and D). Then mark the corresponding letter on the **Answer Sheet 2** with a single line through the center.*

注意：此部分试题请在答题卡 2 上作答。

Passage One

Questions 26 to 29 are based on the passage you have just heard.

26. A) Rent a grave.   B) Burn the body.

     C) Bury the dead near a church.   D) Buy a piece of land for a grave.

27. A) To solve the problem of lack of land.   B) To see whether they have decayed.

C) To follow the Greek religious practice.   D) To move them to a multi-storey graveyard.

28. A) They should be buried lying down.

     B) They should be buried standing up.

     C) They should be buried after being washed.

     D) They should be buried when partially decayed.

29. A) Burning dead bodies to ashes.   B) Storing dead bodies in a remote place.

     C) Placing dead bodies in a bone room.   D) Digging up dead bodies after three years.

Passage Two

Questions 30 to 32 are based on the passage you have just heard.

30. A) Many foreign tourists visit the Unite States every year.

     B) Americans enjoy eating out with their friends.

     C) The United States is a country of immigrants.

     D) Americans prefer foreign foods to their own food.

31. A) They can make friends with people from other countries.

     B) They can get to know people of other cultures and their lifestyles.

     C) They can practise speaking foreign languages there.

     D) They can meet with businessmen from all over the world.

32. A) The couple cook the dishes and the children help them.

     B) The husband does the cooking and the wife serves as the address.

     C) The mother does the cooking while the father and children wait on the guests.

     D) A hired cook prepares the dishes and the family members serve the guests.

Passage Three

Questions 33 to 35 are based on the passage you have just heard.

33. A) He took them to watch a basketball game.

     B) He trained them to play European football.

     C) He let them compete in getting balls out of a basket.

     D) He taught them to play an exciting new game.

34. A) The players found the basket too high to reach.

     B) The players had trouble getting the ball out of the basket.

     C) The players had difficulty understanding the complex rules.

     D) The players soon found the game boring.

35. A) By removing the bottom of the basket.   B) By lowering the position of the basket.

     C) By simplifying the complex rules.   D) By altering the size of the basket.

Section C   Compound Dictation

Directions: *In this section, you will hear a passage three times. When the passage is read for the first time, you should listen carefully for its general idea. When the passage is read for the second time, you are required to fill in the blanks numbered from 36 to 43 with the exact words you have just heard. For blanks numbered from 44 to 46 you are required to fill in the missing information. For these blanks, you can either use the exact words you have just heard or write down the main points in your own words. Finally, when the passage is read for the third time, you should check what you have written.*

注意:此部分试题在答题卡 2 上;请在答题卡 2 上作答。

     For Americans, time is money. They say, "You only get so much time in this life; you'd better use it wisely." The (36)_____ will not be better than the past or present, as Americans are

(37) _____ to see things, unless people use their time for constructive activities. Thus, Americans (38) _____ a "well-organized" person, one has a written list of things to do and a (39) _____ for doing them. The ideal person is punctual and is (40) _____ of other people's time. They do not (41) _____ people's time with conversation or other activity that has no (42) _____, beneficial outcome.

The American attitude toward time is not (43) _____ shared by others, especially non-Europeans. They are more likely to regard time as (44) _____. One of the more difficult things many students must adjust to in the states is the notion that time must be saved whenever possible and used wisely every day. In this context (45) _____. McDonald's, KFC, and other fast food establishments are successful in a country where many people want to spend the least amount of time preparing and eating meals. As McDonald's restaurants (46) _____, bringing not just hamburgers but an emphasis on speed, efficiency, and shiny cleanliness.

Part IV *Reading Comprehension* (*reading in depth*)(*25 minutes*)

Section A

Direction: *In this section, there is a passage with ten blanks. You are required to select one word for each blank from a list of choices given in a word bank following the passage. Read the passage through carefully before making your choices. Each choice in bank is identified by a letter. Please mark the corresponding letter for each item on **Answer Sheet 2** with a single line through the center. **You may not use any of the words in the bank more than once.***

Questions 47 to 56 are based on the following passage.

EI Nino is the name given to the mysterious and often unpredictable change in the climate of the world. This strange __47__ happens every five to eight years. It starts in the Pacific Ocean and is thought to be caused by a failure in the *trade winds*(信风), which affects the ocean currents driven by these winds. As the trade winds lessen in __48__, the ocean temperatures rise, causing the Peru current flowing in from the east to warm up by as much as 5℃.

The warming of the ocean has far-reaching effects. The hot, *humid*(潮湿的) air over the ocean causes severe __49__ thunderstorms. The rainfall is increased across South America, __50__ floods to Peru. In the West Pacific, there are droughts affecting Australia and Indonesia. So while some parts of the world prepare for heavy rains and floods, other parts face drought, poor crops and __51__.

EI Nino usually lasts for about 18 months. The 1982-83 EI Nino brought the most __52__ weather in modern history. Its effect was worldwide and it left more than 2,000 people dead and caused over eight billion pounds __53__ of damage. The 1990 EI Nino lasted until June 1995. scientists __54__ this to be the longest EI Nino for 2,000 years.

Nowadays, weather experts are able to forecast when an EI Nino will __55__, but they are still not __56__ sure what leads to it or what affects how strong it will be.

注意：此部分试题请在答题卡 2 上作答。

A) estimate	B) strength	C) deliberately	D) notify
E) tropical	F) phenomenon	G) stable	H) attraction
I) completely	J) destructive	K) starvation	L) bringing
M) exhaustion	N) worth	O) strike	

ection B

Directions: *There are 2 passages in this section. Each passage is followed by some questions or unfinished statements. For each of them there are four choices marked A), B), C) and D). You should decide on the best choice and mark the corresponding letter on **Answer sheet 2** with a single line through the center.*

Passage One

Questions 57 to 61 are based on the following passage.

Communications technologies are far from equal when it comes to conveying the truth. The first study to compare honesty across a range of communications media has found that people are twice as likely to tell lies in phone conversations as they are in emails. The fact that emails are automatically recorded and can come back to *haunt*（困扰）you appears to be the key to the finding.

Jeff Hancock of Cornell University in Ithaca, New York, asked 30 students to keep a communications diary for a week. In it they noted the number of conversations or email exchanges they had lasting more than 10 minutes, and confessed to how many lies they told. Hancock then worked out the number of lies per conversation for each medium. He found that lies made up 14 per cent of emails, 21 per cent of instant messages, 27 per cent of face-to-face interactions and an astonishing 37 per cent of phone calls.

His results to be presented at the conference on human-computer interaction in Vienna, Austria, in April, have surprised psychologists. Some expected emailers to be the biggest liars reasoning that because deception makes people uncomfortable, the *detachment*（非直接接触）of emailing would make it easier to lie. Others expected people to lie more in face-to-face exchanges because we are most practiced at that form of communication.

But Hancock says it is also crucial whether a conversation is being recorded and could be reread, and whether it occurs in real time. People appear to be afraid to lie when they know the communication could later be used to hold them to account, he says. This is why fewer lies appear in email than on the phone.

People are also more likely to lie in real time—in an instant message or phone call, say—than if they have time to think of a response, says Hancock. He found many lies are *spontaneous*（脱口而出）responses to an unexpected demand, such as: "Do you like my dress?"

Hancock hopes his research will help companies work out the best ways for their employees to communicate. For instance, the phone might be the best medium foe sales where employees are encouraged to stretch the truth. But given his result, work assessment, where honesty is a priority, might be best done using email.

注意:此部分试题请在答题卡 2 上作答。

57. Hancock's study focuses on _____.

    A) the consequences of lying in various communications media

    B) the success of communications technologies in conveying ideas

    C) people's preferences in selecting communications technologies

    D) people 's honesty levels across a range of communications media

58. Hancock's research finding surprised those who believed that _____.

    A) people are less likely to lie in instant messages

    B) people are unlikely to lie in face-to-face interactions

    C) people are most likely to lie in email communication

    D) People are twice as likely to lie in phone conversations

59. According to the passage, why are people more likely to tell the truth through certain media of communication?

    A) They are afraid of leaving behind traces of their lies.

    B) They believe that honesty is the best policy.

    C) They tend to be relaxed when using those media.

    D) They are most practiced at those forms of communication.

60. According to Hancock, the telephone is a preferable medium for promoting sales because _____.

    A) salesmen can talk directly to their customers

    B) salesmen may feel less restrained to exaggerate

    C) salesmen can impress customers as being trustworthy

    D) salesmen may pass on instant messages effectively

61. It can be inferred from the passage that _____.

    A) honesty should be encouraged in interpersonal communications

    B) more employers will use emails to communicate with their employees

    C) suitable media should be chosen for different communication purposes

    D) email is now the dominant medium of communication within a company

Passage Two

Questions 62 to 66 are based on the following passage.

In a country that defines itself by ideals, not by shared blood, who should be allowed to come work and live here? In the wake of the Sept. 11 attacks these questions have never seemed more pressing.

On December 11, 2001, as part of the effort to increase homeland security, federal and local authorities in 14 states staged "Operation Safe Travel" — raids on airports to arrest employees with false *identification*(身份证明). In Salt Lake City there were 69 arrests. But those captured were anything but terrorists, most of them illegal immigrants from Central or South America. Authorities said the undocumented worker's illegal status made them open to *blackmail*(讹诈) by terrorists.

Many immigrants in Salt Lake City were angered by the arrests and said they felt as if they were being treated like disposable goods.

Mayor Anderson said those feelings were justified to a certain extent. "We're saying we want you to work in these places, we're going to look the other way in terms of what our laws are, and then when it's convenient for us, or when we can try to make a point in terms of national security, especially after Sept. 11, then you're disposable. There are whole families being uprooted for all of the wrong reasons," Anderson said.

If Sept. 11 had never happened the airport workers would not have been arrested and could have gone on quietly living in America, probably indefinitely. Ana Castro, a manager at a Ben & Jerry's ice cream shop at the airport, had been working 10 years with the same false Social Security card when she was arrested in the December airport raid. Now she and her family are living under the threat of *deportation*(驱逐出境). Castro's case is currently waiting to be settled. While she awaits the outcome, the government has granted her permission to work here and she has returned to her job at Ben & Jerry's.

62. According to the author, the United States claims to be a nation _____.

    A) composed of people having different values

    B) encouraging individual pursuits

    C) sharing common interests

    D) founded on shared ideals

63. How did the immigrants in Salt Lake City feel about "Operation Safe Travel"?

A) Guilty.　　　　　B) Offended.　　　　　C) Disappointed.　　　　D) Discouraged.

64. Undocumented workers became the target of "Operation Safe Travel" because _____ .

A) evidence was found that they were potential terrorists

B) most of them worked at airports under threat of terrorist attacks

C) terrorists might take advantage of their illegal status

D) they were reportedly helping hide terrorists around the airport

65. By saying ". . . we're going to look the other way in terms of what our laws are" (Line 2，Para. 4)，Mayor Anderson means "_____ ".

A) we will turn a blind eye to your illegal status

B) we will examine the laws in a different way

C) there are other ways of enforcing the law

D) the existing laws must not be ignored

66. What do we learn about Ana Castro from the last paragraph?

A) She will be deported sooner or later.　　　　B) She is allowed to stay permanently.

C) Her case has been dropped.　　　　D) Her fate remains uncertain.

Part V Cloze （15 minutes）

Directions：There are 20 blanks in the following passage. For each blank there are four choices marked A），B），C）and D）on the right side of the paper. You should choose the ONE that best fits into the passage. Then mark the corresponding letter on **Answer Sheet 2** with a single line through the center.

注意：此部分试题请在答题卡 2 上作答。

Do you wake up every day feeling too tired, or even upset? If so, then a new alarm clock could be just for you.

The clock, called SleepSmart, measures your sleep cycle, and waits 67 you to be in your lightest phase of sleep 68 rousing you. Its makers say that should 69 you wake up feeling refreshed every morning.

As you sleep you pass 70 a sequence of sleep states—light sleep, deep sleep and REM (rapid eye movement) sleep—that 71 approximately every 90 minutes. The point in that cycle at which you wake can 72 how you feel later, and may 73 have a greater impact than how much or little you have slept, Being roused during a light phase 74 you are more likely to wake up energetic.

SleepSmart 75 the distinct pattern of brain waves 76 during each phase of sleep, via a headband equipped 77 electrodes （电极）and a microprocessor. This measures the electrical activity of the wearer's brain, in much the 78 way as some machines used for medical and research

67. A) besides　　B) near　　C) for　　D) around

68. A) upon　　　　　　B) before
    C) towards　　　　　D) till

69. A) ensure　　　　　B) assure
    C) require　　　　　D) request

70. A) through　B) into　C) about　D) on

71. A) reveals　　　　　B) reverses
    C) resumes　　　　　D) repeats

72. A) effect　　　　　B) affect
    C) reflect　　　　　D) perfect

73. A) already　　　　　B) every
    C) never　　　　　D) even

74. A) means　　　　　B) marks
    C) says　　　　　D) dictates

75. A) removes　　　　B) relieves
    C) records　　　　D) recalls

76. A) proceeded　　　B) produced
    C) pronounced　　　D) progressed

77. A) by　　B) of　　C) with　　D) over

78. A) familiar　　　　B) similar
    C) identical　　　　D) same

79. A) findings　　　　B) prospects

and communicates wirelessly with a clock unit near the bed. You ___80___ the clock with the latest time at ___81___ you want to be wakened, and it ___82___ *duly* (适时地) wakes you during the last night sleep phase before that.

The ___83___ was invented by a group of students at Brown University in Rhode Island ___84___ a friend complained of waking up tired and performing poorly on a test. " ___85___ sleep-deprived people ourselves, we started thinking of ___86___ to do about it," says Eric Shashoua, a recent college graduate and now chief executive officer of Axon Sleep Research Laboratories, a company created by the students to develop their idea.

C) proposals   D) proposes

80. A) prompt   B) program
    C) plug   D) plan
81. A) where   B) this   C) which   D) that
82. A) then   B) also   C) almost   D) yet
83. A) claim   B) conclusion
    C) concept   D) explanation
84. A) once   B) after   C) since   D) while
85. A) Besides   B) Despite
    C) To   D) As
86. A) what   B) how
    C) whether   D) when

Part Ⅵ *Translation* (*5 minutes*)

Directions: *Complete the sentences on* **Answer Sheet 2** *by translating into English the Chinese given in brackets.*

注意:此部分试题请在答题卡 **2** 上作答,只需写出译文部分。

87. Having spent some time in the city, he had no trouble _____ (找到去历史博物馆的路).

88. _____ (为了挣钱供我上学),Mother often takes on more work than is good for her.

89. The professor required that _____ (我们交研究报告) by Wednesday.

90. The more you explain, _____ (我愈糊涂).

91. Though a skilled worker, _____ (他被公司解雇了) last week because of the economic crisis.

2006 年 12 月全国大学英语四级考试试卷

Part Ⅰ *Writing*（*30 minutes*）

注意：此部分试题在答题卡 1 上作答。

Directions：*For this part，you are allowed 30 minutes to write **Spring Festival Gala on CCTV** according to the outline given below．You should write at least 120 words following the outline given below in Chinese．*

1. 许多人喜欢在除夕夜观看春节联欢晚会
2. 但有些人提出取消春节联欢晚会
3. 在我看来……

Spring Festival Gala on CCTV

Part Ⅱ *Reading Comprehension*（*Skimming and Scanning*）（*15 minutes*）

Six Secrets of High-Energy People

There's an energy crisis in America，and it has nothing to do with fossil fuels. Millions of us get up each morning already weary over what the day holds. "I just can't get started." people say. But it's not physical energy that most of us lack. Sure，we could all use extra sleep and a better diet. But in truth，people are healthier today than at any time in history. I can almost guarantee that if you long for more energy，the problem is not with your body.

What you're seeking is not physical energy. It's emotional energy. Yet，sad to say，life sometimes seems designed to exhaust our supply. We work too hard. We have family obligations. We encounter emergencies and personal crises. No wonder so many of us suffer from emotional fatigue，a kind of utter exhaustion of the spirit.

And yet we all know people who are filled with joy，despite the unpleasant circumstances of their lives. Even as a child I observed people who were poor，or disabled，or ill，but who nonetheless faced life with optimism and vigor. Consider Laura Hillenbrand，who despite an extremely weak body wrote the best-seller *Seabiscuit*. Hillenbrand barely had enough physical energy to drag herself out of bed to write. But she was fueled by having a story she wanted to share. It was emotional energy that helped her succeed.

Unlike physical energy，which is finite and diminishes with age，emotional energy is unlimited and has nothing to do with genes or upbringing. So how do you get it? You can't simply tell yourself to be positive. You must take action. Here are six practical strategies that work.

1. Do something new.

Very little that's new occurs in our lives. The impact of this sameness on our emotional energy is gradual，but huge：It's like a tire with a slow leak. You don't notice it at first，but eventually you'll get a flat. It's up to you to plug the leak—even though there are always a dozen reasons to stay stuck in your dull routines of life. That's where Maura，36，a waitress，found herself a year ago.

Fortunately, Maura had a lifeline — a group of women friends who meet regularly to discuss their lives. Their lively discussions spurred Maura to make small but nevertheless life-altering changes. She joined a gym in the next town. She changed her look with a short haircut and new black T-shirts. Eventually, Maura gathered the courage to quit her job and start her own business.

Here's a challenge: If it's something you wouldn't ordinarily do, do it. Try a dish you've never eaten. Listen to music you'd ordinarily tune out. You'll discover these small things add to your emotional energy.

2. Reclaim life's meaning.

So many of my patients tell me that their lives used to have meaning, but that somewhere along the line things went stale.

The first step in solving this meaning shortage is to figure out what you really care about, and then do something about it. A case in point is Ivy, 57, a pioneer in investment banking. "I mistakenly believed that all the money I made would mean something," she says. "But I feel lost, like a 22-year-old wondering what to do with her life." Ivy's solution? She started a program that shows Wall Streeters how to donate time and money to poor children. In the process, Ivy filled her life with meaning.

3. Put yourself in the fun zone.

Most of us grown-ups are seriously fun-deprived. High-energy people have the same day-to-day work as the rest of us, but they manage to find something enjoyable in every situation. A real estate broker I know keeps herself amused on the job by mentally redecorating the houses she shows to clients. "I love imagining what even the most run-down house could look like with a little tender loving care," she says. "It's a challenge — and the least desirable properties are usually the most fun."

We all define fun differently, of course, but I can guarantee this: If you put just a bit of it into your day, you energy will increase quickly.

4. Bid farewell to guilt and regret.

Everyone's past is filled with regrets that still cause pain. But from an emotional energy point of view, they are dead weights that keep us from moving forward. While they can't merely be willed away, I do recommend you remind yourself that whatever happened is in the past, and nothing can change that. Holding on to the memory only allows the damage to continue into the present.

5. Make up your mind.

Say you've been thinking about cutting your hair short. Will it look stylish — or too extreme? You endlessly think it over. Having the decision hanging over your head is a huge energy drain. Every time you can't decide, you burden yourself with alternatives. Quit thinking that you have to make the right decision; instead, make a choice and don't look back.

6. Give to get.

Emotional energy has a kind of magical quality; the more you give, the more you get back. This is the difference between emotional and physical energy. With the latter, you have to get it to be able to give it. With the former, however, you get it by giving it.

Start by asking everyone you meet, "How are you?" as if you really want to know, then listen to the reply. Be the one who hears. Most of us also need to smile more often. If you don't smile at the person you love first thing in the morning, you're sucking energy out of your relationship. Finally, help another person — and make the help real, concrete. Give a massage(按摩) to someone you love, or cook her dinner, Then, expand the circle to work. Try asking yourself what you'd do if your goal were to be helpful rather than efficient.

After all, if it's true that what goes around comes around, why not make sure that what's circulating around you is the good stuff?

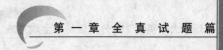

1. The energy crisis in America discussed here mainly refers to a shortage of fossil fuels.

2. People these days tend to lack physical energy.

3. Laura Hillenbrand is an example cited to show how emotional energy can contribute to one's success in life.

4. The author believes emotional energy is inherited and genetically determined.

5. Even small changes people make in their lives can help increase their emotional energy.

6. Ivy filled her life with meaning by launching a program to help poor children.

7. The real-estate broker the author knows is talented in home redecoration.

8. People holding on to sad memories of the past will find it difficult to _____.

9. When it comes to decision-making. One should make a quick choice without _____.

10. Emotional energy is in a way different from physical energy in that the more you give, _____.

Part III *Listing Comprehension* (*35 minutes*)

ection A

11. A) Plan his budget carefully. B) Give her more information.
    C) Ask someone else for advice. D) Buy a gift for his girlfriend.

12. A) She'll have some chocolate cake. B) She'll take a look at the menu.
    C) She'll go without dessert. D) She'll prepare the dinner.

13. A) The man can speak a foreign language.
    B) The woman hopes to improve her English.
    C) The woman knows many different languages.
    D) The man wishes to visit many more countries.

14. A) Go to the library. B) Meet the woman.
    C) See Professor Smith. D) Have a drink in the bar.

15. A) She isn't sure when Professor Bloom will be back.
    B) The man shouldn't be late for his class.
    C) The man can come back sometime later.
    D) She can pass on the message for the man.

16. A) He has a strange personality. B) He's got emotional problems.
    C) His illness is beyond cure. D) His behavior is hard to explain.

17. A) The tickets are more expensive than expected.
    B) The tickets are sold in advance at half price.
    C) It's difficult to buy the tickets on the spot.
    D) It's better to buy the tickets beforehand.

18. A) He turned suddenly and ran into a tree.
    B) He was hit by a fallen box from a truck.
    C) He drove too fast and crashed into a truck.
    D) He was trying to overtake the truck ahead of him.

Questions 19 to 21 are based on the conversation you have just heard.

19. A) To go boating on the St. Lawrence River. B) To go sightseeing in Quebec Province.
    C) To call on a friend in Quebec City. D) To attend a wedding in Montreal.

20. A) Study the map of Quebec Province. B) Find more about Quebec Province.
    C) Brush up on her French. D) Learn more about the local customs.

21. A) It's most beautiful in summer.

B) It has many historical buildings.

C) It was greatly expanded in the 18th century.

D) It's the only French-speaking city in Canada.

Questions 22 to 25 are based on the conversation you have just heard.

22. A) It was about a little animal.   B) It took her six years to write.

   C) It was adapted from a fairy tale.   D) It was about a little girl and her pet.

23. A) She knows how to write best-selling novels.

   B) She can earn a lot of money by writing for adults.

   C) She is able to win enough support from publishers.

   D) She can make a living by doing what she likes.

24. A) The characters.   B) Her ideas.   C) The readers.   D) Her life experiences.

25. A) She doesn't really know where they originated.

   B) She mainly drew on stories of ancient saints.

   C) They popped out of her childhood dreams.

   D) They grew out of her long hours of thinking.

Section B

Passage One

Questions 26 to 28 are based on the passage you have just heard.

26. A) Monitor students' sleep patterns.

   B) Help students concentrate in class.

   C) Record students' weekly performance.

   D) Ask students to complete a sleep report.

27. A) Declining health.   B) Lack of attention.

   C) Loss of motivation.   D) Improper behavior.

28. A) They should make sure their children are always punctual for school.

   B) They should ensure their children grow up in a healthy environment.

   C) They should help their children accomplish high-quality work.

   D) They should see to it that their children have adequate sleep.

Passage Two

Questions 29 to 32 are based on the passage you have just heard.

29. A) She stopped being a homemaker.   B) She became a famous educator.

   C) She became a public figure.   D) She quit driving altogether.

30. A) A motorist's speeding.   B) Her running a stop sign.

   C) Her lack of driving experience.   D) A motorist's failure to concentrate.

31. A) Nervous and unsure of herself.   B) Calm and confident of herself.

   C) Courageous and forceful.   D) Distracted and reluctant.

32. A) More strict training of women drivers.

   B) Restrictions on cell phone use while driving.

   C) Improved traffic conditions in cities.

   D) New regulations to ensure children's safety.

Passage Three

Questions 33 to 35 are based on the passage you have just heard.

33. A) They haven't devoted as much energy to medicine as to space travel.

   B) Three are too many kinds of cold viruses for them to identify.

C) It is not economical to find a cure for each type of cold.

D) They believe people can recover without treatment.

34. A) They reveal the seriousness of the problem.

B) They indicate how fast the virus spreads.

C) They tell us what kind of medicine to take.

D) They show our body is fighting the virus.

35. A) It actually does more harm than good.

B) It causes damage to some organs of our body.

C) It works better when combined with other remedies.

D) It helps us to recover much sooner.

ection C   Compound Dictation

注意:此部分试题在答题卡 2 上;请在答题卡 2 上作答。

You probably have noticed that people express similar ideas in different ways depending on the situation they are in. This is very (36)_____. All languages have two general levels of (37)_____: a formal level and an informal level. English is no (38)_____. The difference in these two levels is the situation in which you use a (39)_____ level. Formal language is the kind of language you find in textbooks, (40)_____ books and in business letters. You would also use formal English in compositions and (41)_____ that you write in school. Informal language is used in conversation with (42)_____, family members and friends, and when we write (43)_____ notes or letters to close friends. Formal language is different from informal language in several ways. First, formal language tends to be more polite. (44)_____. For example, I might say to a friend or a family member "Close the door, please", (45)_____.

Another difference between formal and informal language is some of the vocabulary. (46)_____ Let's say that I really like soccer. If I am talking to my friend, I might say "I am just crazy about soccer", but if I were talking to my boss, I would probably say "I really enjoy soccer".

Part IV *Reading Comprehension* (*reading in depth*) (*25 minutes*)

ection A

Questions 47 to 56 are based on the following passage.

The flood of women into the job market boosted economic growth and changed U. S. society in many ways. Many in-home jobs that used to be done __47__ by women — ranging from family shopping to preparing meals to doing __48__ work—still need to be done by someone. Husbands and children now do some of these jobs, a __49__ that has changed the target market for many products. Or a working woman may face a crushing "poverty of time" and look for help elsewhere, creating opportunities for producers of frozen meals, child care centers, dry cleaners, financial services, and the like.

Although there is still a big wage __50__ between men and women, the income working women __51__ gives them new independence and buying power. For example, women now __52__ about half of all cars. Not long ago, many cars dealers __53__ women shoppers by ignoring them or suggesting that they come back with their husbands. Now car companies have realized that women are __54__ customers. It's interesting that some leading Japanese car dealers were the first to __55__ pay attention to women customers. In Japan, fewer women have jobs or buy cars—the Japanese society is still very much male-oriented. Perhaps it was the __56__ contrast with Japanese society that prompted American firms to pay more attention to women buyers.

注意:此部分试题请在答题卡 2 上作答。

A) scale	B) retailed	C) generate	D) extreme	E) technically
F) affordable	G) situation	H) really	I) potential	J) gap
K) voluntary	L) excessive	M) insulted	N) purchase	O) primarily

 ection B

Passage One

Questions 57 to 61 are based on the following passage.

Reaching new peaks of popularity in North America is Iceberg Water which is harvested from icebergs off the coast of Newfoundland, Canada.

Arthur von Wiesenberger, who carries the title Water Master, is one of the few water critics in North America. As a boy, he spent time in the larger cities of Italy, France and Switzerland, where bottled water is consumed daily. Even then, he kept a water journal, noting the brands he liked best. "My dog could tell the difference between bottled and tap water," he says.

But is plain tap water all that bad? Not at all. In fact, New York's municipal water for more than a century was called the champagne of tap water and until recently considered among the best in the world in terms of both taste and purity. Similarly, a magazine in England found that tap water from the Thames River tasted better than several leading brands of bottled water that were 400 times more expensive.

Nevertheless, soft-drink companies view bottled water as the next battle-ground for market share—despite the fact that over 25 percent of bottled water comes from tap water: PepsiCo's Aquafina and Coca-Cola's Dasani are both purified tap water rather than spring water.

As diners thirst for leading brands, bottlers and restaurateurs *salivate*(垂涎)over the profits. A restaurant's typical mark-up on wine is 100 to 150 percent, whereas on bottled water it's often 300 to 500 percent. But since water is much cheaper than wine, and many of the fancier brands aren't available in stores, most dines don't notice or care.

As a result, some restaurants are turning up the pressure to sell bottled water. According to an article in *The Street Journal*, some of the more shameless tactics include placing attractive bottles on the table for a visual sell, listing brands on the menu without prices, and pouring bottled water without even asking the dinners if they want it.

Regardless of how it's sold, the popularity of bottled water taps into our desire for better health, our wish to appear cultivated, and even a longing for lost purity.

57. What do we know about Iceberg Water from the passage?
    A) It is a kind of iced water.　　　　B) It is just plain tap water.
    C) It is a kind of bottled water.　　　D) It is a kind of mineral water.
58. By saying "My dog could tell the difference between bottled and tap water" (Line 4 Para 2), Von Wiesenberger wants to convey the message that _____.
    A) plain tap water is certainly unfit for drinking
    B) bottled water is clearly superior to tap water
    C) bottled water often appeals more to dogs' taste
    D) dogs can usually detect a fine difference in taste
59. The "fancier brands" (Line 3 Para 5) refers to _____.

A) tap water from the Thames River

B) famous wines not sold in ordinary stores

C) PepsiCo's Aquafina and Coca-Cola's Dasani

D) expensive bottled water with impressive names

60. Why are some restaurants turning up the pressure to sell bottled water?

A) Bottled water brings in huge profits.

B) Competition from the wine industry is intense.

C) Most diners find bottled water affordable.

D) Bottled water satisfied diners' desire to be fashionable.

61. According to passage, why is bottled water so popular?

A) It is much cheaper than wine.

B) It is considered healthier.

C) It appeals to more cultivated people.

D) It is more widely promoted in the market.

Passage Two

Questions 62 to 66 are based on the following passage.

As we have seen, the focus of medical care in our society has been shifting from curing disease to preventing disease-especially in terms of changing our many unhealthy behaviors, such as poor eating habits, smoking, and failure to exercise. The line of thought involved in this shift can be pursued further. Imagine a person who is about the right weight , but does not eat very *nutritious*(有营养的) foods, who feels OK but exercises only occasionally, who goes to work every day, but is not an outstanding worker, who drinks a few beers at home most nights but does not drive while drunk , and who has no chest pains or abnormal blood counts, but sleeps a lot and often feels tired. This person is not ill. He may not even be at risk for any particular disease. But we can imagine that this person could be a lot healthier.

The field of medicine has not traditionally distinguished between someone who is merely "not ill" and someone who is in excellent health and pays attention to the body's special needs. Both types have simply been called "well". In recent years, however, some health specialists have begun to apply the terms "well" and "wellness" only to those who are actively striving to maintain and improve their health. People who are well are concerned with nutrition and exercise, and they make a point of monitoring their body's condition. Most important, perhaps, people who are well take active responsibility for all matters related to their health. Even people who have a physical disease or *handicap*(缺陷) may be "well," in this new sense, if they make an effort to maintain the best possible health they can in the face of their physical limitations. "Wellness" may perhaps best be viewed not as a state that people can achieve, but as an ideal that people can strive for. People who are well are likely to be better able to resist disease and to fight disease when it strikes. And by focusing attention on healthy ways of living, the concept of wellness can have a beneficial impact on the ways in which people face the challenges of daily life.

62. Today medical care is placing more stress on _____ .

A) keeping people in a healthy physical condition

B) monitoring patients' body functions

C) removing people's bad living habits

D) ensuring people's psychological well-being

63. In the first paragraph, people are reminded that _____ .

A) good health is more than not being ill

B) drinking, even if not to excess, could be harmful

C) regular health checks are essential to keeping fit

D) prevention is more difficult than cure

64. Traditionally, a person is considered "well" if he _____.

   A) does not have any unhealthy living habits

   B) does not have any physical handicaps

   C) is able to handle his daily routines

   D) is free from any kind of disease

65. According to the author, the true meaning of "wellness" is for people _____.

   A) to best satisfy their body's special needs

   B) to strive to maintain the best possible health

   C) to meet the strictest standards of bodily health

   D) to keep a proper balance between work and leisure

66. According to what the author advocates, which of the following groups of people would be considered healthy?

   A) People who have strong muscles as well as slim figures.

   B) People who are not presently experiencing any symptoms of disease.

   C) People who try to be as healthy as possible, regardless of their limitations.

   D) People who can recover from illness even without seeking medical care.

Part Ⅴ *Cloze* (*15 minutes*)

Language is the most astonishing behavior in the animal kingdom. It is the species-typical behavior that sets humans completely __67__ from all other animals. Language is a means of communication, __68__ it is much more than that. Many animals can __69__. The dance of the honeybee communicates the location of flowers __70__ other members of the *hive* (蜂群). But human language permits communication about anything, __71__ things like *unicorn* (独角兽) that have never existed. The key __72__ in the fact that the units of meaning, words, can be __73__ together in different ways, according to __74__, to communicate different meanings.

Language is the most important learning we do. Nothing __75__ humans so much as our ability to communicate abstract thoughts, __76__ about the university, the mind, love, dreams, or ordering a drink. It is an immensely complex __77__ that we take for granted. Indeed, we are not aware of most __78__ of our speech and understanding. Consider what happens when one person is speaking to __79__. The speaker has to translate thoughts into __80__ language. Brain

67.	A) apart	B) off	C) up	D) down
68.	A) so	B) but	C) or	D) for
69.	A) transfer		B) transmit	
	C) convey		D) communicate	
70.	A) to	B) from	C) over	D) on
71.	A) only	B) almost	C) even	D) just
72.	A) stays	B) situates	C) hides	D) lies
73.	A) stuck		B) strung	
	C) rung		D) consisted	
74.	A) rules		B) scales	
	C) laws		D) standards	
75.	A) combines		B) contains	
	C) defines		D) declares	
76.	A) what		B) whether	
	C) while		D) if	
77.	A) prospect		B) progress	
	C) process		D) produce	
78.	A) aspects		B) abstracts	
	C) angles		D) assumptions	
79.	A) anybody		B) another	
	C) other		D) everybody	
80.	A) body		B) gesture	
	C) written		D) spoken	
81.	A) growing		B) fixing	

imaging studies suggest that the time from thoughts to the __81__ of speech is extremely fast. Only 0. 04 seconds! The listener must hear the sounds to __82__ out what the speaker means. He must use the sounds of speech to __83__ the words spoken, understand the pattern of __84__ of the words (sentences), and finally __85__ the meaning. This takes somewhat longer, a minimum of about 0. 5 seconds. But __86__ started, it is of course a continuous process.

C) beginning   D) building
82. A) put   B) take   C) draw   D) figure
83. A) identify   B) locate
    C) reveal   D) discover
84. A) performance   B) organization
    C) design   D) layout
85. A) prescribe   B) justify
    C) utter   D) interpret
86. A) since   B) after   C) once   D) until

Part Ⅵ *Translation* (*5 minutes*)

87. Specialists in intercultural studies says that it is not easy to _____（适应不同文化中的生活）.

88. Since my childhood I have found that _____（没有什么比读书对我更有吸引力）.

89. The victim _____（本来会有机会活下来）if he had been taken to hospital in time.

90. Some psychologists claim that people _____（出门在外时可能会感到孤独）.

91. The nation's population continues to rise _____（以每年 1200 万人的速度）.

2007 年 6 月全国大学英语四级考试试卷

Part I *Writing* (*30 minutes*)

注意:此部分试题在答题卡 1 上。

Directions: *For this part, you are allowed 30 minutes to write an announcement to welcome students to join a club. You should write at least 120 words following the outline given below in Chinese.*

1. 本社团的主要活动内容
2. 参加本社团的好处
3. 如何参加本社团

Welcome to Our Club

Part II *Reading Comprehension* (*Skimming and Scanning*) (*15 minutes*)

Protect Your Privacy When Job-hunting Online

Identity theft and identity fraud are terms used to refer to all types of crime in which someone wrongfully obtains and uses another person's personal data in some way that involves fraud or deception, typically for economic gain.

The numbers associated with identity theft are beginning to add up fast these days. A recent General Accounting Office report estimates that as many as 750,000 Americans are victims of identity theft every year. And that number may be low, as many people choose not to report the crime even if they know they have been victimized.

Identity theft is "an absolute epidemic," states Robert Ellis Smith, a respected author and advocate of privacy. "It's certainly picked up in the last four or five years. It's worldwide. It affects everybody, and there's very little you can do to prevent it and, worst of all, you can't detect it until it's probably too late."

Unlike your fingerprints, which are unique to you and cannot be given to someone else for their use, your personal data, especially your social security number, your bank account or credit card number, your telephone calling card number, and other valuable identifying data, can be used, if they fall into the wrong hands, to personally profit at your expense. In the United States and Canada, for example, many people have reported that unauthorized persons have taken funds out of their bank or financial accounts, or in the worst cases, taken over their identities altogether, running up vast debts and committing crimes while using the victims' names. In many cases, a victim's losses may include not only out-of-pocket financial losses, but substantial additional financial costs associated with trying to restore his reputation in the community and correcting erroneous information for which the criminal is responsible.

According to the FBI, identity theft is the number one fraud committed on the Internet. So how do job seekers protect themselves while continuing to circulate their resumes online? The key to a successful online job search is learning to manage the risks. Here are some tips for staying safe while conducting a job search on the Internet.

1. Check for a privacy policy.

If you are considering posting your resume online, make sure the job search site you are considering has a privacy policy, like CareerBuilder.com. The policy should spell out how your information will be used, stored and whether or not it will be shared. You may want to think twice about posting your resume on a site that automatically shares your information with others. You could be opening yourself up to unwanted calls from *solicitors*（推销员）.

When reviewing the site's privacy policy, you'll be able to delete your resume just as easily as you posted it. You won't necessarily want your resume to remain out there on the Internet once you land a job. Remember, the longer your resume remains posted on a job board, the more exposure, both positive and not-so-positive, it will receive.

2. Take advantage of site features.

Lawful job search sites offer levels of privacy protection. Before posting your resume, carefully consider your job search objectives and the level of risk you are willing to assume.

CareerBuilder.com, for example, offers three levels of privacy from which job seekers can choose. The first is standard posting. This option gives job seekers who post their resumes the most visibility to the broadest employer audience possible.

The second is *anonymous*（匿名的）posting. This allows job seekers the same visibility as those in the standard posting category without any of their contact information being displayed. Job seekers who wish to remain anonymous but want to share some other information may choose which pieces of contact information to display.

The third is private posting. This option allows a job seeker to post a resume without having it searched by employers. Private posting allows job seekers to quickly and easily apply for jobs that appear on CareerBuilder.com without retyping their information.

3. Safeguard your identity.

Career experts say that one of the ways job seekers can stay safe while using the Internet to search out jobs is to conceal their identities. Replace your name on your resume with a *generic*（泛指的）identifier, such as "Intranet Developer Candidate," or "Experienced Marketing Representative."

You should also consider eliminating the name and location of your current employer. Depending on your title, it may not be all that difficult to determine who you are once the name of your company is provided. Use a general description of the company such as "Major auto manufacturer." or "International packaged goods supplier."

If your job title is unique, consider using the generic equivalent instead of the exact title assigned by your employer.

4. Establish an email address for your search.

Another way to protect your privacy while seeking employment online is to open up an email account specifically for your online job search. This will safeguard your existing email box in the event someone you don't know gets hold of your email address and shares it with others.

Using an email address specifically for your job search also eliminates the possibility that you will receive unwelcome emails in your primary mailbox. When naming your new email address, be sure that it doesn't contain references to your name or other information that will give away your identity. The best solution is an email address that is relevant to the job you are seeking such as Salesmgr2004 @ provider.com.

5. Protect your references.

If your resume contains a section with the names and contact information of your references, take it out. There's no sense in safeguarding your information while sharing private contact information of your references.

6. Keep *confidential*(机密的) information confidential.

Do not, under any circumstances, share your social security, driver's license, and bank account numbers or other personal information, such as race or eye color. Honest employers do not need this information with an initial application. Don't provide this even if they say they need it in order lo conduct a background check. This is one of the oldest tricks in the book—don't fall for it.

1. Robert Ellis Smith believes identity theft is difficult to detect and one can hardly do anything to prevent it.

2. In many cases, identity theft not only causes the victims' immediate financial losses but costs them a lot to restore their reputation.

3. Identity theft is a minor offence and its harm has been somewhat overestimated.

4. It is important that your resume not stay online longer than is necessary.

5. Of the three options offered by CareerBuilder.com in Suggestion 2, the third one is apparently most strongly recommended.

6. Employers require applicants to submit very personal information on background checks.

7. Applicants are advised to use generic names for themselves and their current employers when seeking employment online.

8. Using a special email address in the job search can help prevent you from receiving _____.

9. To protect your references, you should not post online their _____.

10. According to the passage, identity theft is committed typically for _____.

Part Ⅲ *Listening Comprehension* (*35 minutes*)

ection A

11. A) It could help people of all ages to avoid cancer.
    B) It was mainly meant for cancer patients.
    C) It might appeal more to viewers over 40.
    D) It was frequently interrupted by commercials.

12. A) The man is fond of traveling.
    B) The woman is a photographer.
    C) The woman took a lot of pictures at the contest.
    D) The man admires the woman's talent in writing.

13. A) The man regrets being absent-minded.   B) The woman saved the man some trouble.
    C) The man placed the reading list on a desk.   D) The woman emptied the waste paper basket.

14. A) He quit teaching in June.   B) He has left the army recently.
    C) He opened a restaurant near the school.   D) He has taken over his brother's business.

15. A) She seldom reads books from cover to cover.
    B) She is interested in reading novels.
    C) She read only part of the book.
    D) She was eager to know what the book was about.

16. A) She was absent all week owing to sickness.
    B) She was seriously injured in a car accident.
    C) She called to say that her husband had been hospitalized.
    D) She had to be away from school to attend to her husband.

17. A) The speakers want to rent the Smiths' old house.

    B) The man lives two blocks away from the Smiths.

    C) The woman is not sure if she is on the right street.

    D) The Smiths' new house is not far from their old one.

18. A) The man had a hard time finding a parking space.

    B) The woman found they had got to the wrong spot.

    C) The woman was offended by the man's late arrival.

    D) The man couldn't find his car in the parking lot.

Questions 19 to 22 are based on the conversation you have just heard.

19. A) The hotel clerk had put his reservation under another name.

    B) The hotel clerk insisted that he didn't make any reservation.

    C) The hotel clerk tried to take advantage of his inexperience.

    D) The hotel clerk couldn't find his reservation for that night.

20. A) A grand wedding was being held in the hotel.

    B) There was a conference going on in the city.

    C) The hotel was undergoing major repairs.

    D) It was a busy season for holiday-makers.

21. A) It was free of charge on weekends.   B) It had a 15% discount on weekdays.

    C) It was offered to frequent guests only.   D) It was 10% cheaper than in other hotels.

22. A) Demand compensation from the hotel.   B) Ask for an additional discount.

    C) Complain to the hotel manager.   D) Find a cheaper room in another hotel.

Questions 23 to 25 are based on the conversation you have just heard.

23. A) An employee in the city council at Birmingham.

    B) Assistant Director of the Admissions Office.

    C) Head of the Overseas Students Office.

    D) Secretary of Birmingham Medical School.

24. A) Nearly fifty percent are foreigners.   B) About fifteen percent are from Africa.

    C) A large majority are from Latin America.   D) A small number are from the Far East.

25. A) She will have more contact with students.   B) It will bring her capability into fuller play.

    C) She will be more involved in policy-making.   D) It will be less demanding than her present job.

Section B

Passage 1

Questions 26 to 28 are based on the passage you have just heard.

26. A) Her parents thrived in the urban environment.

    B) Her parents left Chicago to work on a farm.

    C) Her parents immigrated to America.

    D) Her parents set up an ice-cream store.

27. A) He taught English in Chicago.   B) He was crippled in a car accident.

    C) He worked to become an executive.   D) He was born with a limp.

28. A) She was fond of living an isolated life.   B) She was fascinated by American culture.

    C) She was very generous in offering help.   D) She was highly devoted to her family.

Passage 2

Questions 29 to 32 are based on the passage you have just heard.

29. A) He suffered a nervous breakdown.   C) He was seriously injured.

B) He was wrongly diagnosed.   D) He developed a strange disease.

30. A) He was able to talk again.   B) He raced to the nursing home.
    C) He could tell red and blue apart.   D) He could not recognize his wife.

31. A) Twenty-nine days.   B) Two and a half months.
    C) Several minutes.   D) Fourteen hours.

32. A) They welcomed the publicity in the media.
    B) They avoided appearing on television.
    C) They released a video of his progress.
    D) They declined to give details of his condition.

Passage 3

Questions 33 to 35 are based on the passage you have just heard.

33. A) For people to share ideas and show farm products.
    B) For officials to educate the farming community.
    C) For farmers to exchange their daily necessities.
    D) For farmers to celebrate their harvests.

34. A) By bringing an animal rarely seen on nearby farms.
    B) By bringing a bag of grain in exchange for a ticket.
    C) By offering to do volunteer work at the fair.
    D) By performing a special skill at the entrance.

35. A) They contribute to the modernization of American farms.
    B) They help to increase the state governments' revenue.
    C) They provide a stage for people to give performances.
    D) They remind Americans of the importance of agriculture.

Section C   Compound Dictation

Students' pressure sometimes comes from their parents. Most parents are well (36)_____,
but some of them aren't very helpful with the problems their sons and daughters have in (37)_____
to college, and a few of them seem to go out of their way to add to their children's difficulties.

For one thing, parents are often not (38)_____ of the kinds of problems their children face.
They don't realize that the (39)_____ is keener, that the required (40)_____ of work are
higher, and that their children may not be prepared for the change. (41)_____ to seeing A's and
B's on high school report cards, they may be upset when their children's first (42)_____ college
grades are below that level. At their kindest, they may gently (43)_____ why John or Mary isn't
doing better, whether he or she is trying as hard as he or she should, and so on. (44)_____.

Sometimes parents regard their children as extensions of themselves and (45)_____. In their
involvement and identification with their children, they forget that everyone is different and that each
person must develop in his or her own way. They forget that their children. (46)_____.

Part IV   *Reading Comprehension* (*reading in depth*) (*25 minutes*)

Section A

Questions 47 to 56 are based on the following passage.

Years ago, doctors often said that pain was a normal part of life. In particular, when older patients
__47__ of pain, they were told it was a natural part of aging and they would have to learn to live with it.

Times have changed. Today, we take pain __48__. Indeed, pain is now considered the fifth vital sign, as important as blood pressure, temperature, breathing rate and pulse in ___49___ a person's well-being. We know that *chronic*(慢性的) pain can *disrupt*(扰乱的) a person's life, causing problems that ___50___ from missed work to depression.

Thai's why a growing number of hospitals now depend upon physicians who ___51___ in pain medicine. Not only do we evaluate the cause of the pain, which can help us treat the pain better, but we also help provide comprehensive therapy for depression and other psychological and social ___52___ related to chronic pain. Such comprehensive therapy often ___53___ the work of social workers, *psychiatrists*(心理医生) and psychologists, as well as specialists in pain medicine.

This modern ___54___ for pain management has led to a wealth of innovative treatments which are more effective and with fewer side effects than ever before. Decades ago, there were only a ___55___ number of drugs available, and many of them caused ___56___ side effects in older people, including dizziness and fatigue. This created a double-edged sword: the medications helped relieve the pain but caused other problems that could be worse than the pain itself.

注意:此部分试题请在答题卡 2 上作答。

A) result	B) involves	C) significant	D) range	E) relieved
F) issues	G) seriously	H) magnificent	I) determining	J) limited
K) gravely	L) complained	M) respect	N) prompting	O) specialize

ection B

Passage 1

Questions 57 to 61 are based on the following passage.

I've been writing for most of my life. The book *Writing Without Teachers* introduced me to one distinction and one practice that has helped my writing processes tremendously. The distinction is between the creative mind and the critical mind. While you need to employ both to get to a finished result, they cannot work in parallel no matter how much we might like to think so.

Trying to criticize writing on the fly is possibly the single greatest barrier to writing that most of us encounter. If you are listening to that 5th grade English teacher correct your grammar while you are trying to capture a *fleeting*(稍纵即逝的) thought, the thought will die. If you capture the fleeting thought and simply share it with the world in raw form, no one is likely to understand. You must learn to create first and then criticize if you want to make writing the tool for thinking that it is.

The practice that can help you past your learned bad habits of trying to edit as you write is what Elbow calls "free writing." In free writing, the objective is to get words down on paper non-stop, usually for 15-20 minutes. No stopping, no going back, no criticizing. The goal is to get the words flowing. As the words begin to flow, the ideas will come out from the shadows and let themselves be captured on your notepad or your screen.

Now you have raw materials that you can begin to work with using the critical mind that you've persuaded to sit on the side and watch quietly. Most likely, you will believe that this will take more time than you actually have and you will end up staring blankly at the page as the deadline draws near.

Instead of staring at a blank screen start filling it with words no matter how bad. Halfway through your available time, stop and rework your raw writing into something closer to finished product. Move back and forth until you run out of time and the final result will most likely be far better than your current practices.

57. When the author says the creative mind and the critical mind "cannot work in parallel" (Line 4 Para.

1) in the writing process, he means _____.

A) no one can be both creative and critical

B) they cannot be regarded as equally important

C) they are in constant conflict with each other

D) one cannot use them at the same time

58. What prevents people from writing on is _____.

A) putting their ideas in raw form

B) attempting to edit as they write

C) ignoring grammatical soundness

D) trying to capture fleeting thoughts

59. What is the chief objective of the first stage of writing?

A) To organize one's thoughts logically.

B) To choose an appropriate topic.

C) To get one's ideas down.

D) To collect raw materials.

60. One common concern of writers about "free writing" is that _____.

A) it overstresses the role of the creative mind

B) it takes too much time to edit afterwards

C) it may bring about too much criticism

D) it does not help them to think clearly

61. In what way does the critical mind help the writer in the writing process?

A) It refines his writing into better shape.

B) It helps him to come up with new ideas.

C) It saves the writing time available to him.

D) It allows him to sit on the side and observe.

Passage 2

Questions 62 to 66 are based on the following passage.

I don't ever want to talk about being a woman scientist again. There was a time in my life when people asked constantly for stories about what it's like to work in a field dominated by men. 1 was never very good at telling those stories because truthfully I never found them interesting. What I do find interesting is the origin of the universe, the shape of space-time and the nature of black holes.

At 19, when I began studying astrophysics, it did not bother me in the least to be the only woman in the classroom. But while earning my Ph.D. at MIT and then as a post-doctor doing space research, the issue started to bother me. My every achievement—jobs, research papers, awards—was viewed through the lens of *gender*(性别) politics. So were my failures. Sometimes, when I was pushed into an argument on left brain *versus*(相对于) right brain, or nature versus *nurture*(培育), I would instantly fight fiercely on my behalf and all womankind.

Then one day a few years ago, out of my mouth came a sentence that would eventually become my reply to any and all provocations: I don't talk about that anymore. It took me 10 years to get back the confidence I had at 19 and to realize that I didn't want to deal with gender issues. Why should curing sexism be yet another terrible burden on every female scientist? After all, I don't study sociology or political theory.

Today I research and teach at Barnard, a women's college in New York City. Recently, someone asked me how many of the 45 students in my class were women. You cannot imagine my satisfaction at being able to answer. 45. I know some of my students worry how they will manage their scientific research and a desire for children. And I don't dismiss those concerns. Still, I don't tell them "war" stories. Instead, I have given them this: the visual of their physics professor heavily pregnant doing physics experiments. And in turn they have given me the image of 45 women driven by a love of science. And that's a sight worth talking about.

62. Why doesn't the author want to talk about being a woman scientist again?

A) She feels unhappy working in male-dominated fields.

B) She is fed up with the issue of gender discrimination.

C) She is not good at telling stories of the kind.

D) She finds space research more important.

63. From Paragraph 2，we can infer that people would attribute the author's failures to _____ .

A) the very fact that she is a woman

B) her involvement in gender politics

C) her over-confidence as a female astrophysicist

D) the burden she bears in a male-dominated society

64. What did the author constantly fight against while doing her Ph. D. and post-doctoral research?

A) Lack of confidence in succeeding in space science.

B) Unfair accusations from both inside and outside her circle.

C) People's stereotyped attitude towards female scientists.

D) Widespread misconceptions about nature and nurture.

65. Why does the author feel great satisfaction when talking about her class?

A) Female students no longer have to bother about gender issues.

B) Her students' performance has brought back her confidence.

C) Her female students can do just as well as male students.

D) More female students are pursuing science than before.

66. What docs the image the author presents to her students suggest?

A) Women students needn't have the concerns of her generation.

B) Women have more barriers on their way to academic success.

C) Women can balance a career in science and having a family.

D) Women now have fewer problems pursuing science career.

Part V *Cloze* (*15 minutes*)

An earthquake hit Kashmir on Oct. 8. 2005. It took some 75,000 lives, __67__ 130,000 and left nearly 3.5 million without food, jobs or homes. __68__ overnight, scores of tent villages bloomed __69__ the region, tended by international aid organizations, military __70__ and aid groups working day and night to shelter the survivors before winter set __71__ .

Mercifully, the season was mild. But with the __72__ of spring, the refugees will be moved again. Camps that __73__ health care, food and shelter for 150,000 survivors have begun to close as they were __74__ intended to be permanent.

For most of the refugees, the thought of going back brings __75__ emotions. The past six months have been difficult. Families of __76__ many as 10

67. A) injured   B) ruined
    C) destroyed   D) damaged

68. A) Altogether   B) Almost
    C) Scarcely   D) Surely

69. A) among   B) above
    C) amid   D) across

70. A) ranks   B) equipment
    C) personnel   D) installations

71. A) out   B) in   C) on   D) forth

72. A) falling   B) emergence
    C) arrival   D) appearing

73. A) strengthened   B) aided
    C) transferred   D) provided

74. A) never   B) once   C) ever   D) yet

75. A) puzzled   B) contrasted
    C) doubled   D) mixed

76. A) like   B) as   C) so   D) too

people have had to shelter __77__ a single tent and share cookstoves and bathing __78__ with neighbors. "They are looking forward to the clean water of their rivers," officials say. "They are __79__ of free fresh fruit. They want to get back to their herds and start __80__ again." But most will be returning to __81__ but heaps of ruins. In many villages, electrical __82__ have not been repaired, nor have roads. Aid workers __83__ that it will take years to rebuild what the earthquake took __84__. And for the thousands of survivors, the __85__ will never be complete.

Yet the survivors have to start somewhere. New homes can be built __86__ the stones, bricks and beams of old ones. Spring is coming and it is a good time to start again.

77. A) by   B) below   C) under   D) with
78. A) facilities   B) instruments   C) implements   D) appliances
79. A) seeking   B) dreaming   C) longing   D) searching
80. A) producing   B) cultivating   C) farming   D) nourishing
81. A) anything   B) something   C) everything   D) nothing
82. A) lines   B) channels   C) paths   D) currents
83. A) account   B) measure   C) estimate   D) evaluate
84. A) aside   B) away   C) up   D) out
85. A) reservation   B) retreat   C) replacement   D) recovery
86. A) from   B) through   C) upon   D) onto

Part Ⅶ *Translation* (*5 minutes*)

87. The finding of this study failed to _____ (将人们的睡眠质量考虑在内).
88. The prevention and treatment of AIDS is _____ (我们可以合作的领域).
89. Because of the leg injury, the athlete _____ (决定退出比赛).
90. To make donations or for more information, please _____ (按以下地址和我们联系).
91. Please come here at ten tomorrow morning _____ (如果你方便的话).

2007 年 12 月全国大学英语四级考试试卷

Part Ⅰ *Writing*（*30 minutes*）

注意：此部分试题在答题卡 1 上作答。

Directions：*For this part，you are allowed 30 minutes to write a short essay on the topic of **What Electives to Choose**. You should write at least 120 words following the outline given below in Chinese.*

1. 各大学为学生开设了各种各样的选修课
2. 学生出于各种原因选择不同的选修课
3. 以我自己为例

What Electives to Choose

Part Ⅱ *Reading Comprehension*（*Skimming and Scanning*）（*15 minutes*）

Universities Branch Out

As never before in their long history, universities have become instruments of national competition as well as instruments of peace. They are the place of the scientific discoveries that move economies forward, and the primary means of educating the talent required to obtain and maintain competitive advantage. But at the same time, the opening of national borders to the flow of goods, services, information and especially people has made universities a powerful force for global integration, mutual understanding and geopolitical stability.

In response to the same forces that have driven the world economy, universities have become more self-consciously global: seeking students from around the world who represent the entire range of cultures and values, sending their own students abroad to prepare them for global careers, offering courses of study that address the challenges of an interconnected world and *collaborative*（合作的）research programs to advance science for the benefit of all humanity.

Of the forces shaping higher education none is more sweeping than the movement across borders. Over the past three decades the number of students leaving home each year to study abroad has grown at an annual rate of 3.9 percent, from 800,000 in 1975 to 2.5 million in 2004. Most travel from one developed nation to another, but the flow from developing to developed countries is growing rapidly. The reverse flow, from developed to developing countries, is on the rise, too. Today foreign students earn 30 percent of the doctoral degrees awarded in the United States and 38 percent of those in the United Kingdom. And the number crossing borders for undergraduate study is growing as well, to 8 percent of the undergraduates at America's best institutions and 10 percent of all undergraduates in the U.K. In the United States, 20 percent of the newly hired professors in science and engineering are foreign-born, and in China many newly hired faculty members at the top research universities received their graduate education abroad.

Universities are also encouraging students to spend some of their undergraduate years in another country. In Europe, more than 140,000 students participate in the Erasmus program each year, taking courses for credit in one of 2,200 participating institutions across the continent. And in the United States, institutions are helping place students in the summer *internships*(实习) abroad to prepare them for global careers. Yale and Harvard have led the way, offering every undergraduate at least one international study or internship opportunity—and providing the financial resources to make it possible.

Globalization is also reshaping the way research is done. One new trend involves sourcing portions of a research program to another country. Yale professor and Howard Hughes Medical Institute investigator Tian Xu directs a research center focused on the genetics of human disease at Shanghai's Fudan University, in collaboration with faculty colleagues from both schools. The Shanghai center has 95 employees and graduate students working in a 4,300-square-meter laboratory facility. Yale faculty, post-doctors and graduate students visit regularly and attend video-conference seminars with scientists from both campuses. The arrangement benefits both countries; Xu's Yale lab is more productive, thanks to the lower costs of conducting research in China, and Chinese graduate students, post-doctors and faculty get on-the-job training from a world-class scientist and his U.S. team.

As a result of its strength in science, the United States has consistently led the world in the commercialization of major new technologies, from the mainframe computer and the integrated circuit of the 1960s to the Internet *infrastructure*(基础设施) and applications software of the 1990s. The link between university-based science and industrial application is often indirect but sometimes highly visible: Silicon Valley was intentionally created by Stanford University, and Route 128 outside Boston has long housed companies spun off from MIT and Harvard. Around the world, governments have encouraged copying of this model, perhaps most successfully in Cambridge, England, where Microsoft and scores of other leading software and biotechnology companies have set up shop around the university.

For all its success, the United States remains deeply hesitant about sustaining the research-university model. Most politicians recognize the link between investment in science and national economic strength, but support for research funding has been unsteady. The budget of the National Institutes of Health doubled between 1998 and 2003, but has risen more slowly than inflation since then. Support for the physical sciences and engineering barely kept pace with inflation during that same period. The attempt to make up lost ground is welcome, but the nation would be better served by steady, predictable increases in science funding at the rate of long-term GDP growth, which is on the order of inflation plus 3 percent per year.

American politicians have great difficult recognizing that admitting more foreign students can greatly promote the national interest by increasing international understanding. Adjusted for inflation, public funding for international exchanges and foreign-language study is well below the levels of 40 years ago. In the wake of September 11, changes in the visa process caused a dramatic decline in the number of foreign students seeking admission to U.S. universities, and a corresponding surge in enrollments in Australia, Singapore and the U.K. Objections from American university and the business leaders led to improvements in the process and a reversal of the decline, but the United States is still seen by many as unwelcoming to international students.

Most Americans recognize that universities contribute to the nation's well-being through their scientific research, but many fear that foreign students threaten American competitiveness by taking their knowledge and skills back home. They fail to grasp that welcoming foreign students to the United States has two important positive effects: first, the very best of them stay in the States and—like immigrants throughout history—strengthen the nation; and second, foreign students who study in the United States become ambassadors for many of its most *cherished*(珍视) values when they return home. Or at least they understand them better. In America as elsewhere, few instruments of foreign policy are as effective in promoting peace and stability as welcoming international university students.

1. From the first paragraph we know that present-day universities have become _____.
   A) more and more research-oriented   B) in-service training organizations
   C) more popularized than ever before   D) a powerful force for global integration

2. Over the past three decades, the enrollment of overseas students has increased _____.
   A) by 2.5 million   B) by 800,000
   C) at an annual rate of 3.9 percent   D) at an annual rate of 8 percent

3. In the United States, how many of the newly hired professors in science and engineering are foreign-born?
   A) 10%   B) 20%   C) 30%   D) 38%

4. How do Yale and Harvard prepare their undergraduates for global careers?
   A) They organize a series of seminars on world economy.
   B) They offer them various courses in international politics.
   C) They arrange for them to participate in the Erasmus program.
   D) They give them chances for international study or internship.

5. An example illustrating the general trend of universities' globalization is _____.
   A) Yale's collaboration with Fudan University on genetic research
   B) Yale's helping Chinese universities to launch research projects
   C) Yale's student exchange program with European institutions
   D) Yale's establishing branch campuses throughout the world

6. What do we learn about Silicon Valley from the passage?
   A) It houses many companies spun off from MIT and Harvard.
   B) It is known to be the birthplace of Microsoft Company.
   C) It was intentionally created by Stanford University.
   D) It is where the Internet infrastructure was built up.

7. What is said about the U.S. federal funding for research?
   A) It has increased by 3 percent.   B) It has been unsteady for years.
   C) It has been more than sufficient.   D) It doubled between 1998 and 2003.

8. The dramatic decline in the enrollment of foreign students in the U.S after September 11 was caused by _____.

9. Many Americans fear that American competitiveness may be threatened by foreign students who will _____.

10. The policy of welcoming foreign students can benefit the U.S. in that the very best of them will stay and _____.

Part III *Listening Comprehension* (*35 minutes*)

Section A

11. A) She used to be in poor health.   B) She was popular among boys.
    C) She was somewhat overweight.   D) She didn't do well at high school.

12. A) At the airport.   B) In a restaurant.
    C) In a booking office.   D) At the hotel reception.

13. A) Teaching her son by herself.   B) Having confidence in her son.
    C) Asking the teacher for extra help.   D) Telling her son not to worry.

14. A) Have a short break.   B) Take two weeks off.
    C) Continue her work outdoors.   D) Go on vacation with the man.

15. A) He is taking care of his twin brother.   B) He has been feeling ill all week.
    C) He is worried about Rod's health.   D) He has been in perfect condition.

16. A) She sold all her furniture before she moved house.
    B) She still keeps some old furniture in her new house.
    C) She plans to put all her old furniture in the basement.
    D) She brought a new set of furniture from Italy last month.

17. A) The woman wondered why the man didn't return the book.
    B) The woman doesn't seem to know what the book is about.
    C) The woman doesn't find the book useful any more.
    D) The woman forgot lending the book to the man.

18. A) Most of the man's friends are athletes.   B) Few people share the woman's opinion.
    C) The man doesn't look like a sportsman.   D) The woman doubts the man's athletic ability.

Questions 19 to 22 are based on the conversation you have heard.

19. A) She has packed it in one of her bags.   B) She is going to get it at the airport.
    C) She has probably left it in a taxi.   D) She is afraid that she has lost it.

20. A) It ends in winter.   B) It will cost her a lot.
    C) It will last one week.   D) It depends on the weather.

21. A) The plane is taking off soon.   B) The taxi is waiting for them.
    C) There might be a traffic jam.   D) There is a lot of stuff to pack.

22. A) At home.   B) At the airport.
    C) In the man's car.   D) By the side of a taxi.

Questions 23 to 25 are based on the conversation you have just heard.

23. A) She is thirsty for promotion.   B) She wants a much higher salary.
    C) She is tired of her present work.   D) She wants to save travel expenses.

24. A) Translator.   B) Travel agent.
    C) Language instructor.   D) Environment engineer.

25. A) Lively personality and inquiring mind.   B) Communication skills and team spirit.
    C) Devotion and work efficiency.   D) Education and experience.

 ection B

Passage One

Questions 26 to 29 are based on the passage you have just heard.

26. A) They care a lot about children.   B) They need looking after in their old age.
    C) They want to enrich their life experience.   D) They want children to keep them company.

27. A) They are usually adopted from distant places.
    B) Their birth information is usually kept secret.
    C) Their birth parents often try to conceal their birth information.
    D) Their adoptive parents don't want them to know their birth parents.

28. A) They generally hold bad feelings towards their birth parents.
    B) They do not want to hurt the feelings of their adoptive parents.
    C) They have mixed feelings about finding their natural parents.
    D) They are fully aware of the expenses involved in the search.

29. A) Early adoption makes for closer parent-child relationship.
    B) Most people prefer to adopt children from overseas.
    C) Understanding is the key to successful adoption.

D) Adoption has much to do with love.

Passage Two

Questions 30 to 32 are based on the passage you have just heard.

30. A) He suffered from mental illness.

B) He bought *The Washington Post*.

C) He turned a failing newspaper into a success.

D) He was once a reporter for a major newspaper.

31. A) She was the first woman to lead a big U. S. publishing company.

B) She got her first job as a teacher at the University of Chicago.

C) She committed suicide because of her mental disorder.

D) She took over her father's position when he died.

32. A) People came to see the role of women in the business world.

B) Katharine played a major part in reshaping Americans' mind.

C) American media would be quite different without Katharine.

D) Katharine had exerted an important influence on the world.

Passage Three

Questions 33 to 35 are based on the passage you have just heard.

33. A) It'll enable them to enjoy the best medical care.

B) It'll allow them to receive free medical treatment.

C) It'll protect them from possible financial crises.

D) It'll prevent the doctors from overcharging them.

34. A) They can't immediately get back the money paid for their medical cost.

B) They have to go through very complicated application procedures.

C) They can only visit doctors who speak their native languages.

D) They may not be able to receive timely medical treatment.

35. A) They don't have to pay for the medical services.

B) They needn't pay the entire medical bill at once.

C) They must send the receipts to the insurance company promptly.

D) They have to pay a much higher price to get an insurance policy.

Section C

More and more of the world's population are living in towns or cities. The speed at which cities are growing in the less developed countries is (36)＿＿＿＿＿＿＿. Between 1920 and 1960 big cities in developed countries (37)＿＿＿＿＿＿ two and a half times in size, but in other parts of the world the growth was eight times their size.

The (38)＿＿＿＿＿ size of growth is bad enough, but there are now also very (39)＿＿＿＿＿＿ signs of trouble in the (40)＿＿＿＿＿ of percentages of people living in towns and percentages of people working in industry. During the nineteenth century cities grew as a result of the growth of industry. In Europe the (41)＿＿＿＿＿ of people living in cities was always smaller than that of the (42)＿＿＿＿＿ working in factories. Now, however, the (43)＿＿＿＿＿ is almost always true in the newly industrialized world: (44)＿＿＿＿＿＿＿＿＿＿＿＿＿.

Without a base of people working in industry, these cities cannot pay for their growth; (45)＿＿＿＿ ＿＿＿＿＿＿＿＿＿＿＿＿＿＿. There has been little opportunity to build water supplies or other facilities. (46)＿＿＿＿＿＿＿＿＿＿＿＿＿＿＿＿, a growth in the number of hopeless and despairing parents and starving children.

Part Ⅳ *Reading Comprehension*（*Reading in Depth*）（*25 minutes*）

ection A

Questions 47 to 56 are based on the following passage.

As war spreads to many corners of the globe, children sadly have been drawn into the center of conflicts. In Afghanistan, Bosnia, and Colombia, however, groups of children have been taking part in peace education ___47___. The children, after learning to resolve conflicts, took on the ___48___ of peacemakers. The Children's Movement for Peace in Colombia was even *nominated*（提名）for the Nobel Peace Prize in 1998. Groups of children ___49___ as peacemakers studied human rights and poverty issues in Colombia, eventually forming a group with five other schools in Bogota known as The Schools of Peace.

The classroom ___50___ opportunities for children to replace angry, violent behaviors with ___51___, peaceful ones. It is in the classroom that caring and respect for each person empowers children to take a step ___52___ toward becoming peacemakers. Fortunately, educators have access to many online resources that are ___53___ useful when helping children along the path to peace. The Young Peacemakers Club, started in 1992, provides a Website with resources for teachers and ___54___ on starting a Kindness Campaign. The World Centers of Compassion for Children International call attention to children's rights and how to help the ___55___ of war. Starting a Peacemakers' Club is a praiseworthy venture for a class and one that could spread to other classrooms and ideally affect the culture of the ___56___ school.

注意:此部分试题请在答题卡 2 上作答。

A) acting	B) assuming	C) comprehensive	D) cooperative
E) entire	F) especially	G) forward	H) images
I) information	J) offers	K) projects	L) respectively
M) role	N) technology	O) victims	

ection B

Passage One

Questions 57 to 61 are based on the following passage.

By almost any measure, there is a boom in Internet-based instruction. In just a few years, 34 percent of American universities have begun offering some form of distance learning（DL）, and among the larger schools, it's close to 90 percent. If you doubt the popularity of the trend, you probably haven't heard of the University of Phoenix. It grants degrees entirely on the basis of online instruction. It enrolls 90,000 students, a statistic used to support its claim to be the largest private university in the country.

While the kinds of instruction offered in these programs will differ, DL usually signifies a course in which the instructors post *syllabi*（课程大纲）, reading assignments, and schedules on Websites, and students send in their assignments by e-mail. Generally speaking, face-to-face communication with an instructor is minimized or eliminated altogether.

The attraction for students might at first seem obvious. Primarily, there's the convenience promised by courses on the Net: you can do the work, as they say, in your *pajamas*（睡衣）. But figures indicate that the reduced effort results in a reduced commitment to the course. While dropout rate for all freshmen at American universities is around 20 percent, the rate for online students is 35 percent. Students themselves seem to understand the weaknesses inherent in the setup. In a survey conducted for eCornell, the DL division of Cornell University, less than a third of the respondents expected the quality of the online course to be as good as the classroom course.

Clearly, from the schools' perspective, there's a lot of money to be saved. Although some of the more ambitious programs require new investments in servers and networks to support collaborative software, most DL courses can run on existing or minimally *upgraded*(升级) systems. The more students who enroll in a course but don't come to campus, the more school saves on keeping the lights on in the classrooms, paying doorkeepers, and maintaining parking lots. And, while there's evidence that instructors must work harder to run a DL course for a variety of reasons, they won't be paid any more, and might well be paid less.

57. What is the most striking feature of the University of Phoenix?

    A) All its courses are offered online.

    B) Its online courses are of the best quality.

    C) It boasts the largest number of students on campus.

    D) Anyone taking its online courses is sure to get a degree.

58. According to the passage , distance learning is basically characterized by _____ .

    A) a considerable flexibility in its academic requirements

    B) the great diversity of students' academic backgrounds

    C) a minimum or total absence of face-to-face instruction

    D) the casual relationship between students and professors

59. Many students take Internet-based courses mainly because they can _____ .

    A) earn their academic degrees with much less effort

    B) save a great deal on traveling and boarding expenses

    C) select courses from various colleges and universities

    D) work on the required courses whenever and wherever

60. What accounts for the high drop-out rates for online students?

    A) There is no strict control over the academic standards of the courses.

    B) The evaluation system used by online universities is inherently weak.

    C) There is no mechanism to ensure that they make the required effort.

    D) Lack of classroom interaction reduces the effectiveness of instruction.

61. According to the passage, universities show great enthusiasm for DL programs for the purpose of _____ .

    A) building up their reputation   B) cutting down on their expenses

    C) upgrading their teaching facilities   D) providing convenience for students

Passage Two

Questions 62 to 66 are based on the following passage.

In this age of Internet chat, videogames and reality television, there is no shortage of mindless activities to keep a child occupied. Yet, despite the competition, my 8-year-old daughter Rebecca wants to spend her leisure time writing short stories. She wants to enter one of her stories into a writing contest, a competition she won last year.

As a writer I know about winning contests, and about losing them. I know what it is like to work hard on a story only to receive a rejection slip from the publisher. I also know the pressure of trying to live up to a reputation created by previous victories. What if she doesn't win the contest again? That's the strange thing about being a parent. So many of our own past scars and dashed hopes can surface.

A *revelation*(启示)came last week when I asked her, "Don't you want to win again?" "No," she replied, "I just want to tell the story of an angel going to first grade."

I had just spent weeks correcting her stories as she *spontaneously*(自发地) told them. Telling myself that I was merely an experienced writer guiding the young writer across the hall, I offered suggestions for characters, conflicts and endings for her tales. The story about a fearful angel starting first grade was quickly "guided" by me into the tale of a little girl with a wild imagination taking her first music lesson. I had turned her contest into my contest without even realizing it.

Staying back and giving kids space to grow is not as easy as it looks. Because I know very little about farm animals who use tools or angels who go to first grade, I had to accept the fact that I was *co-opting* （借用） my daughter's experience.

While stepping back was difficult for me, it was certainly a good first step that I will quickly follow with more steps, putting myself far enough a way to give her room but close enough to help if asked. All the while I will be reminding myself that children need room to experiment, grow and find their own voices.

62. What do we learn from the first paragraph?

A) Children do find lots of fun in many mindless activities.

B) Rebecca is much too occupied to enjoy her leisure time.

C) Rebecca draws on a lot of online materials for her writing.

D) A lot of distractions compete for children's time nowadays.

63. What did the author say about her own writing experience?

A) She did not quite live up to her reputation as a writer.

B) Her way to success was full of pains and frustrations.

C) She was constantly under pressure of writing more.

D) Most of her stories had been rejected by publishers.

64. Why did Rebecca want to enter this year's writing contest?

A) She believed she possessed real talent for writing.

B) She was sure of winning with her mother's help.

C) She wanted to share her stories with readers.

D) She had won a prize in the previous contest.

65. The author took great pains to refine her daughter's stories because _____.

A) she believed she had the knowledge and experience to offer guidance

B) she did not want to disappoint Rebecca who needed her help so much

C) she wanted to help Rebecca realize her dream of becoming a writer

D) she was afraid Rebecca's imagination might run wild while writing

66. What's the author's advice for parents?

A) A writing career, though attractive, is not for every child to pursue.

B) Children should be allowed freedom to grow through experience.

C) Parents should keep an eye on the activities their kids engage in.

D) Children should be given every chance to voice their opinions.

Part V *Cloze* (*15 minutes*)

One factor that can influence consumers is their mood state. Mood may be defined __67__ a temporary and mild positive or negative feeling that is generalized and not tied __68__ any particular circumstance. Moods should be __69__

67. A) as   B) about   C) by   D) with

68. A) over   B) under   C) to   D) up

69. A) derived   B) descended

     C) divided   D) distinguished

70. A) related   B) referred

from emotions which are usually more intense, __70__ to specific circumstances, and often conscious. __71__ one sense, the effect of a consumer's mood can be thought of in __72__ the same way as can our reactions to the __73__ of our friends — when our friends are happy and "up", that tends to influence us positively, __74__ when they are "down", that can have a __75__ impact on us. Similarly, consumers operating under a __76__ mood state tend to react to *stimuli*(刺激因素) in a direction __77__ with that mood state. Thus, for example, we should expect to see __78__ in a positive mood state evaluate products in more of a __79__ manner than they would when not in such a state. __80__, mood states appear capable of __81__ a consumer's memory.

Moods appear to be __82__ influenced by marketing techniques. For example, the rhythm, pitch, and __83__ of music has been shown to influence behavior such as the __84__ of time spent in supermarkets or __85__ to purchase products. In addition, advertising can influence consumers' moods which, in __86__, are capable of influencing consumer' reactions to products.

C) attached   D) associated

71. A) On   B) Of   C) In   D) By
72. A) thus   B) much   C) even   D) still
73. A) signal   B) gesture   C) view   D) behavior
74. A) for   B) but   C) unless   D) provided
75. A) relative   B) decisive
    C) negative   D) sensitive
76. A) given   B) granted   C) fixed   D) driven
77. A) resistant   B) persistent
    C) insistent   D) consistent
78. A) consumer   B) businessmen
    C) retailers   D) manufacturer
79. A) casual   B) critical
    C) serious   D) favorable
80. A) However   B) Otherwise
    C) Moreover   D) Nevertheless
81. A) lifting   B) enhancing
    C) raising   D) cultivating
82. A) readily   B) rarely
    C) cautiously   D) currently
83. A) step   B) speed   C) band   D) volume
84. A) extent   B) amount   C) scope   D) range
85. A) facilities   B) capacities
    C) reflections   D) intensions
86. A) turn   B) total   C) detail   D) depth

Part Ⅵ Translation (5 minutes)

87. _____ (多亏了一系列的新发明), doctors can treat this disease successfully.

88. In my sixties, one change I notice is that _____ (我比以前更容易累了).

89. I am going to purchase this course, _____ (无论我要作出什么样的牺牲).

90. I would prefer shopping online to shopping in a department store because _____ (它更加方便和省时).

91. Many Americans live on credit, and their quality of life _____ (是用他们能够借到多少来衡量的), not how much they can earn.

2008 年 6 月全国大学英语四级考试试卷

Part Ⅰ Writing (30 minutes)

注意:此部分试题在答题卡 1 上。

Directions: For this part, you are allowed 30 minutes to write a short essay on the topic of **Recreational Activities**. You should write at least 120 words following the outline given below in Chinese.

1. 娱乐活动多种多样
2. 娱乐活动可能使人们受益,也可能有危害性
3. 作为大学生,我的看法

Recreational Activities

Part Ⅱ Reading Comprehension (Skimming and Scanning) (15 minutes)

Media Selection for Advertisements

After determining the target audience for a product or service, advertising agencies must select the appropriate media for the advertisement. We discuss here the major types of media used in advertising. We focus our attention on seven types of advertising: television, newspapers, radio, magazines, out-of-home, Internet, and direct mail.

Television

Television is an attractive medium for advertising because it delivers mass audiences to advertisers. When you consider that nearly three out of four Americans have seen the game show *Who Wants to Be a Millionaire*? you can understand the power of television to communicate with a large audience. When advertisers create a brand, for example, they want to impress consumers with the brand and its image. Television provides an ideal vehicle for this type of communication. But television is an expensive medium, and not all advertisers can afford to use it.

Television's influence on advertising is fourfold. First, narrow-casting means that television channels are seen by an increasingly narrow segment of the audience. The Golf Channel, for instance, is watched by people who play golf. Home and Garden Television is seen by those interested in household improvement projects. Thus, audiences are smaller and more *homogeneous*(具有共同特点的) than they have been in the past. Second, there is an increase in the number of television channels available to viewers, and thus, advertisers. This has also resulted in an increase in the sheer number of advertisements to which audiences are exposed. Third, digital recording devices allow audience members more control over which commercials they watch. Fourth, control over programming is being passed from the networks to local cable operators and satellite programmers.

Newspapers

After television, the medium attracting the next largest annual ad revenue is newspapers. The New

York Times, which reaches a national audience, accounts for $1 billion in ad revenue annually. It has increased its national *circulation*（发行量） by 40% and is now available for home delivery in 168 cities. Locally, newspapers are the largest advertising medium.

Newspapers are a less expensive advertising medium than television and provide a way for advertisers to communicate a longer, more detailed message to their audience than they can through television. Given new production techniques, advertisements can be printed in newspapers in about 48 hours, meaning newspapers are also a quick way of getting the message out. Newspapers are often the most important form of news for a local community, and they develop a high degree of loyalty from local reader.

Radio

Advertising on radio continues to grow. Radio is often used in conjunction with outdoor *bill-boards* （广告牌） and the Internet to reach even more customers than television. Advertisers are likely to use radio because it is a less expensive medium than television, which means advertisers can afford to repeal their ads often. Internet companies are also turning to radio advertising. Radio provides a way for advertisers to communicate with audience members at all times of the day. Consumers listen to radio on their way to school or work, at work, on the way home, and in the evening hours.

Two major changes — satellite and Internet radio — will force radio advertisers to adapt their methods. Both of these radio forms allow listeners to tune in stations that are more distant than the local stations they could receive in the past. As a result, radio will increasingly attract target audiences who live many miles apart.

Magazines

Newsweeklies, women's titles, and business magazines have all seen increases in advertising because they attract the high-end market. Magazines are popular with advertisers because of the narrow market that they deliver. A broadcast medium such as network television attracts all types of audience members, but magazine audiences are more homogeneous. If you read *Sports Illustrated*, for example, you have much in common with the magazine's other readers. Advertisers see magazines as an efficient way of reaching target audience members.

Advertisers using the print media — magazines and newspapers — will need to adapt to two main changes. First, the Internet will bring larger audiences to local newspaper. These audiences will be more diverse and geographically *dispersed*（分散） than in the past. Second, advertisers will have to understand how to use an increasing number of magazines for their target audiences. Although some magazines will maintain national audiences, a large number of magazines will entertain narrower audiences.

Out-of-home advertising

Out-of-home advertising, also called place-based advertising, has become an increasingly effective way of reaching consumers, who are more active than ever before. Many consumers today do not sit at home and watch television. Using billboards, newsstands, and bus shelters for advertising is an effective way of reaching these on-the-go consumers. More consumers travel longer distances to and from work, which also makes out-of-home advertising effective. Technology has changed the nature of the billboard business, making it a more effective medium than in the past. Using digital printing, billboard companies can print a billboard in 2 hours, compared with 6 days previously. This allows advertisers more variety in the types of messages they create because they can change their messages more quickly.

Internet

As consumers become more comfortable with online shopping, advertisers will seek to reach this market. As consumers get more of their news and information from the Internet, the ability of television and radio to get the word out to consumers will decrease. The challenge to Internet advertisers is to create ads that audience members remember.

Internet advertising will play a more prominent role in organizations' advertising in the near future. Internet audiences tend to be quite homogeneous, but small. Advertisers will have to adjust their methods to reach these audiences and will have to adapt their persuasive strategies to the online medium as well.

Direct mail

A final advertising medium is direct mail, which uses mailings to consumers to communicate a client's message. Direct mail includes newsletters, postcards and special promotions. Direct mail is an effective way to build relationships with consumers. For many businesses, direct mail is the most effective form of advertising.

1. Television is an attractive advertising medium in that _____.
   A) it has large audiences
   B) it appeals to housewives
   C) it helps build up a company's reputation
   D) it is affordable to most advertisers
2. With the increase in the number of TV channels, _____.
   A) the cost of TV advertising has decreased
   B) the number of TV viewers has increased
   C) advertisers' interest in other media has decreased
   D) the number of TV ads people can see has increased
3. Compared with television, newspapers as an advertising medium _____.
   A) earn a larger annual ad revenue
   B) convey more detailed messages
   C) use more production techniques
   D) get messages out more effectively
4. Advertising on radio continues to grow because _____.
   A) more local radio stations have been set up
   B) modern technology makes it more entertaining
   C) it provides easy access to consumers
   D) it has been revolutionized by Internet radio
5. Magazines are seen by advertisers as an efficient way to _____.
   A) reach target audiences
   B) appeal to educated people
   C) attract diverse audiences
   D) convey all kinds of messages
6. Out-of-home advertising has become more effective because _____.
   A) billboards can be replaced within two hours
   B) consumers travel more now than ever before
   C) such ads have been made much more attractive
   D) the pace of urban life is much faster nowadays
7. The challenge to Internet advertisers is to create ads that are _____.
   A) quick to update   B) pleasant to look at   C) easy to remember   D) convenient to access
8. Internet advertisers will have to adjust their methods to reach audiences that tend to be _____.
9. Direct mail is an effective form of advertising for businesses to develop _____.
10. This passage discusses how advertisers select _____ for advertisements.

Part III *Listening Comprehension* (*35 minutes*)

Section A

11. A) Give his ankle a good rest.   B) Treat his injury immediately.

C) Continue his regular activities.   D) Be careful when climbing steps.

12. A) On a train.   B) On a plane.

C) In a theater.   D) In a restaurant.

13. A) A tragic accident.   B) A sad occasion.

C) Smith's unusual life story.   D) Smith's sleeping problem.

14. A) Review the details of all her lessons.

B) Compare notes with his classmates.

C) Talk with her about his learning problems.

D) Focus on the main points of her lectures.

15. A) The man blamed the woman for being careless.

B) The man misunderstood the woman's apology.

C) The woman offered to pay for the man's coffee.

D) The woman spilt coffee on the man's jacket.

16. A) Extremely tedious.   B) Hard to understand.

C) Lacking a good plot.   D) Not worth seeing twice.

17. A) Attending every lecture.   B) Doing lots of homework.

C) Reading very extensively.   D) Using test-taking strategies.

18. A) The digital TV system will offer different programs.

B) He is eager to see what the new system is like.

C) He thinks it unrealistic to have 500 channels.

D) The new TV system may not provide anything better.

Questions 19 to 22 are based on the conversation you have just heard.

19. A) A notice by the electricity board.   B) Ads promoting electric appliances.

C) The description of a thief in disguise.   D) A new policy on pensioners' welfare.

20. A) Speaking with a proper accent.   B) Wearing an official uniform.

C) Making friends with them.   D) Showing them his ID.

21. A) To be on the alert when being followed.

B) Not to leave senior citizens alone at home.

C) Not to let anyone in without an appointment.

D) To watch out for those from the electricity board.

22. A) She was robbed near the parking lot.   B) All her money in the bank disappeared.

C) The pension she had just drawn was stolen.   D) She was knocked down in the post office.

Questions 23 to 25 are based on the conversation you have just heard.

23. A) Marketing consultancy.   B) Professional accountancy.

C) Luxury hotel management.   D) Business conference organization.

24. A) Having a good knowledge of its customs.   B) Knowing some key people in tourism.

C) Having been to the country before.   D) Being able to speak Japanese.

25. A) It will bring her potential into full play.   B) It will involve lots of train travel.

C) It will enable her to improve her Chinese.   D) It will give her more chances to visit Japan.

ection B

Passage One

Questions 26 to 28 are based on the passage you have just heard.

26. A) The lack of time.   B) The quality of life.

C) The frustrations at work.   D) The pressure on working families.

27. A) They were just as busy as people of today.

    B) They saw the importance of collective efforts.

    C) They didn't complain as much as modern man.

    D) They lived a hard life by hunting and gathering.

28. A) To look for creative ideas of awarding employees.

    B) To explore strategies for lowering production costs.

    C) To seek new approaches to dealing with complaints.

    D) To find effective ways to give employees flexibility.

Passage Two

Question 29 to 31 are based on the passage you have just heard.

29. A) Family violence.   B) The Great Depression.

    C) Her father's disloyalty.   D) Her mother's bad temper.

30. A) His advanced age.   B) His children's efforts.

    C) His improved financial condition.   D) His second wife's positive influence.

31. A) Love is blind.   B) Love breeds love.

    C) Divorce often has disastrous consequences.   D) Happiness is hard to find in blended families.

Passage Three

Question 32 to 35 are based on the passage you have just heard.

32. A) It was located in a park.   B) Its owner died of a heart attack.

    C) It went bankrupt all of a sudden.   D) Its potted plants were for lease only.

33. A) Planting some trees in the greenhouse.   B) Writing a want ad to a local newspaper.

    C) Putting up a Going Out of Business sign.   D) Helping a customer select some purchases.

34. A) Opening an office in the new office park.

    B) Keeping better relations with her company.

    C) Developing fresh business opportunities.

    D) Building a big greenhouse of his own.

35. A) Owning the greenhouse one day.   B) Securing a job at the office park.

    C) Cultivating more potted plants.   D) Finding customers out of town.

Section C　Compound Dictation

    We're now witnessing the emergence of an advanced economy based on information and knowledge. Physical (36)_____ , raw materials, and capital are no longer the key (37)_____ in the creation of wealth. Now, the (38)_____ raw material in our economy is knowledge. Tomorrow's wealth depends on the development and exchange of knowledge. And (39)_____ entering the workforce offer their knowledge, not their muscles. Knowledge workers get paid for their education and their ability to learn. Knowledge workers (40)_____ in mind work. They deal with symbols: words, (41)_____ , and data.

    What does all this mean for you? As a future knowledge worker, you can expect to be (42)_____ , processing, as well as exchanging in formation. (43)_____ , three out of four jobs involve some form of mind work, and that number will increase sharply in the future. Management and employees alike (44)_____ .

    In the new world of work, you can look forward to being in constant training (45)_____ . You can also expect to be taking greater control of your career. Gone are the nine-to-five jobs, lifetime security, predictable promotions, and even the conventional workplace, as you are familiar with. (46)_____ . And don't wait for someone to "empower" you. You have to empower yourself.

Part IV Reading Comprehension (reading in depth) (25 minutes)

ection A

Questions 47 to 56 are based on the following passage.

Some years ago I was offered a writing assignment that would require three month of travel through Europe. I had been abroad a couple of times, but I could hardly __47__ to know my way around the continent. Moreover, my knowledge of foreign languages was __48__ to a little college French.

I hesitated. How would I, unable to speak the language, __49__ unfamiliar with local geography or transportation systems, set up __50__ and do research? It seemed impossible, and with considerable __51__, I sat down to write a letter begging off. Halfway through, a thought ran through my mind: *you can't learn if you don't try.* So I accepted the assignment.

There were some bad __52__. But by the time I had finished the trip I was an experienced traveler. And ever since, I have never hesitated to head for even the most remote of places, without guides or even __53__ bookings, confident that somehow I will manage.

The point is that the new, the different, is almost by definition __54__. But each time you try something, you learn, and as the learning piles up, the world opens to you.

I've learned to ski at 40, and flown up the Rhine River in a __55__. And I know I'll go on doing such things. It's not because I'm braver or more daring than others. I'm not. But I'll accept anxiety as another name for challenge and I believe I can __56__ wonders.

注意:此部分试题请在答题卡 **2** 上作答。

A) accomplish	B) advanced	C) balloon	D) claim
E) constantly	F) declare	G) interviews	H) limited
I) manufacture	J) moments	K) news	L) reduced
M) regret	N) scary	O) totally	

Section B

Passage One

Questions 57 to 61 are based on the following passage.

Global warming may or may not be the great environmental crisis of the 21st century, but — regardless of whether it is or isn't—we won't do much about it. We will argue over it and may even, as a nation, make some fairly solemn-sounding commitments to avoid it. But the more dramatic and meaningful these commitments seem, the less likely they are to be observed.

Al Gore calls global warming an "inconvenient truth" as if merely recognizing it could put us on a path to a solution. But the real truth is that we don't know enough to relieve global warming, and— without major technological breakthroughs—we can't do much about it.

From 2003 to 2050, the world's population is projected to grow from 6.4 billion to 9.1 billion, a 42% increase. If energy use per person and technology remain the same, total energy use and greenhouse gas emissions (mainly, CO_2) will be 42% higher in 2050. But that's too low, because societies that grow richer use more energy. We need economic growth unless we condemn the world's poor to their present poverty and freeze everyone else's living standards. With modest growth, energy use and greenhouse emissions more than double by 2050.

No government will adopt rigid restrictions on economic growth and personal freedom (limits on electricity usage, driving and travel) that might cut back global warming. Still, politicians want to show they're "doing something." Consider the *Kyoto protocol*（京都议定书）. It allowed countries that joined to punish those that didn't. But it hasn't reduced CO_2 emissions（up about 25% since 1990），and many *signatories*（签字国）didn't adopt tough enough policies to hit their 2008-2012 targets.

The practical conclusion is that if global warming is a potential disaster，the only solution is new technology. Only an aggressive research and development program might find ways of breaking our dependence on fossil fuels or dealing with it.

The trouble with the global warming debate is that it has become a moral problem when it's really engineering one. The inconvenient truth is that if we don't solve the engineering problem，we're helpless.

57. What is said about global warming in the first paragraph?
    A) It may not prove an environmental crisis at all.
    B) It is an issue requiring worldwide commitments.
    C) Serious steps have been taken to avoid or stop it.
    D) Very little will be done to bring it under control.

58. According to the author's understanding，what is Al Gore's view on global warming?
    A) It is a reality both people and politicians are unaware of.
    B) It is a phenomenon that causes us many inconveniences.
    C) It is a problem that can be solved once it is recognized.
    D) It is an area we actually have little knowledge about.

59. Greenhouse emissions will more than double by 2050 because of _____ .
    A) economic growth
    B) wasteful use of energy
    C) the widening gap between the rich and poor
    D) the rapid advances of science and technology

60. The author believes that，since the signing of the Kyoto Protocol，_____ .
    A) politicians have started to do something to better the situation
    B) few nations have adopted real tough measures to limit energy use
    C) reductions in energy consumption have greatly cut back global warming
    D) international cooperation has contributed to solving environmental problems

61. What is the message the author intends to convey?
    A) Global warming is more of a moral issue than a practical one.
    B) The ultimate solution to global warming lies in new technology.
    C) The debate over global warming will lead to technological breakthroughs.
    D) People have to give up certain material comforts to stop global warming.

Passage Two

Questions 62 to 66 are based on the following passage.

Someday a stranger will read your e-mail without your permission or scan the Websites you've visited. Or perhaps someone will casually glance through your credit card purchases or cell phone bills to find out your shopping preferences or calling habits.

In fact，it's likely some of these things have already happened to you. Who would watch you without your permission? It might be a spouse，a girlfriend，a marketing company，a boss，a cop or a criminal. Whoever it is，they will see you in a way you never intended to be seen——the 21st century equivalent of being caught naked.

Psychologists tell us boundaries are healthy，that it's important to reveal yourself to friends，family and lovers in stages，at appropriate times. But few boundaries remain. The digital bread *crumbs*（碎屑）

you leave everywhere make it easy for strangers to reconstruct who you are, where you are and what you like. In some cases, a simple Google search can reveal what you think. Like it or not, increasingly we live in a world where you simply cannot keep a secret.

The key question is: Does that matter?

For many Americans, the answer apparently is "no."

When opinion polls ask Americans about privacy, most say they are concerned about losing it. A survey found an overwhelming pessimism about privacy, with 60 percent of respondents saying they feel their privacy is "slipping away, and that bothers me."

But people say one thing and do another. Only a tiny fraction of Americans change any behaviors in an effort to preserve their privacy. Few people turn down a discount at *tollbooths*(收费站) to avoid using the EZ – Pass system that can track automobile movements. And few turn down supermarket loyalty cards. Privacy economist Alessandro Acquisti has run a series of tests that reveal people will surrender personal information like Social Security numbers just to get their hands on a pitiful 50-cents-off *coupon* (优惠卷).

But privacy does matter—at least sometimes. It's like health; when you have it, you don't notice it. Only when it's gone do you wish you'd done more to protect it.

62. What does the author mean by saying "the 21st century equivalent of being caught naked" (Lines 3-4, Para. 2)?

A) People's personal information is easily accessed without their knowledge.

B) In the 21st century people try every means to look into others' secrets.

C) People tend to be more frank with each other in the information age.

D) Criminals are easily caught on the spot with advanced technology.

63. What would psychologists advise on the relationships between friends?

A) Friends should open their hearts to each other.

B) Friends should always be faithful to each other.

C) There should be a distance even between friends.

D) There should be fewer disputes between friends.

64. Why does the author say "we live in a world where you simply cannot keep a secret" (Line 5. Para. 3)?

A) Modem society has finally evolved into an open society.

B) People leave traces around when using modern technology.

C) There are always people who are curious about others' affairs.

D) Many search engines profit by revealing people's identities.

65. What do most Americans do with regard to privacy protection?

A) They change behaviors that might disclose their identity.

B) They use various loyalty cards for business transactions.

C) They rely more and more on electronic devices.

D) They talk a lot but hardly do anything about it.

66. According to the passage, privacy is like health in that _____.

A) people will make every effort to keep it

B) its importance is rarely understood

C) it is something that can easily be lost

D) people don't cherish it until they lose it

Part V Cloze (15 minutes)

Universities are institutions that teach a wide variety of subjects at advanced levels. They also carry out research work aimed __67__ extending man's knowledge of these subjects. The emphasis given to each of these functions __68__ from university to university, according to the views of the people in __69__ and according to the resources available. The smaller and newer universities do not __70__ the staff or equipment to carry out the __71__ research projects possible in larger institutions. __72__ most experts agree that some research activity is __73__ to keep the staff and their students in __74__ with the latest developments in their subjects.

Most students attend a university mainly to __75__ the knowledge needed for their chosen __76__. Educationists believe that this aim should not be the __77__ one. Universities have always aimed to produce men and women __78__ judgment and wisdom as well as knowledge. For this reason, they __79__ students to meet others with differing __80__ and to read widely to __81__ their understanding in many fields of study. __82__ a secondary school course, a student should be interested enough in a subject to enjoy gaining knowledge for its own __83__. He should be prepared to __84__ sacrifices to study his chosen __85__ in depth. He should have an ambition to make some __86__ contribution to man's knowledge.

67. A) at   B) by   C) to   D) in
68. A) turns   B) ranges   C) moves   D) varies
69. A) prospect   B) place
    C) control   D) favor
70. A) occupy   B) possess   C) involve   D) spare
71. A) maximum   B) medium
    C) virtual   D) vast
72. A) But   B) As   C) While   D) For
73. A) natural   B) essential
    C) functional   D) optional
74. A) coordination   B) accordance
    C) touch   D) grasp
75. A) acquire   B) accept   C) endure   D) ensure
76. A) procession   B) profession
    C) possession   D) preference
77. A) typical   B) true   C) mere   D) only
78. A) with   B) under   C) on   D) through
79. A) prompt   B) provoke
    C) encourage   D) anticipate
80. A) histories   B) expressions
    C) interests   D) curiosities
81. A) broaden   B) lengthen
    C) enforce   D) specify
82. A) Amid   B) Over   C) After   D) Upon
83. A) object   B) effect   C) course   D) sake
84. A) take   B) suffer   C) make   D) pay
85. A) field   B) target   C) scope   D) goal
86. A) radical   B) meaningful
    C) truthful   D) initial

Part VI Translation (5 minutes)

87. Our efforts will pay off if the results of the research _____. (能应用于新技术的开发)

88. I can't boot my computer now. Something _____ (一定出了毛病) with its operation system.

89. Leaving one's job, _____ (不管是什么工作), is a difficult change, even for those who look forward to retiring.

90. _____ (与我成长的地方相比), this town is more prosperous and exciting.

91. _____ (直到他完成使命) did he realize that he was seriously ill.

第二章 实战模拟篇

本章采编了五套高保真大学英语四级模拟试题,供考前进行自我检测。这五套题的写作部分尽量体现近年来常考到的几种典型写作模式;其他各项测试内容均严格按照国家大学英语四级测试要求设计。所以,在此建议考生能按照所给定的时间进行"封闭式"强化训练,提高单位时间内做题的速度和效率,以便能熟练地把握做题时间,更好地应对未来的四级测试。

New College English Model Test One

Part I Writing (30 minutes)

Directions: *For this part, you are allowed 30 minutes to write a short essay "Why Do College Students Take A Part-Time Job?". You should write at least 120 words following the outline given below.*

1. 最近几年越来越多的大学生加入打工的队伍
2. 造成大学生打工的可能原因
3. 大学生打工应注意的一些事项

Why Do College Students Take A Part-Time Job?

_____

_____

_____

...

Part II Reading Comprehension (Skimming and Scanning) (15 minutes)

Fantasy Flight: Chiaki Mukai, Japan's First Female Astronaut

Raised by a working mother in Gunma Prefecture, a place known for dry winds and tough women, Chiaki Mukai decided she wanted to become a doctor while she was still in elementary school. At 32, she was a *cardiovascular*(心血管的) surgeon and chief resident at the Keio Hospital in Tokyo. Then she saw the newspaper ad that changed her life.

The beginning of a dream

The National Space Development Agency of Japan (NASDA) was looking for astronauts. What really shocked Chiaki, as she prefers to be known, was that there were no gender restrictions.

She suffered for three day. Weightlessness has much to offer scientific research, she thought. If I don't try, I'll regret it for the rest of my life.

"I had no idea what to expect," Chiaki said, giving one of her trademark smiles. "But I started two training programs the day I sent in my application. First, I started learning English. Then I began working out with weights."

Her English study program was entirely self-constructed. She made English labels for everything in the house. "I wanted it to seem like I was living in an English-speaking country," she explained. She answered the phone in English. She read English-language books. In August 1985, NASDA chose three payload specialists for the 1992 Spacelab-J launch — Mamoru Mohri, Takao Doi, and Chiaki Mukai. Chiaki's journey to the stars had begun.

The journey to space

"You can never give up," Chiaki says. "The life of Marie Curie taught me that. I read time and again how she struggled with her home, her children, and her scientific dream. And she achieved her goals — even though it cost her life."

"My mother is the same kind of woman. She didn't want to depend on someone else for her livelihood, so she opened a *haberdashery*(男子服饰用品店) in our hometown. She still runs it."

Chiaki's mother didn't blink an eye when her daughter told her of being chosen as an astronaut. "You never know what life's going to deal you," she said to Chiaki. "So you must do what you really want to."

Once she started her training for space, Chiaki's *roster*(名单) of heroes grew longer. "Yuri Gagarin was the pioneer," she said. "I have immense respect for him. And Neil Armstrong — it was really great, what he did. That must have been a 'fantastic voyage'. But then all the people I worked with at NASA and NASDA are heroes in their won way. So how do I choose."

Chiaki gestured at the *bustle*(喧嚣) of Tokyo outside the window. "From here, we can't see very much. But from 300 miles up, you realize how small the earth is. But you know what, I first learned that in Orlando, Florida — at Disneyworld."

Which brings Chiaki to another of her heroes: Walt Disney. Like Chiaki, he was a dreamer. And he shared his dreams of fantastic worlds with others. She is fascinated buy the way his movies, gentle and natural, teach us about humanity.

"Disney, and science fiction writers like Arthur C. Clarke, realized the Earth is just a small planet without having to go into space. Their accomplishment is much greater in a way than ours. We saw with our eyes. They saw with their minds' eyes."

The first Japanese astronaut to fly an American space shuttle was Mamoru Mohri, who went as payload specialist on the Spacelab-J, a flight funded largely by Japan. Chiaki and Takao Doi backed him up.

After Mohri's flight touched down, Chiaki journeyed back to Japan to begin work in the microgravity lab at Tsukuba. But word soon came that she had been chosen as payload specialist for the International Microgravity Laboratory-2 (IML-2), so she returned to take up0 training where she'd paused.

"Mohri was chosen to fly the Japanese-funded space shuttle, so there was never any doubt that he'd go. But the IML-2 was an international flight. NASA didn't have to choose me. And there were half-a-dozen well-qualified alternatives who could have gone in my place. The pressure as tremendous."

Chiaki says she had a hard time understanding jokes told in southern accents. "Flying is fine. *Acronyms*(首字母缩拼词) are easy to learn, so you don't even have to speak in sentences. But jokes. Whew! Or tales about family. Any time the subject strayed from work, I was in trouble."

In preparation for her flight, Chiaki took more than a thousand of the training flights that give passengers twenty seconds of weightlessness. "Twenty seconds is nothing like the real thing," Chiaki says ruefully. "No matter how many times you do it."

The dream came true

On 8 July 1994, a quarter of a century after Neil Armstrong and Buzz Aldrin walked on the surface of the moon, the IML-2 mission blasted off. Soon the shuttle Columbia was in orbit, and Chiaki's work began. Before the shuttle touched down two weeks later, she had appeared on children's television, played *midwife*(接生婆) to a brood of *newts*(蝾螈), used her own body to record the effects of weightlessness on human beings——82 experiments in all.

"Way out there, looking down at the curvature of the earth, I couldn't help thinking what a small world this is. Compared to all of outer space, Earth is like one tiny *plankton*(浮游生物) swimming in a vast ocean. Yet look at the power of mankind. Look where we are, 300 miles above the surface. We're so very fragile, yet so very strong."

"Back on earth, I made an astounding discovery. When you let go of things, they drop! I was constantly reminded of Earth's tremendous pull. For nearly three days after touchdown, every step reminded me of gravity. Every move I made was a tussle with weight. Yet after three days, my body adjusted. Isn't that marvelous?" While scientists continue to research the many implications of weightlessness, Chiaki envisions great medical benefits from microgravitational situations. *Rehabilitation* (康复) would make tremendous strides, she maintains. "People with handicaps in full gravity might not have them in zero gravity conditions. They could practice movements at zero, 0.25 G, 0.5 G, and so on until they were competent at normal gravity."

To understand the functions of the eye, we remove all light, Chiaki explains. To understand the functions of the ear, we remove all sound, and work from there. So she ways that removing the weight of gravity will bring mankind new understanding of how the human body works.

The impossible dream

Cervantes is another Chiaki hero... or perhaps we should say Don Quixote. "I love *Man of La Mancha*. I cry every time I see it." She hums: "To dream the impossible dream...."

"I like the way they translated that song into Japanese," she says. "Instead of 'impossible dream', and means that as soon as you have fulfilled one dream, another even more vivid dream forms."

She stands in her grey-green double-breasted suit and thrusts out a hand. Her grasp is firm, like her vision. With a smile, she strides away. Back to her laboratory in Tsukuba. Where she'll work regular 12-hour days... reaching for the stars.

1. Raised by a working mother, Chiaki Mukai dreamed of becoming an astronaut when she was still a child.
2. Chiaki Mukai was surprised to learn that women could also apply for the position of an astronaut.
3. Chiaki Mukai's mother was against her daughter's choice because she thought that being an astronaut was dangerous.
4. Chiaki Mukai was the first Japanese astronaut to fly a space shuttle.
5. Chiaki Mukai was chosen by NASA because she was female and warm-hearted.
6. Seen from the outer space, the earth is much smaller than the other planets or stars.
7. After returning from her flight, Chiaki Mukai had difficulty in adjusting to the gravity on the earth.
8. Being in a situation of weightlessness will help mankind further understand _____.
9. According to Chiaki Mukai, the impossible dream or unreachable dream means once one has realized one dream, _____.
10. To Chiaki Mukai, her next dream may be _____.

Part III *Listening Comprehension* (*35 minutes*)

ection A

11. A) The flight has been canceled.　　　　　B) The plane is late.

C) The plane is on time.   D) The tickets for this flight have been sold out.

12. A) He is not to blame.   B) It was his fault.

C) He will accept all responsibility.   D) He will be more careful next time.

13. A) She has been dismissed for her poor performance.

B) She has been fired by the company.

C) She has been granted leave for one month.

D) She has been offered a new job.

14. A) There will be heavy fog in all areas.   B) There will be heavy rain by midnight.

C) There will be heavy fog in the east.   D) There will be fog in all areas by midnight.

15. A) She's scornful.   B) She's angry.

C) She's sympathetic.   D) She's worried.

16. A) He likes the job of a dish-washer because it pays well.

B) He thinks it's important to have a good job from the beginning.

C) He hates to be a dish-washer because it's boring.

D) He would work as a dish-washer in summer if he has to.

17. A) She must learn to understand John's humor better.

B) She enjoys John's humor a great deal.

C) She doesn't appreciate John's humor.

D) She thinks John is not funny enough.

18. A) Joan may have taken a wrong train.   B) Joan won't come to the conference.

C) Joan will miss the next conference.   D) Joan may be late for the opening speech.

Questions 19 to 22 are based on the conversation you have just heard.

19. A) The election for senator.   B) The election for treasurer.

C) The election for secretary.   D) The election for president.

20. A) They're competing against each other in an election.

B) The man is writing the woman's speech.

C) The woman is planning the man's campaign.

D) The man is interviewing the woman.

21. A) Junior class treasurer.   B) President.

C) Senior class treasurer.   D) Vice president.

22. A) Make posters.   B) Write a speech.

C) Answer questions.   D) Study chemistry.

Questions 23 to 25 are based on the conversation you have just heard.

23. A) Because they are interesting.

B) Because they are required by the school.

C) Because they are beneficial for future work.

D) Because they are needed to apply for scholarship.

24. A) They don't have enough money to pay high fees.

B) They have learned too many grammar rules.

C) They can't deal with the assignment of reading and writing.

D) They have great difficulties in communication with native speakers.

25. A) Financial problems.

B) Heavy burden of part-time jobs.

C) Not having enough time for work due to partying.

D) Lack of right attitude and skills in classroom work.

Section B

Passage One

Questions 26 to 28 are based on the passage you have just heard.

26. A) Love.   B) Violence.   C) Conflict.   D) Mystery.

27. A) The main character remains the same.

    B) The main character dies in the end.

    C) The main character gains his ends.

    D) The main character undergoes a change.

28. A) We can learn how bad persons can improve themselves.

    B) We can learn how to deal with people.

    C) We can understand life a little better.

    D) We can find better ways to cope with conflicts.

Passage Two

Questions 29 to 32 are based on the passage you have just heard.

29. A) How to start a university.   B) How colleges have changed in America.

    C) The American Revolution.   D) The world famous colleges in America.

30. A) In 1636.   B) In 1638.   C) In 1836.   D) In 1782.

31. A) Latin and Greek.   B) English and French.

    C) French and German.   D) Latin, Greek, French, and German.

32. A) Colleges and universities are smaller than before.

    B) All college students study to become teachers or ministers.

    C) Different kinds of colleges and universities have been set up to meet the needs of students.

    D) Early schools are not alike.

Passage Three

Questions 33 to 35 are based on the passage you have just heard.

33. A) The idea that it reached out to "the end of the world".

    B) The idea that it would be too hot at the equator.

    C) The idea that it is too large.

    D) Both A and B.

34. A) There is less salt in the Atlantic Ocean than in any other oceans of the world.

    B) The water of the Atlantic Ocean is saltier than that of the Pacific Ocean.

    C) The water of the Atlantic Ocean is saltier than that of any other place in the world.

    D) The Atlantic Ocean has more salt than water in it.

35. A) The Saltiest Ocean in the World.   B) The Atlantic Ocean.

    C) The Atlantic—A Lonely Ocean.   D) The Water of the Ocean.

Section C Compound Dictation

    Working relations with other people at the place of work include relationships with fellow employees, workers or colleagues. A major part of work or job (36)＿＿＿＿＿ comes from "getting on" with others at work. Work relations will also include those between the "boss" and yourself: management-employee relations are not always straightforward, (37)＿＿＿＿＿ as the management's (38)＿＿＿＿＿ of your performance can be (39)＿＿＿＿＿ to your future career.

    There will always be (40)＿＿＿＿＿ about which employees will want to talk to the management. In small businesses the "boss" will (41)＿＿＿＿＿ work alongside his workers. Anything, which needs

to be (42)_____ out, will be done face-to-face as soon as a problem arises. There may be no formal meetings or (43)_____. The larger the business, the less direct contact there will be between employees and management. (44)_____.
Some companies have specially organized consultative committees for this purpose.

In many countries of the world today, especially in large firms, employees join a trade union and ask the union to represent them to the management. (45)_____.
The process through which unions negotiate with management on behalf of their members is called "collective bargaining". (46)_____.
Occasionally a firm will refuse to recognize the right of a union to negotiate for its members and a dispute over union recognition will arise.

Part Ⅳ *Reading Comprehension*（*Reading in Depth*）（*25 minutes*）

ection A

Questions 47 to 56 are based on the following passage.

The motor vehicle has killed and disabled more people in its brief history than any bomb or weapon ever invented. Much of the blood on the street flows __47__ from uncivil behavior of drivers who refuse to respect the legal and moral rights of others. So the *massacre*（残杀）on the road may be __48__ as a social problem. In fact, the enemies of society on wheels are rather harmless people just ordinary people acting carelessly, you might say. But it is a __49__ both of law and common morality that carelessness is no excuse when one's actions could bring death or damage to others. A __50__ of the killers go even beyond carelessness to total negligence.

Researchers have estimated that as many as 80 per cent of all automobile accidents can be attributed to the psychological condition of the driver. Emotional upsets can distort drivers' reactions, slow their judgement, and blind them to dangers that might otherwise be __51__. The experts warn that it is vital for every driver to make a conscious effort to keep one's emotions under control. Yet the irresponsibility that accounts for much of the problem is not __52__ to drivers. Street walkers regularly __53__ traffic regulations, they are at fault in most vehicle walker accidents; and many cyclists even believe that they are not __54__ to the basic rules of the road.

Significant legal advances have been made towards safer driving in the past few years. Safety standards for vehicle have been raised both at the point of manufacture and through periodic road-worthiness __55__. In addition, speed limits have been lowered. Due to these measures, the accident rate has decreased. But the accident experts still worry because there has been little or no improvement in the way drivers behave. The only real and lasting solution, say the experts, is to convince people that driving is a skilled task requiring constant care and concentration. Those who fail to do all these things __56__ a threat to those with whom they share the road.

A) inspections	I) violate
B) implications	J) essentially
C) minority	K) confined
D) insight	L) perceived
E) present	M) referred
F) subject	N) principle
G) reserved	O) evident
H) ultimately	

Section B

Passage One

Questions 57 to 61 are based on the following passage.

In cities with rent control, the city government sets the maximum rent that a landlord can charge for an apartment. Supporters of rent control argue that it protects people who are living in apartments. Their rent cannot increase; therefore, they are not in danger of losing their homes. However, the critics say that after a long time, rent control may have negative effects. Landlords know that they cannot increase their profits. Therefore, they invest in other businesses where they can increase their profits. They do not invest in new buildings which would also be rent-controlled.

As a result, new apartments are not built. Many people who need apartments cannot find any. According to the critics, the end result of rent control is a shortage of apartments in the city. Some theorists argue that the minimum wage law can cause problems in the same way. The federal government sets the minimum that an employer must pay workers. The minimum helps people who generally look for unskilled, low-paying jobs. However, if the minimum is high, employers may hire fewer workers. They will replace workers with machinery. The price, which is the wage that employers must pay, increases. Therefore, other things being equal, the number of workers that employers want decreases. Thus, critics claim, an increase in the minimum wage may cause unemployment. Some poor people may find themselves without jobs instead of with jobs at the minimum wage.

Supporters of the minimum wage say that it helps people keep their dignity. Because of the law, workers cannot sell their services for less than the minimum. Furthermore, employers cannot force workers to accept jobs at unfair wages.

Economic theory predicts the results of economic decisions such as decisions about farm production, rent control, and the minimum wage. The predictions may be correct only if "other things are equal". Economists do not agree on some of the predictions. They also do not agree on the value of different decisions. Some economists support a particular decision while others criticize it. Economists do agree, however, that there are no simple answers to economic questions.

57. There is the possibility that setting maximum rent may _____.
   A) cause a shortage of apartments
   B) worry those who rent apartments as homes
   C) increase the profits of landlords
   D) encourage landlords to invest in building apartment

58. According to the critics, rent control _____.
   A) will always benefit those who rent apartments
   B) proves to be of vital importance to the low-income groups
   C) will bring negative effects in the long run
   D) is necessary especially in protecting those unemployed

59. The problem of unemployment will arise _____.
   A) if the minimum wage is set too high   B) if the minimum wage is set too low
   C) if the workers are unskilled   D) if the maximum wage is set

60. The passage tells us _____.
   A) the relationship between supply and demand
   B) the possible results of government controls
   C) the necessity of government control

D) the urgency of getting rid of government controls

61. Which of the following statements is NOT true?

    A) The results of economic decisions cannot always be predicted.

    B) Minimum wage can not always protect employees.

    C) Economic theory can predict the results of economic decisions if other factors are not changing.

    D) Economic decisions should not be based on economic theory.

Passage Two

Questions 62 to 66 are based on the following passage.

Beauty has always been regarded as something praiseworthy. Almost everyone thinks attractive people are happier and healthier, have better marriages and have more respectable occupations. Personal consultants give them better advice for finding jobs. Even judges are softer on attractive *defendants*(被告). But in the executive circle, beauty can become a liability.

While attractiveness is a positive factor for a man on his way up the executive ladder, it is harmful to a woman.

Handsome male executives were perceived as having more integrity than plainer men; effort and ability were thought to account for their success.

Attractive female executives were considered to have less integrity than unattractive ones; their success was attributed not to ability but to factors such as luck.

All unattractive women executives were thought to have more integrity and to be more capable than the attractive female executives. Interestingly, though, the rise of the unattractive overnight successes was attributed more to personal relationships and less to ability than was that of attractive overnight successes.

Why are attractive women not thought to be able? An attractive woman is perceived to be more *feminine*(阴柔的) and an attractive man more *masculine*(阳刚之气的) than the less attractive ones. Thus, an attractive woman has an advantage in traditionally female jobs, but an attractive woman in a traditionally masculine position appears to lack the "masculine" qualities required.

This is true even in politics. "When the only clue is how he or she looks, people treat men and women differently," says Anne Bowman, who recently published a study on the effects of attractiveness on political candidates. She asked 125 undergraduates to rank two groups of photographs, one of men and one of women, in order of attractiveness. The students were told the photographs were of candidates for political offices. They were asked to rank them again, in the order they would vote for them.

The results showed that attractive males utterly defeated unattractive men, but the women who had been ranked most attractive invariably received the fewest votes.

62. The word "liability" (Line 4, Para. 1) most probably means "_____".

    A) misfortune   B) instability   C) disadvantage   D) burden

63. In traditionally female jobs, attractiveness _____.

    A) reinforces the feminine qualities required

    B) makes women look more honest and capable

    C) is of primary importance to women

    D) often enables women to succeed quickly

64. Bowman's experiment reveals that when it comes to politics, attractiveness _____.

    A) turns out to be an obstacle to men

    B) affects men and women alike

    C) has as little effect on men as on women

D) is more of an obstacle than a benefit to women

65. It can be inferred from the passage that people's views on beauty are often _____.

A) practical   B) prejudiced   C) old-fashioned   D) radical

66. The author writes this passage to _____.

A) discuss the negative aspects of being attractive

B) give advice to job-seekers who are attractive

C) demand equal rights for women .

D) emphasize the importance of appearance

Part IV *Cloze* (*15 minutes*)

The first man who cooked his food, instead of eating it raw, lived so long ago that we have no idea who he was or where he lived. We do know, ___67___, that for thousands of years food was always eaten cold and ___68___. Perhaps the cooked food was heated accidentally by a ___69___ fire or by the molten *lava*(熔岩) from an *erupting*(喷发的) ___70___. When people first tasted food that had been cooked, they found it tasted better. However, ___71___ after this discovery, cooked food must have remained a rarity ___72___ man learned how to make and ___73___ fire.

Primitive men who lived in hot ___74___ could depend on the heat of the sun to cook their food. For example, in the desert areas of the southwestern United States, the Indians cooked their food by placing it on a flat ___75___ in the hot sun. They cooked pieces of meat and thin cakes of corn meal in this ___76___. We guess that the earliest kitchen ___77___ was a stick ___78___ which a piece of meat could be attached and held over a fire. Later this stick was ___79___ by an iron rod which could be turned frequently to cook the meat ___80___ all sides.

Cooking food in water was ___81___ before man learned to make water containers that could not be ___82___ by fire.

The ___83___ cooking pots were reed or grass baskets in which soups and stews could be cooked. ___84___ 166 B. C. the Egyptians had learned to

67. A) thus   B) however
     C) otherwise   D) consequently

68. A) raw   B) crude
     C) coarse   D) fresh

69. A) forest   D) range
     C) kitchen   D) solar

70. A) chimney   B) volcano
     C) blast   D) valley

71. A) through   B) since
     C) soon   D) even

72. A) when   B) which
     C) until   D) as

73. A) switch   B) glow
     C) light   D) lighten

74. A) regions   B) districts
     C) communities   D) grounds

75. A) stone   B) board
     C) table   D) cupboard

76. A) fashion   B) zone
     C) sector   D) belt

77. A) appliance   B) instrument
     C) tool   D) equipment

78. A) by   B) over
     C) on   D) to

79. A) supported   B) replaced
     C) converted   D) transferred

80. A) around   B) on
     C) over   D) at

81. A) incapable   B) unavoidable
     C) impossible   D) unpopular

82. A) broken   B) destroyed
     C) steamed   D) pierced

83. A) last   B) latest
     C) earliest   D) latter

make mere ___85___ cooking pots out of sandstone. Many years later，the Eskimos learned to make ___86___ pans.

84. A) As early as   B) As well as
    C) As long as   D) As far as
85. A) temporary   B) permanent
    C) stable   D) steady
86. A) similar   B) uniform
    C) likely   D) identical

Part Ⅵ Translation（*5 minutes*）

87. It was essential that _____（申请表要在截止日期之前寄回）.

88. _____（面对严重的疾病），she has shown great courage.

89. She doesn't talk much，but _____（言之有理）.

90. It has not been made clear _____（这条路什么时候通车）.

91. The *riot*（暴乱）is said _____（由于政府的住房政策引起的）.

New College English Model Test Two

Part Ⅰ Writing (30 minutes)

Directions：*For this part，you are allowed 30 minutes to write a short essay "Is Frustration A Bad Thing?" You should write at least 120 words following the outline given below.*

1. 有些人认为挫折是坏事
2. 更多的人并不这么看
3. 在我看来……

Is Frustration A Bad Thing?

_____

_____

_____

...

Part Ⅱ Reading Comprehension (Skimming and Scanning) (15 minutes)

American Karoshi(过劳死)

Workaholics(工作狂) in America

A thin，40-something man with scattered white hair and *wan*(苍白的) complexion looked up from his notebook in a church basement on Manhattan's Upper West Side.

"Hi，I'm Emerson，" he said，"and I'm addicted to work."

"Hi，Emerson，" answered his companions.

Emerson is a lecturer at a major university in the New York area. In addition to his course load，he developed two new classes last semester，submitted a book-length manuscript for publication and served as executive director of a small not-for-profit corporation. "In my own eyes I'm a lazy *sloth*(懒惰的人)，" he declared. He even agonized over coming to this evening's Workaholics Anonymous meeting. He couldn't shake the thought of running home to update his telephone list. "I just feel compelled to do this，" he said. "It's insanity."

What makes workaholics of Americas

Emerson is not alone. His condition is a product of the society that surrounds him. Joan Feldman of an investment firm in Tower 2 of the World Trade Center barely got out of the building after the first airliner crashed into Tower 1 on 11 September. While hurrying down the stairs from the 88th floor，she heard an announcement over the Center's public-address system ordering employees back to work. "I would be dead，" said Ms Feldman when asked what would have happened if she had obeyed.

America's obsession with work has reached epidemic proportions，according to Dr Bryan E. Robinson，family therapist and author of the 1998 book，*Chained To the Desk*（New York University Press）. He believes that workaholism is a disease that kills people and ruins families. In New York，time is money，and since one's worth is measured by ability to earn，overwork isn't just a good idea，it's the law of supply and demand. According to psychiatrist Dr Jay B. Rohrlich，in Hollywood where one's appearance is *paramount*（至高无上的）, the same problems might manifest themselves in *anorexia*（厌食症）. But in New York, where working excessively to achieve success is the norm, people go overboard. "When your drive controls you, instead of you controlling it, it can be the sign of underlying problems," he points out.

That equation is reinforced by new technologies which make workaholics of all of us. When Marilyn Machlowitz wrote *Workaholics* in 1980, things were very different. "We didn't have faxes, cell phones, cell phones with e-mail, beepers, Palm Pilots. Workaholics used to be the people who world work anytime, anywhere. What has changed is that it has become the norm to be on call 24/7. Now that's something that doesn't cause anyone to blink. Globalization has really changed a lot of our work habits." People in the financial industry check in with London when they arrive for work in the morning and don't stop until the *Nikkei*（日经指数）starts up at eight or nine in the evening. "The demand has increased to a point where it may be faster than people are hardwired to handle. And we haven't seen all that high-tech has to offer yet, either." Twenty years ago we had enforced downtime, noted Ms Machlowitz: "If we had to send a draft of a document to someone, we had time before they received it in the mail, read it and mailed it back demanding changes. That time has collapsed to nothing. 'Right away' has a new definition."

A study on workaholics

A study recently conducted by the health insurer Oxford Health Plans found that one in five Americans show up for work whether they're ill, injured or have a medical appointment. This same obsession keeps one in five Americans from taking their vacation—a failure which has been found to put individuals at risk of early death. "*Vacationitis*（假日病）" may come from fear of returning to find someone else at your desk, or the idea that everything will collapse in your absence.

Workaholics Anonymous publishes a list of telltale signs including: working more than 40 hours a week; taking work with you to bed, on weekends and on vacation; talking about work more than any other subject; believing its' okay to work long hours if you love what you do; thinking about working while driving, falling asleep or when others are talking.

To New Yorkers, of course, these are simply the habits of successful people. The International Labor Office released findings that after passing the Japanese as the world's most overworked population in the mid-1990s, Americans have pulled way ahead of the pack. Americans now work an average of 1,979 hours a year, about three-and-a-half weeks more than the Japanese, six-and-a-half weeks more than the British and about twelve-and-a-half weeks more than their German counterparts.

Patrick Cleary of the National Association of Manufacturers told the *New York Times*, "We don't see this necessarily as bad news at all," pointing out that the increase in hours coincided with a strong economic performance. Companies often compensate for America's chronic shortage of skilled laborers with demands of forced overtime. But while an inflated salary can dull the pains of overwork, excessive job stress can cause permanent *degenerative*（不断恶化的）damage to the heart.

Workaholics deserve more attention

In Japan, if a "salary man" is found slumped over his keyboard in the morning, it triggers survivors to call for a Karoshi investigation to determine whether the death was caused by overwork. In New York the *coroner*（验尸官）would call the same condition heart failure.

Cardiac *disease*（心脏病）is a complex malady affected by diet, activity, smoking, drinking and stress—and it occurs in epidemic proportions in the US. But coroners and judges refuse to entertain the notion that inordinate work stress can cause death. "If someone is working 14 hours a day, that person is not going to be eating right," said one physician at New York's Beth Israel Medical Center, who asked that his name not be revealed. "They're not going to have time for a nice home-cooked meal. That means fast food and increased *cholesterol*(胆固醇). Secondly, the time constraints will not permit them to exercise. And if the person is a workaholic, often they're going to be a smoker or, if they're really stressed out, a drinker."

An explosion in karoshi cases accompanied Japan's economic boom in the early 1980s. Since karoshi was legally recognized in the 1980s, 30,000 Japanese have been diagnosed as victims. The large number of work-related deaths spurred Tokyo to legislate a national pension system for surviving members of karoshi victims' families. But Washington continues to fail to react to such stimuli.

US courts give no money to damage claims by overworked Americans. The law seems to suggest that if everyone is overworked to the point of *debilitation*(虚弱), none therefore warrants compensation. This makes America's Protestant work ethic a Puritan plague and affirms anthropologist Marshall Sahlins's comment that the market system has handed down to human beings a sentence of "life at hard labor".

1. From his appearance, we know that Emerson was exhausted by his work.
2. Besides his work as a lecturer at a major university, Emerson also ran a corporation to earn more money.
3. According to the author, there are few people who are so addicted to work like Emerson.
4. Dr. Bryan E Robinson believes that workaholism is also a disease which can be cured with medicine.
5. The author believes that new technologies contribute to the workaholics of modern people.
6. People maybe suffer from vacationitis because they don't want to waste money during vacations.
7. According to the findings released by the International Labour Office, the British people occupy the third place among the world's most overworked population.
8. If a "salary man" is found slumped over his keyboard, his death may be caused by _____, a term preferably used in the US.
9. One physician at New York's Beth Israel Medical Center believed that if a person is a workaholic, more often than not, he will be a _____ .
10. Unlike Japan, the US still fails to legislate a national pension system for _____ .

Part Ⅲ *Listening Comprehension* (*35 minutes*)

Section A

11. A) The man thinks travelling by air is quite safe.
    B) Both speakers feel nervous when flying.
    C) The woman never travels by plane.
    D) The speakers feel sad about the serious loss of life.
12. A) In an office.　　　　　　　　B) In a restaurant.
    C) At a railway station.　　　　　D) At the information desk.
13. A) Fix the shelf.　　B) Paint the shelf.　　C) Write the letter.　　D) look for the pen.
14. A) It gives a 30% discount to all customers.　　B) It is run by Mrs. Winter's husband.
    C) It hires Mrs. Winter as an adviser.　　　　　D) It encourages husbands to shop on their own.
15. A) Long exposure to the sun.　　　　B) Lack of sleep.
    C) Too tight a hat.　　　　　　　　　D) Long working hours.
16. A) His English is still poor after ten years in America.
    B) He doesn't mind speaking English with an accent.
    C) He doesn't like the way Americans speak.

D) He speaks English as if he were a native speaker.

17. A) An auto mechanic.　　　　　　　　　　B) An electrician.

　　C) A carpenter.　　　　　　　　　　　　D) A telephone repairman.

18. A) They both enjoyed watching the game.

　　B) The man thought the results were beyond their expectations.

　　C) They both felt good about the results of the game.

　　D) People were surprised at their winning the game.

Questions 19 to 22 are based on the conversation you have just heard.

19. A) They may not be able to take their vacation.

　　B) It may snow during their vacation.

　　C) They need more money.

　　D) They may miss graduation.

20. A) They are going skiing.　　　　　　　　B) Their plans include other friends.

　　C) They will drive together.　　　　　　　D) Their reservations have been canceled.

21. A) Because of the possibility of bad weather.

　　B) Because of the faculty's contracts.

　　C) Because of the summer schedule of classes.

　　D) Because of' the date for graduation.

22. A) He might lose his financial aid.　　　　B) He doesn't want to attend summer classes.

　　C) He had already missed too many.　　　D) He's afraid he might not graduate.

Questions 23 to 25 are based on the conversation you have just heard.

23. A) His friend.　　　B) His sister.　　　C) His mother.　　　D) His colleague.

24. A) A small place with a nice view of the city.

　　B) A spacious apartment that includes cable TV.

　　C) An apartment downtown with free parking.

　　D) An apartment outside the downtown area.

25. A) He should be careful when using his credit cards.

　　B) He ought to sell his car to save money.

　　C) He should stop spending money on entertainment.

　　D) He ought to find a cheaper apartment in the downtown area.

Section B

Passage One

Questions 26 to 28 are based on the passage you have just heard.

26. A) The poor places are getting richer.　　B) The rich places are getting richer.

　　C) The poor places are getting poorer.　　D) Both B and C.

27. A) The poor are unemployed.

　　B) All the poor have no land.

　　C) The poor have no houses in big cities.

　　D) There is no hope for the poor in the village.

28. A) Rural unemployment.　　　　　　　　B) Urban unemployment.

　　C) No housing in the villages.　　　　　　D) No foreign aid in the villages.

Passage Two

Questions 29 to 32 are based on the passage you have just heard.

29. A) The increasing output of tobacco.

B) The rapid development of cigarette-making machine.

C) The rapid development of cigarette-making factories.

D) The great number of people engaged in cigarette producing.

30. A) Forty-three.　　　B) Thirty-one.　　　C) Seventy-five.　　　D) Forty-six.

31. A) Income, years of schooling, and job type.

B) Income and work environment.

C) Education and mood.

D) Occupation and influence of family members.

32. A) City people smoke less than people living on farms.

B) The better-educated men tend to smoke more heavily than those with lower income.

C) The better-educated women tend to smoke more heavily.

D) A well-paid man is likely to smoke more packs of cigarettes per day.

Passage Three

Questions 33 to 35 are based on the passage you have just heard.

33. A) It's very far from the heart of the city.

B) It's at the crossroads of 42nd Street and 5th Avenue in the heart of the city.

C) It's at the 42nd Street and 5th Avenue crossing.

D) Its doors face the 42nd Street and other Avenues.

34. A) There are so many books to work with in the library.

B) It's impossible to grow grass and trees in the heart of New York.

C) The library's cost are going down.

D) The library needs more books and paintings.

35. A) Because it is one of New York's most valuable buildings.

B) Because it contains all our knowledge.

C) Because there are a lot of rooms, in which readers can sit and think in comfort.

D) Because well-known New York writers and artists are trying to use it.

Section C

From the top of Temple IV, dense jungle *canopy*(遮篷) spreads to the horizon in every direction. Some 215 feet below lies Tikal, the greatest of the Mayan cities, much of it still (36)_____ by trees that have swallowed Temple IV up to the base of its (37)_____ .

(38)_____ of archaeologists have worked to *excavate*(挖掘) this vast city since a Spanish governor rediscovered it in 1848. They're still at work today, clearing trees from nearby temples, searching for (39)_____ to how the ancient Maya lived and what caused them to (40)_____ their great cities six centuries before the Spanish conquest. New inscriptions, villages, even (41)_____ cities are being discovered every year, (42)_____ great excitement among archaeologists.

The latest and most (43)_____ find was announced on Sept. 8: the discovery of a nearly intact 170-room palace buried at Cancuen, 70 miles south of Tikal. (44)_____ _____. It's so large, in fact, that previous expeditions to Cancuen mistook it for a great jungle-covered hill.

(45)_____ .

But what to make of a city abandoned so swiftly? Dr. Hammond finds evidence that the city was in the midst of a massive expansion project when its inhabitants suddenly left. Hammond thinks (46)_____ _____ "Just before the collapse, there are more Maya around than ever before, and they're packed into cities that are larger, more numerous, and more closely spaced," he says.

Part Ⅳ *Reading Comprehension*（*Reading in Depth*）（*25 minutes*）

Section A

Questions 47 to 56 are based on the following passage.

Man will never conquer space. Such a statement may sound *ludicrous*（荒唐的），after we have made such long ___47___ into space. Yet it expresses a truth that our forefathers knew and we have forgotten one that our descendants must learn again, in heartbreak and loneliness.

Our age is in many ways unique, full of ___48___ that never occurred before and may never come again. They distort our thinking, making us believe that what is true now will be true forever, though perhaps on a large ___49___ . Because we have *annihilated*（消除）distance on this planet, we imagine that we can do the same in space. The truth is ___50___ , and we will see it more clearly if we forget the present and turn our minds toward the past.

To our ancestors, the vastness of the earth was a(n) ___51___ factor in their thoughts and lives. No man could ever see more than a tiny ___52___ of the earth. Only a lifetime ago, parents waved farewell to their emigrating children, knowing they would never see them again.

Now, within one ___53___ generation, all this has changed. Psychologically as well as physically, there are no longer any remote places on earth. When a friend leaves for what was once a distant country, he cannot feel the same sense of *irrevocable*（无法改变的）___54___ that saddened our forefathers. We know that he is only hours away by jetliner, and we have merely to reach for the telephone to hear his voice.

When the satellite communication network is fully established, it will be as easy to see friends on the far side of the earth as to talk to them on the other side of the town. Then the world will ___55___ no more. From a world that has become too small, we are moving out into one that will be forever too large, whose ___56___ will recede from us always more swiftly than we can reach out toward them.

A) frontiers	I) scale
B) extensions	J) exclusive
C) incredible	K) otherwise
D) ambitious	L) fraction
E) shrink	M) diverse
F) isolate	N) separation
G) dominant	O) phenomena
H) strides	

Section B

Passage One

Questions 57 to 61 are based on the following passage.

It is 3a. m. Everything on the university campus seems ghostlike in the quiet, misty darkness — everything except the computer center. Here, twenty students *rumpled*（弄皱的，散乱的）and *bleary-eyed* （视力模糊不清的），sit staring at their consoles, tapping away on the terminal keys. With eyes glued to the video screen, they tap on for hours. For the rest of the world, it might be the middle of the night, but here time does not exist. This is a world to itself. These young computer "hackers" are pursuing a kind of compulsion, a drive so consuming that it overshadows nearly every other part of their lives and forms the focal point of their existence. They are compulsive computer programmers. Some of these students have been at the console for thirty hours or more without a break for meals or sleep. Some have fallen asleep on sofas and lounge chairs in the computer center, trying to catch a few winks but are reluctant to get too far away from their beloved machines.

Most of these students don't have to be at the computer center in the middle of the night. They aren't working on assignments. They are there because they want to be — they are irresistibly drawn there.

And they are not alone. There are hackers at computer centers all across the country. In their extreme form, they focus on nothing else. They drop out of school and lose contact with friends; they might have difficulty finding jobs, choosing instead to wander from one computer center to another.

"I remember one hacker. We literally had to carry him off his chair to feed him and put him to sleep. We really feared for his health," says a computer science professor at MIT.

Computer science teachers are now more aware of the implications of this hacker phenomenon and are on the lookout for potential hackers and cases of computer *addiction*(沉溺, 上瘾) that are already severe. They know that the case of the hackers is not just the story of one person's relationship with a machine. It is the story of a society's relationship to the so-called thinking machines, which are becoming almost *ubiquitous*(到处存在的).

57. We can learn from the passage that those at the computer center in the middle of the night are _____.

A) students working on a program they have to complete before dawn

B) students using computers to amuse themselves

C) hard-working computer science majors

D) students deeply fascinated by the computer

58. Which of the following is NOT true of those young computer "hackers"?

A) Most of them are top students majoring in computer programming.

B) For them, computer programming is the sole purpose for their life.

C) They can stay with the computer at the center for nearly three days on end.

D) Their "love" for the computer is so deep that they want to be near their machines even when they sleep.

59. It can be reasonably inferred from the passage that _____.

A) the "hackers" are largely dependent on their teachers to take care of their routine life

B) university computer centers are open to almost everyone

C) university computer centers are expecting outstanding programmers out of the "hackers"

D) the "hacker" phenomenon is partly attributed to the insufficiency of the computer centers

60. The author's attitude towards the "hacker" phenomenon can be described as _____.

A) subjective   B) prejudiced   C) anxious   D) disgusted

61. Which of the following may be a most appropriate title for the passage?

A) The Charm of Computer Science.

B) A New Type of Electronic Toys.

C) Computer Programming, A Worthwhile Cause.

D) Computer Addicts.

Passage Two

Questions 62 to 66 are based on the following passage.

The age of gilded *youth*(纨绔子弟) is over. Today's under-thirties are the first generation for a century who can expect a lower living standard than their parents. Research into the lifestyle and prospects of people born since 1970 shows that they are likely to face a lifetime of longer working hours, lower job security and higher taxes than the previous generation. When they leave work late in the evening they will be more likely to return to a small rented flat than to a house of their own. When, eventually, they retire it will be on pensions far lower in real terms than those of their immediate *forebears*(祖先,祖宗).

The findings are revealed in a study of the way the ageing of Britain's population is affecting different generations. Anthea Tinker, professor of social gerontology at King's College London, who carried out much of the work, said the growth of the proportion of people over 50 had reversed the traditional flow of wealth from older to younger generations. "Today's older middle-aged and elderly are becoming the new winners," she said. "They made relatively small contributions in tax but now make relatively big claims on the welfare system. Generations born in the last three to four decades face the prospect of handing over more than a third of their lifetime's earnings to care for them".

The *surging*(激增) number of older people, many living alone, has also increased demand for property and pushed up house prices. While previous generations found it easy to raise a *mortgage*(抵押), today's under-thirties have to live with their parents or rent. If they can afford to buy a home it is more likely to be a flat than a house. Laura Lenox-Conyngham, 28, grew up in a large house and her mother did not need to work. Unlike her wealthy parents, she graduated with student and postgraduate loan debts of £13,000. She now earns about £20,000 a year, preparing food to be photographed for magazines. Her home is a one-bedroom flat in central London and she sublets the lounge sofa bed to her brother. "My father took pity and paid off my student debts," she said. "But I still have no pension and no chance of buying a property for at least a couple of years—and then it will be something small in a bad area. My only hope is the traditional one of meeting a rich man." Tinker's research reveals Lenox-Conyngham is representative of many young professionals, especially in London, Manchester, Edinburgh and Bristol.

62. By saying "the growth of the proportion of people over 50 had reversed the traditional flow of wealth from older to younger generations" (Lines 3 - 4, Para. 2), Anthea Tinker really means that _____.

    A) currently wealth flows from old generation to younger generation

    B) traditionally wealth flows from younger generation to old generation

    C) with the increasingly big population of over 50, the trend arises that wealth flows from younger generation to old generation

    D) with more and more people of over 50, traditions have been reversed

63. Why are today's older middle-aged and elderly becoming the new winners?

    A) Because they contributed a small portion in tax but enjoy more on the welfare system.

    B) Because they contributed a lot in tax and now can claim much on the welfare system.

    C) Because they made small contributions, but now can make money easily.

    D) Because they outnumber younger generation and enjoy more privileges in the present society.

64. Which factor pushed up house prices?

    A) Many young men, who live alone, have increased demand for houses.

    B) Many young men need to rent more houses.

    C) It is easy to apply for a mortgage for young generation.

    D) The number of older people, many of whom live alone, becomes bigger and bigger.

65. In what way does Laura Lenox-Conyngham make her living?

A) By taking photographs for magazines.

B) By marrying a rich man.

C) By subletting the lounge sofa-bed to her brother.

D) By preparing food for photographs for some magazines.

66. We can conclude from the passage that _____ .

A) today's under-thirties are leading a miserable life in Britain

B) Laura Lenox-Conyngham's attitude to work and life represents that of many young professionals in Britain

C) life can get harder for under-thirties in Britain

D) elders enjoy extremely high living standard in Britain

Part Ⅴ *Cloze* (*15 minutes*)

The industrial societies have been extremely productive during the last two centuries. The economic advance has been __67__ . During this __68__ short period of time, greater changes in people's __69__ have occurred than in the thousands of years __70__ preceded. From about 8000 B.C. , when the agricultural __71__ of the human race began, __72__ 1776 A.D. , the beginning of the American Revolution, people grew hardly any richer __73__ . The Americans of 1776 used the same energy __74__ as the Romans of 1 A.D.. Both the ancient Romans and Americans of 200 years ago could travel about the same short distance in a day. Both had about the same annual income and the same life __75__ . During the past 200 years the world population has increased 6 times, the annual world __76__ has increased 80 times, and the distance a person can travel has __77__ 1,000 times. There __78__ also been much recent progress on art, culture, learning, and science. Such changes have led to a high __79__ of production and __80__ of the economy. Economists fear that within the next 100 to 150 years, the earth's __81__ will become very __82__ . Their fears are partly __83__ , but we should not be afraid. Industrial civilization __84__ new knowledge. By advancing knowledge, we not only __85__ new forms of resources, but we also find

67. A) particular   B) excellent
    C) remarkable   D) excessive

68. A) approximately   B) relatively
    C) roughly   D) normally

69. A) circumstances   B) environments
    C) situations   D) conditions

70. A) which   B) when
    C) where   D) whenever

71. A) stage   B) era
    C) phase   D) century

72. A) to   B) in
    C) up to   D) until

73. A) above all   B) after all
    C) in all   D) at all

74. A) origin   B) capacity
    C) potential   D) source

75. A) scope   B) duration
    C) span   D) stretch

76. A) outset   B) output
    C) outlet   D) outcome

77. A) brought up   B) gone up
    C) built up   D) picked up

78. A) has   B) is
    C) have   D) having

79. A) ratio   B) proportion
    C) rate   D) percentage

80. A) decline   B) depression
    C) recession   D) growth

81. A) resources   B) sources
    C) stocks   D) deposits

82. A) scarce   B) rare
    C) unusual   D) precious

ways to economize their use. Advanced modern knowledge can feed the hungry people of the world and improve their ___86___ of living.

83. A) transformed   B) converted
   C) modified   D) justified
84. A) applies for   B) allows for
   C) adapts to   D) accounts for
85. A) generate   B) create
   C) manufacture   D) yield
86. A) level   B) cost
   C) standard   D) grade

Part Ⅵ *Translation* (*5 minutes*)

87. You should know that pride will _____ (妨碍你成功).

88. The estimate that _____ (多达三分之一的求职者没有找到工作) proved to be false.

89. I can use a computer, but _____ (一说到修理计算机)，I know nothing about it.

90. He _____ (本来可以选择另一种职业)，but at the time, he didn't have enough money.

91. Should this happen again, _____ (会有什么后果)?

New College English Model Test Three

Part Ⅰ *Writing*（*30 minutes*）

Directions：*For this part，you are allowed 30 minutes to write a short essay "Scholarship Budgets". You should write at least 120 words following the outline given below.*

以下表格中列出了某大学生在某学期中获得奖学金（total：3000 RMB yuan）的开支预算，请根据表中的信息，就以下几个方面做出简要的说明：

1. 简要描述这位同学奖学金的预算开支情况

2. 你认为这样开支合理吗？请说明理由

3. 若是你，你应如何分配这笔钱

Items	Expenses（RMB *yuan*）
daily necessities（food，bus fare，soap，towel，toothpaste，etc.）	300
clothing	600
books and VCDS	200
trip	500
inviting friends	600
online chat and entertainment，computer games，etc.	400
date	400
TOTAL	￥3,000

Scholarship Budgets

_____

_____

...

Part Ⅱ *Reading Comprehension*（*Skimming and Scanning*）（*15 minutes*）

Can We Live Without Our Mobiles?

Are you a mobile phone addict?

HELLO. My name is Damian and I'm a mobile-phone addict. I am here today to face the truth about my condition and hope that by speaking out I can help others to overcome their own problems.

The casual observer probably couldn't detect anything wrong with me. I have a respectable appearance and my behavior in public isn't shocking or conspicuous. I hadn't even realized myself that I was a mobile phonoholic，until the past few days. But I have just spent two of those days conducting an experiment that has revealed the awful reality. I have suffered mentally and physically. And my experience has convinced me that I am only one of millions of fellow addicts. You may well be one yourself.

I have just attempted to live my life without a mobile phone. I was one of four people asked to *eschew*(回避) my phone for two days. Russell Crowe was not officially part of our group, but maybe he was trying a similar thing in a New York hotel lately. If he had used his mobile, rather than the hotel phone, to call his wife in Sydney he might have been able to secure a connection and wouldn't have been so enraged that he threw a phone at a clerk and ended up *handcuffed*(拷上手铐) in a Manhattan court.

The magic power of mobile phones

Mobile phones have been the biggest agent of change in the daily behavior of Britons in the past decade. Today there are more than 55 million mobile phone subscribers in Britain, a huge leap from less than 10 million users in 1997. As the size of the handsets has diminished, their influence has grown, altering the speed and frequency of our communication with each other, quickening the pace of decision-making and altering radically the way we plan our working and social lives.

As the coverage of mobile phones has extended, so the world has shrunk; now it has been announced that we will soon even be able to use them on the London Underground. There will be nowhere beyond their reach (and, even as an addict, I dread this. The only thing worse than a mobile phone train bore will surely be someone exposing their sweaty *armpits*(腋窝) to lift their phone to their ear and *yabber*(急促而含混不清地说话). "'ello darlin'. I'm underground.... I said I'M UNDERGROUND! Amazin' innit?")

Two days without a mobile phone

Switching it off at the beginning of Day I was strange. For the past few years I have done this only when boarding an aircraft. Even on holiday—and this may strike you as rather sad—I put the phone on silent and annoy my wife by checking it at least every few hours.

Dorothy Rowe, a clinical psychologist, tells me that this sort of behavior is consistent with extroverts "who need reassurance that other people are thinking of them. Your degree of self-confidence will determine how much you worry about it." Worry about it? Me? Don't be ridiculous. I check only out of idle curiosity. I'm not a needy control freak or anything.

I should have left the phone at home, or at least put it in a drawer for two days. But I couldn't bring myself to do that, so I left it sitting on my desk. For the first few hours of *abstinence*(节制) I kept involuntarily picking it up and looking at the display to see if I had any messages or had missed a call, only to see that it was, of course, switched off.

When I had got used to the fact that it was off, I still picked it up, turned it over in my hand and fiddled with it, like a smoker fidgeting with a packet of cigarettes. I realized that I had a whole routine of nervous *tics*(不自觉的习惯行为) involving my phone and that these were *exacerbated*(加剧) by my desire to use it. I took these to be the physical effects of undergoing the process of withdrawal.

My 40-minute walk home at the end of the day is normally a time for making calls, mostly to friends or family. Now that I was banned from doing this, the phone felt as if it was torching a hole in my pocket. I was desperate to use it. My fingers *twitched*(抽搐).

These two days were mostly office-bound and I didn't need to use my phone to do my job. I can't imagine how I would have been able to operate if I had been out on a story. Like anyone working on the hoof away from the office the phone is glued to my ear and I can make and receive dozens of calls a day.

Can we live without this machine?

How did we ever work without mobile phones? I dimly recall the beginning of my career, more than a dozen years ago, constantly searching for phone boxes, laboriously leaving messages and placing hourly check calls to my editors.

Many mobile calls we make in our private lives are certainly unnecessary. But the convenience of a phone is undeniable. I wasted 15 minutes trying to locate an address in my car because I couldn't call and ask for directions. I also bought the wrong skin cream for my son because I couldn't make a call home from Boots.

Rowe suggests that being hooked on our mobile phones may not have made us better at communicating, particularly in our personal lives. "Our communication is not necessarily better. A good rule used to be that if you were angry with somebody you wrote them a letter but, rather than post it straight away, you slept on it. The trouble with instant mobile phone communication is that you can act on impulses that you will later regret."

When I switched the phone back on after two days I found I had three messages and four texts. OK, so I was a bit put out that there were not more. I had missed the chance to do a phone interview that I had been trying to secure for two weeks and an invitation to a last-minute lunch. Frustrating, but to be honest, no more than that.

However, I was relieved to have the phone back on. My fingers soon stopped twitching. I sent some trivial texts and made a couple of meaningless calls and that cheered me up.

I remain convinced that the phone is a crucial tool for work, but realize that otherwise it is often just a pointless security blanket: "Hi, darlin. I'm on my way home. Just leaving the office now. Love you. Byeeeee."

So do I have the strength of character to stop using it as such? Of course I do. I just choose not to. As I said, I'm not a needy person.

1. The author had long realized that he was a mobile phonoholic.
2. The author and other three people conducted an experiment, trying to live without their mobile phones for two days.
3. To Britons, mobile phones have been the greatest invention in the past decade.
4. According to the author, mobile phones will be able to cover everywhere.
5. At the beginning the author felt comfortable turning his mobile phone off because nobody could bother him any longer.
6. From the experiment the author realized that having a mobile phone or not wouldn't make any difference to him in his work.
7. Although many calls we make are absolutely unnecessary, mobile phones can surely bring us convenience.
8. Rowe believes that being addicted to our mobile phones may not boost our skills in _____.
9. After turning his mobile phone on again, the author felt _____.
10. The author's attitude towards mobile phone is that _____ for work, but is often meaningless in other respects.

Part III *Listening Comprehension* (*35 minutes*)

Section A

11. A) Swimming.   B) Playing.   C) Boating.   D) Playing table tennis.
12. A) To remind him of the data he should take to the conference.
    B) To see if he is ready for the coming conference.
    C) To tell him something about the conference.
    D) To help him prepare for the conference.

13. A) The long wait.   B) The broken-down computer.

    C) The mistakes in her telephone bill.   D) The bad telephone service.

14. A) They spent three hundred dollars on their vacation.

    B) They drew more money than they should have from the bank.

    C) They lost their bankbook.

    D) They had only three hundred dollars in the bank.

15. A) To find out her position in the company.

    B) To apply for a job.

    C) To offer her a position in the company.

    D) To make an appointment with the sales manager.

16. A) He is surprised.   B) He feels very happy.

    C) He is indifferent.   D) He feels very angry.

17. A) He hasn't cleaned his room since Linda visited him.

    B) Linda is the only person who ever comes to see him.

    C) He's been too busy to clean his room.

    D) Cleaning is the last thing he wants to do.

18. A) She is a generous woman by nature.   B) It doesn't have a back cover.

    C) She feels the man's apology is enough.   D) It is no longer of any use to her.

Questions 19 to 22 are based on the conversation you have just heard.

19. A) He was very young when his grandpa was born.

    B) He never played basketball with his grandpa.

    C) He would hang out with his grandpa when his grandpa was 18.

    D) He was too old to play basketball and stuff.

20. A) He was sorry they could never play ball together.

    B) He was sorry he could never tell story to him.

    C) He was sorry he was too old to play basketball and stuff.

    D) He was sorry that he was too occupied with his work.

21. A) unconvincing.   B) persuasive.   C) disgusting.   D) praiseworthy.

22. A) Because they cannot stand the continual nagging of their children.

    B) Because they have to give in to their children's demands.

    C) Because they are deeply moved by their children's honesty.

    D) Because they can be considerate of their children's needs.

Questions 23 to 25 are based on the conversation you have just heard.

23. A) Convince the man to take a rock-climbing course with her.

    B) Find a place to go rock-climbing.

    C) Find out if a rock-climbing course will be offered.

    D) Plan a rock-climbing trip over spring break.

24. A) There is no one to teach them how to do it.

    B) Not very many students are interested in it.

    C) The college doesn't have any rock-climbing equipment.

    D) There are no appropriate places for rock-climbing nearby.

25. A) Selecting the necessary equipment.

    B) Finding a climbing partner.

    C) Increasing upper-body strength.

    D) Discussing popular climbing sites.

ection B

Passage One

Questions 26 to 28 are based on the passage you have just heard.

26. A) Scientists.　　　　B) Greeks.　　　　C) Teachers.　　　　D) Scholars.

27. A) They could not think.　　　　B) They had no pollution.

　　C) They could not dive deep.　　　　D) They had small boats.

28. A) The water turns gray.　　　　B) It grows again.

　　C) Life on earth improves.　　　　D) Life on earth dies.

Passage Two

Questions 29 to 32 are based on the passage you have just heard.

29. A) Practice requires him to be honest.

　　B) Dishonesty is not a virtue.

　　C) Honesty may make him suffer.

　　D) Honesty is the best policy.

30. A) They avoid telling lies and are friendly to others.

　　B) They usually like telling lies.

　　C) They often tell lies for their own sake.

　　D) They prefer their relatives to friends.

31. A) Children are honest by nature.

　　B) Children should be taught to be honest.

　　C) Children should learn to tell harmless lies when necessary.

　　D) Children may learn from experience to be dishonest.

32. A) Evidence—conclusion.　　　　B) Analysis—confirmation.

　　C) Statement—support.　　　　D) Statement—support—restatement.

Passage Three

Questions 33 to 35 are based on the passage you have just heard.

33. A) The United States is quite rich in natural resources.

　　B) The young Americans are well-educated to respect the usefulness of cooperation.

　　C) The Americans are the people with knowledge and skills from many countries.

　　D) The workingman is now enjoying the wonderful life he achieved through struggle.

34. A) The land has an abundance of coal resources.

　　B) The United States has some farmland.

　　C) People from many countries brought with them wealth.

　　D) The workingman laid a firm foundation for the whole nation.

35. A) The education of his children.

　　B) The fight for his existence.

　　C) The problem of cooperation with his children.

　　D) The increase of the value of his own.

Section C

　　Crime has its own cycles, a magazine reported some years ago. Police (36)＿＿＿＿＿＿ that were studied for five years from over 2,400 cities and towns show a surprising (37)＿＿＿＿＿＿ between changes in the season and crime patterns.

　　The pattern of crime has changed very little over a long period of years. Murder reaches its high during July and August, as do other (38)_____ attacks. Murder, in (39)_____, is more than seasonal; it is a weekend crime. It is also a nighttime crime: 62 percent of murders are (40)_____ between 6 p.m. and 6 a.m.

Unlike the summer high in crimes of bodily harm, break and enter or "B and E" has a different cycle. You are most likely to be robbed between 6 p.m. and 2 a.m. on a Saturday night in (41)_____, January, or February. Which is the least criminal month of all? May—except for one strange (42)_____. More dog bites are reported in this month than in any other month of the year.

(43)_____ our intellectual seasonal cycles are completely different from our criminal patterns. Professor Huntington, of the Foundation for the Study of Cycles, (44)_____ _____. In all examples, he found a spring peak and an autumn peak separated by a summer low.

On the other hand, Professor Huntington's studies showed that (45)_____.

Possibly, high temperature and *humidity*(湿度) bring on our strange and surprising summer actions, but police officers are not sure. (46) "_____," they say.

Part Ⅳ *Reading Comprehension* (*Reading in Depth*) (*25 minutes*)

Section A

Questions 47 to 56 are based on the following passage.

On any collecting trip, obtaining the animals is, as a rule, the simplest part of the job. As soon as the local people discover that you are willing to buy live wild creatures, the stuff comes __47__ in; ninety percent is, of course, the more common types, but they do bring an occasional rarity. If you want the __48__ rare stuff, you generally have to go out and find it yourself.

The __49__ difficulty you have when you have got a newly caught animal is not so much the __50__ it might be suffering, but the fact that being caught forces it to exist close to a creature it regards as an enemy of the worst possible sort: yourself. On many __51__ an animal may take beautifully to being in a cage but getting used to the idea of living with people is another matter. This is the difficulty you can only deal with by patience and kindness. For month after month an animal may try to bite you every time you approach its cage, until you __52__ of ever making a favorable impression on it. Then, one day, sometimes without any __53__ warning, it will trot forward and take food from your hand, or allow you to tickle it behind the ears. At such moments you feel that all the waiting in the world was __54__.

Feeding, of course, is one of your main problems. Not only must you have a fairly extensive knowledge of what each animal eats in the wild state, but you have to work out something else when the natural food is unavailable, and then teach your animal to eat it. You also have to provide for their individual likes and dislikes, which vary __55__. I have known a rat which, refusing all normal rat food—fruit, bread, vegetables—lived for three days on a(n) __56__ diet of spaghetti.

A) despair	I) pouring
B) boast	J) occasions
C) really	K) pushing
D) chief	L) settings
E) worthwhile	M) exclusive
F) numerous	N) shock
G) strikingly	O) preliminary
H) enormously	

Section B

Passage One

Questions 57 to 61 are based on the following passage.

Large companies need a way to reach the savings of the public at large. The same problem, on a smaller scale, faces practically every company trying to develop new products and create new jobs. There can be little prospect of raising the sort of sums needed from friends and people we know, and while banks may agree to provide short-term finance, they are generally unwilling to provide money on a permanent basis for long-term projects. So companies turn to public, inviting people to lend them money, or take a share in the business in exchange for a share in future profits. This they do by issuing stocks and shares in the business through The Stock Exchange.

By doing so they can put into circulation the savings of individuals and institution, both at home and overseas. When the saver needs his money back, he does not have to go to the company with whom he originally placed it. Instead, he sells his shares through a stockbroker to some other saver who is seeking to invest his money.

Many of the services needed both by industry and by each of us are provided by the Government or by local authorities. Without hospitals, roads, electricity, telephones, railways, this country could not function. All these require continuous spending on new equipment and new development if they are to serve us properly, requiring more money than is raised through taxes alone. The government, local authorities, and nationalized industries therefore frequently needed to borrow money to finance major capital spending, and they, too, come to The Stock Exchange.

There is hardly a man or woman in this country whose job or whose standard of living does not depend on the ability of his or her employers to raise money to finance new development. In one way or another this new money must come from the savings of the country. The Stock Exchange exists to provide a channel through which these savings can reach those who need finance.

57. Almost all companies involved in new production and development must _____.
    A) rely in their own financial resources
    B) persuade the banks to provide long-term finance
    C) borrow large sums of money from friends and people we know
    D) depend on the population as a whole for finance

58. The money which enables these companies to go ahead with their projects is _____.
    A) repaid to its original owners as soon as possible
    B) raised by the selling of shares in the companies
    C) exchanged for part ownership in The Stock Exchange
    D) invested in different companies on The Stock Exchange

59. When the savers want their money back they _____.
    A) ask another company to obtain their money for them
    B) look for other people to borrow money from
    C) put their shares in the company back on the market
    D) transfer their money to a more successful company

60. All the essential services on which we depend are _____.
    A) run by the Government or our local authorities
    B) in constant need of financial support
    C) financed wholly by rates and taxes

D) unable to provide for the needs of the population

61. The Stock exchange makes it possible for the Government, local authorities and nationalized industries _____.

    A) to borrow as much money as they wish

    B) to make certain everybody saves money

    C) to raise money to finance new developments

    D) to make certain everybody lends money to them

Passage Two

Questions 62 to 66 are based on the following passage.

The liberal view of democratic citizenship that developed in the 17th and 18th centuries was fundamentally different from that of the classical Greeks. The pursuit of private interests, with as little interference as possible from government, was seen as the road to human happiness and progress rather than the public obligations and involvement in the collective community that were emphasized by the Greeks. Freedom was to be realized by limiting the scope of governmental activity and political obligation and not through *immersion*(专注于) in the collective life of the **polis**. The basic role of the citizen was to select governmental leaders and keep the powers and scope of public authority in check. In the liberal view, the rights of citizen against the state were the focus of special emphasis.

Over time, the liberal democratic notion of citizenship developed in two directions. First, there was movement to increase the proportion of members of society who were *eligible*(合格的) to participate as citizens—especially through extending the right of *suffrage*(投票)—and to ensure the basic political equality of all. Second, there was a broadening of the legal activities of government and a use of governmental power to put right imbalances in social and economic life. Political citizenship became an instrument through which groups and classes with sufficient numbers of votes could use the state power to enhance their social and economic well-being.

Within the general liberal view of democratic citizenship, tensions have developed over the degree to which government can and should be used as an instrument for promoting happiness and well-being. Political philosopher Martin Diamond has classified two views of democracy as follows. On the one hand, there is the "libertarian" perspective that stresses the private pursuit of happiness and emphasizes the necessity for restraint on government and protection of individual liberties. On the other hand, there is the "majoritarian" view that emphasizes the "task of the government to uplift and aid the common man against the *malefactors*(作恶者) of great wealth". The tensions between these two views are very evident today. Tax-payer revolts and calls for smaller government and less government regulation clash with demands for greater government involvement in the economic marketplace and the social sphere.

62. The author's primary purpose is to _____.

    A) study ancient concepts of citizenship

    B) contrast different notions of citizenship

    C) criticize modern libertarian democracy

    D) describe the importance of universal suffrage

63. It can be inferred from the passage that the Greek word "poli" in Paragraph 1 means _____.

    A) family life   B) military service

    C) marriage   D) political community

64. The author cites Martin Diamond because the author _____.

    A) regards Martin Diamond as an authority on political philosophy

    B) wishes to *refute*(反驳) Martin Diamond's views on citizenship

C) needs a definition of the term "citizenship"

D) is unfamiliar with the distinction between libertarian and majoritarian concepts of democracy

65. According to the passage，all of the following are characteristics of the liberal idea of government EXCEPT _____ .

A) the emphasis on the rights of private citizenship

B) the activities government may lawfully pursue

C) the obligation of citizens to participate in government

D) the size of the geographical area controlled by a government

66. A majoritarian would be most likely to favor legislation that would _____ .

A) eliminate all restrictions on individual liberty

B) cut spending for social welfare programs

C) provide greater protection for consumers

D) lower taxes on the wealthy and raise taxes for workers

Part Ⅴ *Cloze* (*15 minutes*)

If you were to begin a new job tomorrow，you would bring with you some basic strengths and weaknesses. Success or failure in your work would depend, __67__ a great extent, __68__ your ability to use your strengths and weaknesses to the best __69__ . Of the __70__ importance is your attitude. A person who begins a job __71__ that he isn't going to like it or is sure that he is going to fail is __72__ a weakness which can only hold back his success. __73__ , a person who is secure of his belief __74__ he is probably as __75__ of doing the work as anyone else and who is willing to make a cheerful __76__ at it possesses a certain strength of purpose. The __77__ are that he will do well.

Having the *prerequisite*（首要必备的）skills for a particular job is strength. Lacking those skills is obviously a weakness. A book-keeper who can't add or a carpenter who can't cut a straight line with a saw __78__ hopeless cases.

This book has been designed to help you __79__ the strength and overcome the weakness that you bring to the job of learning. But in order to measure your development，you must first take __80__ of

67. A) on   B) for
     C) of   D) to

68. A) in   B) at
     C) on   D) for

69. A) advantage   B) convenience
     C) benefit   D) interest

70. A) ultimate   B) remote
     C) utmost   D) eventual

71. A) convinced   B) convincing
     C) being convinced   D) having been convinced

72. A) exposing   B) concealing
     C) detecting   D) exhibiting

73. A) On the other hand   B) On the whole
     C) All in all   D) In brief

74. A) which   B) what
     C) that   D) where

75. A) able   B) capable
     C) competent   D) equal

76. A) venture   B) application
     C) attack   D) attempt

77. A) chances   B) prospects
     C) opportunities   D) occasions

78. A) being   B) been
     C) are   D) is

79. A) make the best of   B) get the best of
     C) have the better of   D) get the better of

80. A) stake   B) stick
     C) stock   D) stroke

81. A) Where   B) As

where you stand now. __81__ we get further along in the book，we'll be dealing in some detail with __82__ processes for developing and __83__ learning skills. __84__ , you should stop __85__ your present strengths and weaknesses in three areas that are __86__ to your success or failure in school：your attitude，your reading and communication skills，and your study habits.

C) Unless   D) Until

82. A) specialized   B) special
    C) specified   D) specific

83. A) investigating   B) justifying
    C) complicating   D) strengthening

84. A) For beginning with it   B) For it to begin with
    C) With beginning it   D) To begin with

85. A) examining   B) to examine
    C) being examined   D) having examined

86. A) sufficient   B) peculiar
    C) critical   D) equivalent

Part Ⅵ *Translation* (*5 minutes*)

87. He made a long speech _____ (只暴露出他对这门学科一无所知).

88. The magician _____ (从观众当中随意挑选了几个人) and asked them to help him with the performance.

89. If I were to do it, I _____ (会是另一种做法).

90. The factory has over 1000 staff members, _____ (其中三分之二是女工).

91. _____ (你没有理由不事先告诉他们) that you are going.

New College English Model Test Four

Part Ⅰ *Writing*（*30 minutes*）

Directions：*For this part，you are allowed 30 minutes to write a short essay "Student Use of the Internet".*
You should write at least 120 words following the outline given below.

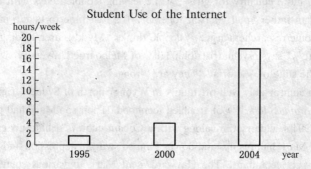

Student Use of the Internet

1. 上图所示的是 1995 年、2000 年和 2004 年某高校大学生上网的情况，请说明其变化
2. 分析其变化的原因
3. 你认为目前大学生在上网方面存在的困难和问题是什么

Student Use of the Internet

_____

_____

_____

...

Part Ⅱ *Reading Comprehension*（*Skimming and Scanning*）（*15 minutes*）

Flirting with Suicide

The death of an Australian boy's dream

The life of David Woods was the stuff of an Australian boy's dream. He played professional rugby league football in a country that treats athletes as idols. At the age of 29, he had a loving family, a girlfriend, a 3-month-old baby, plenty of money, everything to live for. And, for *unfathomable*（高深莫测的）reasons, nothing to live for. On New Year's Day, Woods ran a hose from the exhaust pipe to the window of his Mitsubishi sedan and *asphyxiated*（使窒息）himself. His family still has no idea why. One day he called his mother to announce that he had signed a new contract with his team, Gold Coast, recalls his elder brother, Tony. "Twenty hours later," says Tony, "he gassed himself to death."

The death of David Woods came as a wake-up call to Australia, which is often touted as the ideal place to bring up kids. But the sun, the beaches and the sporting culture are the cheery backdrop to a disturbing trend: young Australian men are now killing themselves at the rate of one a day— triple the rate of 30 years ago. Though most Australians aren't particularly suicidal, their boys are. In 1990 suicide surpassed car accidents as the leading cause of death among males aged 15 to 24. Funloving Australia is now far worse off than Asian nations known for strict discipline. The yearly suicide rate for young Australian males is 2 1/2 times higher than in Japan, Hong Kong or Singapore. It's a "picture of despair, despondency and aimlessness," says Adam Graycar, director of Australia's Institute of Criminology.

A hard struggle for Australian youth

Why boys? A nation of wideopen spaces and rugged individualism, Australia still *lionizes*(把……捧为名人) the film star Gary Cooper model of masculinity: the strong, silent type who never complains, who always gets the job done. In recent years schools and social institutions have concentrated on creating new opportunities and more equality for girls—while leaving troubled boys with the classic *admonition* (告戒) of the Australian father: pull yourself together. It's past time to take a much closer look at the lives of young men, some researchers argue. "People think, 'My kids aren't doing drugs, my kids are at home, my kids are safe'," says psychiatrist John Tiller of Melbourne University, who studied 148 suicides and 206 attempts in the state of Victoria. "They are wrong."

The Haywards, a comfortably well-off family in Wyong, north of Sydney, figured they were dealing with the normal *melodramas*(传奇剧) of troubled teenhood. Their son Mark had put up a poster of rock star Kurt Cobain, a 1994 suicide victim, along with a Cobain quote: "I hate myself and I want to die." "From the age of 12, Mark had his ups and downs—mood swings, depression and low self-esteem," says his father, Stuart, a tax accountant. The Haywards sent Mark to various counselors, none of whom warned that he had suicidal tendencies. By last year Mark was 19, fighting bouts of unemployment and a drug problem. He tried church, struggling to "do the right thing," says his father. Last September Mark dropped out of a *detoxification*(戒毒) program, and apologized to his parents. "I have let you down again," he said. A few days later, his mother found Mark's body in bushland near their home.

In retrospect, Mark Hayward's struggles were far from uncommon. The number of suicides tends to keep pace with the unemployment rate, which for Australians between 15 and 19 has risen from 19 percent in 1978, the first year data were collected, to 28 percent last year. Suicide is especially high among the most marginal: young *Aboriginal*(澳大利亚土著的) men, isolated by poverty, alcoholism and racism. As in other developed countries, Australian families have grown less *cohesive*(聚合在一起的) in recent years, putting young men out into the world at an earlier age. Those who kill themselves often "think it will make it easier for the parents by not being there," says Liz Brunsdon, whose 21-year-old son, Dean, hanged himself three years ago. In fact, she says, Dean's death "threw our family apart because each of us suffered so much that we couldn't help each other."

The deeper mystery is why the universal anguish of growing up should have such particularly devastating effects in Australia. One answer is that the country allows easier access to guns than most other developed Asian nations. (One exception is neighboring New Zealand, where guns are as easy to find, and the suicide rate among young people is even worse.) Australian boys tend to end their lives violently—by shooting or hanging. Girls, by contrast, often take an overdose of drugs, and are more often rescued.

Increasing concerns

Educators now hope to teach adults to recognize youths troubled by suicidal depression and alienation. That is no easy task in a society that generally avoids *introspection*(内省). "Good services do exist in Australia," says child psychologist Marie Bashir, but "the Australian philosophy is: pull your socks up. Get out and play more sport."

To get Australia's attention, psychiatrist Tiller wants the government to sponsor a shock advertising campaign, similar to one that portrays the pain and guilt felt by survivors of people killed in drunkendriving accidents. The ads should make people aware of the threat, and urge them to get help for young men at risk, says Tiller: "We need to teach boys to express themselves. We need to pick them up at 5 years old to prevent a problem in 15 years."

The rising death toll has just begun to force suicide onto the nation's political agenda. Suicide now takes more lives than murder or AIDs. Brendan Nelson, a physician and backbencher in Parliament, recently called for the creation of a National Office for Young People to report to the prime minister on youth concerns. Slowly, Australians are overcoming the old fear of talking openly about a problem that has long been considered taboo. "We have one young person every day ending his life and possibly another four who are not reported as suicides but are killing themselves," says Clyde Begg of the Australian Community Research Organization. "Now, if we don't talk about that, we are *derelict*(不负责任的) in our duty."

Be brave to speak it out

Tony Woods is talking now, but he wasn't always. The brother of the football player who gassed himself to death, Woods says he tried to take his own life at the age of 17 by slashing his wrists with a carving knife after breaking up with a girlfriend. Woods has made it his mission to warn other boys that they may find themselves on the same dangerous path taken by his brother, David. Among other things, he plans to bring professional football players into schools to urge boys to seek counseling for their personal problems. "Boys can't communicate what they feel," says Woods. "They are socialized to be hard, tough, independent men who don't show their feelings. We need to tell them: 'You are worthwhile. Seek help'." It is the kind of simple advice, Tony Woods now believes, that his brother never heard.

1. The most unusual about David Wood's suicide is that nobody knew the reason why he did it.
2. The tragedy of David Wood is compared to cherry backdrop to Australia.
3. According to the author, Australian society is different from Asian societies because car accidents cause most deaths in Asian societies.
4. The neglect of the society contributes a lot to the increase in the suicide of the Australian young men.
5. Mark Hayward's struggles were quite similar to those of David Woods.
6. The number of suicides among young people tends to keep pace with their level of education.
7. One reason for the high suicide rate in Australia is that people can get guns easily.
8. Psychiatrist Tiller urge people to get help for young Australian men by teaching them to _____.
9. Australians are advised to overcome the old taboo of _____.
10. Tony Woods is talking now and considers it his duty to prevent other young Australians from _____.

Part III *Listening Comprehension* (*35 minutes*)

ection A

11. A) The man attended the concert, but didn't like it.
    B) The man was sorry to miss the football game.
    C) The man is more interested in football than in classical music.
    D) The man was sorry that he didn't attend the concert.
12. A) Singing loudly.　　　　　　　　　　B) Listening to music.
    C) Studying.　　　　　　　　　　　　　D) Talking on the phone.
13. A) She can't receive any calls.　　　　B) She can't make any calls.
    C) She can do nothing with the phone.　D) She can't repair the phone.
14. A) Tom is very responsible.　　　　　　B) Tom's words aren't reliable.

C) What Tom said is true.   D) Tom is not humorous at all.

15. A) How to use a camera.   B) How to use a washer.

C) How to use a keyboard.   D) How to use a tape recorder.

16. A) They should put the meeting to an end.

B) They should hold another meeting to discuss the matter.

C) She would like to discuss another item.

D) She wants to discuss the issue again later.

17. A) He believes the Browns have done a sensible thing.

B) He doesn't think the Browns should move to another place.

C) He doesn't think the Browns' investment is a wise move.

D) He believes it is better for the Browns to invest later.

18. A) He may convert it and use it as a restaurant.   B) He may pull it down and build a new restaurant.

C) He may rent it out for use as a restaurant.   D) He may sell it to the owner of a restaurant.

Questions 19 to 22 are based on the conversation you have just heard.

19. A) The rules in English language.   B) Learning English and mathematics.

C) The approach to learning English.   D) Playing soccer needs a lot of exercise.

20. A) To pass the exam.   B) To obtain master's degree at the university.

C) To join the soccer team.   D) To prepare himself for study at the university.

21. A) Rules of playing soccer are confusing.

B) The man needn't learn the rules of English.

C) Languages can not be learned very well in classes.

D) Rules are important for adults in learning languages.

22. A) The woman is an English teacher.

B) The man used to be a good soccer player.

C) The woman has mastered English quite well.

D) The man will realize the importance of practice in learning a language.

Questions 23 to 25 are based on the conversation you have just heard.

23. A) At a park.   B) At the beach.   C) At Dave's house.   D) By a river.

24. A) Six.   B) Seven.   C) Eight.   D) Nine.

25. A) She has been working a lot recently.   B) She has been taking care of her sick mother.

C) She has been taking two night classes.   D) She has been looking for a new job.

 ection B

Passage One

Questions 26 to 28 are based on the passage you have just heard.

26. A) Use of library facilities.   B) Library regulations.

C) Library personnel.   D) Location of the library.

27. A) Book publishers.   B) Librarians.

C) Returning faculty members.   D) New university students.

28. A) Graduate students.   B) Undergraduate students.

C) Professors.   D) Library employees.

Passage Two

Questions 29 to 32 are based on the passage you have just heard.

29. A) Because they like the taste of tar.

B) Because smoking makes them feel relaxed.

C) Because smoking to them means fun.

D) Because smoking is the easiest thing to get addicted to.

30. A) Cigarette ashes.   B) Nicotine.   C) Tar.   D) Not mentioned.

31. A) They are trying to persuade people to buy cigarettes with less tar.

    B) They are trying to persuade people to smoke only a few cigarettes a day.

    C) They are trying to persuade people to smoke only during a break.

    D) They are trying to persuade people to give up smoking entirely.

32. A) Because they are less harmful.   B) Because they cost less.

    C) Because they taste better.   D) Because they last longer.

Passage Three

Questions 33 to 35 are based on the passage you have just heard.

33. A) They need more friends who give them courage.   B) They need more physical exercises.

    C) They need more food.   D) They need special training.

34. A) The shortage of water.   B) The shortage of food.

    C) The condition of weightlessness.   D) The great pressure outside the spacecraft.

35. A) Air.   B) Medicine.   C) Food.   D) Water.

Section C

Teaching involves more than leadership. Some of the teacher's time and effort is (36) _____ toward instruction, some toward evaluation. But it is the teacher as a group leader who creates an (37) _____ organizational structure and good working environment so that instruction and evaluation activities can take place. A group that is (38) _____ disorganized, unclear about its goals, or (39) _____ fighting among its members will not be a good learning group. The leadership pattern includes helping to form and maintain a positive learning environment so that instruction and evaluation activities can take place.

On the first day of class, the teacher faces a room filled with (40) _____. Perhaps a few closely (41) _____ groups and friendships already exist. But there is no sense of group unity, no set of rules for (42) _____ in the group, no feeling of belonging. If teachers are successful leaders, they will help students develop a system of relationships that encourages (43) _____.

Standards and rules must be established that maintain order, ensure justice, and protect individual rights, but do not *contradict*(与……矛盾) school policy. What happens when one student hurts another's individual rights? (44) _____. Students may break rules they did not know existed. If standards are set without input from the class, students may spend a great deal of creative energy in ruining the class environment, finding ways to break rules.

(45) _____.

Regular maintenance is necessary. Conflicts arise. The needs of individual members change. A new kind of learning task requires a new organizational structure. (46) _____.

One task for the teacher is to restore a positive environment by helping students cope with conflict, change, and stress.

Part IV Reading Comprehension (Reading in Depth) (25 minutes)

Section A

Questions 47 to 56 are based on the following passage.

The provision of social care is among the most labor-intensive occupations. BS Social Care has experts in the field and so is sensitive to the varied and highly specific needs of the Care community.

BS Social Care specializes in providing both temporary and __47__ social care staff to organizations which are part of local authorities within the National Health Service, voluntary bodies, charities and private __48__ care providers. Our clients are always looking for staff that have experience in working with people in the following fields: childcare, youth work, older people, mental health, learning __49__, physical disabilities and *vulnerable*（脆弱的）adults.

BS Social Care offers both work that will fit in with your own personal __50__. So, if you are looking for part-time work with __51__ hours, full time work whilst looking for a permanent job, your first *locum*（临时代理）position after qualifying or even extra hours alongside your own job, we will search for the right position to meet your individual needs.

Our in-depth knowledge of local companies will give you that extra advantage when looking for work. Staff seeking permanent placements will benefit from our professional consultants who will help you with *CV*（简历）and pre-interview advice and we will also __52__ on your behalf to get the best possible salary and benefits __53__.

The quality of service we provide depends entirely on our staff. The Leeds branch of BS Social Care is __54__ to delivering the very best service to both clients and care professionals. We thoroughly interview all __55__ before they are made available to work and we also operate a quality management programme to continuously __56__ the abilities of both our care professionals and consultants.

A) package	I) permanent
B) flexible	J) abundant
C) suppressed	K) circumstances
D) committed	L) attendants
E) assess	M) disabilities
F) foster	N) welfare
G) applicants	O) sector
H) negotiate	

Section B

Passage One

Questions 57 to 61 are based on the following passage.

For some time past it has been widely accepted that babies—and other creatures—learn to do things because certain acts lead to "rewards"; and there is no reason to doubt that this is true. But it used also to be widely believed that effective rewards, at least in the early stages, had to be directly related to such basic physiological "drives" as thirst or hunger. In other words, a baby would learn if he got food or drink, some sort of physical comfort, not otherwise.

It is now clear that this is not so. Babies will learn to behave in ways that produce results in the world with no reward except the successful outcome.

Papousek began his studies by using milk in the normal way to "reward" the babies and so teach them to carry out some simple movements, such as turning the head to one side or the other. Then he noticed that a baby who had had enough to drink would refuse the milk but would still go on making the learned response with clear signs of pleasure. So he began to study the children's response in situation where no milk was provided. He quickly found that children as young as four months would learn to turn their heads to right or left if the movement "switched on" a display of lights and indeed that they were capable of learning quite complex turns to bring about this result, for instance, two left or two right, or even to make as many as three turns to one side.

Papousek's light display was placed directly in front of the babies and he made the interesting observation that sometimes they would turn back to watch the lights closely although they would "smile and bubble" when the display came on. Papousek concluded that it was not primarily the sight of the lights that pleased them, it was the success they were achieving in solving the problem, in mastering the skill, and that there exists a fundamental human urge to make sense of the world and bring it under intentional control.

57. According to the author, babies learn to do things which _____.
    A) are directly related to pleasure
    B) will meet their physical needs
    C) will bring them a feeling of success
    D) will satisfy their curiosity

58. Papousek noticed in his studies that a baby _____.
    A) would make learned response when it saw the milk
    B) would carry out learned movements when it had enough to drink
    C) would continue the simple movements without being given milk
    D) would turn its head to right or left when it had enough to drink.

59. In Papousek's experiment babies make learned movements of the head in order to _____.
    A) have the lights turned on   B) be rewarded with milk   C) please their parents   D) be praised

60. The babies would "smile and bubble" at the lights because _____.
    A) the lights were directly related to some basic "drives"
    B) the sight of the lights was interesting
    C) they need not turn back to watch the lights
    D) they succeeded in "switching on" the lights

61. According to Papousek, the pleasure babies get in achieving something is a reflection of _____.
    A) a basic human desire to understand and control the world
    B) the satisfaction of certain physiological needs
    C) their strong desire to solve complex problems
    D) a fundamental human urge to display their learned skills

Passage Two
Questions 62 to 66 are based on the following passage.

Internet voting happens all the time, but usually it's confined to topics such as "Who is the cutest cast member of Party of Five?" Soon, however, people will be able to cast their *ballot*(选票) for President on the Internet. In March, Arizona Democrats will vote online in their state's presidential primary, and Florida and Washington are considering online voting. The military plans to allow a small test group of overseas soldiers to vote via the Internet this November.

The internet voting is growing rapidly. There are civic engagement enthusiasts who see it as a way to prevent the drop in voter turnout. Then there are the Internet *buffs*(爱好者), who think the Internet is going to change everything, so why not politics? Most important are the persons who make the plan for developing software for online voting. Imagine the retail price of that software, then multiply it by every state and city government, and suddenly a lot of Internet capitalists develop a deeply felt concern for increasing voter turnout.

Some problems will arise. Hackers and some politicians could break into a voting database and make the secret ballot not so secret. A massive computer failure would have disastrous consequences. Just as serious, online voting could distort participation levels, at least, to the wealthy and cyber-connected.

In the long run, however, online voting might make little difference. Since the 1960s, the government has made numerous attempts to energize nonvoters by making it easier for them to get to the polls, extending voting hours, lowering the voting age, etc. Still, voter turnout has decreased steadily. Political scientists believe the important cause is the indifference to politics, not the inconvenience of voting. Putting a ballot on the Internet might even further depress turnout by cheapening one of the holy ceremonies of democracy. "The business of democracy," says Curtis Gans, an analyst of voting behavior, "shouldn't be the same as getting your e-mail."

62. Which of the following statements may NOT be the main reason why Internet voting is growing rapidly?
   A) The civic affair enthusiasts take it as a way to increase voter turnout.
   B) Some Internet lovers hope that Internet can change politics.
   C) Some people can make profit from developing software for online voting.
   D) An increasing number of states or cities are considering voting online to help promote Internet voting.

63. Which of the following point is NOT mentioned as the potential problem of Internet voting?
   A) A distance computer failure.
   B) The leaking out of the secret ballots.
   C) The unfair distribution of votes.
   D) The distorted levels of participants.

64. Political scientists believe that the important cause for decreasing voter turnout is _____.
   A) the inconvenience of voting
   B) the commercialization of the voting procedures
   C) the lack of interest and enthusiasm in politics
   D) the insecurity of voting on line due to the constant breakdown of computer systems

65. The writer of this passage seems to suggest _____.
   A) voting online will not radically affect the conventional practice in election campaign
   B) the rapid increase of voting online will gradually change people's concept about voting
   C) voting online will eventually turn out a more promising step to democracy
   D) effective measures should be taken to prevent Internet capitalists from abusing this new form of election

66. It can be inferred from the passage that _____.
   A) online voting has simplified the whole process of voting, making it much cheaper and more efficient
   B) online voting questions can be diverse, ranging from the plainest to the toughest
   C) democracy is counted as something solemn and serious, a matter not done so informally online
   D) lowering the voting age can encourage young people to join politics

Part Ⅴ *Cloze* (*15 minutes*)

The *unauthorized*(未经授权的) copying of computer programs by American businesses alone deprived software publishers of $1.6 billion last year, a figure that swells to nearly $7.5 billion

67. A) base   B) foundation
      C) ground   D) basis

68. A) At   B) On
      C) Through   D) With

when overseas markets are included. "Industry's loss on a global ___67___ is astonishing", says Ken Wasch，head of the US software Publishers Association.

___68___ first glance, software *piracy*(盗版) seems no different from ___69___ of any other copyrighted materials. But software is not really like other intellectual ___70___ . Books and videotapes can be copied only by ___71___ that are relatively ___72___ and expensive，and the product is ___73___ quite as good as the original. Software, on the other hand, is easily ___74___ , and the result is not a scratchy second-generation copy ___75___ a perfect working program.

The rapid growth of electronic networks only ___76___ the problem, for it allows anyone with a computer and a modem to ___77___ software silently and instantaneously. More than 90 countries around the world are already ___78___ to the Internet，a global network that reaches a(n) ___79___ 25 million computer users.

How to 80 this increasingly *rampant*(猖獗 的) piracy? The publisher's first ___81___ was to control it through technical means：by putting ___82___ in their programs ___83___ prevented users from copying them. This ___84___ worked for a while，or at least until determined pirates found ways to ___85___ it. ___86___ the codes also made it difficult for legitimate users to copy programs onto their hard drives.

69. A) which   B) what
     C) that   D) this
70. A) right   B) property
     C) outcome   D) possession
71. A) manners   B) processes
     C) processions   D) courses
72. A) time-consumed   B) timely-consumed
     C) time-consuming   D) timely-consuming
73. A) always   B) usually
     C) often   D) never
74. A) produced   B) created
     C) published   D) duplicated
75. A) but   B) yet
     C) except   D) or
76. A) composes   B) compounds
     C) arouses   D) generates
77. A) dismiss   B) dissolve
     C) distribute   D) divide
78. A) related   B) adapted
     C) connected   D) fallen
79. A) estimated   B) evaluated
     C) exaggerated   D) judged
80. A) combine   B) combat
     C) compete   D) compress
81. A) approach   B) contact
     C) entrance   D) access
82. A) codes   B) clues
     C) signs   D) hints
83. A) or   B) and
     C) but   D) that
84. A) pressure   B) strategy
     C) emphasis   D) attack
85. A) get around   B) get across
     C) get into   D) get along
86. A) Thus   B) Because
     C) But   D) Moreover

Part VI *Translation* (*5 minutes*)

87. They are in favor of _____(采取严格的措施来控制污染).

88. It's reported that by the end of this year the output of cars in this factory _____ _____(将增加大约 10%).

89. He made a suggestion that _____(立即对这台新的电子仪器加以检验).

90. She feels like giving up her job, _____(不顾后果).

91. _____(我们一得出这个结论) than they agreed to it.

New College English Model Test Five

Part Ⅰ Writing (30 minutes)

Directions: *For this part, you are allowed 30 minutes to write a short essay "**A Letter to the Editor-in-chief about A Newly-Published English Magazine**". You should write at least 120 words following the outline given below.*

假设你是李明,请你就一本新近出版的英语学习杂志写一封评价信,内容应涉及杂志的版面设计(layout)、文章内容、难易度、实用性、价格等,可以评价其特色和受欢迎之处,也可以提出你的建议、构想和要求。以下是该杂志的主要栏目,仅供写作时参考:

news channel(新闻频道), humor(幽默故事), tales of life(人生广角), classis prose(经典文选), kaleidoscope(万花筒), learning aid(教与学), easy readings(轻松读物), New CET(Band 4 and 6)(聚焦新四、六级考试), basic grammar(英语语法ABC), corner of literature(文学角), practice in writing(习作园地)等。

A Letter to the Editor-in-chief about A Newly-Published English Magazine

Dear Editor-in-Chief,

_____

_____

_____

...

Sincerely yours,

Li Ming

Part Ⅱ Reading Comprehension (Skimming and Scanning)(15 minutes)

Generation XXL

A society of obese children

Children's impulses haven't changed much in recent decades. But social forces — from the disappearance of home cooking to the rise of fast food and video technology—have converged to make them heavier. Snack and soda companies are spending hundreds of millions a year to promote empty calories, while schools cut back on physical education and outdoor play is supplanted by *Nintendo*(任天堂游戏机) and Internet. By the government's estimate, some 6 million American children are now fat enough to endanger their health. An additional 5 million are on the threshold, and the problem is growing more extreme even as it becomes more widespread. "The children we see today are 30 percent heavier than the ones who were referred to us in 1990," says Dr. Naomi Neufeld, a pediatric *endocrinologist*(儿科内分泌学家) in Los Angeles.

Obese kids suffer both physically and emotionally throughout childhood, and those who remain heavy as adolescents tend to stay that way into adulthood. The resulting illnesses — *diabetes*(糖尿病), heart disease, high blood pressure, several cancers—now claim an estimated half-million American lives each year, while costing us \$100 billion in medical expenses and lost productivity. U. S. Agriculture

Secretary Dan Glickman predicts that obesity will soon rival smoking as a cause of preventable death, and some health experts are calling for national action to combat it. Meanwhile, the challenge for children, and their parents, is to swim against the current.

Until recently, childhood obesity was so rare that no one tracked it closely. Body-mass index (BMI), the height-to-weight ratio used to measure adult weight, seemed irrelevant to people whose bodies are still growing. But that mind-set is changing. In a gesture aimed at parents and *pediatricians*(儿科医师), federal health officials recently published new growth charts that extend the BMI system to children. Unlike the adult charts, which classify anyone with a BMI of 25 or higher as "overweight" and anyone with a BMI of 30 or more as "obese," the childhood charts use population norms from the 1960s to determine healthy weight ranges for kids 2 to 20. According to the new charts, a typical 7-year-old girl stands 4 feet 1 inch tall and weighs 50 pounds, giving her a BMI of 15. By the age of 17, she stands 5 feet 4 and weighs 125 pounds, for a BMI of 21. To spare parents undue alarm over baby fat or the normal weight gain that precedes growth *spurts*(冲刺), the new charts use a broad definition of healthy weight.

The heavy sufferings

Even by these *lenient*(宽松的) standards, the proportion of kids who are overweight jumped from 5 percent in 1964 to nearly 13 percent in 1994, the most recent year on record. If the trend has continued—and many experts believe it has accelerated—one child in three is now either overweight or at risk of becoming so. No race or class has been spared, and many youngsters are already suffering health consequences. Dr. Nancy Krebs, a pediatrician at the University of Colorado, notes that overweight children are now showing up with such problems as fatty liver, a *precursor*(先兆) to *cirrhosis*(硬化), and obstructive sleep *apnea*(呼吸暂停), a condition in which the excess flesh around the throat blocks the airway, causing loud snoring, fitful sleep and a chronic lack of oxygen that can damage the heart and lungs.

Even type 2 diabetes—known traditionally as "adult-onset" diabetes turn up in overweight kids. "Ten years ago I would have told you that type 2 diabetes doesn't occur until after 40," says Dr. Robin Goland of New York's Columbia-Presbyterian Hospital, "Now 30 percent of our pediatric patients are type 2." Unlike type 1 disease, in which the *pancreas*(胰腺) fails to produce the *insulin*(胰岛素) needed to transport sugar from the bloodstream into cells, type 2 diabetes occurs when a person's cells grow resistant to insulin, causing sugar to build up in the blood. Unless it's carefully managed, this obesity-related condition can damage blood vessels within a decade, setting the stage for kidney failure and blindness as well as *amputations*(截肢手术), heart attacks and strokes. And because children are not routinely screened for type 2 disease, Goland worries that many cases are going undiagnosed.

Even if they don't develop diabetes, chronically overweight kids may become prime candidates for heart attacks and strokes. In a recent survey of preschoolers at New York City Head Start Centers, Dr. Christine Williams of Columbia University found that overweight kids as young as 3 and 4 showed signs of elevated blood pressure and *cholesterol*(胆固醇). "There's a lag between the development of obesity and the chronic diseases associated with it," says Dr. William Dietz of the Centers for Disease Control and Prevention. "We're in that trough right now. Very soon we'll see the rate of *cardiovascular*(心脏血管的) disease among teenagers rising."

Obesity—a struggle of the whole society

How does a child end up in this predicament? Genes are clearly part of the story. Nine-year-old Emily Hoffman of Humble, Texas, was born weighing nearly 11 pounds. And though she was raised in ways her pediatricians approved of, everything she ate seemed to turn into fat. By 7 she weighed 180 pounds. But even in kids who are prone to obesity, lifestyle is what triggers it. Felice Ramirez weighed 200 pounds when she started eighth grade in Victoria, Texas, three years ago. And though she has since lost 25, she is constantly influenced in the wrong direction. She has a P.E. class at school, but sitting on the bleachers counts as participation. And though the school cafeteria tries to offer healthy fare, the lines are so long, and the lunch period so short, that kids are often forced to dine on packaged snacks from the vending machines.

These are common temptations. Many schools now feature not only soda and snack machines but on-site outlets for fast-food chains. At the same time, recess and physical education are vanishing from the schools' standard curriculum. Not surprisingly, the proportion of high-school kids in daily gym classes fell from 42 percent to 29 percent during the 90's.

1. The improvement of the living conditions is one social force that makes children heavier.
2. Every year about 50,000 Americans die of diseases resulting from obesity.
3. According to Dan Glickman, obesity will rival smoking as a cause of preventable death in the near future.
4. Childhood obesity was never tracked closely before, the reason of which is that childhood obesity used to be rare.
5. The proportion of kids who are overweight in 1994 jumped 13 percent compared with that in 1964.
6. Type 2 diabetes only occur in adults while type 1 diabetes may occur in children.
7. The research of Dr. Christine Williams shows that overweight kids may become prime candidates for heart attacks and strokes.
8. The author cites the example of Emily Hoffman to show that _____ is/are one cause of overweight.
9. The example of Felice Ramirez shows us that in kids who are prone to obesity _____ is/are a stimulating factor for overweight.
10. Besides the unhealthy food and drink, the vanishing of _____ from the school courses also contributes to the problem of childhood obesity.

Part Ⅲ *Listening Comprehension* (*35 minutes*)

Section A

11. A) At a gas station.   B) At a bank.   C) At a hospital.   D) At a school.
12. A) She wants to win the race.   B) She is tired of losing.
    C) She doesn't want to disappoint her family.   D) Her sister is waiting for her.
13. A) Barry no longer lives in New York.   B) Barry doesn't know how to economize.
    C) The woman called Barry in California.   D) The woman didn't ever meet Barry.
14. A) Two hours.   B) Four hours.   C) Six hours.   D) Eight hours.
15. A) A restaurant.   B) The station.   C) The stadium.   D) A star.
16. A) A play.   B) A movie.   C) A lecture.   D) A concert.
17. A) Three-quarters of an hour.   B) Half an hour.
    C) A quarter of an hour.   D) Ten minutes.
18. A) He fell.   B) He had a fight.   C) He was killed.   D) He was punished.

Questions 19 to 22 are based on the conversation you have just heard.

19. A) A vacation the woman took.   B) French influence in New Orleans.
    C) New Orleans' Mardi Gras Festival.   D) A business trip.
20. A) By bus.   B) By car.   C) By plane.   D) By train.
21. A) The weather.   B) The food.   C) The architecture.   D) The music.
22. A) He was president when the city was purchased.
    B) He led the American forces in a nearby battle.

C) He designed Jackson Square in the French Quarter.

D) He helped found New Orleans.

Questions 23 to 25 are based on the conversation you've just heard.

23. A) Different family backgrounds.　　　B) The generation gap.

　　C) Traveling and studying overseas.　　D) Different interests and hobbies.

24. A) His parents are too strict with him.　　B) His parents are indifferent to politics.

　　C) His parents don't understand him.　　D) His parents always criticize him.

25. A) They were kept away from all the big social activities.

　　B) They were open to current events.

　　C) They didn't seem to know much about their times.

　　D) They were always agreeable to her.

 ection B

Passage One

Questions 26 to 28 are based on the passage you have just heard.

26. A) To prevent disease among military personnel.

　　B) To investigate serious crimes in the military.

　　C) To find ways of identifying bodies of soldiers.

　　D) To store old military journals and diaries.

27. A) Working on DNA.　　　　　　B) Wearing a necklace.

　　C) Taking blood samples.　　　　D) Making identification tags.

28. A) Biology.　　　B) Geology.　　　C) History.　　　D) Political Science.

Passage Two

Questions 29 to 31 are based on the passage you have just heard.

29. A) They can do better than others.

　　B) It is expensive to hire labor.

　　C) They don't like to be helped.

　　D) They don't trust others.

30. A) It publishes books only for children.

　　B) It publishes books about people's pets.

　　C) It uses computers to make up stories.

　　D) It makes the young readers the leading characters in the stories.

31. A) Written by children themselves.

　　B) Personalized story books for children.

　　C) Printed with standard things.

　　D) Published with the help of computers.

Passage Three

Questions 32 to 35 are based on the passage you have just heard.

32. A) Advice about landscaping.

　　B) Hints about saving to buy a house.

　　C) Photographs of the homes of famous people.

　　D) Plans for houses.

33. A) Nineteenth-century American painting.　　B) American architectural history.

　　C) Introduction to economics.　　　　　　D) Eighteenth-century American society.

34. A) There was a shortage of architects.　　　B) They included plans for elaborate house.

C) Builders could not work without one.　　D) They were relatively inexpensive.

35. A) People who restore old houses.　　B) People who sell houses.

C) People who design new houses.　　D) People who want to buy a house.

ection C

The biggest safety threat facing airlines today may not be a terrorist with a gun, but the man with the portable computer in business class. In the last 15 years, (36)_____ have reported well over 100 (37)_____ that could have been caused by electromagnetic interference. The source of this interference remains (38)_____, but increasingly, experts are pointing the (39)_____ at portable electronic devices such as portable computers, radio and cassette players and (40)_____ telephones.

RTCA, an organization which advises the aviation industry, has (41)_____ that all airlines ban such devices from being used during "critical" (42)_____ of flight, particularly take-off and landing. Some experts have gone further, calling for a (43)_____ ban during all flights. Currently, rules on using these devices are left up to individual airlines. And (44)_____, given that many passengers want to work during flights.

The difficulty is predicting how electromagnetic fields might affect an aircraft's computers. (45)_____. But, because they have not been able to reproduce these effects in a laboratory, they have no way of knowing whether the interference might be dangerous or not. (46)_____.

Part Ⅳ　*Reading Comprehension*（*Reading in Depth*）（*25 minutes*）

ection A

Questions 47 to 56 are based on the following passage.

People travel for a lot of reasons. Some tourists go to see battlefields or __47__ shrines. Others are looking for culture, or simply want to have their pictures taken in front of famous places. But most European tourists are looking for a sunny beach to lie on.

Northern Europeans are willing to pay a lot of money and put up with a lot __48__ for the sun because they have so little of it. Residents of cities like London, Copenhagen, and Amsterdam spend a lot of their winter in the dark because the days are so short and much of the rest of the year in the rain. This is the reason the Mediterranean has always attracted them. Every summer, more than 25 million people travel to Mediterranean __49__ and beaches for their vacation. They all come for the same reason: sun.

The huge crowds mean lots of money for the economies of Mediterranean countries. Italy's 30,000 hotels are booked __50__ every summer. And 13 million people camp out on French beaches, parks, and roadsides. Spain's long sandy coastline __51__ more people than anywhere else. 37 million tourists visit yearly, or one tourist for every person living in Spain. But there are signs that the area is getting more tourism than it can __52__. The Mediterranean is already one of the most polluted seas on earth. And with increased tourism, it's getting worse. The French can't figure out what to do with all the __53__ left by campers around St. Tropez. And in many places, swimming is dangerous because of pollution.

None of this, however, is __54__ anyone's fun, The Mediterranean gets more popular every year with tourists. __55__, they don't go there for clean water and solitude. They __56__ traffic jams and seem to like crowded beaches. They don't even mind the pollution. No matter how dirty the water is, the coastline still looks beautiful. And as long as the sun shines, it's still better than sitting in the cold rain in

Berlin, London, or Oslo.

A) appeals	I) garbage
B) handle	J) spoiling
C) Obviously	K) distinguish
D) attracts	L) solid
E) Roughly	M) damages
F) religious	N) resorts
G) tolerate	O) inconveniences
H) encountering	

 ection B

Passage One

Questions 57 to 61 are based on the following passage.

Although language is used to transmit information, the informative functions of language are blended with older and deeper functions so that only a small portion of our everyday speech can be described as purely informative. The ability to use language for strictly informative purposes was probably developed relatively late in the course of *linguistic*(语言上的) evolution.

Long before that time, our ancestors probably made the sorts of cries animals do to express feelings of hunger, fear, loneliness, and the like. Gradually these noises seem to have become more *differentiated* (能区分开的), transforming the cries into language as we know it today.

Although we have developed language in which accurate reports may be given, we still use language as *vocal*(发声的) equivalents of gestures such as crying in pain. When words are used as the vocal equivalent of expressive gestures, language is functioning in presymbolic ways. These presymbolic uses of language co-exist with our symbolic system, so that the talking we do in everyday life is a thorough blending of symbolic and presymbolic language.

What we call social conversation is mainly presymbolic in character. When we are at a large social gathering, for example, we all have to talk. It is typical of these conversations that, except among very good friends, few of the remarks made have any informative value. We talk together about nothing at all and thereby establish a relationship.

There is a principle at work in the selection of the subject matter we consider appropriate for social conversation. Since the purpose of this kind of talk is the establishment of communication, we are careful to select subjects about which agreement is immediately possible. With each new agreement, no matter how commonplace, the fear and suspicion of the stranger wear away, and the possibility of friendship emerges. When further conversation reveals that we have friends or political views or artistic values or hobbies in common, a friend is made, and genuine communication and cooperation can begin.

57. The phrase "older and deeper functions" in the first sentence refers to _____.

A) the grammatical structure of language

B) the expression of emotions through sound

C) the transmission of information through written language

D) the purely informative part of language

58. The author uses the term "presymbolic language" to mean probably _____.

A) language used in accurate reports

B) language that lacks an elaborate grammatical structure

C) language that our ancestors use prehistorically

D) language that is of little informative value

59. With regard to the evolution of language, which of the following statements is TRUE?

A) The origin of language can be traced back to the early man's imitation of noises made by animals.

B) Meaningless cries preceded the origin of language.

C) In the process of evolution, language is mainly non-informative.

D) Originally, language is the indistinguishable forms of cries.

60. The primary value of presymbolic language for humans is that it _____.

A) wipes out human hostility and suspicion

B) permits and aids the smooth functioning of interpersonal relationships

C) kills time in a more casual way

D) helps establish an agreement for genuine cooperation

61. Which of the following statements is TRUE according to the passage?

A) Since language is mainly for information, communication in our daily life is primarily symbolic.

B) In modern times, we tend to use more symbolic languages than presymbolic ones.

C) Before a genuine communication and conversation began, speakers generally accompany symbolic language with presymbolic one.

D) In terms of daily talking it is relatively hard to determine which part of the language is symbolic and which part is presymbolic.

Passage Two

Questions 62 to 66 are based on the following passage.

Do women tend to *devalue*(贬低) the worth of their work? Do they apply different standards to rewarding their own work more critically than they do to rewarding the work of others? These were the questions asked by Michigan State University psychologists Lawrence Messe and Charlene Callahan-Levy. Past experiments had shown that when women were asked to decide how much to pay themselves and other people for the same job, they paid themselves less. Following up on this finding, Messe and Callahan-Levy designed experiments to test several popular explanations of why women tend to get less in pay situations.

One theory the psychologists tested was that women judge their own work more harshly than that of others. The subjects for the experiment testing this theory were men and women from the Michigan State undergraduate student body. The job the subjects were asked to perform for pay was an opinion *questionnaire*(调查表) requiring a number of short essays on campus-related issues. After completing the questionnaire, some subjects were given six dollars in bills and change and were asked to decide payment for themselves. Others were given the same amount and were asked to decide payment for another subject who had also completed the questionnaire.

The psychologists found that, as in earlier experiments, the women paid themselves less than the men paid themselves. They also found that the women paid themselves less than they paid other women and less than the men paid the women. The differences were substantial. The average paid to women by themselves was $2.97. The average paid to men by themselves was $4.06. The average paid to women by others was $4.37. In spite of the differences, the psychologists found that the men and the women in the experiment evaluated their own performances on the questionnaire about equally and better than the expected performances of others.

On the basis of these findings, Messe and Callahan-Levy concluded that women's attachment of a comparatively low monetary value to their work cannot be based entirely on their judgment of their own ability.

62. The experiment designed in the passage would be most relevant to the *formulation*（陈述，表述）of a theory concerning the _____ .

A) generally lower salaries received by women workers in comparison to men

B) reluctance of some women to enter professions that are traditionally dominated by men

C) anxiety expressed by some women workers in dealing with male supervisors

D) prejudices often suffered by women in attempting to enter the workforce

63. How is the research of Messe and Callahan-Levy related to earlier experiments in the same field?

A) It suggests a need to discard methods used in earlier experiments.

B) It tends to weaken the assumptions on which earlier experiments were designed.

C) It suggests that the problem revealed in earlier experiments may be more widespread than previously thought.

D) It helps to explain a phenomenon revealed in earlier experiments.

64. Which of the following statements is supported by the facts stated in the passage?

A) Men tend to pay themselves more than they pay other men for the same work.

B) Women tend to pay men more than they pay other women for the same work.

C) Men tend to pay women less than they pay other men for the same work.

D) None of the above.

65. The work of Messe and Callahan-Levy tends to support which of the following notions?

A) Women are generally less concerned with financial rewards for their work than men are.

B) Men are willing to pay women more than women are willing to pay themselves.

C) Payment for work should generally be directly related to the quality of the work.

D) Women judge their own work more critically than they judge the work of men.

66. It can be inferred from the last paragraph that _____ .

A) it is not always reliable to measure women's ability by how much they earn

B) women would rather attach importance to sacrifices than ask for repayment for their work

C) women tend to assess their ability of work by their own self-worth rather than monetary values

D) women generally remain indifferent to how much money they should obtain from their work

Part V *Cloze* (*15 minutes*)

The standard of living of any country means the average person's share of the goods and services which the country produces. A country's standard of living, therefore, depends on its __67__ to produce wealth. Wealth, in this sense is not money, __68__ we do __69__ live on money but on things that money can buy: "goods" such as food and clothing, and "services" such as transport and __70__ . A country's capacity to __71__ wealth is influenced by many factors, __72__ have an effect on one another. Wealth is dependent __73__ a great

67. A) potential   B) faculty
     C) capability   D) capacity

68. A) for   B) though
     C) but   D) if

69. A) not only   B) neither
     C) either   D) not

70. A) entertainment   B) assignment
     C) attachment   D) achievement

71. A) dominate   B) accumulate
     C) yield   D) assemble

72. A) most of which   B) in which most
     C) which most   D) on which most

73. A) on   B) of

extent ___74___ a country's natural resources. Some regions are ___75___ in coal and minerals, and have a fertile soil and a(n) ___76___ climate; other regions possess perhaps only one of these things, and some regions have ___77___ of them. The U.S.A. is one of the wealthiest regions of the world ___78___ she has vast natural resources within her borders. The Sahara Desert on the other hand, is one of the ___79___ wealthy. ___80___ to natural resources comes the ability to turn them to use. China is perhaps as ___81___ off as the U.S.A. in natural resources, but suffered from civil and ___82___ wars, and for this and other reasons was unable to ___83___ her resources. Another important factor is the technical efficiency of a country's people. Old countries that have numerous skilled craftsmen are better ___84___ to produce wealth than countries whose workers are largely unskilled. Furthermore, wealth also produces wealth. As a country becomes wealthier its people can put their savings into factories and machines, ___85___ which more goods will help workers to ___86___ more goods.

C) to   D) with

74. A) to   B) in
    C) as   D) on
75. A) scarce   B) abundant
    C) generous   D) unusual
76. A) appropriate   B) delicate
    C) favorable   D) flexible
77. A) none   B) nothing
    C) anything but   D) nothing but
78. A) in which   B) of which
    C) for which   D) in that
79. A) last   B) latest
    C) least   D) latter
80. A) Prior   B) Next
    C) As   D) Up
81. A) well   B) good
    C) bad   D) badly
82. A) outer   B) outward
    C) exterior   D) external
83. A) exploit   B) explore
    C) extend   D) expand
84. A) placed   B) located
    C) settled   D) deposited
85. A) in the event of   B) with the exception of
    C) at the expense of   D) as a result of
86. A) make out   B) give out
    C) turn out   D) hold out

Part Ⅵ Translation (*5 minutes*)

87. You can borrow this book _____ (条件是不要把它借给别人).
88. I felt _____ (如释重负) when I heard that she survived the earthquake.
89. The plan was especially supported by those _____ (那些愿意有更多机会说英语的人).
90. Despite the great achievements made by China over the past decade, _____ (还有许多问题亟待解决).
91. It is strange that she _____ (竟然没有看出自己的缺点).

第三章 单项强化篇

该章主要针对阅读、听力、写作和翻译四个方面,进行单独的强化训练。由于完型填空为考生较为熟悉的题型;限于篇幅,本书就不再单独设计练习,随前面的全真和模拟试题一并讲解训练。其他四部分均安排专题训练内容,进行考前强化模拟。单项训练的目的旨在帮助考生更为详细地了解各类测试题目的出题规律和解题技巧,更快地提高单项测试的应试能力。

第一节 阅读演练篇

该部分是强化训练的重中之重,有三部分组成。第一部分是仔细阅读,是考生比较熟悉的题型。与以往其他阅读测试不同的是,四级仔细阅读有其特殊性和解题方法,考生需要经过一定的训练才能摸准四级阅读的"脾气",才能游刃有余地应对。本书精选了历年测试的阅读真题作为训练材料,一来确保训练的效度和高保真度,二来熟悉四级仔细阅读的出题规律和解题技巧。历年指导四级的经验告诉我们,考前做真题是获取高分的一条捷径,也是强化训练的必经之路。本节向考生提供了八天的仔细阅读强化材料,每天按照4篇文章,40分钟来控制阅读时间进行训练。建议在打牢基础的前提下,考前一个月内进行强化阅读训练或回炉复习。第二、三部分是快速阅读和选词填空,是新四级增加的题型。"快速阅读"检测考生"扫描查读"信息的能力,文章篇幅一般在1300字左右。做快速阅读时,关键要找到题干中的核心词,然后确定文章上下的出处,再仔细阅读出处,达到解题的目的。做题时,建议考生先浏览后面的题目,带着问题搜找文章相关细节,通常能比较轻松地找到答案。关于选词填空,由于是差额选词,很多考生有无从下手的感觉。其实,做该题时,先判断填空单词的词性常常是解题的快速有效方法。了解了所需单词的词性再加上对上下文语篇和语法的理解,一般填空题就迎刃而解了。

Part I *Reading Comprehension*(*Reading in Depth*)

八天攻克阅读关(第一天强化)

Passage 1

Educating girls quite possibly yields a higher rate of return than any other investment available in the developing world. Women's education may be unusual territory for economists, but enhancing women's contribution to development is actually as much an economic as a social issue. And economics, with its emphasis on *incentives*(激励), provides guideposts that point to an explanation for why so many girls are deprived of an education.

Parents in low-income countries fail to invest in their daughters because they do not expect them to make an economic contribution to the family: girls grow up only to marry into somebody else's family and bear children. Girls are thus seen as less valuable than boys and are kept at home to do housework while their brothers are sent to school-the *prophecy*(预言) becomes self-fulfilling, trapping women in a *vicious circle*(恶性循环) of neglect.

An educated mother, on the other hand, has greater earning abilities outside the home and faces an entirely different set of choices. She is likely to have fewer but healthier children and can insist on the development of all her children, ensuring that her daughters are given a fair chance. The education of her daughters then makes it much more likely that the next generation of girls, as well as of boys, will be educated and healthy. The vicious circle is thus transformed into a virtuous circle.

Few will dispute that educating women has great social benefits. But it has enormous economic advantages as well. Most obviously, there is the direct effect of education on the wages of female workers. Wages rise by 10 to 20 per cent for each additional year of schooling. Such big returns are impressive by the standard of other available investments, but they are just the beginning. Educating women also has a significant impact on health practices, including family planning.

1. The author argues that educating girls in developing countries is _____.
   A) rewarding   C) expensive   B) troublesome   D) labor-saving
2. By saying "...the prophecy becomes self-fulfilling..."(Para. 2), the author means that _____.
   A) girls will eventually find their goals in life beyond reach
   B) girls will be increasingly discontented with their life at home
   C) girls will be capable of realizing their own dreams
   D) girls will turn out to be less valuable than boys
3. The author believes that a vicious circle can turn into a virtuous circle when _____.
   A) women care more about education
   B) parents can afford their daughters' education
   C) girls can gain equal access to education
   D) a family has fewer but healthier children
4. What does the author say about women's education?
   A) It has aroused the interest of a growing number of economists.
   B) It will yield greater returns than other known investments.
   C) It is now given top priority in many developing countries.
   D) It deserves greater attention than other social issues.
5. The passage mainly discusses _____.
   A) unequal treatment of boys and girls in developing countries
   B) the major contributions of educated women to society
   C) the economic and social benefits of educating women
   D) the potential earning power of well-educated women

Passage 2

Psychiatrists(精神病专家) who work with older parents say that maturity can be an asset in child rearing-older parents are more thoughtful, use less physical discipline and spend more time with their children. But raising kids takes money and energy. Many older parents find themselves balancing their limited financial resources, declining energy and failing health against the growing demands of an active child. Dying and leaving young children is probably the older parents' biggest, and often unspoken, fear. Having late-life children, says an economics professor, often means parents, particularly fathers, "end up retiring much later." For many, retirement becomes an unobtainable dream.

Henry Metcalf, a 54-year-old journalist, knows it takes money to raise kids. But he's also worried that his energy will give out first. Sure, he can still ride bikes with his athletic fifth grader, but he's learned that young at heart doesn't mean young. Lately he's been taking afternoon *naps*(午睡) to keep up his energy. "My body is aging," says Metcalf. "You can't get away from that."

Often, older parents hear the ticking of another kind of biological clock. Therapists who work with middle-aged and older parents say fears about aging are nothing to laugh at. "They worry they'll be mistaken for grandparents, or that they'll need help getting up out of those little chairs in nursery school," says Joann Galst, a New York psychologist. But at the core of those little fears there is often a much bigger one: "that they won't be alive long enough to support and protect their child," she says.

Many late-life parents, though, say their children came at just the right time. After marrying late and undergoing years of *fertility*(受孕) treatment, Marilyn Nolen and her husband, Randy, had twins. "We both wanted children," says Marilyn, who was 55 when she gave birth. The twins have given the couple what they desired for years, "a sense of family."

Kids of older dads are often smarter, happier and more sociable because their fathers are more involved in their lives. "The dads are older, more mature," says Dr. Silber, "and more ready to focus on parenting."

6. Why do psychiatrists regard maturity as an asset in child rearing?
   A) Older parents can better balance their resources against children's demands.
   B) Older parents are usually more experienced in bringing up their children.
   C) Older parents are often better prepared financially.
   D) Older parents can take better care of their children.

7. What does the author mean by saying "For many, retirement becomes an unobtainable dream"(Lines 7-8, Para. 1)?
   A) They have to go on working beyond their retirement age.
   B) They can't get full pension unless they work some extra years.
   C) They can't obtain the retirement benefits they have dreamed of.
   D) They are reluctant to retire when they reach their retirement age.

8. The author gives the example of Henry Metcalf to show that _____.
   A) many people are young in spirit despite their advanced age
   B) taking afternoon naps is a good way to maintain energy
   C) older parents tend to be concerned about their aging bodies
   D) older parents should exercise more to keep up with their athletic children

9. What's the biggest fear of older parents according to New York psychologist Joan Galst?
   A) Being laughed at by other people.   C) Being mistaken for grandparents.
   B) Slowing down of their pace of life.   D) Approaching of death.

10. What do we learn about Marilyn and Randy Nolen?
    A) They thought they were an example of successful fertility treatment.
    B) Not until they had the twins did they feel they had formed a family.
    C) They believed that children born of older parents would be smarter.
    D) Not until they reached middle age did they think of having children.

Passage 3

Interest in pursuing international careers has soared in recent years, enhanced by *chronic*(长久的) personnel shortages that are causing companies to search beyond their home borders for talent.

Professionals seek career experience outside of their home countries for a variety of reasons. They may feel the need to recharge their batteries with a new challenge. They may want a position with more responsibility that encourages creativity and initiative. Or they may wish to expose their children to another culture, and the opportunity to learn a second language.

When applying for a job, one usually has to submit a resume or curriculum vitae(CV). The two terms generally mean the same thing: a one- or two-page document describing one's educational qualifications and professional experience. However, guidelines for preparing a resume are constantly changing. The best advice is to find out what is appropriate regarding the *corporate*（公司）culture, the country culture, and the culture of the person making the hiring decision. The challenge will be to embrace two or more cultures in one document. The following list is a good place to start.

   • Educational requirements differ from country to country. In almost every case of 'cross- border' job hunting, just stating the title of your degree will not be an adequate description. Provide the reader with details about your studies and any related experience.

   • Pay attention to the resume format you use-chronological or reverse-chronological order. Chronological order means listing your 'oldest' work experience first. Reverse-chronological order means listing your current or most recent experience first. Most countries have preferences about which format is most acceptable. If you find no specific guidelines, the general preference is for the reverse-chronological format.

   • If you are submitting your resume in English, find out if the *recipient*（收件人）uses British English or American English because there are variations between the two versions. For example, university education is often referred to as "tertiary education" in the United Kingdom, but this term is almost never used in the United States. A reader who is unfamiliar with these variations may assume that your resume contains errors.

11. Companies are hiring more foreign employees because _____.
    A) they have difficulty finding qualified personnel at home
    B) they find foreign employees are usually more talented
    C) they need original ideas from employees hired overseas
    D) they want to expand their business beyond home borders

12. The author believes that an individual who applies to work overseas _____.
    A) is usually creative and full of initiative
    B) aims to improve his foreign language skills
    C) seeks either his own or his children's development
    D) is dissatisfied with his own life at home

13. When it comes to resume writing, it is best to _____.
    A) know the employer's personal likes and dislikes
    B) follow appropriate guidelines for job hunting
    C) learn about the company's hiring process
    D) take cultural factors into consideration

14. When writing about qualifications, applicants are advised to _____.
    A) provide a detailed description of their study and work experiences
    B) give the title of the university degree they have earned at home
    C) highlight their keen interest in pursuing a 'cross-border' career
    D) stress their academic potential to impress the decision maker

15. According to the author's last piece of advice, the applicants should be aware of _____.
    A) the recipient's preference with regard to the format
    B) the different educational systems in the US and the UK
    C) the differences between the varieties of English
    D) the distinctive features of American and British cultures

Passage 4

   Speeding off in a stolen car, the thief thinks he has got a great catch. But he is in for an unwelcome surprise. The car is fitted with a remote *immobiliser*（锁止器）, and a radio signal from a control centre miles away will ensure that once the thief switches the engine off, he will not be able to start it again.

The idea goes like this. A control box fitted to the car contains a mini-cellphone, a micro-processor and memory, and a *GPS*（全球定位系统）satellite positioning receiver. If the car is stolen, a coded cellphone signal will tell the control centre to block the vehicle's engine management system and prevent the engine being restarted.

In the UK, a set of technical fixes is already making life harder for car thieves. 'The pattern of vehicle crime has changed,' says Martyn Randall, a security expert. He says it would only take him a few minutes to teach a person how to steal a car, using a bare minimum of tools. But only if the car is more than 10 years old.

Modern cars are far tougher to steal, as their engine management computer won't allow them to start unless they receive a unique ID code beamed out by the *ignition*（点火）key. In the UK, technologies like this have helped achieve a 31% drop in vehicle-related crime since 1997.

But determined criminals are still managing to find other ways to steal cars, often by getting hold of the owner's keys. And key theft is responsible for 40% of the thefts of vehicles fitted with a tracking system.

If the car travels 100 metres without the driver confirming their ID, the system will send a signal to an operations centre that it has been stolen. The hundred metres minimum avoids false alarms due to inaccuracies in the GPS signal.

Staff at the centre will then contact the owner to confirm that the car really is missing, and keep police informed of the vehicle's movements via the car's GPS unit.

16. What's the function of the remote immobilizer fitted to a car?
    A) To allow the car to lock automatically when stolen.
    B) To prevent the car thief from restarting it once it stops.
    C) To help the police make a surprise attack on the car thief.
    D) To prevent car theft by sending a radio signal to the car owner.

17. By saying 'The pattern of vehicle crime has changed' (Lines 1-2. Para. 3) Martyn Randall suggests that _____ .
    A) self-prepared tools are no longer enough for car theft
    B) the thief has to make use of computer technology
    C) it takes a longer time for the car thief to do the stealing
    D) the thief has lost interest in stealing cars over 10 years old

18. What is essential in making a modern car tougher to steal?
    A) A GPS satellite positioning receiver.   B) A unique ID card.
    C) A special cell phone signal.   D) A coded ignition key.

19. Why does the tracking system set a 100-metre minimum before sending an alarm to the operations centre?
    A) To give the driver time to contact the operations centre.
    B) To allow for possible errors in the GPS system.
    C) To keep police informed of the car's movements.
    D) To leave time for the operations centre to give an alarm.

20. What will the operations centre do first after receiving an alarm?
    A) Start the tracking system.   B) Locate the missing car.
    C) Contact the car owner.   D) Block the car engine.

攻克阅读关（第二天强化）

Passage 5

On average, American kids ages 3 to 12 spent 29 hours a week in school, eight hours more than they did in 1981. They also did more household work and participated in more of such organized activities as soccer and *ballet*（芭蕾舞）. Involvement in sports, in particular, rose almost 50% from 1981 to 1997: boys now spend an average of four hours a week playing sports; girls log half that time. All in all, however, children's leisure time dropped from 40% of the day in 1981 to 25%.

"Children are affected by the same time *crunch*（危机）that affects their parents," says Sandra Hofferth, who headed the recent study of children's timetable. A chief reason, she says, is that more mothers are working outside the home. (Nevertheless, children in both double-income and "male breadwinner" households spent comparable amounts of time interacting with their parents, 19 hours and 22 hours respectively. In contrast, children spent only 9 hours with their single mothers.)

All work and no play could make for some very messed-up kids. "Play is the most powerful way a child explores the world and learns about himself," says T. Berry Brazelton, professor at Harvard Medical School. Unstructured play encourages independent thinking and allows the young to negotiate their relationships with their peers, but kids ages 3 to 12 spent only 12 hours a week engaged in it.

The children sampled spent a quarter of their rapidly decreasing "free time" watching television. But that, believe it or not, was one of the findings parents might regard as good news. If they're spending less time in front of the TV set, however, kids aren't replacing it with reading. Despite efforts to get kids more interested in books, the children spent just over an hour a week reading. Let's face it, who's got the time?

21. By mentioning "the same time crunch"(Line 1, Para. 2) Sandra Hofferth means _____.
    A) children have little time to play with their parents
    B) children are not taken good care of by their working parents
    C) both parents and children suffer from lack of leisure time
    D) both parents and children have trouble managing their time

22. According to the author, the reason given by Sandra Hofferth for the time crunch is _____.
    A) quite convincing   B) partially true
    C) totally groundless   D) rather confusing

23. According to the author a child develops better if _____.
    A) he has plenty of time reading and studying
    B) he is left to play with his peers in his own way
    C) he has more time participating in school activities
    D) he is free to interact with his working parents

24. The author is concerned about the fact that American kids _____.
    A) are engaged in more and more structured activities
    B) are increasingly neglected by their working mothers
    C) are spending more and more time watching TV
    D) are involved less and less in household work

25. We can infer from the passage that _____.
    A) extracurricular activities promote children's intelligence
    B) most children will turn to reading with TV sets switched off

C) efforts to get kids interested in reading have been fruitful

D) most parents believe reading to be beneficial to children

Passage 6

Henry Ford, the famous U. S. inventor and car manufacturer, once said, "The business of America is business." By this he meant that the U. S. way of life is based on the values of the business world.

Few would argue with Ford's statement. A brief glimpse at a daily newspaper vividly shows how much people in the United States think about business. For example, nearly every newspaper has a business section, in which the deals and projects, finances and management, stock prices and labor problems of corporations are reported daily. In addition, business news can appear in every other section. Most national news has an important financial aspect to it. Welfare, foreign aid, the federal budget, and the policies of the Federal Reserve Bank are all heavily affected by business. Moreover, business news appears in some of the unlikeliest places. The world of arts and entertainment is often referred to as "the entertainment industry" or "show business."

The positive side of Henry Ford's statement can be seen in the prosperity that business has brought to U. S. life. One of the most important reasons so many people from all over the world come to live in the United States is the dream of a better job. Jobs are produced in *abundance*(大量地) because the U. S. economic system is driven by competition. People believe that this system creates more wealth, more jobs, and a materially better way of life.

The negative side of Henry Ford's statement, however, can be seen when the word business is taken to mean big business. And the term big business-referring to the biggest companies, is seen in opposition to labor. Throughout U. S. history working people have had to fight hard for higher wages, better working conditions, and the fight to form unions. Today, many of the old labor disputes are over, but there is still some employee anxiety. Downsizing-the laying off of thousands of workers to keep expenses low and profits high-creates feelings of insecurity for many.

26. The United States is a typical country _____.

    A) which encourages free trade at home and abroad

    B) where people's chief concern is how to make money

    C) where all businesses are managed scientifically

    D) which normally works according to the federal budget

27. The influence of business in the U. S. is evidenced by the fact that _____.

    A) most newspapers are run by big businesses

    B) even public organizations concentrate on working for profits

    C) Americans of all professions know how to do business

    D) even arts and entertainment are regarded as business

28. According to the passage, immigrants choose to settle in the U. S. , dreaming that _____.

    A) they can start profitable businesses there

    B) they can be more competitive in business

    C) they will make a fortune overnight there

    D) they will find better chances of employment

29. Henry Ford's statement can be taken negatively because _____.

    A) working people are discouraged to fight for their rights

    B) there are many industries controlled by a few big capitalists

    C) there is a conflicting relationship between big corporations and labor

    D) public services are not run by the federal government

30. A company's efforts to keep expenses low and profits high may result in _____.

    A) reduction in the number of employees   B) improvement of working conditions

    C) fewer disputes between labor and management   D) a rise in workers' wages

Passage 7

    Professor Smith recently persuaded 35 people, 23 of them women, to keep a diary of all their absent-minded actions for a fortnight. When he came to analyse their embarrassing *lapses*（差错）in a scientific report, he was surprised to find that nearly all of them fell into a few groupings, nor did the lapses appear to be entirely *random*（随机的）.

    One of the women, for instance, on leaving her house for work one morning threw her dog, her earrings and tried to fix a dog biscuit on her ear. "The explanation for this is that the brain is like a computer," explains the professor. "People programme themselves to do certain activities regularly. It was the woman's custom every morning to throw her dog two biscuits and then put on her earrings. But somehow the action got reversed in the program." About one in twenty of the incidents the volunteers reported were these "programme assembly failures."

    Altogether the volunteers logged 433 unintentional actions that they found themselves doing-an average of twelve each, There appear to be peak periods in the day when we are at our *zaniest*（荒谬可笑的）. These are two hours some time between eight a. m. and noon, between four and six p. m. with a smaller peak between eight and ten p.m. "Among men the peak seems to be when a changeover in brain 'programmes' occurs, as for instance between going to and from work." Women on average reported slightly more lapses-12. 5 compared with 10. 9 for men-probably because they were more reliable reporters.

    A startling finding of the research is that the absent-minded activity is a hazard of doing things in which we are skilled. Normally, you would expect that skill reduces the number of errors we make. But trying to avoid silly slips by concentrating more could make things a lot worse-even dangerous.

31. In his study Professor Smith asked the subjects _____.

    A) to keep track of people who tend to forget things

    B) to report their embarrassing lapses at random

    C) to analyze their awkward experiences scientifically

    D) to keep a record of what they did unintentionally

32. Professor Smith discovered that _____.

    A) certain patterns can be identified in the recorded incidents

    B) many people were too embarrassed to admit their absent-mindedness

    C) men tend to be more absent-minded than women

    D) absent-mindedness is an excusable human weakness

33. "Programme assembly failures"(Line 6, Para. 2) refers to the phenomenon that people _____.

    A) often fail to programme their routines beforehand

    B) tend to make mistakes when they are in a hurry

    C) unconsciously change the sequence of doing things

    D) are likely to mess things up if they are too tired

34. We learn from the third paragraph that _____.

    A) absent-mindedness tends to occur during certain hours of the day

    B) women are very careful to perform actions during peak periods

    C) women experience more peak periods of absent-mindedness

    D) men's absent-mindedness often results in funny situations

35. It can be concluded from the passage that _____ .

    A) people should avoid doing important things during peak periods of lapses

    B) hazards can be avoided when people do things they are good at

    C) people should be careful when programming their actions

    D) lapses cannot always be attributed to lack of concentration

Passage 8

It's no secret that many children would be healthier and happier with adoptive parents than with the parents that nature dealt them. That's especially true of children who remain in abusive homes because the law blindly favors biological parents. It's also true of children who suffer for years in *foster homes*(收养孩子的家庭) because of parents who can't or won't care for them but refuse to give up *custody*(监护) rights.

Fourteen-year-old Kimberly Mays fits neither description, but her recent court victory could eventually help children who do. Kimberly has been the object of an angry custody baffle between the man who raised her and her biological parents, with whom she has never lived. A Florida judge ruled that the teenager can remain with the only father she's ever known and that her biological parents have "no legal claim" on her.

The ruling, though it may yet be reversed, sets aside the principle that biology is the primary determinant of parentage. That's an important development, one that's long overdue.

Shortly after birth in December 1978, Kimberly Mays and another infant were mistakenly switched and sent home with the wrong parents. Kimberly's biological parents, Ernest and Regina Twigg, received a child who died of a heart disease in 1988. Medical tests showed that the child wasn't the Twiggs'own daughter, but Kimt only was, thus sparking a custody battle with Robert Mays. In 1989, the two families agreed that Mr. Mays would maintain custody with the Twiggs getting visiting rights. Those rights were ended when Mr. Mays decided that Kimberly was being harmed.

The decision to leave Kimberly with Mr. Mays rendered her suit debated. But the judge made clear that Kimberly did have standing to *sue*(起诉) on her own behalf. Thus he made clear that she was more than just property to be handled as adults saw fit.

Certainly, the biological link between parent and child is fundamental. But biological parents aren't always preferable to adoptive ones, and biological parentage does not convey an absolute ownership that cancels all the rights of children.

36. What was the primary consideration in the Florida judge's ruling? _____

    A) The biological link.   B) The child's benefits.

    C) The traditional practice.   D) The parents' feelings.

37. We can learn from the Kimberly case that _____ .

    A) children are more than just personal possessions of their parents

    B) the biological link between parent and child should be emphasized

    C) foster homes bring children more pain and suffering than care

    D) biological parents shouldn't claim custody rights after their child is adopted

38. The Twiggs claimed custody rights to Kimberly because _____ .

    A) they found her unhappy in Mr. Mays' custody

    B) they regarded her as their property

    C) they were her biological parents

    D) they felt guilty about their past mistake

39. Kimberly had been given to Mr. Mays _____ .

A) by sheer accident   B) out of charity

C) at his request   D) for better care

40. The author's attitude towards the judge's ruling could be described as _____.

     A) doubtful   B) critical   C) cautious   D) supportive

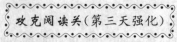

攻克阅读关(第三天强化)

Passage 9

A recent study, published in last week's Journal of the American Medical Association, offers a picture of how risky it is to get a lift from a teenage driver. Indeed, a 16-year-old driver with three or more passengers is three times as likely to have a fatal accident as a teenager driving alone. By contrast, the risk of death for drivers between 30 and 59 decreases with each additional passenger.

The authors also found that the death rates for teenage drivers increased dramatically after 10 p. m., and especially after midnight. With passengers in the car, the driver was even more likely to die in a late-night accident.

Robert Foss, a scientist at the University of North Carolina Highway Safety Research Center, says the higher death rates for teenage drivers have less to do with "really stupid behavior" than with just a lack of driving experience. "The basic issue," he says, "is that adults who are responsible for issuing licenses fail to recognize how complex and skilled a task driving is."

Both he and the author of the study believe that the way to *mitigate*(使……缓解)the problem is to have states institute so-called graduated licensing systems in which getting a license is a multistage process. A graduated license requires that a teenager first prove himself capable of driving in the presence of an adult, followed by a period of driving with night or passenger restrictions before graduating to full driving privileges.

Graduated licensing systems have reduced teenage driver crashes, according to recent studies. About half of the states now have some sort of graduated Licensing system in place, but only 10 of those states have restrictions on passengers. California is the strictest, with a *novice*(新手)driver prohibited from carrying any passenger under 20(without the presence of an adult over 25)for the first six months.

41. Which of the following situations is most dangerous according to the passage?

     A) Adults giving a lift to teenagers on the highway after 10 p. m.

     B) A teenager driving after midnight with passengers in the car.

     C) Adults driving with three or more teenage passengers late at night.

     D) A teenager getting a lift from a stranger on the highway at midnight.

42. According to Robert Foss, the high death rate of teenage drivers is mainly due to _____.

     A) their frequent driving at night   B) their improper way of driving

     C) their lack of driving experience   D) their driving with passengers

43. According to Paragraph 3, which of the following statements is TRUE?

     A) Teenagers should spend more time learning to drive.

     B) Driving is a skill too complicated for teenagers to learn.

     C) Restrictions should be imposed on teenagers applying to take driving lessons.

     D) The licensing authorities are partly responsible for teenagers' driving accidents.

44. A suggested measure to be taken to reduce teenagers' driving accidents is that _____.

     A) driving in the presence of an adult should be made a rule

B) they should be prohibited from taking on passengers

C) they should not be allowed to drive after 10 p. m.

D) the licensing system should be improved

45. The present situation in about half of the states is that the graduated licensing system _____.

    A) is under discussion   B) is about to be set up

    C) has been put into effect   D) has been perfected

Passage 10

If you know exactly what you want, the best route to a job is to get specialized training. A recent survey shows that companies like the graduates in such fields as business and health care who can go to work immediately with very little on-the-job training.

That's especially true of booming fields that are challenging for workers. At Cornell's School of Hotel Administration, for example, bachelor's degree graduates get an average of four or five job offers with salaries ranging from the high teens to the low 20s and plenty of chances for rapid advancement. Large companies, especially, like a background of formal education coupled with work experience.

But in the long run, too much specialization doesn't pay off. Business, which has been flooded with MBAs, no longer considers the degree an automatic stamp of approval. The MBA may open doors and command a higher salary initially, but the impact of a degree washes out after five years.

As further evidence of the *erosion*（销蚀）of *corporate*（公司的）faith in specialized degrees, Michigan State's Scheetz cites a pattern in corporate hiring practices. Although companies tend to take on specialists as new hires, they often seek out generalists for middle and upper-level management. "They want someone who isn't *constrained*（限制）by nuts and bolts to look at the big picture," says Scheetz.

This sounds suspiciously like a formal statement that you approve of the liberal-arts graduate. Time and again labor-market analysts mention a need for talents that liberal-arts majors are assumed to have: writing and communication skills, organizational skills, open-mindedness and adaptability, and the ability to analyze and solve problems. David Birch claims he does not hire anybody with an MBA or an engineering degree, "I hire only liberal-arts people because they have a less-than-canned way of doing things," says Birch. Liberal-arts means an academically thorough and strict program that includes literature, history, mathematics, economics, science, human behavior—plus a computer course or two. With that under your belt, you can feel free to specialize "A liberal-arts degree coupled with an MBA or some other technical training is a very good combination in the marketplace," says Scheetz.

46. What kinds of people are in high demand on the job market?

    A) Students with a bachelor's degree in humanities.

    B) People with an MBA degree from top universities.

    C) People with formal schooling plus work experience.

    D) People with special training in engineering.

47. By saying "...but the impact of a degree washes out after five years"(Line 3, Para, 3), the author means _____.

    A) most MBA programs fail to provide students with a solid foundation

    B) an MBA degree does not help promotion to managerial positions

    C) MBA programs will not be as popular in five years' time as they are now

    D) in five years people will forget about the degree the MBA graduates have got

48. According to Scheetz's statement(Lines 4-5, Para. 4), companies prefer _____.

    A) people who have a strategic mind

    B) people who are talented in fine arts

C) people who are ambitious and aggressive

D) people who have received training in mechanics

49. David Birch claims that he only hires liberal-arts people because _____.

    A) they are more capable of handling changing situations

    B) they can stick to established ways of solving problems

    C) they are thoroughly trained in a variety of specialized fields

    D) they have attended special programs in management

50. Which of the following statements does the author support?

    A) Specialists are more expensive to hire than generalists.

    B) Formal schooling is less important than job training.

    C) On-the-job training is, in the long run, less costly.

    D) Generalists will outdo specialists in management.

Passage 11

About six years ago I was eating lunch in a restaurant in New York City when a woman and a young boy sat down at the next table. I couldn't help overhearing parts of their conversation. At one point the woman asked: "So, how have you been?" And the boy-who could not have been more than seven or eight years old—replied. "Frankly, I've been feeling a little depressed lately."

This incident stuck in my mind because it confirmed my growing belief that children are changing. As far as I can remember, my friends and I didn't find out we were "depressed" until we were in high school.

The evidence of a change in children has increased steadily in recent years. Children don't seem childlike anymore. Children speak more like adults, dress more like adults and behave more like adults than they used to.

Whether this is good or bad is difficult to say, but it certainly is different. Childhood as it once was no longer exists. Why?

Human development is based not only on *innate*(天生的) biological states, but also on patterns of access to social knowledge. Movement from one social role to another usually involves learning the secrets of the new status. Children have always been taught adult secrets, but slowly and in stages: traditionally, we tell sixth graders things we keep hidden from fifth graders.

In the last 30 years, however, a secret-*revelation*(揭示) machine has been installed in 98 percent of American homes. It is called television. Television passes information, and *indiscriminately*(不加区分地), to all viewers alike, be they children or adults. Unable to resist the temptation, many children turn their attention from printed texts to the less challenging, more vivid moving pictures.

Communication through print, as a matter of fact, allows for a great deal of control over the social information to which children have access. Reading and writing involve a complex code of symbols that must be memorized and practiced. Children must read simple books before they can read complex materials.

51. According to the author, feeling depressed is _____.

    A) a sure sign of a psychological problem in a child

    B) something hardly to be expected in a young child

    C) an inevitable part of children's mental development

    D) a mental scale present in all humans, including children

52. Traditionally, a child is supposed to learn about the adult world _____.

    A) through contact with society   B) gradually and under guidance

    C) naturally and by biological instinct   D) through exposure to social information

53. The phenomenon that today's children seem adult-like is attributed by the author to _____.

    A) the widespread influence of television

    B) the poor arrangement of teaching content

    C) the fast pace of human intellectual development

    D) the constantly rising standard of living

54. Why is the author in favor of communication through print for children?

    A) It enables children to gain more social information.

    B) It develops children's interest in reading and writing.

    C) It helps children to memorize and practice more.

    D) It can control what children are to learn.

55. What does the author think of the change in today's children?

    A) He feels amused by their premature behavior.

    B) He thinks it is a phenomenon worthy of note.

    C) He considers it a positive development.

    D) He seems to be upset about it.

Passage 12

"Opinion" is a word that is used carelessly today. It is used to refer to matters of taste, belief, and judgment. This casual use would probably cause little confusion if people didn't attach too much importance to opinion. Unfortunately, most do attach great importance to it. "I have as much right to my opinion as you to yours, " and "'Everyone's entitled to his opinion," are common expressions. In fact, anyone who would challenge another's opinion is likely to be branded intolerant.

Is that label accurate? Is it intolerant to challenge another's opinion? It depends on what definition of opinion you have in mind. For example, you may ask a friend "'What do you think of the new Ford cars?" And he may reply, "In my opinion, they're ugly." In this case, it would not only be intolerant to challenge his statement, but foolish. For it's obvious that by opinion he means his personal preference, a matter of taste. And as the old saying goes, "It's pointless to argue about matters of taste."

But consider this very different use of the term. A newspaper reports that the Supreme Court has delivered its opinion in a controversial case. Obviously the justices did not state their personal preferences, their mere likes and dislikes. They stated their considered judgment, painstakingly arrived at after thorough inquiry and deliberation.

Most of what is referred to as opinion falls somewhere between these two extremes. It is not an expression of taste. Nor is it careful judgment. Yet it may contain elements of both. It is a view or belief more or less casually arrived at, with or without examining the evidence. Is everyone entitled to his opinion? Of course, this is not only permitted, but guaranteed. We are free to act on our opinions only so long as, in doing so, we do not harm others.

56. Which of the following statements is TRUE, according to the author?

    A) Everyone has a right to hold his own opinion.

    B) Free expression of opinions often leads to confusion.

    C) Most people tend to be careless in forming their opinions.

    D) Casual use of the word "opinion" often brings about quarrels.

57. According to the author, who of the following would be labored as intolerant?

    A) Someone who turns a deaf ear to others' opinions.

    B) Someone who can't put up with others' tastes.

    C) Someone who values only their own opinions.

D) Someone whose opinion harms other people.

58. The new Ford cars are cited as an example to show that _____.

    A) it is foolish to criticize a famous brand

    B) one should not always agree to others' opinions

    C) personal tastes are not something to be challenged

    D) it is unwise to express one's likes and dislikes in public

59. Considered judgment is different from personal preference in that _____.

    A) it is stated by judges in the court   B) it reflects public likes and dislikes

    C) it is a result of a lot of controversy   D) it is based on careful thought

60. As indicated in the passage, being free to act on one's opinion _____.

    A) means that one can ignore other people's criticism

    B) means that one can impose his preferences on others

    C) doesn't mean that one has the right to do things at will

    D) doesn't mean that one has the right to charge others without evidence

攻克阅读关（第四天强化）

Passage 13

    I'm usually fairly skeptical about any research that concludes that people are either happier or unhappier or more or less certain of themselves than they were 50 years ago. While any of these statements might be true, they are practically impossible to prove scientifically. Still, I was struck by a report which concluded that today's children are significantly more anxious than children in the 1950s. In fact, the analysis showed, normal children ages 9 to 17 exhibit a higher level of anxiety today than children who were treated for mental illness 50 years ago.

    Why are America's kids so stressed? The report cites two main causes: increasing physical isolation—brought on by high divorce rates and less involvement in community, among other things—and a growing perception that the world is a more dangerous place.

    Given that we can't turn the clock back, adults can still do plenty to help the next generation cope.

    At the top of the list is *nurturing*（培育）a better appreciation of the limits of individualism. No child is an island. Strengthening social ties helps build communities and protect individuals against stress.

    To help kids build stronger connections with others, you can pull the plug on TVs and computers. Your family will thank you later. They will have more time for face-to-face relationships, and they will get more sleep.

    Limit the amount of *virtual*（虚拟的）violence your children are exposed to. It's not just video games and movies; children see a lot of murder and crime on the local news.

    Keep your expectations for your children reasonable. Many highly successful people never attended Harvard or Yale.

    Make exercise part of your daily routine. It will help you cope with your own anxieties and provide a good model for your kids. Sometimes anxiety is unavoidable. But it doesn't have to ruin your life.

61. The author thinks that the conclusions of any research about people's state of mind are _____.

    A) surprising   B) confusing   C) illogical   D) questionable

62. What does the author mean when he says, "we can't turn the clock back"(Line 1, Para. 3)?

    A) It's impossible to slow down the pace of change.

B) The social reality children are facing cannot be changed.

C) Lessons learned from the past should not be forgotten.

D) It's impossible to forget the past.

63. According to an analysis, compared with normal children today, children treated as mentally ill 50 years ago _____ .

A) were less isolated physically

B) were probably less self-centered

C) probably suffered less from anxiety

D) were considered less individualistic

64. The first and most important thing parents should do to help their children is _____ .

A) to provide them with a safer environment

B) to lower their expectations for them

C) to get them more involved socially

D) to set a good model for them to follow

65. What conclusion can be drawn from the passage?

A) Anxiety, though unavoidable, can be coped with.

B) Children's anxiety has been enormously exaggerated.

C) Children's anxiety can be eliminated with more parental care.

D) Anxiety, if properly controlled, may help children become mature.

Passage 14

It is easier to negotiate initial salary requirement because once you are inside, the organizational *constraints*（约束）influence wage increases. One thing, however, is certain: your chances of getting the raise you feel you deserve are less if you don't at least ask for it. Men tend to ask for more, and they get more, and this holds true with other resources, not just pay increases. Consider Beth's story:

I did not get what I wanted when I did not ask for it. We had *cubicle*（小隔间）offices and window offices. I sat in the cubicles with several male colleagues. One by one they were moved into window offices, while I remained in the cubicles. Several males who were hired after me also went to offices. One in particular told me he was next in line for an office and that it had been part of his negotiations for the job. I guess they thought me content to stay in the cubicles since I did not voice my opinion either way.

It would be nice if we all received automatic pay increases equal to our merit, but "nice" isn't a quality attributed to most organizations. If you feel you deserve a significant raise in pay, you'll probably have to ask for it.

Performance is your best bargaining *chip*（筹码）when you are seeking a raise. You must be able to demonstrate that you deserve a raise. Timing is also a good bargaining chip. If you can give your boss something he or she needs（a new client or a sizable contract, for example）just before merit pay decisions are being made, you are more likely to get the raise you want.

Use information as a bargaining chip too. Find out what you are worth on the open market. What will someone else pay for your services?

Go into the negotiations prepared to place your chips on the table at the appropriate time and prepared to use communication style to guide the direction of the interaction.

66. According to the passage, before taking a job, a person should _____ .

A) demonstrate his capability

B) give his boss a good impression

C) ask for as much money as he can

D) ask for the salary he hopes to get

67. What can be inferred from Beth's story?

A) Prejudice against women still exists in some organizations.

B) If people want what they deserve, they have to ask for it.

C) People should not be content with what they have got.

D) People should be careful when negotiating for a job.

68. We can learn from the passage that _____.

    A) unfairness exists in salary increases

    B) most people are overworked and underpaid

    C) one should avoid overstating one's performance

    D) most organizations give their staff automatic pay raises

69. To get a pay raise, a person should _____.

    A) advertise himself on the job market

    B) persuade his boss to sign a long-term contract

    C) try to get inside information about the organization

    D) do something to impress his boss just before merit pay decisions

70. To be successful in negotiations, one must _____.

    A) meet his boss at the appropriate time

    B) arrive at the negotiation table punctually

    C) be good at influencing the outcome of the interaction

    D) be familiar with what the boss likes and dislikes

Passage 15

When families gather for Christmas dinner, some will stick to formal traditions dating back to Grandma's generation. Their tables will be set with the good dishes and silver, and the dress code will be Sunday-best.

But in many other homes, this china-and-silver elegance has given way to a *stoneware*（粗陶）-and-stainless informality, with dresses assuming an equally casual-Friday look. For hosts and guests, the change means greater simplicity and comfort. For makers of fine china in Britain, it spells economic hard times.

Last week Royal Doulton, the largest employer in Stoke-on-Trent, announced that it is eliminating 1,000 jobs—one-fifth of its total workforce. That brings to more than 4,000 the number of positions lost in 18 months in the *pottery*（陶瓷）region. Wedgwood and other pottery factories made cuts earlier.

Although a strong pound and weak markets in Asia play a role in the downsizing, the layoffs in Stoke have their roots in earthshaking social shifts. A spokesman for Royal Doulton admitted that the company "has been somewhat slow in catching up with the trend" toward casual dining. Families eat together less often, he explained, and more people eat alone, either because they are single or they eat in front of television.

Even dinner parties, if they happen at all, have gone casual. In a time of long work hours and demanding family schedules, busy hosts insist, rightly, that it's better to share a takeout pizza on paper plates in the family room than to wait for the perfect moment or a "real" dinner party. Too often, the perfect moment never comes. Iron a fine-patterned tablecloth? Forget it. Polish the silver? Who has time?

Yet the loss of formality has its down side. The fine points of *etiquette*（礼节）that children might once have learned at the table by observation or instruction from parents and grandparents（"Chew with your mouth closed." "Keep your elbows off the table."）must be picked up elsewhere. Some companies now offer etiquette seminars for employees who may be competent professionally but clueless socially.

71. The trend toward casual dining has resulted in _____.

    A) bankruptcy of fine china manufacturers   B) shrinking of the pottery industry

    C) restructuring of large enterprises   D) economic recession in Great Britain

72. Which of the following may be the best reason for casual dining?
    A) Family members need more time to relax.
    B) Busy schedules leave people no time for formality.
    C) People want to practice economy in times of scarcity.
    D) Young people won't follow the etiquette of the older generation.

73. It can be learned from the passage that Royal Doulton is _____.
    A) a retailer of stainless steel tableware   B) a dealer in stoneware
    C) a pottery chain store   D) a producer of fine china

74. The main cause of the layoffs in the pottery industry is _____.
    A) the increased value of the pound   B) the economic recession in Asia
    C) the change in people's way of life   D) the fierce competition at home and abroad

75. Refined table manners, though less popular than before in current social life, _____.
    A) are still a must on certain occasions   B) are bound to return sooner or later
    C) are still being taught by parents at home   D) can help improve personal relationships

Passage 16

Some houses are designed to be smart. Others have smart designs. An example of the second type of house won an Award of Excellence from the American Institute of Architects.

Located on the shore of Sullivan's Island off the coast of South Carolina, the award-winning cube-shaped beach house was built to replace one smashed to pieces by *Hurricane*（飓风）Hugo 10 years ago. In September 1989, Hugo struck South Carolina, killing 18 people and damaging or destroying 36,000 homes in the state.

Before Hugo, many new houses built along South Carolina's shoreline were poorly constructed, and enforcement of building codes wasn't strict, according to architect Ray Huff, who created the cleverly-designed beach house. In Hugo's wake, all new shoreline houses are required to meet stricter, better-enforced codes. The new beach house on Sullivan's Island should be able to withstand a Category 3 hurricane with peak winds of 179 to 209 kilometers per hour.

At first sight, the house on Sullivan's Island looks anything but hurricane-proof. Its redwood shell makes it resemble "a large party *lantern*（灯笼）" at night, according to one observer. But looks can be deceiving. The house's wooden frame is reinforced with long steel rods to give it extra strength.

To further protect the house from hurricane damage, Huff raised it 2.7 meters off the ground on timber pilings-long, slender columns of wood anchored deep in the sand. Pilings might appear insecure, but they are strong enough to support the weight of the house. They also elevate the house above storm surges. The pilings allow the surges to run under the house instead of running into it. "These swells of water come ashore at tremendous speeds and cause most of the damage done to beach-front buildings," said Huff.

Huff designed the timber pilings to be partially concealed by the house's ground-to-roof shell. "The shell masks the pilings so that the house doesn't look like it's standing with its pant legs pulled up," said Huff. In the event of a storm surge, the shell should break apart and let the waves rush under the house, the architect explained.

76. After the tragedy caused by Hurricane Hugo, new houses built along South Carolina's shore line are required _____.
    A) to be easily reinforced   B) to look smarter in design
    C) to meet stricter building standards   D) to be designed in the shape of cubes

77. The award-winning beach house is quite strong because _____.

A) it is strengthened by steel rods　　　B) it is made of redwood

C) it is in the shape of a shell　　　D) it is built with timber and concrete

78. Huff raised the house 2.7 meters off the ground on timber pilings in order to _____.

A) withstand peak winds of about 200 km/hr　B) anchor stronger pilings deep in the sand

C) break huge sea waves into smaller ones　D) prevent water from rushing into the house

79. The main function of the shell is _____.

A) to strengthen the pilings of the house　B) to give the house a better appearance

C) to protect the wooden frame of the house　D) to slow down the speed of the swelling water

80. It can be inferred from the passage that the shell should be _____.

A) fancy-looking　　　B) waterproof

C) easily breakable　　　D) extremely strong

攻克阅读关(第五天强化)

Passage 17

A is for always getting to work on time.

B is for being extremely busy.

C is for the *conscientious*(勤勤恳恳的) way you do your job.

You may be all these things at the office, and more. But when it comes to getting ahead, experts say, the ABCs of business should include a P, for politics, as in office politics.

Dale Carnegie suggested as much more than 50 years ago: Hard work alone doesn't ensure career advancement. You have to be able to sell yourself and your ideas, both publicly and behind the scenes. Yet, despite the obvious rewards of engaging in office politics-a better job, a raise, praise-many people are still unable—or unwilling—to "play the game."

"People assume that office politics involves some *manipulative*(工于心计的) behavior," says Deborah Comer, an assistant professor of management at Hofstra University. "But politics derives from the word 'polite'. It can mean lobbying and forming associations. It can mean being kind and helpful, or even trying to please your superior, and then expecting something in return."

In fact, today, experts define office politics as proper behavior used to pursue one's own self-interest in the workplace. In many cases, this involves some form of socializing within the office environment-not just in large companies, but in small workplaces as well.

"The first thing people are usually judged on is their ability to perform well on a consistent basis," says Nell P. Lewis, a management psychologist. "But if two or three candidates are up for a promotion, each of whom has reasonably similar ability, a manager is going to promote the person he or she likes best. It's simple human nature."

Yet, psychologists say, many employees and employers have trouble with the concept of politics in the office. Some people, they say, have an idealistic vision of work and what it takes to succeed. Still others associate politics with *flattery*(奉承), fearful that, if they speak up for themselves, they may appear to be flattering their boss for favors.

Experts suggest altering this negative picture by recognizing the need for some self-promotion.

81. "Office politics"(Line 2, Para. 4) is used in the passage to refer to _____.

A) the code of behavior for company staff

B) the political views and beliefs of office workers

C) the interpersonal relationships within a company

D) the various qualities required for a successful career

82. To get promoted, one must not only be competent but _____.

A) give his boss a good impression B) honest and loyal to his company

C) get along well with his colleagues D) avoid being too outstanding

83. Why are many people unwilling to "play the game"(Line 4, Para. 5)?

A) They believe that doing so is impractical.

B) They feel that such behavior is unprincipled.

C) They are not good at manipulating colleagues.

D) They think the effort will get them nowhere.

84. The author considers office politics to be _____.

A) unwelcome at the workplace

B) bad for interpersonal relationships

C) indispensable to the development of company culture

D) an important factor for personal advancement

85. It is the author's view that _____.

A) speaking up for oneself is part of human nature

B) self-promotion does not necessarily mean flattery

C) hard work contributes very little to one's promotion

D) many employees fail to recognize the need of flattery

Passage 18

As soon as it was revealed that a reporter for Progressive magazine had discovered how to make a hydrogen bomb, a group of *firearm*(火器) fans formed the National Hydrogen Bomb Association, and they are now lobbying against any legislation to stop Americans from owning one.

"The Constitution," said the association's spokesman, "gives everyone the right to own arms. It doesn't spell out what kind of arms. But since anyone can now make a hydrogen bomb, the public should be able to buy it to protect themselves."

"Don't you think it's dangerous to have one in the house, particularly where there are children around?"

"The National Hydrogen Bomb Association hopes to educate people in the safe handling of this type of weapon. We are instructing owners to keep the bomb in a locked cabinet and the *fuse*(导火索) separately in a drawer."

"Some people consider the hydrogen bomb a very fatal weapon which could kill somebody."

The spokesman said, "Hydrogen bombs don't kill people-people kill people. The bomb is for self-protection and it also has a deterrent effect. If somebody knows you have a nuclear weapon in your house, they're going to think twice about breaking in."

"But those who want to ban the bomb for American citizens claim that if you have one locked in the cabinet, with the fuse in a drawer, you would never be able to assemble it in time to stop an *intruder*(侵入者)."

"Another argument against allowing people to own a bomb is that at the moment it is very expensive to build one. So what your association is backing is a program which would allow the middle and upper classes to acquire a bomb while poor people will be left defenseless with just handguns."

86. According to the passage, some people started a national association so as to _____.

A) block any legislation to ban the private possession of the bomb

B) coordinate the mass production of the destructive weapon

C) instruct people how to keep the bomb safe at home

D) promote the large-scale sale of this newly invented weapon

87. Some people oppose the ownership of H-bombs by individuals on the grounds that _____.

A) the size of the bomb makes it difficult to keep in a drawer

B) most people don't know how to handle the weapon

C) people's lives will be threatened by the weapon

D) they may fall into the hands of criminals

88. By saying that the bomb also has a deterrent effect the spokesman means that it _____.

A) will frighten away any possible intruders

B) can show the special status of its owners

C) will threaten the safety of the owners as well

D) can kill those entering others' houses by force

89. According to the passage, opponents of the private ownership of H-bombs are very much worried that _____.

A) the influence of the association is too powerful for the less privileged to overcome

B) poorly-educated Americans will find it difficult to make use of the weapon

C) the wide use of the weapon will push up living expenses tremendously

D) the cost of the weapon will put citizens on an unequal basis

90. From the tone of the passage we know that the author is _____.

A) doubtful about the necessity of keeping H-bombs at home for safety

B) unhappy with those who vote against the ownership of H-bombs

C) not serious about the private ownership of H-bombs

D) concerned about the spread of nuclear weapons

Passage 19

Sign has become a scientific hot button. Only in the past 20 years have specialists in language study realized that signed languages are unique—a speech of the hand. They offer a new way to probe how the brain generates and understands language, and throw new light on an old scientific controversy: whether language, complete with grammar, is something that we are born with, or whether it is a learned behavior. The current interest in sign language has roots in the pioneering work of one rebel teacher at Gallaudet University in Washington, D.C., the world's only liberal arts university for deaf people.

When Bill Stokoe went to Gallaudet to teach English, the school enrolled him in a course in signing. But Stokoe noticed something odd: among themselves, students signed differently from his classroom teacher.

Stokoe had been taught a sort of gesture code, each movement of the hands representing a word in English. At the time, American Sign Language(ASL) was thought to be no more than a form of *pidgin English*(混杂英语). But Stokoe believed the "hand talk" his students used looked richer. He wondered: Might deaf people actually have a genuine language? And could that language be unlike any other on Earth? It was 1955, when even deaf people dismissed their signing as "substandard". Stokoe's idea was academic *heresy*(异端邪说).

It is 37 years later. Stokoe-now devoting his time to writing and editing books and journals and to producing video materials on ASL and the deaf culture-is having lunch at a cafe near the Gallaudet campus and explaining how he started a revolution. For decades educators fought his idea that signed languages are natural languages like English, French and Japanese. They assumed language must be based on speech, the *modulation*(调节) of sound. But sign language is based on the movement of hands, the modulation of space. "What I said," Stokoe explains, "is that language is not mouth stuff- it's brain stuff."

91. The study of sign language is thought to be _____.

    A) a new way to look at the learning of language

    B) a challenge to traditional views on the nature of language

    C) an approach to simplifying the grammatical structure of a language

    D) an attempt to clarify misunderstanding about the origin of language

92. The present growing interest in sign language was stimulated by _____.

    A) a famous scholar in the study of the human brain

    B) a leading specialist in the study of liberal arts

    C) an English teacher in a university for the deaf

    D) some senior experts in American Sign Language

93. According to Stokoe, sign language is _____.

    A) a substandard language   B) a genuine language

    C) an artificial language   D) an international language

94. Most educators objected to Stokoe's idea because they thought _____.

    A) sign language was not extensively used even by deaf people

    B) sign language was too artificial to be widely accepted

    C) a language should be easy to use and understand

    D) a language could only exist in the form of speech sounds

95. Stokoe's argument is based on his belief that _____.

    A) sign language is as efficient as any other language

    B) sign language is derived from natural language

    C) language is a system of meaningful codes

    D) language is a product of the brain

Passage 20

    It came as something of a surprise when Diana, Princess of Wales, made a trip to Angola in 1997, to support the Red Cross's campaign for a total ban on all anti-personnel landmines. Within hours of arriving in Angola, television screens around the world were filled with images of her comforting victims injured in explosions caused by landmines. "I knew the statistics," she said. "But putting a face to those figures brought the reality home to me; like when I met Sandra, a 13- year-old girl who had lost her leg, and people like her."

    The Princess concluded with a simple message: "We must stop landmines". And she used every opportunity during her visit to repeat this message.

    But, back in London, her views were not shared by some members of the British government, which refused to support a ban on these weapons. Angry politicians launched an attack on the Princess in the press. They described her as "very ill-informed" and a "*loose cannon*（乱放炮的人）."

    The Princess responded by brushing aside the criticisms: "This is a *distraction*（干扰）we do not need. All I'm trying to do is help."

    Opposition parties, the media and the public immediately voiced their support for the Princess. To make matters worse for the government, it soon emerged that the Princess's trip had been approved by the Foreign Office, and that she was in fact very well-informed about both the situation in Angola and the British government's policy regarding landmines. The result was a severe embarrassment for the government.

    To try and limit the damage, the Foreign Secretary, Malcolm Rifkind, claimed that the Princess's views on landmines were not very different from government policy, and that it was "working towards" a worldwide ban. The Defense Secretary, Michael Portillo, claimed the matter was "a misinterpretation or misunderstanding."

For the Princess, the trip to this war-torn country was an excellent opportunity to use her popularity to show the world how much destruction and suffering landmines can cause. She said that the experience had also given her the chance to get closer to people and their problems.

96. Princess Diana paid a visit to Angola in 1997 _____.
    A) to voice her support for a total ban of landmines
    B) to clarify the British government's stand on landmines
    C) to investigate the sufferings of landmine victims there
    D) to establish her image as a friend of landmine victims

97. What did Diana mean when she said "…putting a face to those figures brought the reality home to me"(Line 5, Para. 1)?
    A) She just couldn't bear to meet the landmine victims face to face.
    B) The actual situation in Angola made her feel like going back home.
    C) Meeting the landmine victims in person made her believe the statistics.
    D) Seeing the pain of the victims made her realize the seriousness of the situation.

98. Some members of the British government criticized Diana because _____.
    A) she was ill-informed of the government's policy
    B) they were actually opposed to banning landmines
    C) she had not consulted the government before the visit
    D) they believed that she had misinterpreted the situation in Angola

99. How did Diana respond to the criticisms?
    A) She paid no attention to them.   B) She made more appearances on TV.
    C) She met the 13-year-old girl as planned.   D) She rose to argue with her opponents.

100. What did Princess Diana think of her visit to Angola?
    A) It had caused embarrassment to the British government.
    B) It had brought her closer to the ordinary people.
    C) It had greatly promoted her popularity.
    D) It had affected her relations with the British government.

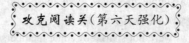

攻克阅读关(第六天强化)

Passage 21

Scratchy throats, stuffy noses and body aches all spell misery, but being able to tell if the cause is a cold or *flu*(流感) may make a difference in how long the misery lasts.

The American Lung Association(ALA) has issued new guidelines on combating colds and the flu, and one of the keys is being able to quickly tell the two apart. That's because the prescription drugs available for the flu need to be taken soon after the illness sets in. As for colds, the sooner a person starts taking over-the-counter remedy, the sooner relief will come.

The common cold and the flu are both caused by viruses. More than 200 viruses can cause cold symptoms, while the flu is caused by three viruses-flu A, B and C. There is no cure for either illness, but the flu can be prevented by the flu vaccine, which is, for most people, the best way to fight the flu, according to the ALA.

But if the flu does strike, quick action can help. Although the flu and common cold have many similarities, there are some obvious signs to look for.

Cold symptoms such as stuffy nose, runny nose and scratchy throat typically develop gradually, and adults and teens often do not get a fever. On the other hand, fever is one of the characteristic features of the flu for all ages. And in general, flu symptoms including fever and chills, sore throat and body aches come on suddenly and are more severe than cold symptoms.

The ALA notes that it may be particularly difficult to tell when infants and preschool age children have the flu. It advises parents to call the doctor if their small children have flu-like symptoms.

Both cold and flu symptoms can be eased with over-the-counter medications as well. However, children and teens with a cold or flu should not take aspirin for pain relief because of the risk of Reye *syndrome*(综合症), a rare but serious condition of the liver and central nervous system.

There is, of course, no vaccine for the common cold. But frequent hand washing and avoiding close contact with people who have colds can reduce the likelihood of catching one.

101. According to the author, knowing the cause of the misery will help _____.
    A) shorten the duration of the illness
    B) the patient buy medicine over the counter
    C) the patient obtain cheaper prescription drugs
    D) prevent people from catching colds and the flu
102. We learn from the passage that _____.
    A) one doesn't need to take any medicine if he has a cold or the flu
    B) aspirin should not be included in over-the-counter medicines for the flu
    C) delayed treatment of the flu will harm the liver and central nervous system
    D) over-the-counter drugs can be taken to ease the misery caused by a cold or the flu
103. According to the passage, to combat the flu effectively, _____.
    A) one should identify the virus which causes it
    B) one should consult a doctor as soon as possible
    C) one should take medicine upon catching the disease
    D) one should remain alert when the disease is spreading
104. Which of the following symptoms will distinguish the flu from a cold? _____
    A) A stuffy nose.   B) A high temperature.
    C) A sore throat.   D) A dry cough.
105. If children have flu-like symptoms, their parents _____.
    A) are advised not to give them aspirin
    B) should watch out for signs of Reye syndrome
    C) are encouraged to take them to hospital for vaccination
    D) should prevent them from mixing with people running a fever

Passage 22

In a time of low academic achievement by children in the United States, many Americans are turning to Japan, a country of high academic achievement and economic success, for possible answers. However, the answers provided by Japanese preschools are not the ones Americans expected to find. In most Japanese preschools, surprisingly little emphasis is put on academic instruction. In one investigation, 300 Japanese and 210 American preschool teachers, child development specialists, and parents were asked about various aspects of early childhood education. Only 2 percent of the Japanese *respondents*(答问卷者) listed "to give children a good start academically" as one of their top three reasons for a society to have preschools. In contrast, over half the American respondents chose this as one of their top three choices. To prepare children for successful careers in first grade and beyond, Japanese schools do not teach reading, writing, and mathematics, but rather skills such as persistence, concentration, and the ability to function as a member of a group. The vast majority of young Japanese children are taught to read at home by their parents.

In the recent comparison of Japanese and American preschool education, 91 percent of Japanese respondents chose providing children with a group experience as one of their top three reasons for a society to have preschools. Sixty-two percent of the more individually *oriented*（强调个性发展的）Americans listed group experience as one of their top three choices. An emphasis on the importance of the group seen in Japanese early childhood education continues into elementary school education.

Like in America, there is diversity in Japanese early childhood education. Some Japanese kindergartens have specific aims, such as early musical training or potential development. In large cities, some kindergartens are attached to universities that have elementary and secondary schools.

Some Japanese parents believe that if their young children attend a university-based program, it will increase the children's chances of eventually being admitted to top-rated schools and universities. Several more progressive programs have introduced free play as a way out for the heavy intellectualizing in some Japanese kindergartens.

106. We learn from the first paragraph that many Americans believe _____.

A) Japanese parents are more involved in preschool education than American parents

B) Japan's economic success is a result of its scientific achievements

C) Japanese preschool education emphasizes academic instruction

D) Japan's higher education is superior to theirs

107. Most Americans surveyed believe that preschools should also attach importance to _____.

A) problem solving   B) group experience

C) parental guidance   D) individually-oriented development

108. In Japan's preschool education, the focus is on _____.

A) preparing children academically   B) developing children's artistic interests

C) tapping children's potential   D) shaping children's character

109. Free play has been introduced in some Japanese kindergartens in order to _____.

A) broaden children's horizon   B) cultivate children's creativity

C) lighten children's study load   D) enrich children's knowledge

110. Why do some Japanese parents send their children to university-based kindergartens?

A) They can do better in their future studies.

B) They can accumulate more group experience there.

C) They can be individually oriented when they grow up.

D) They can have better chances of getting a first-rate education.

Passage 23

Lead deposits, which accumulated in soil and snow during the 1960's and 70's, were primarily the result of leaded gasoline emissions originating in the United States. In the twenty years that the Clean Air Act has mandated unleaded gas use in the United States, the lead accumulation world-wide has decreased significantly.

A study published recently in the journal Nature shows that air-borne leaded gas emissions from the United States were the leading contributor to the high concentration of lead in the snow in Greenland. The new study is a result of the continued research led by Dr. Charles Boutron, an expert on the impact of heavy metals on the environment at the National Center for Scientific Research in France. A study by

Dr. Boutron published in 1991 showed that lead levels in *arctic*（北极的） snow were declining.

In his new study，Dr. Boutron found the ratios of the different forms of lead in the leaded gasoline used in the United States were different from the ratios of European，Asian and Canadian gasoline and thus enabled scientists to *differentiate*（分区） the lead sources. The dominant lead ratio found in Greenland snow matched that found in gasoline from the United States.

In a study published in the journal Ambio，scientists found that lead levels in soil in the North-eastern United States had decreased markedly since the introduction of unleaded gasoline.

Many scientists had believed that the lead would stay in soil and snow for a longer period.

The authors of the Ambio study examined samples of the upper layers of soil taken from the same sites of 30 forest floors in New England，New York and Pennsylvania in 1980 and in 1990.

The forest environment processed and redistributed the lead faster than the scientists had expected.

Scientists say both studies demonstrate that certain parts of the *ecosystem*（生态系统） respond rapidly to reductions in atmospheric pollution，but that these findings should not be used as a license to pollute.

111. The study published in the journal Nature indicates that _____ .
   A) the Clean Air Act has not produced the desired results
   B) lead deposits in arctic snow are on the increase
   C) lead will stay in soil and snow longer than expected
   D) the US is the major source of lead pollution in arctic snow

112. Lead accumulation worldwide decreased significantly after the use of unleaded gas in the US _____ .
   A) was discouraged   B) was enforced by law
   C) was prohibited by law   D) was introduced

113. How did scientists discover the source of lead pollution in Greenland?
   A) By analyzing the data published in journals like Nature and Ambio.
   B) By observing the lead accumulations in different parts of the arctic area.
   C) By studying the chemical elements of soil and snow in Northeastern America.
   D) By comparing the chemical compositions of leaded gasoline used in various countries.

114. The authors of the Ambio study have found that _____ .
   A) forests get rid of lead pollution faster than expected
   B) lead accumulations in forests are more difficult to deal with
   C) lead deposits are widely distributed in the forests of the US
   D) the upper layers of soil in forests are easily polluted by lead emissions

115. It can be inferred from the last paragraph that scientists _____ .
   A) are puzzled by the mystery of forest pollution
   B) feel relieved by the use of unleaded gasoline
   C) still consider lead pollution a problem
   D) lack sufficient means to combat lead pollution

Passage 24

Exercise is one of the few factors with a positive role in long-term maintenance of body weight. Unfortunately，that message has not gotten through to the average American，who would rather try switching to "light" beer and low-calorie bread than increase physical exertion. The Centers for Disease Control，for example，found that fewer than one-fourth of overweight adults who were trying to shed pounds said they were combining exercise with their diet.

In rejecting exercise，some people may be discouraged too much by calorie-expenditure charts；for example，one would have to briskly walk three miles just to work off the 275 calories in one delicious Danish *pastry*(小甜饼)。Even exercise professionals concede half a point here. "Exercise by itself is a very tough way to lose weight," says York Onnen, program director of the President's Council on Physical Fitness and Sports.

Still，exercise's supporting role in weight reduction is vital. A study at the Boston University Medical Center of overweight police officers and other public employees confirmed that those who dieted without exercise regained almost all their old weight，while those who worked exercise into their daily routine maintained their new weight.

If you have been *sedentary*(极少活动的) and decide to start walking one mile a day，the added exercise could burn an extra 100 calories daily. In a year's time，assuming no increase in food intake，you could lose ten pounds. By increasing the distance of your walks gradually and making other dietary adjustments，you may lose even more weight.

116. What is said about the average American in the passage?
    A) They tend to exaggerate the healthful effect of "light" beer.
    B) They usually ignore the effect of exercise on losing weight.
    C) They prefer "light" beer and low-calorie bread to other drinks and food.
    D) They know the factors that play a positive role in keeping down body weight.

117. Some people dislike exercise because _____.
    A) they think it is physically exhausting
    B) they find it hard to exercise while on a diet
    C) they don't think it possible to walk 3 miles every day
    D) they find consulting caloric-expenditure charts troublesome

118. "Even exercise professionals concede half a point here"(Line 3，Para. 2) means "They _____."
    A) agree that the calories in a small piece of pastry can be difficult to work off by exercise
    B) partially believe diet plays a supporting role in weight reduction
    C) are not fully convinced that dieting can help maintain one's new weight
    D) are not sufficiently informed of the positive role of exercise in losing weight

119. What was confirmed by the Boston University Medical Center's study?
    A) Controlling one's calorie intake is more important than doing exercise.
    B) Even occasional exercise can help reduce weight.
    C) Weight reduction is impossible without exercise.
    D) One could lose ten pounds in a year's time if there's no increase in food intake.

120. What is the author's purpose in writing this article?
    A) To justify the study of the Boston University Medical Center.
    B) To stress the importance of maintaining proper weight.
    C) To support the statement made by York Onnen.
    D) To show the most effective way to lose weight.

攻克阅读关(第七天强化)

Passage 25

Is there enough oil beneath the Arctic National Wildlife *Refuge*(保护区)(ANWR) to help secure America's energy future? President Bush certainly thinks so. He has argued that tapping ANWR's oil would help ease California's electricity crisis and provide a major boost to the country's energy independence. But no one knows for sure how much crude oil lies buried beneath the frozen earth, with the last government survey, conducted in 1998, projecting output anywhere from 3 billion to 16 billion barrels.

The oil industry goes with the high end of the range, which could equal as much as 10% of U. S. consumption for as long as six years. By pumping more than 1 million barrels a day from the reserve for the next two to three decades, lobbyists claim, the nation could cut back on imports equivalent to all shipments to the U. S. from Saudi Arabia. Sounds good. An oil boom would also mean a multibillion-dollar *windfall*(意外之财)in tax revenues, *royalties*(开采权使用费) and leasing fees for Alaska and the Federal Government. Best of all, advocates of drilling say, damage to the environment would be insignificant. "We've never had a documented case of an oil rig chasing deer out onto the pack ice." says Alaska State Representative Scott Ogan.

Not so fast, say environmentalists. Sticking to the low end of government estimates, the National Resources Defense Council says there may be no more than 3.2 billion barrels of economically recoverable oil in the coastal plain of ANWR, a drop in the bucket that would do virtually nothing to ease America's energy problems. And consumers would wait up to a decade to gain any benefits, because drilling could begin only after much bargaining over leases, environmental permits and regulatory review. As for ANWR's impact on the California power crisis, environmentalists point out that oil is responsible for only 1% of the Golden State's electricity output -and just 3% of the nation's.

121. What does President Bush think of tapping oil in ANWR?

A) It will exhaust the nation's oil reserves.

B) It will help secure the future of ANWR.

C) It will help reduce the nation's oil imports

D) It will increase America's energy consumption

122. We learn from the second paragraph that the American oil industry _____.

A) believes that drilling for oil in ANWR will produce high yields

B) tends to exaggerate America's reliance on foreign oil

C) shows little interest in tapping oil in ANWR

D) expects to stop oil imports from Saudi Arabia

123. Those against oil drilling in ANWR argue that _____.

A) it can cause serious damage to the environment

B) it can do little to solve U.S. energy problems

C) it will drain the oil reserves in the Alaskan region

D) it will not have much commercial value

124. What do the environmentalists mean by saying "Not so fast"(Line 1, Para.3)?

A) Oil exploitation takes a long time.　　　B) The oil drilling should be delayed.

C) Don't be too optimistic.　　　D) Don't expect fast returns.

125. It can be learned from the passage that oil exploitation beneath ANWR's frozen earth _____.

A) remains a controversial issue　　　B) is expected to get under way soon

C) involves a lot of technological problems　　　D) will enable the U. S. to be oil independent

Passage 26

"Tear'em apart!" "Kill the fool!" " Murder the *referee*(裁判)!"

These are common remarks one may hear at various sporting events. At the time they are made, they may seem innocent enough. But let's not kid ourselves. They have been known to influence behavior in such a way as to lead to real bloodshed. Volumes have been written about the way words affect us. It has been shown that words having certain *connotations*(含义) may cause us to react in ways quite foreign to what we consider to be our usual humanistic behavior. I see the term "opponent" as one of those words. Perhaps the time has come to delete it from sports terms.

The dictionary meaning of the term "opponent" is "adversary"; "enemy"; "one who opposes your interests." Thus, when a player meets an opponent, he or she may tend to treat that opponent as an enemy. At such times, winning may dominate one's intellect, and every action, no matter how gross, may be considered justifiable. I recall an incident in a handball game when a referee refused a player's request for a time out for a glove change because he did not considered them wet enough. The player proceeded to rub his gloves across his wet T-shirt and then exclaimed. "Are they wet enough now?"

In the heat of battle, players have been observed to throw themselves across the court without considering the consequences that such a move might have on anyone in their way. I have also witnessed a player reacting to his opponent's international and illegal blocking by deliberately hitting him with the ball as hard as he could during the course of play. Off the court, they are good friends. Does that make any sense? It certainly gives proof of a court attitude which departs from normal behavior.

Therefore, I believe it is time we *elevated*(提升) the game to the level where it belongs thereby setting an example to the rest of the sporting world. Replacing the term "opponent" with "associate" could be an ideal way to start.

The dictionary meaning of the term "associate" is "colleague"; "friend"; "companion." Reflect a moment! You may soon see and possibly feel the difference in your reaction to the term "associate" rather than "opponent."

126. Which of the following statements best expresses the author's view?
    A) Aggressive behavior in sports can have serious consequences.
    B) The words people use can influence their behavior.
    C) Unpleasant words in sports are often used by foreign athletes.
    D) Unfair judgments by referees will lead to violence on the sports field.

127. Harsh words are spoken during games because the players _____.
    A) are too eager to win
    B) are usually short-tempered and easily offended
    C) cannot afford to be polite in fierce competitions
    D) treat their rivals as enemies

128. What did the handball player do when he was not allowed a time out to change his gloves?
    A) He refused to continue the game.
    B) He angrily hit the referee with a ball.
    C) He claimed that the referee was unfair.
    D) He wet his gloves by rubbing them across his T-shirt.

129. According to the passage, players, in a game, may _____.
    A) deliberately throw the ball at anyone illegally blocking their way
    B) keep on screaming and shouting throughout the game
    C) lie down on the ground as an act of protest
    D) kick the ball across the court with force

130. The author hopes to have the current situation in sports improved by _____.
    A) calling on players to use clean language on the court
    B) raising the referee's sense of responsibility

C) changing the attitude of players on the sports field

D) regulating the relationship between players and referees

Passage 27

Consumers are being confused and misled by the *hodge-podge*(大杂烩) of environmental claims made by household products, according to a "green labeling" study published by Consumers International Friday.

Among the report's more *outrageous*(令人无法容忍的) findings-a German fertilizer described itself as "earthworm friendly", a brand of flour said it was "non-polluting" and a British toilet paper claimed to be "environmentally friendlier".

The study was written and researched by Britain's National Consumer Council(NCC) for lobby group Consumer International. It was funded by the German and Dutch governments and the European Commission.

"While many good and useful claims are being made, it is clear there is a long way to go in ensuring shoppers are adequately informed about the environmental impact of products they buy," said Consumers International director Anna Fielder.

The 10-country study surveyed product packaging in Britain, Western Europe, Scandinavia and the United States. It found that products sold in Germany and the United Kingdom made the most environmental claims on average.

The report focused on claims made by specific products, such as *detergent*(洗涤剂), insect sprays and by some garden products. It did not test the claims, but compared them to labeling guidelines set by the International Standards Organization(ISO) in September, 1999.

Researchers documented claims of environmental friendliness made by about 2,000 products and found many too vague or too misleading to meet ISO standards.

"Many products had specially-designed labels to make them seem environmentally friendly, but in fact many of these symbols mean nothing," said report researcher Philip Page.

"Laundry detergents made the most number of claims with 158. Household cleaners were second with 145 separate claims, while paints were third on our list with 73. The high numbers show how very confusing it must be for consumers to sort the true from the misleading." he said.

The ISO labeling standards ban vague or misleading claims on product packaging, because terms such as "environmentally friendly" and "non-polluting" cannot be verified. "What we are now pushing for is to have multinational corporations meet the standards set by the ISO." said Page.

131. According to the passage, the NCC found it outrageous that _____.

A) all the products surveyed claim to meet ISO standards

B) the claims made by products are often unclear or deceiving

C) consumers would believe many of the manufactures' claim

D) few products actually prove to be environment friendly

132. As indicated in this passage, with so many good claims, the consumers _____.

A) are becoming more cautious about the products they are going to buy

B) are still not willing to pay more for products with green labeling

C) are becoming more aware of the effects different products have on the environment

D) still do not know the exact impact of different products on the environment

133. A study was carried out by Britain's NCC to _____.

A) find out how many claims made by products fail to meet environmental standards

B) inform the consumers of the environmental impact of the products they buy

C) examine claims made by products against ISO standards

D) revise the guidelines set by the International Standards Organization

134. What is one of the consequences caused by the many claims of household products?

A) They are likely to lead to serious environmental problems.

B) Consumers find it difficult to tell the true from the false.

C) They could arouse widespread anger among consumer.

D) Consumers will be tempted to buy products they don't need.

135. It can be inferred from the passage that the lobby group Consumer International wants to _____ .

A) make product labeling satisfy ISO requirements

B) see all household products meet environmental standards

C) warn consumers of the danger of so-called green products

D) verify the efforts of non-polluting products

Passage 28

Two hours from the tall buildings of Manhattan and Philadelphia live some of the world's largest black bears. They are in northern Pennsylvania's Pocono Mountains, a home they share with an abundance of other wildlife.

The streams, lakes, *meadows*(草地), mountain ridges and forests that make the Poconos an ideal place for black bears have also attracted more people to the region. Open spaces are threatened by plans for housing estates and important *habitats*(栖息地) are endangered by highway construction. To protect the Poconos' natural beauty from irresponsible development, The Nature *Conservancy*(大自然保护协会) named the area one of America's "Last Great Places".

Operating out of a century-old schoolhouse in the village of Long Pond, Pennsylvania, the conservancy's Bud Cook is working with local people and business leaders to balance economic growth with environmental protection. By forging partnerships with people like Francis Altemose, the Conservancy has been able to protect more than 14,000 acres of environmentally important land in the area.

Altemose's family has farmed in the Pocono area for generations. Two years ago Francis worked with the Conservancy to include his farm in a county farmland protection program. As a result, his family's land can be protected from development and the Altemoses will be better able to provide a secure financial future for their 7-year-old grandson.

Cook attributes the Conservancy's success in the Poconos to having a local presence and a commitment to working with local residents.

"The key to protecting these remarkable lands is connecting with the local community," Cook said. "The people who live there respect the land. They value quiet forests, clear streams and abundant wildlife. They are eager to help with conservation effort."

For more information on how you can help The Nature Conservancy protect the Poconos and the world's other "Last Great Places," please call 1-888-564 6864, or visit us on the World Wide Web at www.tnc.org.

136. The purpose in naming the Poconos as one of America's "Last Great Places" is to _____ .

A) gain support from the local community   B) protect it from irresponsible development

C) make it a better home for black bears   D) provide financial security for future generations

137. We learn from the passage that _____ .

A) the population in the Pocono area is growing

B) wildlife in the Pocono area is dying out rapidly

C) the security of the Pocono residents is being threatened

D) farmlands in the Pocono area are shrinking fast

138. What is important in protecting the Poconos according to Cook?

    A) The setting up of an environmental protection website.

    B) Support from organizations like The Nature Conservancy.

    C) Cooperation with the local residents and business leaders.

    D) Inclusion of farmlands in the region's protection program.

139. What does Bud Cook mean by "having a local presence"(Line 1, Para. 5)?

    A) Financial contributions from local business leaders.

    B) Consideration of the interests of the local residents.

    C) The establishment of a wildlife protection foundation in the area.

    D) The setting up of a local Nature Conservancy branch in the Pocono area.

140. The passage most probably is _____.

    A) an official document   B) a news story

    C) an advertisement   D) a research report

攻克阅读关（第八天强化）

Passage 29

Just five one-hundredths of an inch thick, light golden in color and with a perfect "saddle curl," the Lay's potato chip seems an unlikely weapon for global domination. But its maker, Frito-Lay, thinks otherwise. "Potato chips are a snack food for the world," said Salman Amin, the company's head of global marketing. Amin believes there is no corner of the world that can resist the charms of a Frito-Lay potato chip.

Frito-Lay is the biggest snack maker in America, owned by PepsiCo, and accounts for over half of the parent company's $ 3 billion annual profits. But the U.S. snack food market is largely saturated, and to grow, the company has to look overseas.

Its strategy rests on two beliefs: first a global product offers economies of scale with which local brands cannot compete. And second, consumers in the 21st century are drawn to "global" as a concept. "Global" does not mean products that are consciously identified as American, but ones than consumes——especially young people—see as part of a modern, *innovative*(创新的)world in which people are linked across cultures by shared beliefs and tastes. Potato chips are an American invention, but most Chinese, for instance, do not know that Frito-Lay is an American company. Instead, Riskey, the company's research and development head, would hope they associate the brand with the new world of global communications and business.

With brand perception, a crucial factor, Riskey ordered a redesign of the Frito-Lay *logo*(标识). The logo, along with the company's long-held marketing image of the "irresistibility" of its chips, would help facilitate the company's global expansion.

The executives acknowledge that they try to swing national eating habits to a food created in America, but they deny that amounts to economic imperialism. Rather, they see Frito-Lay as spreading the benefits of free enterprise across the world. "We're making products in those countries, we're adapting them to the tastes of those countries, building businesses and employing people and changing lives," said Steve Reinemund, PepsiCo's chief executive.

141. It is the belief of Frito-Lay's head of global marking that _____.

    A) potato chips can hardly be used as a weapon to dominate the world market

    B) their company must find new ways to promote domestic sales.

    C) the light golden color enhances the charm of their company's potato chips

    D) people the world over enjoy eating their company's potato chips

142. What do we learn about Frito-Lay from Paragraph 2?

    A) Its products use to be popular among overseas consumers.

    B) Its expansion has caused fierce competition in the snack marker.

    C) It gives half of its annual profits to its parent company.

    D) It needs to turn to the world market for development.

143. One of the assumptions on which Frito-Lay bases its development strategy is that _____.

    A) consumers worldwide today are attracted by global brands

    B) local brands cannot compete successfully with American brands

    C) products suiting Chinese consumers' needs bring more profits

    D) products identified as American will have promising market value

144. Why did Riskey have the Frito-Lay logo redesigned?

    A) To suit changing tastes of young consumers.

    B) To promote the company's strategy of globalization.

    C) To change the company's long-held marketing image.

    D) To compete with other American chip producers.

145. Frito-Lay's executives claim that the promoting of American food in the international market _____.

    A) won't affect the eating habits of the local people

    B) will lead to economic imperialism

    C) will be in the interest of the local people

    D) won't spoil the taste of their chips

Passage 30

In communities north of Denver, residents are pitching in to help teachers and administrators as the Vrain school District tries to solve a $13.8 million budget shortage blamed on mismanagement. "We're worried about our teachers and principals, and we really don't want to lose them because of this," one parent said. "If we can help ease their financial burden, we will."

Teachers are grateful, but know it may be years before the district is *solvent*(有综合能力的). They feel really good about the parent support, but they realize it's impossible for them to solve this problem.

The 22,000-student district discovered the shortage last month. "It's extraordinary. Nobody would have imagined something happening like this at this level," said State Treasurer Mike Coffman.

Coffman and district officials last week agreed on a state emergency plan freeing yp a $9.8 million loan that enabled the *payroll*(工资单) to be met for 2,700 teachers and staff in time for the holidays.

District officials also took $1.7 million from student-activity accounts of its 38 schools.

At Coffman's request, the District Attorney has begun investigating the district's finances. Coffman says he wants to know whether district officials hid the budget shortage until after the November election, when voters approved a $212 million bond issue for schools.

In Frederick, students' parents are buying classroom supplies and offering to pay for groceries and utilities to keep first-year teachers and principals in their jobs.

Some $36,000 has been raised in donations from Safeway. A Chevrolet dealership donated $10,000 and forgave the district's $10,750 bill for renting the driver educating cars. IBM contributed

4,500 packs of paper.

"We employ thousands of people in this community," said Mitch Carson, a hospital chief executive, who helped raise funds. "We have children in the school, and we see how they could be affected."

At Creek High School, three students started a website that displays newspaper articles, district information and an email *forum*(论坛). "Rumors about what's happening to the district are moving at lighting speed," said a student. "We wanted to know the truth, and spread that around instead."

146. What has happened to the Vrain School District?

    A) A huge financial problem has arisen.

    B) Many schools there are mismanaged.

    C) Lots of teachers in the district are planning to quit.

    D) Many administrative personnel have been laid off.

147. How did the residents in the Vrain School District respond to the budget shortage?

    A) They felt somewhat helpless about it.   B) They accused those responsible for it.

    C) They pooled their efforts to help solve it.   D) They demanded a thorough investigation.

148. In the view of State Treasurer Mike Coffman, the educational budget shortage is _____.

    A) unavoidable   B) unthinkable

    C) insolvable   D) irreversible

149. Why did Coffman request an investigation?

    A) To see if there was a deliberate cover-up of the problem.

    B) To find out the extent of the consequences of the case.

    C) To make sure that the school principals were innocent.

    D) To stop the voters approving the $212 million bong issue.

150. Three high school students started a website in order to _____.

    A) attract greater public attention to their needs

    B) appeal to the public for contributions and donations

    C) expose officials who neglected their duties

    D) keep people properly informed of the crisis

Passage 31

"Humans should not try to avoid stress any more than they would shun food, love or exercise." said Dr. Hans Selye, the first physician to document the effects of stress on the body. While there's no question that continuous stress is harmful, several studies suggest that challenging situations in which you're able to rise to the occasion can be good for you.

In a 2001 study of 158 hospital nurses, those who faced considerable work demands but coped with the challenge were more likely to say they were in good health than those who felt they couldn't get the job done.

Stress that you can manage also boost *immune*(免疫的) function. In a study at the Academic Center for Dentistry in Amsterdam, researchers put volunteers through two stressful experiences. In the first, a timed task that required memorizing a list followed by a short test, subjects believed they had control over the outcome. In the second, they weren't in control: They had to sit through a *gory*(血淋淋的) video on surgical procedures. Those who did well on the memory test had an increase in levels of immunoglobulin A, an antibody that's the body's first line of defense against germs. The video-watchers experienced a downturn in the antibody.

Stress prompts the body to produce certain stress hormones. In short bursts these hormones have a positive effect, including improved memory function. "They can help nerve cells handle information and put it into storage," says Dr. Bruce McEwen of Rockefeller University in New York. But in the long run these hormones can have a harmful effect on the body and brain.

"Sustained stress is not good for you," says Richard Morimoto, a researcher at Northwestern University in Illinois studying the effects of stress on *longevity*(长寿), "It's the occasional burst of stress or brief exposure to stress that could be protective."

151. The passage is mainly about _____.

    A) the benefits of manageable stress   B) how to avoid stressful situations

    C) how to cope with stress effectively   D) the effects of stress hormones on memory

152. The word "shun"(Line 1, Para. 1) most probably means _____.

    A) cut down on   B) stay away from   C) run out of   D) put up with

153. We can conclude from the study of the 158 nurses in 2001 that _____.

    A) people under stress tend to have a poor memory

    B) people who can't get their job done experience more stress

    C) doing challenging work may be good for one's health

    D) stress will weaken the body's defense against germs

154. In the experiment described in Paragraph 3, the video-watchers experienced a downturn in the antibody because _____.

    A) the video was not enjoyable at all   B) the outcome was beyond their control

    C) they knew little about surgical procedures   D) they felt no pressure while watching the video

155. Dr. Bruce McEwen of Rockefeller University believes that _____.

    A) a person's memory is determined by the level of hormones in his body

    B) stress hormones have lasting positive effects on the brain

    C) short bursts of stress hormones enhance memory function

    D) a person's memory improves with continued experience of stress.

Passage 32

If you want to teach your children how to say sorry, you must be good at saying it yourself, especially to your own children. But how you say it can be quite tricky.

If you say to your children "I'm sorry I got angry with you, but..." what follows that "but" can render the apology ineffective: "I had a bad day" or "your noise was giving me a headache" leaves the person who has been injured feeling that he should be apologizing for his bad behavior in expecting an apology.

Another method by which people appear to apologize without actually doing so is to say "I'm sorry you're upset"; this suggests that you are somehow at fault for allowing yourself to get upset by what the other person has done.

Then there is the general, all covering apology, which avoids the necessity of identifying a specific act that was particularly hurtful or insulting, and which the person who is apologizing should promise never to do again. Saying "I'm useless as a parent" does not commit a person to any specific improvement.

These pseudo-apologies are used by people who believe saying sorry shows weakness, Parents who wish to teach their children to apologize should see it as a sign of strength, and therefore not resort to these pseudo-apologies.

But even when presented with examples of genuine *contrition*(悔悟), children still need help to become aware of the complexities of saying sorry. A three-year-old might need help in understanding that other children feel pain just as he does, and that hitting a playmate over the head with a heavy toy requires an apology. A six-year-old might need reminding that spoiling other children's expectations can require an apology. A 12-year-old might need to be shown that raiding the biscuit tin without asking permission is acceptable, but that borrowing a parent's clothes without permission is not.

156. If a mother adds "but" to an apology,_____.

    A) she doesn't feel that she should have apologized.

    B) she does not realize that the child has been hurt

    C) the child may find the apology easier to accept

    D) the child may feel that he owes her an apology

157. According to the author, saying "I'm sorry you're upset" most probably means "_____".

    A) You have good reason to get upset

    B) I'm aware you're upset, but I'm not to blame

    C) I apologize for hurting your feelings

    D) I'm at fault for making you upset

158. It is not advisable to use the general, all-covering apology because _____.

    A) it gets one into the habit of making empty promises

    B) it may make the other person feel guilty

    C) it is vague and ineffective

    D) it is hurtful and insulting

159. We learn from the last paragraph that in teaching children to say sorry _____.

    A) the complexities involved should be ignored

    B) their ages should be taken into account

    C) parents need to set them a good example

    D) parents should be patient and tolerant

160. It can be inferred from the passage that apologizing properly is _____.

    A) a social issue calling for immediate attention   B) not necessary among family members

    C) a sign of social progress   D) not as simple as it seems

Part Ⅱ *Reading Comprehension (Skimming and Scanning)*

Passage 1

The Hidden Keys to Job Search Success

    In order to find the ideal job in today's job market, a personal self-assessment is essential. Comments from job hunters who have been successful reveal that getting a better job depends on the job seekers' ability to package their special talents and sell them to potential employers. To do this effectively you must get to know yourself.

What You Must Know and Why

Ask yourself:

    Do I know all of my personal skills and talents?

    Can I quickly summarize my background, experience, accomplishments, and strengths?

    What are my interests, likes, dislikes, and preferences?

    What are my goals, objectives, and expectations?

    Getting to know yourself is one of the most basic and vital elements of the whole job search process. Your own personal database provides you with the basic self-assessment information needed to sell yourself to potential employers. In today's lean market you cannot afford to leave any stone unturned. If you leave any talents and capabilities unmentioned in interviews, you are shortchanging yourself.

Many job seekers have said that knowing their skills, talents and capabilities was the key that helped unlock the door to a larger world of job opportunities. To learn more about yourself, ask yourself the key question: Do I really know myself, all of my skills and talents? You may say, "Of course." But think again.

When was the last time you asked yourself if you like variety or are comfortable with a set routine? If you prefer a set routine, you certainly wouldn't want to work in a network newsroom. On the other hand, if you like variety, you might well lose your mind if you were to take a job as a telephone operator. If you pass out at the sight of blood, by all means don't fill out an application to be a *paramedic*(护理人员). If you were born with raw nerves, an air traffic controller position is not for you. Are you the curious sort? By all means, be a researcher, a private investigator, or a *diagnostician*(诊断专家). If you prefer not to work with people, you should avoid working in sales or customer service.

In your effort to find the ideal job, it is very important to make sure that the job you choose matches the kind of person you are — your interests, skills, experience, and abilities. If you choose a job or profession to please someone else, in the end you will likely displease yourself and others as well.

Knowing who you are allows you to know your:
Strengths
Interests
Weaknesses
Skills and talents
Attitude about work
Personal traits
Job preferences
Goals and objectives
Likes and dislikes
Expectations
Incorporate this information with your:
Education
Special training
Work history and experience
Accomplishments

The end result is a knowledgeable focused individual, someone who knows who they are, where they're going, and how to get there. Most important, they know what skills, experience, abilities, and talents they have to present to a prospective employer.

In some 30 years of dealing with job seekers at all levels, one fact constantly surfaces in comments from successful job hunters: Obtaining the ideal job depends upon the job seekers' ability to sell their talents and skills to the employer. Ask yourself if you would purchase anything major — an automobile, a home, or a computer, for instance — from a salesperson who was hesitant or unsure about his or her product. If this salesperson was vague about the product's history and performance, and in general didn't know its advantages, surely you would be inclined to look elsewhere for this merchandise. There are, of course, the rare exceptions of those so skilled they can *bluff*(哄骗) their way through any sale, whether it be selling iceboxes to North pole residents, or *mink coats*(貂皮衣) in the Sahara desert.

Unless you are one of this rare breed, you'll need to have the right questions and answers prepared for your interviews. Put yourself in your future employer's position. That employer will want to know what you can do and how well you are capable of performing. The answers to such questions must come from you, your resume, and your interviews, as well as from phone discussions that will occur and references you will provide. Knowing how to communicate and present your talents is essential if you want to get to first base in your search for the ideal job.

Obtaining the ideal job necessitates communicating to an employer what you are capable of doing and what you have successfully accomplished in the past. You will be judged on how you present this information in:

Writing

Telephone conversations

Interviews

The image you project

Many job seekers think of the first two points but seem to take their image for granted. This is a mistake, because if the image you project to an employer isn't a good match for the position and the company, your resume and your interview won't get you the job. Remember, creating your image starts with your resume and telephone conversation, continues throughout the interview and selection process, and doesn't end until your follow-up closing discussions.

If you're being considered for a position as director of *protocol*（协议）for the state of California, don't wear a *seersucker*（泡泡纱）suit with a flowered tie. If you do, no accomplishment, connection, or skill will be enough to overcome the *lackluster*（暗淡的）social image you portray.

In discussions with many job seekers, I find many have been so busy working that they have had little time to spend on questions of self-assessment, such as what kind of job they really want and what their real skills, abilities, and talents have in common with their job preferences. You may want to discuss this subject with close business and professional associates, friends, a spouse, or others who know you well. Should you decide to seek professional counseling in the self-assessment process, be sure to seek a qualified professional.

While developing your interests, job preferences, and career plans, keep in mind that they will vary as conditions in your life change. If you have been laid off, for instance, your immediate need may be driven by the necessity to find a job as soon as possible to support yourself and others who are dependent on you. If you are in this situation, do not lose sight of your long-term goals; do not accept a *marginal*（边缘的）or lower-level position unless it becomes necessary to do so. The exception, of course, is economic necessity and/or a job that will attain your longer-term goals or one more suitable to your interests. In a lean competitive market it is important to be flexible and, most of all, to know your strengths and how to package and present them.

The Self-Assessment Process: 12 Steps

To perform your self-assessment, utilize the following 12 steps. The end result will be your own personal evaluation and database of total skills, experience, capabilities, and talents. You will want to identify all of the items described in steps 1 through 8. In step 9 you will complete your assessment outline. In steps 10 and 11, you will test your results and apply them to job market needs. For those who need extra help or assistance in the self-assessment process, step 12 provides for assistance.

Step 1: Decide what type of job you want; define your interests.

Step 2: Find job categories that match or relate to your interests.

Step 3: Identify your personal job satisfaction factors.

Step 4: Identify your strengths and weaknesses.

Step 5. Identify your skills and skill levels.

Step 6: Identify your personal traits.

Step 7: Recognize your transferable skills.

Step 8: Identify your accomplishments.

Step 9: Create your personal assessment outline.

Step 10: Test your results and apply them to job market needs.

Step 11: Gather job information(a double check).

Step 12: Assess your skills and seek career counseling.

For sentences 1-7, mark Y, N, NG; fill in the missing information for sentences 8-10.

1. _____ Whether you can find a better job in today's lean market depends largely on your self-assessment.

2. _____ The market is not so fair today, even if you have skills, talents and capabilities you are not always sure to find an ideal job without any important social relations.

3. _____ To learn more about yourself, you can be sure enough to ask yourself the questions about your skills and talents.

4. _____ Family background should be taken into account when you get to know yourself.

5. _____ An employer can judge a job seeker through writing, telephone conversations, interviews as well as the image he or she presents.

6. _____ Your self-image starts from your outward appearance, so wearing the right clothing can guarantee a successful job interview.

7. _____ Job seekers should also learn to be flexible as conditions will change.

8. In your effort to find the ideal job, it is very important to ensure that the job you choose _____ — your interests, skills, experiences, and abilities.

9. You need to have the right questions and answers prepared for the interview, as the future employer wants to know _____.

10. In the self-assessment process, step _____ can help you know what you have successfully done in the past.

Passage 2

The Truth about Recycling

Since 1960 the amount of municipal waste being collected in America has nearly tripled, reaching 245 m tonnes in 2005. According to European Union statistics, the amount of municipal waste produced in western Europe increased by 23% between 1995 and 2003, to reach 577 kg per person(So much for the plan to reduce waste per person to 300 kg by 2000).

As the volume of waste has increased, so have recycling efforts. In 1980 America recycled only 9.6% of its municipal rubbish; today the rate stands at 32%. A similar trend can be seen in Europe, where some countries, such as Austria and the Netherlands, now recycle 60% or more of their municipal waste. Britain's recycling rate, at 27%, is low, but it is improving fast, having nearly doubled in the past three years.

Even so, when a city introduces a curbside recycling program, the sight of all those recycling carts *trundling*(转动) around can raise doubts about whether the collection and transportation of waste materials requires more energy than it saves. "We are constantly being asked: Is recycling worth doing on environmental grounds?" says Julian Parfitt, principal analyst at Waste & Resources Action Program (WRAP), a non-profit British company that encourages recycling and develops markets for recycled materials.

The Benefit of Recycling

Studies that look at the entire life cycle of a particular material can shed light on this question in a particular case, but WRAP decided to take a broader look. It asked the Technical University of Denmark and the Danish Topic Centre on Waste to conduct a review of 55 life-cycle analyses, all of which were selected because of their rigorous methodology. The researchers then looked at more than 200 *scenarios* (方案), comparing the impact of recycling with that of burying or burning particular types of waste material. They found that in 83% of all scenarios that included recycling, it was indeed better for the environment.

Based on this study, WRAP calculated that Britain's recycling efforts reduce its carbon-dioxide emissions by 10-15 m tonnes per year. That is equivalent to a 10% reduction in Britain's annual carbon-dioxide emissions from transport, or roughly equivalent to taking 3.5 m cars off the roads. Similarly, America's Environmental Protection Agency estimates that recycling reduced the country's carbon emissions by 49m tonnes in 2005.

Recycling has many other benefits, too. It conserves natural resources. It also reduces the amount of waste that is buried or burnt, hardly ideal ways to get rid of the stuff(Landfills take up valuable space and emit methane, a potent greenhouse gas; and although *incinerators*(焚化炉) are not as polluting as they once were, they still produce harmful emissions, so people dislike having them around).

But perhaps the most valuable benefit of recycling is the saving in energy and the reduction in greenhouse gases and pollution that result when scrap materials are substituted for virgin feedstock. "If you can use recycled materials, you don't have to mine ores, cut trees and drill for oil as much," says Jeffrey Morris of Sound Resource Management, a consulting firm based in Olympia, Washington.

Extracting metals from ore, in particular, is extremely energy-intensive. Recycling aluminum, for example, can reduce energy consumption by as much as 95%. Savings for other materials are lower but still substantial: about 70% for plastics, 60% for steel, 40% for paper and 30% for glass. Recycling also reduces emissions of pollutants that can cause smog, acid rain and the *contamination*(污染物) of waterways.

The China Question

Much recyclable material can be processed locally, but ever more is being shipped to developing nations, especially China. The country has a large appetite for raw materials and that includes scrap metals, waste paper and plastics, all of which can be cheaper than virgin materials. In most cases, these waste materials are recycled into consumer goods or packaging and returned to Europe and America via container ships. With its hunger for resources and the availability of cheap labor, China has become the largest importer of recyclable materials in the world.

But the practice of shipping recyclables to China is controversial. Especially in Britain, politicians have voiced the concern that some of those exports may end up in landfills. Many experts disagree. According to Pieter van Beukering, an economist who has studied the trade of waste paper to India and waste plastics to China: "As soon as somebody is paying for the material, you bet it will be recycled."

In fact, Dr van Beukering argues that by importing waste materials, recycling firms in developing countries are able to build larger factories and achieve economies of scale, recycling materials more efficiently and at lower environmental cost. He has witnessed as much in India, he says, where dozens of inefficient, polluting paper mills near Mumbai were transformed into a smaller number of far more productive and environmentally friendly factories within a few years.

Still, compared with Western countries, factories in developing nations may be less tightly regulated, and the recycling industry is no exception. China especially has been plagued by countless illegal-waste imports, many of which are processed by poor migrants in China's coastal regions. They dismantle and recycle anything from plastic to electronic waste without any protection for themselves or the environment.

The Chinese government has banned such practices, but migrant workers have spawned a mobile cottage industry that is difficult to wipe out, says Aya Yoshida, a researcher at Japan's National Institute for Environmental Studies who has studied Chinese waste imports and recycling practices. Because this type of industry operates largely under the radar, it is difficult to assess its overall impact. But it is clear that processing plastic and electronic waste in a crude manner releases toxic chemicals, harming people and the environment—the opposite of what recycling is supposed to achieve.

Waste—A Design Flaw

Under pressure from environmental groups, such as the Silicon Valley Toxics Coalition, some computer-makers have established rules to ensure that their products are recycled in a responsible way. Hewlett-Packard has been a leader in this and even operates its own recycling factories in California and Tennessee. Dell, which was once criticized for using prison labor to recycle its machines, now takes back its old computers for no charge. And last month Steve Jobs detailed Apple's plans to eliminate the use of toxic substances in its products.

This is an unusual case, however. More generally, one of the biggest barriers to more efficient recycling is that most products were not designed with recycling in mind. Improving this problem may require a complete rethinking of industrial processes, says William McDonough, an architect and the co-author of a book published in 2002 called *"Cradle to Cradle: Remaking the Way We Make Things"*. Along with Michael Braungart, his fellow author and a chemist, he lays out a vision for establishing "closed-loop" cycles where there is no waste. Recycling should be taken into account at the design stage, they argue, and all materials should either be able to return to the soil safely or be recycled indefinitely.

If done right, there is no doubt that recycling saves energy and raw materials, and reduces pollution. But as well as trying to recycle more, it is also important to try to recycle better. As technologies and materials evolve, there is room for improvement and cause for optimism. In the end, says Ms Krebs, "waste is really a design flaw".

For sentences 1–7, mark Y, N, NG; fill in the missing information for sentences 8–10.

1. _____ With the increasing volume of waste, the recycling efforts seem to be lagging behind.

2. _____ WRAP is gaining huge profits from encouraging recycling and developing markets for recycled materials.

3. _____ America reduced more carbon emissions than Britain by recycling in 2005.

4. _____ Landfills can be very space-consuming and produce huge greenhouse gases.

5. _____ Large amount of raw materials were consumed in China because it is easier to process them.

6. _____ To process plastic and electronic waste in a crude manner will do harm to the workers and the environment.

7. _____ Nowadays recycling is inefficient because most product designers haven't taken recycling into account.

8. Among over 200 scenarios of waste treatment, most had proved that recycling was better for the environment than _____.

9. Other than landfills and incinerators, recycling has more benefits as it reduces the amount of waste that is buried or burnt and conserves _____.

10. William McDonough suggested that recycling should be taken into account in products designing so that all materials should be able to _____.

Passage 3

English, the Most Widely Used Language

Geographically the most widespread language on earth is English, and it is second only to Mandarin Chinese in the number of people who speak it. English is the national language of the United Kingdom, the United States, Australia, and New Zealand. It is one of the two national languages of Canada. It is an official or semiofficial language in such countries as South Africa and India. Members of the diplomatic corps in most lands have some knowledge of English. English has long been the language of commerce, and it is becoming the language of international relations as well.

Characteristics of English

English vocabulary is larger than that of any other language. There are more than 600,000 words in the largest dictionaries of the English language.

Some English words have been passed on from generation to generation as far back as scholars can trace. These words, such as *woman*, *man*, *sun*, *hand*, *love*, *go*, and *eat*, express basic ideas and feelings. Later, many words were borrowed from other languages, including Arabic, French, German, Greek, Italian, Latin, Russian, and Spanish. For example, *algebra*（代数）is from Arabic, *fashion* from French, piano from Italian, and *canyon*（峡谷）from Spanish.

A number of words, such as *doghouse and splashdown*（太空船在海上溅落）, were formed by combining other words. New words are also created by blending words. For example, motor and hotel were blended into *motel*（汽车旅馆）. Words can be shortened to form new words, as was done with "history" to form "story". Words called acronyms are formed by using the first letter or letters of several words. The word *radar*（雷达）is an acronym for *radio detection and ranging*.

Pronunciation and spelling in English sometimes seem illogical or inconsistent. Many words are spelled similarly though pronounced differently. Examples include *cough*, *though*, *and through*. Other words, such as *blue*, *crew*, *to*, *too*, *you and shoe*, have similar pronunciations but are spelled differently. Many of these variations show changes that occurred during the development of English. The spelling of some words remained the same through the centuries, though their pronunciation changed.

Grammar is the set of principles used to create sentences. These principles define the elements used to assemble sentences and the relationships between the elements. The elements include parts of *speech* （词性）and *inflections*（词形的变化）.

Parts of speech are the word categories of the English language. Scholars do not all agree on how to describe the parts of speech. The traditional description lists eight classes: nouns, pronouns, verbs, adjectives, adverbs, conjunctions and interjections. The most important relationships of the parts of speech include subject and verb, verb and *predicate*（谓语）, and *modifier*（修饰语）and the word modified.

Grammar also defines the order in which parts of speech may be used. The subject of a sentence usually comes first in the word order in English. It is generally followed by the verb and then the object. Single words that modify nouns are usually placed before the noun, but phrases that modify nouns are usually placed after the noun. Words that modify verbs can be put before or after the verb.

The Development of English

The history of the English language can be divided into three main periods. The language of the first period, which began about 500 A.D. and ended about 1100 A.D., is called Old English. During the next period, from about 1100 to 1485, the people spoke Middle English. The language of the period from about 1485 to the present is known as Modern English.

Old English was mainly a mixture of the Germanic languages of the Angles, Jutes, and Saxons. Old English resembles modern German more than it does modern English. Old English had many inflections, as does modern German, and its word order and pronunciation resembled those of modern German.

Middle English began to develop after 1066 A.D. when England was conquered by the Normans, a people from the area in France that is now called Normandy. Their leader, William the Conqueror, became king of England. The Normans took control of all English institutions, including the government and the church.

Most of the English people continued to speak English. However, many of the members of the upper class in England learned Norman French because they wanted influence and power. The use of French words eventually became fashionable in England. The English borrowed thousands of these words and made them part of their own language. The French-influenced language of England during this period is now called Middle English.

The Normans *intermarried* (通婚) with the English and, through the years, became increasingly distant—socially, economically, and culturally—from France. The Normans began to speak English in daily life. By the end of the 1300's, the French influence had declined sharply in England. English was used again in the courts and in business affairs, where French had replaced it.

Eventually Modern English developed. By about 1485, English had lost most of its Old English inflections, and its pronunciation and word order closely resembled those of today. During this period, the vocabulary of English expanded by borrowing words from many other languages. Beginning in the 1600's, the language spread throughout the world as the English explored and *colonized* (使成为殖民地) Africa, Australia, India, and North America. Different dialects of the English language developed in these areas.

Today, English is the international language of science and technology. English is also used throughout the world in business and diplomacy.

Varieties of English

The British writer George Bernard Shaw once remarked that "England and America are two countries separated by the same language." This humorous statement is a simple way of noting that the English language is not the same everywhere it is spoken. It is a living, evolving language that attains distinctive qualities in different environments. An American tourist in London, in search of public transportation, takes the underground rather than a subway. In a hotel the tourist takes the lift up to his room, not an elevator.

British English. What might be called the standard English of Britain is the speech of the educated people who live in London and the southeastern part of England. But this is only one of the regional dialects that has, over the centuries, achieved more extensive use than others. Other dialects include the class dialect *London Cockney* (伦敦土话) and Northern dialects, Midland dialects, Southwestern dialects, Welsh dialects, Lowland and Highland Scottish, Cornish, and Irish.

American English. In spite of the standardizing effects of radio and television, there are still a number of dialect regions across the United States. Significant contributions have been made to the creation of new dialects by black Americans and Hispanics. Neither of these groups, however, has a uniform dialect. Each has its regional variations. The influence of the United States on Canadian English has been strong because there is no natural boundary between the two countries. Most Americans would be hard pressed to distinguish the English used in the western provinces of Canada from that spoken in the United States.

Australia and New Zealand. Both Australia and New Zealand were settled by the British, and the

English language taken there came from a variety of British dialects. New terms were coined to describe the unusual plants and animals, and some words were picked up from the speech of *the native aborigines* (澳洲之原始居民) in Australia and *Maoris*(毛利人) in New Zealand. There is little regional variation in Australia, but there is significant social variation, as in Britain. The language of New Zealand is quite similar to that of Australia.

South Asia. It is made up of the countries of India, Pakistan, Bangladesh, Sri Lanka, Nepal, and Bhutan. The area is a vast complex of *ethnic*(种族的) and *linguistic*(语言的) differences: there are more than 1,600 dialects and languages in India alone. English, brought by a colonizing nation, became a second language. Today it exhibits wide diversity, depending on the background of those who adopt it and the native vocabularies they bring to it.

South Africa. The oldest British settlement in Africa, has two accepted European languages—English and Afrikans, or Cape Dutch. Although the English spoken in South Africa differs somewhat from standard British English, its speakers do not regard it as a separate dialect. Residents have added many Afrikanerisms to the language to denote features of the landscape.

Elsewhere in Africa—the most *multilingual*(多语言的) area of the world --English helps answer the needs of wider communication. It functions as an official language in Botswana, Lesotho, Swaziland, Zimbabwe, Zambia, Malawi, Uganda, and Kenya. The West African states of the Gambia, Sierra Leone, Nigeria, Ghana, and Liberia have English as the official language.

For sentences 1 - 7, mark Y, N, NG; fill in the missing information for sentences 8 - 10.

1. _____ The word "fashion" is of Spanish origin, so is the word "radar".

2. _____ From the inconsistency of its spelling and pronunciation, we can trace how English words have changed in its long history.

3. _____ As to grammar rules in English, scholars seem to have different ways in explaining the parts of speech.

4. _____ The word order and pronunciation of Old English are very much like those of modern German.

5. _____ Most Americans would find striking differences between American English and the English used in the western provinces of Canada.

6. _____ Sooner or later British English and American English will become totally different languages.

7. _____ English show a number of varieties in South Asian countries because people there are from different backgrounds and they put native vocabularies into English.

8. _____ are the word categories of the English language. The traditional description lists _____ classes.

9. The three main periods in the history of English language are _____, _____, _____.

10. The English language was enriched in Australia and New Zealand chiefly through _____ to describe the unusual plants and animals and _____ from the speech of the native aborigines.

Passage 4

Understanding Happiness

For thousands of years, people have been debating the meaning of happiness and how to find it. From the ancient Greeks and Romans to current day writers and professors, the debate about happiness continues. What makes someone happy? In what parts of the world are people the happiest? Why even study happiness?

The Greek philosopher Aristotle said that a person's highest happiness comes from the use of his or her intelligence. Religious books such as the Koran and Bible discuss faith as a form of happiness. The British scientist Charles Darwin believed that all species were formed in a way so as to enjoy happiness. And, the United States *Declaration of Independence* guarantees "life, liberty and the pursuit of happiness" as a basic human right. People throughout history may have had different ideas about happiness. But today, many people are still searching for its meaning.

How do you study something like happiness? You could start with the World Database of Happiness at Erasmus University in Rotterdam, The Netherlands. This set of information includes how to define and measure happiness. It also includes happiness averages in countries around the world and compares that information through time.

Some findings are not surprising. For example, the database suggests that married people are happier than single people. People who like to be with other people are happier than unsocial people. But other findings are less expected: People with children are equally happy as couples without children. And wealthier people are only a little happier than poorer people. This database also shows that studying happiness no longer involves just theories and ideas. Economists, psychiatrists, doctors and social scientists are finding ways of understanding happiness by examining real sets of information.

Positive psychology is the new term for a method of scientific study that tries to examine the things that make life worth living instead of life's problems. Traditional psychology generally studies negative situations like mental suffering and sickness. But positive psychology aims to study the strengths that allow people and communities to do well. Martin Seligman is the director of the Positive Psychology Center at the University of Pennsylvania in Philadelphia. He says positive psychology has three main concerns: positive emotions, positive individual qualities and positive organizations and communities.

There is also an increasing amount of medical research on the physical qualities of happiness. Doctors can now look at happiness at work in a person's brain using a method called magnetic *resonance imaging* (核磁共振成像), or MRI. For example, an MRI can show how one area of a person's brain activates when he or she is shown happy pictures. A different area of the brain becomes active when the person sees pictures of terrible subjects. Doctors are studying brain activity to better understand the physical activity behind human emotions. This research may lead to better understanding of depression and other mental problems.

Happiness is an extremely popular subject for books. If you search for "happiness" on the Website of the online bookseller, Amazon.com, you will find more than 200,000 results. Experts from several areas of study recently published books on the subject. The historian Darrin McMahon examines the development of happiness in *Happiness: A History*. Mr. McMahon looks at two thousand years of politics and culture in western countries. He says it is only in recent history that people think of happiness as a natural human right and it was not until the Enlightenment period in the eighteenth century Europe that people began to think they had the power to find happiness themselves. Darrin McMahon notes that in demanding happiness, people may think something is wrong with them or others if they are not happy. He sees the pressure to be happy as actually creating unhappiness.

Dan Gilbert teaches psychology at Harvard University in Massachusetts. He recently published *Stumbling on Happiness*. Mr. Gilbert looks at the way the human mind is different from other animals because we can think about the future and use our imaginations. He also explains how our minds can trick us in a way that creates difficulties in making happy choices for the future. For example, a person might think that buying a new car would make him or her happy even though the last car the person bought did not. So, events that we believe will bring us happiness bring us less than we think. And, events we fear will make us unhappy make us less unhappy than we believe. The book provides valuable information on the surprising ways in which our minds work. Here is a quotation of Mr. Gilbert talking about this "impact bias." It was taken from the Big Think Website. "Most of the time when people are wrong about how they'll feel about the future, they're wrong in the direction of thinking that things will matter to them more than they really do. We are remarkable at our ability to adjust and adapt to almost any situation; but we seem not to know this about ourselves. And so we mistakenly predict that good things will make us happy... really happy for a really long time. While bad things, they'll just *slay*(杀害) us. It turns out neither of these things is by and large true."

Why is studying happiness important? There are many answers to this question. One has to do with understanding happiness in order to create better public policies. Richard Layard is a British economist and lawmaker who studies this subject. His research is influenced by the eighteenth century thinker Jeremy Bentham. Mr. Bentham believed that the goal of public policy was to create the "greatest happiness for the greatest number." Richard Layard has looked at the relation between happiness and a country's wealth. He questions why people in western countries are no happier than they were fifty years ago although they now earn more money. Mr. Layard believes that part of the problem is that economics and public policy tend to measure a country's success by the amount of money it makes. He notes that happiness depends on more than the purchasing power of a person or a nation. Mr. Layard says that public policy should also help people improve the things that lead to happiness such as job security and health. To help improve public health policies in Britain, Mr. Layard has pressed the British government to spend more money on mental health treatment centers. He argues that by helping people recover from mental illness, the government can make a big step in the effort to increase happiness.

1. What can be inferred from the first paragraph?
   A) The meaning of happiness was found thousands of years ago.
   B) Happiness is an everlasting topic for discussion.
   C) The ancient Greeks and Romans were the happiest people.
   D) Current day scholars are good at making people happy.
2. The Bible tells us happiness comes from _____.
   A) the application of one's intelligence   B) the strong belief in religion
   C) a certain way of enjoyment   D) the guarantee of life and liberty
3. Which of the following information may NOT be covered by the World Database of Happiness?
   A) The way of defining happiness.   B) The measurement of happiness.
   C) The method of creating happiness.   D) The comparison of happiness averages.
4. The findings of the database imply that couples without children are _____.
   A) as happy as people with children   B) as happy as single people
   C) happier than unsocial people   D) a little happier than poor people
5. As an approach of scientific study, positive psychology focuses on _____.
   A) mental suffering   B) psychological sickness
   C) power that prevents people from winning   D) strengths that enable people to succeed
6. MRI is used in the study of happiness in order to _____.
   A) find out the physical quantities of happiness.   B) look at the images formed in people's brain
   C) study the reaction of the brain to happiness   D) understand the pictures of terrible subjects.
7. When did people start to believe in their ability to find happiness according to Mr. McMahon?
   A) 200,000 years ago.   B) 2,000 years ago.
   C) In recent years.   D) In the 18th century.
8. Mr. Gilbert suggests the difference between human mind and animals lies in the fact that we can

think about the future and _____.

9. One of the reasons for studying happiness is to _____.

10. Richard Layard indicates that happiness depends on other things as well as _____.

Passage 5

Dolphins: Senses

Vision

Bottlenose dolphins can see equally well above and under water. A number of other species, including the killer whales, are known to have the same capability. This is not true for all dolphin and whale species, though.

The river dolphins, who live in very murky waters, have eyes that seem to be adapted for above water vision only. There are some indications that these species may even be virtually blind.

The dolphin eye is *optimized*（使达到最佳）for underwater vision. In the human eye, most of the *refraction*（折射）is done by the *cornea*（角膜）, while additional focusing is done by the lens. Underwater the human eye loses most of its refractive power and the lens cannot compensate for that. Underwater we cannot get a clear picture: we are extremely far-sighted underwater. In the dolphin eye, the refractive power of the lens has become greatly increased, because the lens is located further forward and is completely *spherical*（球形的）.

The dolphin eye looks a lot like a fish eye. The dolphin pupil is rather special: instead of a round hole that narrows in bright light, there is a kind of "lid"（called operculum）that slides down, covering the centre of the pupil, leaving narrow slits on its edges. These narrow slits may give the dolphin more depth of vision above water and therefore better vision. Special adaptations in the edges of the lens may also improve above water vision.

The dolphin *retina*（视网膜）has both rods and cones like the human eye. The rods are the most sensitive to light and play a major role in vision under low light conditions. The cones are more sensitive to light and also play a role in color vision. Color vision in dolphins is probably poorly developed, though. There are indications that the dolphin eye is insensitive to red light.

The dolphin eye has a well developed reflective layer behind the retina. This indicates that the dolphin eye is adapted for vision in poor light conditions, not unlike the cat.

The dolphin cornea is organized differently than most mammal eyes: instead on one high-sensitivity area（or yellow spot）, the dolphin eye has two such areas. One may be associated with forward vision and the other with lateral（sideways）vision.

Hearing

Dolphins have tiny external ear opening, which are barely visible, just behind the eyes. These openings probably have no or only a limited function in hearing. The acoustic faculty in dolphins is well developed. The auditory systems in the brain are highly developed and much larger than for instance in humans. This strong development of the auditory systems of the brain is at least in part an explanation for the large brains in dolphins. The auditory nerve has double the amount of nerve fibers compared to the human auditory nerve. Bottlenose dolphins can hear sounds with frequencies between 75 Hz and 150 kHz （in humans the range is 10 Hz to 16-20 kHz）. Dolphins are most sensitive for sounds between 40 and 70 kHz.

In dolphins, the sound is conducted to the middle ear mainly via the blubber, which is an excellent sound conductor, and the lower jaw. The lower jaw of the dolphin is filled with a fatty tissue, which conducts sound quite well. This tissue extends from a thin area of the lower jaw to the inner ears. Experiments in which a sound-absorbing *hood*（头罩）of neoprene was placed over the lower jaw showed that dolphins with the hood in place had considerable difficulty in hearing.

The middle ear *cavities*(空穴) of dolphins are independently suspended and surrounded by air-filled spaces. This reduces the contact with the surrounding bone and can probably help the dolphin in directional hearing. The middle ear in dolphins serves 2 functions：one is to *stiffen*(使强化) the sound transmission system，optimizing it for high frequencies. The other is to balance the pressure between the inner ear and the external environment. The pressure of a given sound in water is about 60 times as high as the same sound intensity in air.

Touch

Dolphins are very *tactile*(有触觉的) animals. Their skin is very sensitive to touch. It is unclear if there are also pain and temperature receptors in their skin.

The areas that are most sensitive to touch are around the blowhole and the eyes and the upper and lower lips，near the corner of the mouth. The *snout*(动物的口鼻部)，melon and lower jaw are somewhat less sensitive while the skin on the back and tail stock are the least sensitive areas of the body.

Neonate dolphins have small "whiskers" which may have a function as a touch sensor. Some river dolphin species have whiskers even as adults. This may help them locate prey at close range.

Taste

Partly because dolphins swallow their food whole，many people assumed they have no sense of taste. It is unclear if bottlenose dolphins have *taste-buds*(味蕾) in their tongue. Taste-buds have been found in other dolphin species，though. Individual dolphins have developed preferences for specific fish species. If that is related to taste or to consistency of the fish is unclear.

Dolphins seem to be able to detect certain chemicals in the water. There may be some form of chemical communication in dolphins：chemicals excreted(排泄) by one dolphin can be tasted in the water by other.

For sentences 1-7，mark Y，N，NG ；fill in the missing information for sentences 8-10.

1. _____ All dolphin and whale species can see equally well above and under water.
2. _____ Some river dolphins may even be virtually blind.
3. _____ The whale eye has a well developed reflective layer(tapetum lucidum) behind the retina.
4. _____ Dolphins have large external ear openings，which are easily seen，just behind the eyes.
5. _____ Some scientists believe that there are also pain and temperature receptors in dolphin's skin.
6. _____ The skin on the back of dolphins is a part that is the least sensitive.
7. _____ All dolphins have taste-buds in their tongue.
8. Underwater the human eye will lose _____.
9. The fatty tissue extends from a thin area of the lower jaw to _____.
10. The function of Neonate dolphins' small "whiskers" is similar to a _____.

Passage 6

Will We Run Out of Water?

Picture a "ghost ship" sinking into the sand，left to rot on dry land by a receding sea. Then imagine dust storms sweeping up toxic pesticides and chemical fertilizers from the dry seabed and spewing them across towns and villages.

Seem like a scene from a movie about the end of the world? For people living near the Aral sea in Central Asia，it's all too real. Thirty years ago，government planners diverted the rivers that flow into the sea in order to irrigate farmland. As a result，the sea has shrunk to half its original size，*stranding*(使搁浅) ships on dry land. The seawater has tripled in salt content and become polluted，killing all 24 native species of fish.

Similar large-scale efforts to redirect water in other parts of the world have also ended in ecological crisis, according to numerous environmental groups. But many countries continue to build massive dams and irrigation systems, even though such projects can create more problems than they fix. Why? People in many parts of the world are desperate for water, and more people will need more water in the next century.

"Growing populations will worsen problems with water," says Peter H. Gleick, an environmental scientist at the Pacific Institute for studies in Development, Environment, and Security, a research organization in California. He fears that by the year 2025, as many as one-third of the world's projected 8.3 billion people will suffer from water shortages.

Where Water Goes

Only 2.5 percent of all water on Earth is freshwater, water suitable for drinking and growing food, says Sandra Postel, director of the Global Water Policy Project in Amherst, Mass. Two-thirds of this freshwater is locked in glaciers and ice caps. In fact, only a tiny percentage of freshwater is part of the water cycle, in which water evaporates and rises into the atmosphere and then condenses and falls back to Earth as precipitation(rain or snow).

Some precipitation runs off land to lakes and oceans, and some becomes groundwater, water that seeps into the earth. Much of this renewable freshwater ends up in remote places like the Amazon river basin in Brazil, where few people live. In fact, the world's population has access to only 12,500 cubic kilometers of freshwater — about the amount of water in Lake Superior. And people use half of this amount already. "If water demand continues to climb rapidly," says Postel, "there will be severe shortages and damage to the aquatic(水的) environment."

Close to Home

Water *woes*(灾难) may seem remote to people living in rich countries like the United States. But Americans could face serious water shortages, too, especially in areas that rely on groundwater. Groundwater accumulates in *aquifers*(地下储水层), layers of sand and gravel that lie between soil and bedrock.(For every liter of surface water, more than 90 liters are hidden underground.) Although the United States has large aquifers, farmers, ranchers, and cities are tapping many of them for water faster than nature can *replenish*(补充) it. In northwest Texas, for example, over-pumping has shrunk groundwater supplies by 25 percent, according to Postel.

Americans may face even more urgent problems from pollution. Drinking water in the United States is generally safe and meets high standards. Nevertheless, one in five Americans every day unknowingly drinks tap water contaminated with bacteria and chemical wastes, according to the Environmental Protection Agency. In Milwaukee, 400,000 people fell ill in 1993 after drinking tap water tainted with *cryptosporidium*(隐孢子虫), a microbe that causes fever, *diarrhea*(腹泻) and vomiting.

The Source

Where do contaminants come from? In developing countries, people dump raw sewage into the same streams and rivers from which they draw water for drinking and cooking; about 250 million people a year get sick from water-borne diseases.

In developed countries, manufacturers use 100,000 chemical compounds to make a wide range of products. Toxic chemicals pollute water when released untreated into rivers and lakes.(Certain compounds, such as *polychlorinated biphenyls*(多氯化联二苯), or PCBs, have been banned in the United States.)

But almost everyone contributes to water pollution. People often pour household cleaners, car antifreeze, and paint *thinners*（稀释剂）down the drain; all of these contain hazardous chemicals. Scientists studying water in the San Francisco Bay reported in 1996 that 70 percent of the pollutants could be traced to household waste.

Farmers have been criticized for overusing herbicides and pesticides, chemicals that kill weeds and insects. Farmers also use nitrates, nitrogen-rich fertilizer that helps plants grow but that can wreak *havoc* （大破坏）on the environment. Nitrates are swept away by surface runoff to lakes and seas. Too many nitrates "over-enrich" these bodies of water, encouraging the buildup of algae, or microscopic plants that live on the surface of the water. Algae deprive the water of oxygen that fish need to survive, at times choking off life in an entire body of water.

What's the Solution?

Water expert Gleick advocates conservation and local solutions to water-related problems; governments, for instance, would be better off building small-scale dams rather than huge and disruptive projects like the one that ruined the Aral Sea.

"More than 1 billion people worldwide don't have access to basic clean drinking water," says Gleick. "There has to be a strong push on the part of everyone—governments and ordinary people—to make sure we have a resource so fundamental to life."

For sentences 1-7, mark Y, N, NG ; fill in the missing information for sentences 8-10.

1. _____ That the huge water projects have diverted the rivers causes the Aral Sea to shrink.
2. _____ The construction of massive dams and irrigation projects do more good than harm.
3. _____ The chief causes of water shortage are population growth and water pollution.
4. _____ The problems Americans face concerning water are ground water shrinkage and tap water pollution.
5. _____ According to the passage all water pollutants come from household waste.
6. _____ The people living in the United States have to exploit the domestic energy resources already within her reach to deal with the water crisis.
7. _____ Water expert Gleiek has come up with the best solution to water-related problems.
8. According to Peter H. Gleick, by the year 2025, as many as _____ of the world's people will suffer from water shortages.
9. Two-thirds of the freshwater on Earth is locked in _____ .
10. In agriculture, _____ used by farmers can be detrimental to environment.

Passage 7
Policy on Student Privacy Rights

Policy Statement
Under the Family Educational Rights and Privacy Act(FERPA), you have the right to:
◆ inspect and review your education records;
◆ request an amendment to your education records if you believe they are inaccurate or misleading;
◆ request a hearing if your request for an amendment is not resolved to your satisfaction;
◆ consent to disclosure of personally identifiable information from your education records, except to the extent that FERPA authorizes disclosure without your consent;
◆ file a complaint with the U. S. Department of Education Family Policy Compliance Office if you believe your fights under FERPA have been violated.

1. Inspection

What are education records?

Education records are records maintained by the university that are directly related to students. These include biographic and demographic data, application materials, course schedules, grades and work-study records. The term does not include:

◆ information contained in the private files of instructors and administrators, used only as a personal memory aid and not accessible or revealed to any other person except a temporary substitute for the maker of the record;

◆ Campus Police records;

◆ employment records other than work-study records;

◆ medical and psychological records used solely for treatment purposes;

◆ records that only contain information about individuals after they have left the university;

◆ any other records that do not meet the above definition of education records.

How do I inspect my education records?

◆ Complete an Education Inspection and Review Request Form(available online as a PDF document or from The HUB, 12C Warner Hall) and return it to The HUB.

◆ The *custodian*(监管人) of the education record you wish to inspect will contact you to arrange a mutually convenient time for inspection, not more than 45 days after your request. The custodian or designee will be present during your inspection.

◆ You will not be permitted to review financial information, including your parents' financial information; or confidential letters of recommendation, if you have *waived*(放弃) your right to inspect such letters.

◆ You can get copies of your education records from the office where they are kept for 25 cents per page, prepaid.

2. Amendment

How do I amend my educational records?

◆ Send a written, signed request for amendment to the Vice President for Enrollment, Carnegie Mellon University, 610 Warner Hall, Pittsburgh, PA 15213. Your request should specify the record you want to have amended and the reason for amendment.

◆ The university will reply to you no later than 45 days after your request. If the university does not agree to amend the record, you have a right to a hearing on the issue.

3. Hearing

How do I request a hearing?

◆ Send a written, signed request for a hearing to the Vice President for Enrollment, Carnegie Mellon University, 610 Warner Hall, Pittsburgh, PA 15213. The university will schedule a hearing no later than 45 days after your request.

How will the hearing be conducted?

◆ A university officer appointed by the Vice President for Enrollment, who is not affiliated with your enrolled college will conduct the hearing.

◆ You can bring others, including an attorney, to the hearing to assist or represent you. If your attorney will be present, you must notify the university ten days in advance of the hearing so that the university can arrange to have an attorney present too, if desired.

◆ The university will inform you of its decision, in writing, including a summary of the evidence presented and the reasons for its decision, no later than 45 days after the hearing.

◆ If the university decides not to amend the record, you have a right to add a statement to the record that explains your side of the story.

4. Disclosure

Carnegie Mellon generally will not disclose personally identifiable information from your education records without your consent except for directory information and other exceptions specified by law.

What is directory information?

Directory information is personally identifiable information of a general nature that may be disclosed without your consent, unless you specifically request the university not to do so. It is used for purposes like compiling campus directories.

If you do not want your directory information to be disclosed, you must notify The HUB, 12C Warner Hall, in writing within the first 15 days of the semester.

Notifying The HUB covers only the disclosure of centralized records. Members of individual organizations such as fraternities, sororities(妇女联谊会), athletics, etc. must also notify those organizations to restrict the disclosure of directory information.

Carnegie Mellon has defined directory information as the following:

◆ your full name
◆ local/campus address
◆ local/campus telephone number
◆ email user ID and address
◆ major, department, college
◆ class status(freshman, sophomore, junior, senior, undergraduate, or graduate)
◆ dates of attendance(semester begin and end dates)
◆ enrollment status(full, half, or part time)
◆ date(s) of graduation
◆ degrees awarded
◆ sorority or fraternity affiliation

For students participating in intercollegiate athletics, directory information also includes:

◆ height, weight
◆ sport of participation

What are the other exceptions?

Under FERPA, Carnegie Mellon may release personally identifiable information from your education records without your prior consent to:

◆ school officials with legitimate educational interests;
◆ certain federal officials in connection with federal program requirements;
◆ organizations involved in awarding financial aid;
◆ state and local officials who are legally entitled to the information;
◆ testing agencies such as the Educational Testing Service, for the purpose of developing,
◆ validating, researching and administering tests;
◆ accrediting(授权与) agencies, in connection with their accrediting functions;

◆ parents of dependent students(as defined in section 152 of the Internal Revenue Service Code);

◆ appropriate parties in a health or safety emergency, if necessary to protect the health or safety of the student or other individuals;

◆ officials of another school in which the student seeks or intends to enroll;

◆ victims of violent crimes or non-forcible sexual offenses(the results of final student disciplinary proceedings);

◆ parents or legal guardians of students under 21 years of age(information regarding violations of university drug and alcohol policies);

◆ courts(records relevant to legal actions initiated by students, parents or the university).

5. Complaints

If you believe the university has not complied with FERPA, you can file a complaint with the:

Family Policy Compliance Office

Department of Education

400 Maryland Avenue, S. W.

Washington, DC 20202 -4605

For sentences 1–7, mark Y, N, NG ; fill in the missing information for sentences 8–10.

1. _____ This article has university students as its target audience.

2. _____ Under FERPA, students are entitled to request an amendment to their education records whenever they wish.

3. _____ The education records are kept by the students themselves.

4. _____ A student's demand for the inspection of his records must be met within a month.

5. _____ When the request for an amendment is refused by the university, the student may ask for a hearing.

6. _____ The university is free to disclose the Directory information of students without their consent.

7. _____ In a hearing for the amendment of education records, both the student and the university may hire attorneys.

8. If a student feels that his rights under PERPA has been violated, he could file a _____ with the U.S. Department of Education Family Policy Compliance Office.

9. A student who wants to inspect his education records must fill out a(n) _____.

10. The directory information for intercollegiate athletes include additional information such as _____ _____.

Passage 8

Raising Wise Consumers

Almost anyone with a profit motive is marketing to innocents. Help your kids understand it's OK not to have it all. Here are five strategies for raising wise consumers.

1. Lead by example

While you may know that TV commercials stimulate desire for consumer goods, you'll have a hard time selling your kids on the virtues of turning off the tube if you structure your own days around the latest *sitcom*(情景喜剧) or reality show.

The same principle applies to money matters. It does no good to lecture your kids about spending, saving and sharing when doing out their pocket money if you spend every free weekend afternoon at the mall. If you suspect your own spending habits are out of *whack*（不正常的）, consider what financial advisor Nathan Dungan says in his book *Wasteful Sons and Material Girls: How Not to Be Your Child's ATM*. "In teaching your child about money, few issues are as critical as your own regular consumer decisions," he writes. "In the coming weeks, challenge yourself to say no to your own wants and to opt for less expensive options."

2. Encourage critical thinking

With children under six or seven, start by telling them, "Don't believe everything you see," says Linda Millar, vice-president of Education for Concerned Children's Advertisers, a nonprofit group of 26 Canadian companies helping children and their families by media. Show them examples of false or exaggerated advertising claims, such as a breakfast cereal making you bigger and stronger.

Shaft Graydon, a media educator and past president of Media Watch, suggests introducing children to the "marketing that doesn't show"—the *mascots*（吉祥物）and web-sites that strengthen brand loyalty, the trading toys that cause must-have-it fever and the celebrity *endorsements*（签名）. "Explain that advertisers pay millions of dollars for celebrities to endorse a product, and that the people who buy the product end up sharing the cost," she says.

3. Supervise with sensitivity

According to a survey conducted by Media Awareness Network in 2001, nearly 70 per cent of children say parents never sit with them while they surf the Net and more than half say parents never check where they've been online. The states for TV habits paint a similar picture. A 2003 Canadian Teachers' Federation study of children's media habits found that roughly 30 per cent of children in Years Three to Six claim that no adult has input into their selection of TV shows; by Year Eight, the figure rises to about 60 per cent.

"Research suggests that kids benefit more from having parents watch with them than having their viewing time limited," says Craydon, noting that many children have TV sets in their bedrooms, which effectively free them from parental supervision. And what exactly does "supervision" mean? "Rather than ridiculing your child's favorite show, game or website, which will only create distance between you, you can explain media messages conflict with the values you'd like to develop in your child," Craydon says.

If you're put off by coarse language in a TV show, tell your child that hearing such language sends the(false) message that this is the way most people communicate when under stress. If violence in a computer game disturbs you, point out that a steady diet of onscreen violence can weaken sensitivity towards real life violence. "And when you do watch a show together," adds Graydon, "discuss some of the hidden messages, both good and bad."

4. Say no without guilt

I'm not proud to admit it, but when Tara asked me if I could take her shopping, I ended up saying yes. More precisely, I told her that if she continued to work hard and do well in school, I would take her over the school holidays. The holidays have now passed and I still haven't taken her, but I have no doubt she'll remind me of it soon enough. When I do take her, I intend to set firm limits(both on the price and the clothing items) before we walk into the store.

Still, I wonder why I gave in so quickly to Tara's request. Author Thompson says that my status as a baby boomer may provide a clue. "We boomer parents spring from a consumer culture in which having the right stuff helps you fit in," she explains. "Our research has shown that even parents in poor homes will buy Game Boys over necessities." In fact, 68 per cent of parents routinely give in to their kids' requests.

To counteract this tendency, Graydon says parents have to "learn, or relearn, how to say no." And what if the child calls you a miser or reminds you that her best friend has four Barbies(芭比娃娃) and she doesn't even have one? Graydon suggests practicing this mantra(祷文): "We create our own family rules according to our family values. We create our own family rules according to our own family values. We create..."

5. Offer alternatives

As parents know, saying "You can't have that" only intensifies a kid's desire for whatever "that" is. Rather than arbitrarily restricting their TV or computer time to protect them from media influence, Jeff Derevensky, a professor of applied child psychology at McGjll University, suggests creating a list of mutually acceptable alternatives. "If you want to encourage your children to build towers or play board games, be prepared to participate," he says. "Many kids will do these activities with their parents but not with other kids."

Miranda Hughes, a part-time physician and mother of four, fills her home with such basics as colored pencils and paints, craft materials, board and card games, building toys, a piano with the lid permanently open, sheet music(活页乐谱) and books of all kinds. "I also offer my own time whenever possible," she says. Although Hughes has a television in her house, "complete with 150 channels," she says her kids watch only about an hour a week. "I haven't had to implement any rules about TV or computer use," she says. "There's usually something else my kids would rather be doing."

For sentences 1-7, mark Y, N, NG; fill in the missing information for sentences 8-10.

1. _____ This passage outlines five strategies for making parents wise consumers.
2. _____ It is useful to lecture your kids about spending, saving and sharing when doing out their pocket money if you spend every free weekend afternoon at the mall.
3. _____ According to Nathan Dungan, in teaching your child about money, the most important issue is your own buying decisions.
4. _____ People are often deceived by false or exaggerated advertising claims.
5. _____ It is revealed by research that it is more beneficial to kids if their parents watch TV programs with them than having their viewing time limited.
6. _____ According to a research, 68 per cent of parents routinely satisfy their kids' demands.
7. _____ Miranda Hughes' kids watch TV only about an hour a week because she has made rules against her kids doing that.
8. According to a survey, _____ of the children investigated say that parents never check where they've been online.
9. The fact that many children have TV sets in their bedrooms effectively prevents them from _____ ____ by their parents.
10. Jeff Derevensky suggests that parents create a list of mutually acceptable options to protect children from _____.

Part Ⅲ *Reading Comprehension (Blanks-Filling)*

Passage 1

consultant	reliability	option	conduct	retails
dulls	president	occasions	category	hinders
acquisition	discipline	underlying	assume	consist

The universities have trained the intellectual pioneers of our civilization—the priests, the lawyers, the statesmen, the doctors, the men of science, and the men of letters. The (1)_____ of business now requires intellectual imagination of the same type as that which in former times has mainly passed into those other occupations.

There is one great difficulty which (2)_____ all the higher types of human effort. In modern times this difficulty has even increased in its possibilities for evil. In any large organization the younger men, who are *novices*（新手）, must be set to jobs which (3)_____ in carrying out fixed duties in obedience to orders. No (4)_____ of a large corporation meets his youngest employee at his office door with the offer of the most responsible job which the work of that corporation includes. The young men are set to work at a fixed routine, and only occasionally even see the president as he passes in and out of the building. Such work is a great (5)_____. It *imparts*（传授）knowledge, and it produces (6)_____ of character; also it is the only work for which the young men, in that novice stage, are fit, and it is the work for which they are hired. There can be no criticism of the custom, but there may be an unfortunate effect: *prolonged*（长久的）routine work (7)_____ the imagination.

The way in which a university should function in the preparation for an intellectual career, is by promoting the imaginative consideration of the various general principles (8)_____ that career. Its students thus pass into their period of technical apprenticeship with their imaginations already practiced in connecting details with general principles.

Thus the proper function of a university is the imaginative (9)_____ of knowledge. Apart from this importance of the imagination, there is no reason why businessmen, and other professional men, should not pick up their facts bit by bit as they want them for particular (10)_____. A university is imaginative or it is nothing—at least nothing useful.

Passage 2

occupied	impression	considerable	barrier	ornament
automatically	permanent	spectator	concerned	undergo
sustain	excessively	devices	essentially	fundamental

The distinctive architectural feature of the typical Broadway theatre is that two almost independent buildings are constructed side by side in such a way that they face and open into each other. The audience sits in the auditorium structure and watches the actors perform in the stage house. This separation is more than an *aesthetic*（审美的）(1)_____, because the building codes require that a physical (2)_____ protects the audience from a fire starting on the stage. A fire-proof wall, rather than a mere *partition*（隔离墙）, separates the structures, and this separation is completed by a fire-proof curtain that is furnished in such a way as to fall (3)_____ in case of fire. Automatic fire doors similarly close all other openings between the two structures. The building codes keep such openings to a minimum.

This separation came about in the nineteenth century as a result of theatre fires. It has produced (4)_____ architectural change from previous centuries without making much change in the appearance of the building. Most theatres of the sixteenth to eighteenth centuries were remodeled from banquet halls, tennis courts, and other *rectangular*（长方形的）halls, and remained (5)_____ a single wooden structure with a thin partition for the *proscenium*（舞台前部的）wall.

So far as the audience is (6)_____, a theatre is primarily a place for entertainment. In the theatre the audience is enabled to (7)_____ a vivid emotional experience similar to that undergone by the characters in the play. The audience approaches the theatre with the expectation of some sort of excitement, or emotional vividness. The architect and the decorator try to (8)_____ and increase this excitement and anticipation as the (9)_____ moves through the theatre. One of the familiar architectural devices for this effect is spaciousness of lobby and auditorium. Color and ornamentation are other (10)_____ for the same purpose, as seen in almost all theatres built before the nineteenth century.

Passage 3

isolated	processes	foster	nourished	considerably
repeatedly	attain	compel	intellectually	handicapped
demonstrated	theoretically	reared	asserted	roughly

There are two factors which determine an individual's intelligence. The first is the sort of brain he is born with. Human brains differ (1)_____, some being more capable than others. But no matter how good a brain he has to begin with, an individual will have a low order of intelligence unless he has opportunities to learn. So the second factor is what happens to the individual—the sort of environment in which he is (2)_____. If an individual is (3)_____ environmentally, it is likely that his brain will fail to develop and he will never (4)_____ the level of intelligence of which he is capable.

The importance of environment in determining an individual's intelligence can be (5)_____ by the case history of the identical twins, Peter and Mark X. Being identical, the twins had identical brains at birth, and their growth (6)_____ were the same. When the twins were three months old, their parents died, and they were placed in separate (7)_____ homes. Peter was reared by parents of low intelligence in an (8)_____ community with poor educational opportunities. Mark was reared in the home of well-to-do parents who had been to college. He was read to as a child, sent to good schools, and given every opportunity to be stimulated(9)_____. This environmental difference continued until the twins were in their late teens, when they were given tests to measure their intelligence. Mark's I. Q was 125, twenty-five points higher than the average and fully forty points higher than his identical brother. Given equal opportunities, the twins, having identical brains, would have tested at (10)_____ the same level.

Passage 4

motivation	enterprise	specifically	unlikely	overseas
identified	withdrawn	charms	,innovative	accounts
resistant	scale	facilitate	brilliant	crucial

Just five one-hundredths of an inch thick, light golden in color and with a perfect "saddle curl," the Lay's potato chip seems an (1)_____ weapon for global domination. But its maker Frito-Lay thinks otherwise. "Potato chips are a snack food for the world," said Salman Amin, the company's head of global marketing. Amin believes there is no corner of the world that can resist the (2)_____ of a Frito-Lay potato chip.

Frito-Lay is the biggest snack maker in America owned by Pepsi Co and (3)_____ for over half of the parent company's $ 3 billion annual profits. But the U. S. snack food market is largely saturated, and to grow, the company has to look (4)_____.

Its strategy rests on two beliefs: first a global product offers economies of (5)_____ with which local brands cannot compete. And second, consumers in the 21st century are drawn to "global" as a concept. "Global"does not mean products that are consciously (6)_____ as American, but ones that consumes—especially young people—see as part of a modern, (7)_____ world in which people are linked across cultures by shared beliefs and tastes. Potato chips are an American invention, but most Chinese, for instance, do not know that Frito-Lay is an American company. Instead, Riskey, the company's research and development head, would hope they associate the brand with the new world of global communications and business.

With brand perception a (8)_____ factor, Riskey ordered a redesign of the Frito-Lay *logo*（标识）. The logo, along with the company's long-held marketing image of the "irresistibility"of its chips would help (9)_____ the company's global expansion.

The executives acknowledge that they try to swing national eating habits to a food created in America, but they deny that amounts to economic imperialism. Rater, they see Frito-Lay as spreading the benefits of free (10)_____ across the world. "We're making products in those countries, we're adapting them to the tastes of those countries, building businesses and employing people and changing lives," said Steve Reinemund, PepsiCo's chief executive.

Passage 5

undoubtedly	*infinitely*	*foreseeable*	*fantastic*	*monitor*
perspectives	*abandoned*	*resolved*	*automated*	*route*
distract	*attached*	*economical*	*authorities*	*attached*

Some pessimistic experts feel that the automobile is bound to fall into disuse. They see a day in the not-too-distant future when all autos will be (1)_____ and allowed to rust. Other (2)_____, however, think the auto is here to stay. They hold that the car will remain a leading means of urban travel in the (3)_____ future.

The motorcar will (4)_____ change significantly over the next 30 years. It should become smaller, safer, and more (5)_____ , and should not be powered by the gasoline engine. The car of the future should be far more pollution-free than present types.

Regardless of its power source, the auto in the future will still be the main problem in urban traffic *congestion*（拥挤）. One proposed solution to this problem is the (6)_____ highway system.

When the auto enters the highway system, a *retractable*（可伸缩的）arm will drop from the auto and make contact with a rail, which is similar to those powering subway trains electrically. Once (7)_____ to the rail, the car will become electrically powered from the system, and control of the vehicle will pass to a central computer. The computer will then (8)_____ all of the car's movements.

The driver will use a telephone to dial instructions about his destination into the system. The computer will calculate the best (9)_____ , and reserve space for the car all the way to the correct exit from the highway. The driver will then be free to relax and wait for the *buzzer*（蜂鸣器）that will warn him of his coming exit. It is estimated that an automated highway will be able to (10)_____ 10,000 vehicles per hour, as opposed to the 1,500 to 2,000 vehicles that can be carried by a present-day highway.

第二节 写作演练篇

该部分针对大学英语四级测试的特点和各类题型，以国家四级测试写作部分的真题为例，以参考样文的形式,向考生展示四级写作的特点和固有的模式。纵观多年的四级写作,尽管题目在变,但基础写作的基本要领大致是一样的。四级写作特有的"三段式"模式,要求考生能非常熟练地驾驭主题句、发展句和句子间的连贯性等内在写作要素。考生可以通过熟悉样文,仔细揣摩写作套路,领会相关写作要素是如何运用的。更重要的是,通过参考样文,习得凝练的语言表达,提高语言文字的表达和驾驭能力。建议考生先不要急于看范文,每一个题目先动笔写一写,然后再对照范文,这样就能更快地掌握写作的要领。(备注:有关新四级作文部分请参考第一章真题答案部分)

Sample Composition 1

Volunteers Wanted(2006 年 6 月)

1. 校学生会将组织一次暑假志愿者活动,现招募志愿者
2. 本次志愿者活动的目的、活动安排等
3. 报名条件及联系方式

The Students' Union is organizing a voluntary program for the coming summer vacation. As is known to all, the 2008 Beijing Olympic Games need more English-speaking taxi drivers. The Student Union will open free English classes for them to improve their basic English communication skills. Now volunteers are wanted.

The following is the brief introduction to this program. First, its chief purpose is to help taxi drivers manage simple daily oral communications so that they can communicate easily with the foreign guests. Volunteers will work 15 days as English teachers from July 10 to July 24. There will be two hours teaching in the morning and 2 hours for oral practice in the afternoon. The Students' Union will provide the volunteers with three meals a day and transportation from and to the university during the class days.

The volunteers are requested to speak fluent English. Those with English teaching experience are preferable. Besides the English skills, we expect the volunteers to be patient, open-minded with a loving heart. Please contact us at telephone number 7654321 or write to us through Email at volunteer @ university. edu. cn before June 21. An interview will be held on June 22 for all candidates.

Sample Composition 2

Should the University Campus be Open to Tourists? (2005 年 12 月)

1. 名校校园正成为旅游新热点
2. 校园是否应对公众开放,人们看法不同
3. 我认为……

Nowadays, many famous university campuses have become one of the popular tourist attractions. It has been shown on TV and on the radio that every year thousands and thousands of middle school students visit Tsing Hua University and Peking University and other famous universities in China. In the place far away from the capital city, the local students also visit the universities famous in their own provinces.

So far as the present situation is concerned, is it a good or bad thing to open the university campus for tourists? Different people have different opinions. On the one hand, some people argue that it is a good thing for the students to visit these famous university campuses in that it can enable the middle school students to get more first-hand information and to stimulate their great interests and academic pursuits. On the other hand, others hold a negative view about this phenomenon. In their opinion, opening universities to tourists will have a negative effect because it will not only spoil the environment but also undermine the intellectual atmosphere.

In my opinion, tourism to universities does more harm than good. The campus is mainly a place for study. With the increasing tourism on campus, it will ruin the academic atmosphere and disturb the peaceful learning environment.

Sample Composition 3

Teacher's Day(2005 年 6 月)

1. 向老师表达节日祝贺
2. 从一件难忘的事来回忆老师的教诲和无私的奉献
3. 我如何回报老师的关爱

Teacher's Day

It is Teacher's Day today, a time to honor all teachers. So first of all, I extend my best wishes to all my beloved and respectable teachers and express my sincere gratitude for their patient instructions and loving care.

The day reminds me of my middle school match teacher, who gave me strength, helped me regain my confidence and guided me to success. During my days in middle school, my mother died and life was hard for me from that time on. I still remembered one day when I was in junior middle school, I got a bad cold, coughing all day and all night. Just as I longed for my mother's love, my math teacher helped me to the hospital, accompanying me while I was in hospital, feeding me food and medicine, reading stories and arranging class work. My eyes welled up with tears the moment I thought of her encouraging words and her tender love shown to me. It was my math teacher who warmed my already cooled heart, and helped boost my self-esteem, helping me with my school work, inspiring me when confronting failures and difficulties and rewarding me for any slightest progress I made.

Now, I am a university student. Thanks to my dear teacher' selfless love, I have achieved my dream and am on the way to future success. On this special occasion, I will pledge to all my teachers that I will cherish my time at school and make every effort to prove worthy of my devotion and make myself useful to society.

Sample Composition 4

A Campaign Speech(2004 年 12 月)

1. 你认为自己具备了什么条件(能力、性格、爱好等)可以胜任学生会主席的工作
2. 如果当选,你将为本校学生做些什么

A Campaign Speech

Dear fellow students,

I am grateful that you offer me the chance to speak here. I am impressed by the speeches of the previous candidates. Yet, I want to prove myself better for the post of chairman.

First of all, I have a pleasant personality. Last year I was the dorm director of our building and I managed to get along with all the students well. I have acquired working experience and communication skills which I consider as the most essential for the coordinator of the whole student union.

Secondly, I'm always ready to create. At present our union is very well organized. However our activity schedule is slightly monotonous. I am willing to add some vivid elements into it in order to make our campus life more enjoyable.

If I am elected the chairman, I promise I will become your voice and build the student union into a bridge between the students and the university.

I'm your best choice, vote for me, vote for yourself, thank you!

Sample Composition 5

A Brief Introduction to a Tourist Attraction(2004 年 6 月)

Your introduction should include:

- some welcoming words
- the schedule for the day
- a description of the place the tourists will be visiting

(e. g. a scenic spot or a historical site, etc.)

A Brief Introduction to a Tourist Attraction

Good morning, ladies and gentlemen! My name is Chen Hui. You may call me by my English name John if you like. It's my honor to be given the opportunity to act as your tour guide today. Please allow me to give you a warm welcome. Welcome to Suzhou, paradise on earth! I hope you will have a good time here.

As you know, Suzhou is famous for her gardens. Therefore, the place you will be visiting today is the Lingering Garden. The meaning of the name is "long lasting between heaven and earth". The garden is composed of four sections. Its middle section is the garden's highlight. The western section is based on large rockeries and gives a rough feeling. The northern section has a view of natural mountain villages. The eastern section has many magnificent and spacious halls, pavilions and corridors. All these form a splendid garden area with alternating spaces, each with its own characteristics. As a result, many small and large courtyards can be observed: a garden in a garden, a view in a view. I am sure you will enjoy yourselves here.

Since I have made all the arrangements for your journey in Suzhou, I'd like to tell you about today's schedule. At 8 a.m. we will be taking a sightseeing bus to go to the scenic spot. From 8:30 a.m. to 12 noon, we will be visiting parts of the scenic spot. From 12 noon to 1 p.m. we will be having lunch, and then from 1 p.m. to 4:30 p.m. We will be visiting the rest of the scenic spot. After that, we will return to the hotel. That's the schedule for today's tour.

Sample Composition 6

A Letter of Inquiry(2003 年 12 月)

Write a letter in reply to a friend's inquiry about applying for admission to your college or university.

1. 建议报考的专业及理由；
2. 报考该专业的基本条件；
3. 应当如何备考。

A Letter of Reply to a Friend

December 27, 2003

Dear Zhàng Ming,

I am glad to receive your letter. In my opinion, as you are an arts student, I advise you to choose English language as an option. Firstly, foreign language department is one of the biggest departments in our school, which has many distinguished professors and the best teaching facilities. What's more important, students majoring in English in particular are in high demand now in the labor market owing partly to China's entrance to the WTO and the successful bidding for hosting the 2008 Olympic Games. Thus, you need not worry more about finding an ideal job.

In order to study at the Foreign Language Department, you have to meet the following requirements. First, the entrance to our English department demands a good command of English language, especially the spoken English because there is an additional oral test. Secondly, you have to be proficient in the use of our native language—Chinese since there is huge amount of bi-lingual translation work if you are enrolled. What's more important, you have to pass the necessary entrance examination so that you can have the possibility to be taken in by the school.

As far as the preparation work is concerned, you are supposed to prepare well for all the essential subjects so that you can meet the necessary requirements imposed by the entrance examination. In addition, these basic subjects can lay a good foundation for your future success since language involves various aspects of our life. As for the language, I think, besides the practice of such basic skills as listening, reading, writing, speaking and so on, you should attach more importance to spoken English. Listening to the native speakers by radio or TV and trying to imitate their pronunciation and tone prove to be a good way to quickly improve your ability. If you have further questions, please feel free to write to me. Wish you success!

Sincerely yours,

Li Ming

Sample Composition 7

The Day My Classmate Fell Ill (or Got Injured) (2003 年 9 月)

1. 简单叙述一下这位同学生病(或受伤)的情况
2. 同学、老师和我是如何帮助他/她的
3. 人与人之间的这种相互关爱给我的感受是……

The Day My Classmate Fell Ill (or Got Injured)

I have a classmate named Angel, who is a lovely and bright girl. She is popular with all the classmates. One day, news came that Angel had got blood cancer. It really shocked everybody. When I saw her in the hospital, I could not help crying. She was so thin, so weak, and it seemed that only skin and bones were left. Her face was so pale. Even so, she gave us a big smile to comfort us.

We decided to help her save her life. Angel's family was not very rich and could not afford the operation. All the classmates and teachers began to raise money in school. Some called the media for help. In the end, we succeeded in raising the money for the first operation. We will keep trying until Angel is cured.

Many people offered as much help as they could even though they did not know Angel. I am really touched by this. There is love everywhere as long as we seek for it.

Sample Composition 8

An Eye-Witness Account of a Traffic Accident (2003 年 6 月)

假设你在某日某时某地目击一起车祸,就此写一份见证书。见证书必须包括以下几点:

1. 车祸发生的时间及地点
2. 所见到的车祸情况
3. 对车祸原因的分析

An Eye-Witness Account of a Traffic Accident

When I was going back home from college at four o'clock in the afternoon last Friday, that is June 13th, 2003, I witnessed a terrible car accident. The accident took place on the Middle Fuxin Road.

As far as I could remember, I was walking on the pavement and a blue Santana swiftly passed by. When it approached a truck parked on the roadside, suddenly, a girl stepped out from behind the truck. On seeing the girl, the car driver pulled a sudden brake. But it was too late. The girl was hit by the car and bounced off at least three meters. Then she lay on the road, her legs seemingly injured. The police and the ambulance arrived in less than five minutes and the girl was sent to hospital immediately.

That is all I had seen. To me the main cause of the accident might be like this: The girl was just about to walk to the other side of the road when the car moved near. But for the big car, she should have seen the approaching danger. Unfortunately, her view was blocked by the huge vehicle, which eventually led to the tragedy.

Sample Composition 9

It Pays to Be Honest(2002 年 12 月)

1. 当前社会上存在许多不诚实的现象
2. 诚实利人利己,做人应该诚实

It Pays to Be Honest

The other day, when I was reading newspaper, I found a very surprising report that people tell between two hundred and three hundred lies every day. I wondered if that could be true. Think about this problem further, I find that it is not difficult to find dishonest people around us. Nowadays, people try to get benefits by dishonest means. For example, some students copy the exercises done by others or cheat on examinations in order to get good marks. The same thing may be said of a merchant who tries to get rich by deceiving customers. Those people may succeed for a time, but sooner or later, they will be caught. In the end, dishonesty will bring them nothing but troubles.

Therefore, as the English proverb goes: Honesty is the best policy. For one thing, if we want to be trusted and respected by our friends, we must be honest. For another, if we want to succeed in our work, the first quality we should have is honesty. So whatever our aim is, we must work honestly to attain it. It can not only benefit us, but also benefit other people, even the whole society.

Sample Composition 10

Student Use of Computers(2002 年 6 月)

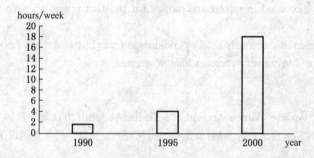

Average number of hours a student spends on the computer per week

1. 上图所示为 1990 年、1995 年、2000 年某校大学生使用计算机的情况,请描述其变化;
2. 请说明这些变化的原因(可从计算机的用途、价格或社会发展等方面加以说明);
3. 你认为目前大学生在计算机使用中有什么困难或问题。

Student Use of Computers

In modem times, computer has become a very useful tool of communication. And its use is more and more popular. This is reflected obviously on university students. The average number of hours a student spends on the computer per week is an eloquent indication. In 1990, the average number was only less than 2, but in 1995, it had increased to more than four. And in 2000, it reached more than 18. The consequence is that the rate of the average number of hours a student spends on the computer per week is rising more and more rapidly.

Why does this phenomenon appear? The reasons are as follows. First, the development of industry has lowered the price of computer. So more families could afford it. Second, the use of computer is more and more common in every area. And people need it much more than before. Third, the computer will become the requirement for studying and living. That means it'll be a very commonplace tool like TV set, bike and so on.

But now, not every student could own a computer because the price is still a little high for most of the students. And most of them who have owned computers are not very familiar to the use of computer. The difficulties exist all the time, but they will all be solved. So we hope, every one could use a computer easily and use it like a simple tool in life.

Sample Composition 11
A Letter to the University President(2002 年 1 月)

假设你是李明,请你就本校食堂的状况给校长写一封信,内容应涉及食堂的饭菜质量、价格、环境、服务等,可以是表扬,可以是批评建议,也可以兼而有之。

A Letter to the University President

January 12th, 2002

Dear Mr. President,

It is really my pleasure to have this opportunity to write to you. My name is Li Ming, a freshman major in Mathematics. I'm writing this letter just to report something about the canteen service on our campus.

Before I came to Beijing my parents were really worried about my new life here. Because I came from south China, where the food is quite different from that in the north. However, since my college life began, I have found that the food in our canteen is much better than I expected. There are various kinds of food, and I can not only have a balanced diet everyday, but also save a lot of money. I think the prices are also reasonable, and we have a lot of choices. Thirdly, the stuff member of our canteen are all very kind to us, they not only introduce the recipe of the food, but also give us some recommendations.

But here I also want to provide a suggestion. There are more and more students on campus, so can we have one or two new canteens to solve the problem.

Thank you for reading my letters!

Sincerely yours,

Li Ming

Sample Composition 12
A Letter to a Schoolmate(2001 年 6 月)

Write a letter to Xiao Wang, a schoolmate of yours who is going to visit you during the week-long holiday. You should write at least 100 words according to the suggestions given below in Chinese.

1. 表示欢迎
2. 提出对度假安排的建议
3. 提醒应注意的事项

A Letter to a Schoolmate

June 23, 2001

Dear Xiao Wang,

I'm very glad to know that you will come to visit me during the summer holiday. I haven't seen you for a long time, so I miss you very much. You let me make the traveling plan for us, so I want to tell you something about my plan.

At first, I think we can go shopping. Tianjin is very famous for commerce. If you come here, you must go shopping at Binjiang Street and Heping Road that are very prosperous and have various goods. Then we can go to Tianjin broadcast and TV tower from which you can see all the beautiful sights in Tianjin. If you want to visit Tianjin University and Nankai University, it's very convenient. Tianjin has many other places that are very worth seeing, like the Old Culture Street, the Food Street, the Natural Museum, the Science and Technology Museum and so on. There are many strange and beautiful houses that made and lived by foreigners before the liberation of China there. Many famous people lived there and the streets have a very long history. I think you will feel interested in it. I can also let you eat some traditional and delicious food in Tianjin. But you must bear in mind something, if you want to go outside by yourself, you must take a Tianjin map with you, because the roads in Tianjin are not straight, and you may easily lose your way.

I'm looking forward to your coming and give my best wishes to you and your family.

Sincerely yours,

Zhang Ying

Sample Composition 13

How to Succeed in a Job Interview? （2000 年 12 月）

1. 面试在求职过程中的作用
2. 取得面试成功的因素：仪表、举止谈吐、能力、专业知识、自信、实事求是……

How to Succeed in a Job Interview?

Nowadays, when people want to find a job, they always have job interview. So a job interview has become more and more important in our society. Interview has the advantage of being the most natural situation. It is easier to build up a relationship with the interviewee, and he will feel at ease and will answer questions more fully and more naturally. In this way the interviewer is likely to find out a great deal about the interviewee. On the other hand, there are disadvantages as well. The interviewer may be so strongly affected by his own feelings that he will be unable to judge by a proper standard. His feelings may drive him to make the final decision. It is not necessary for us to feel bad if we have failed in an interview, because it is only a matter of choice, instead of right or wrong.

If we want to succeed in a job interview, we have to remember the following factors. Firstly, we should pay more attention to our appearance. We should dress more formally, which is a kind of respect for the interviewer. Secondly, we should talk in a proper way, with good manners and confidence. Thirdly, we should try our best to show our ability as much as possible.

If we can bear those factors in mind, we are more likely to succeed.

Sample Composition 14

Is a Test of Spoken English Necessary?

1. 很多人认为有必要举行英语口语考试，理由是……
2. 也有人持不同意见，……
3. 我的看法和打算

Is a Test of Spoken English Necessary?

A test of spoken English will be included as an optional component of the College English Test

(CET). Their statement is that to master English is not only to recite the words, phrases and grammars, but also do lots of oral practice. The necessity is also attributed to today's educational environment, which attach more importance to the marks of examinations but less to the abilities of the students. A large number of students who have learned English many years cannot even speak a complex sentence concerning our daily life. So the test of spoken English can change this condition by making the students pay more attention to their oral English.

On the contrary, there are also many people who view it as an opposite one. In their opinions, the test is not reasonable because the abilities of expression are quite different. To judge the English level only by a test is sometimes unfair.

As far as I am concerned, I think it is interesting and it is a good challenge. So I welcome this test. I will study hard to improve my oral English. And I expect to do the best in the test.

Sample Composition 15

How I Finance My College Education?

1. 上大学的费用(tuition and fees)可以通过多种途径解决
2. 哪种途径适合于我(说明理由)

How I Finance My College Education

As I enter the college, a new world comes to me. I have to face more things than before. Among them, there's an important one that can help me finish the four years education, that is the tuition and fees of the college.

How can we students get money for that?

We can certainly get it from our parents. That is a traditional way. But for some poor families, especially some in the countryside, the cost of four years education is still a big problem. Nowadays, things are different. More and more students want to be independent from their parents and pay their way through college. It really can lessen the load of the family to some extent.

As for me, the best way I think to get the money is loaning from the bank. We can get the whole tuition each year and have to pay back after four years' schooling as well as just 3% interest rate per year in addition after we graduate from college. I also advocate doing an odd job during our vacations as a supplement to my tuition on condition that it will not affect my academic study.

Sample Composition 16

Reading Selectively Or Extensively? (1999 年 6 月)

1. 有人认为读书要有选择
2. 有人认为应当博览群书
3. 我的看法

Reading Selectively Or Extensively?

Reading books is very important for us, because books can provide the knowledge which can make society develop, and by reading books you can acquire all kinds of knowledge. However, since there are so many books in the world, we should read selectively or extensively?

Some people think that we should read selectively. Firstly, life is limited, and it is impossible for us to read all kinds of books. Secondly, not all the books can benefit us. Some kinds of books, such as cartoon books, popular novels and magazines only can entertain us and make us feel relaxed in our spare time. Thirdly, everyone has special interest while reading, so we could select different books to read according to our personal interests.

On the other hand, in modem society, people are supposed to have more knowledge than their ancestors to deal with the colorful world. The society is developing faster and faster, if we confine our knowledge only to our major or our study field, we couldn't keep up with the changes around us. So some people suggest we read extensively so as to get much more knowledge and not to become a person like Rip Van Winkle.

As far as I'm concerned, I think we'd better read both selectively and extensively. Thus, we can not only become a knowledgeable person in our own field, but also become a well-informed and qualified modem man.

第三节　翻译演练篇

该题型属于新四级增加的内容,所占比例仅占总分的 5%,测试的重点是各类语法项目和某些惯用法。主要包括各类从句(如:状语从句、定语从句等)、虚拟语气、倒装结构、比较级、各类非谓语动词形式、固定搭配结构、介词短语等。应该说此类翻译不是纯粹意义上的自由翻译,而是在一定约束范围内,利用给定的语言结构,确定要考查的内容。所以,做题时,一定要看清楚要考查的"题眼",就会大大提高解题的命中率。

Translation Test One

Part Ⅴ　Translation

Complete the sentences by translating into English the Chinese given in brackets.

1. A word processor is much better than a typewriter because it enables you to _____ (更容易的输入和编辑你的文本).
2. I send you my best regards _____ (值此幸福时刻).
3. We don't know _____ (为什么那个地区如此多的人不喜欢穿颜色鲜艳的衣服).
4. _____ (要是他们在后天我们启程之前赶到), we should have a wonderful dinner party.
5. It's high time we _____ (我们采取有效措施控制日益上涨的物价).

Translation Test Two

Part Ⅴ　Translation

Complete the sentences by translating into English the Chinese given in brackets.

1. If people feel hopeless, they don't bother _____ (获取成功所需要的技能).
2. While crossing the mountain area, all the men carried guns lest _____ (遭到野兽的袭击).
3. Investigators agreed that _____ (乘客一定是在飞机坠毁的瞬间死的).
4. We have to be fully aware of the false advertisements which are designed to make money _____ (以牺牲消费者的利益为代价).
5. As regards language learning, people often doubt _____ (是否值得付出这么多艰辛的劳动).

Translation Test Three

Part Ⅴ　Translation

Complete the sentences by translating into English the Chinese given in brackets.

1. The world would be an infinitely better place if the powerful nations _____ (用一半的金钱和辛劳致力于解决) such problems as poverty, hunger and war as they do to the space race.

2. _____（从汽车的数量来判断）, there were not many people at the club yet.

3. Research findings show we spend about two hours dreaming every night, _____（不论我们白天做过什么）.

4. _____（他此行的所见所闻）gave him a very deep impression.

5. Singer as she is, Marie has always preferred _____（喜欢自己做衣服）to buying them in the shops.

Translation Test Four

Part Ⅴ　Translation

Complete the sentences by translating into English the Chinese given in brackets.

1. All substances, _____（不论是固体还是液体）, take up space.

2. Let's take action to protect wildlife. Learning to live _____（与所有的野生动植物和睦相处）is part of modern civilization.

3. If the horse wins tomorrow, _____（在过去的三年里,它就赢了20场比赛）.

4. The reason I plan to go is _____（是因为若我不去,她会很失望的）.

5. In view of their purchasing power, I have no objection to _____（他们做出那样的购买决定）.

Translation Test Five

Part Ⅴ　Translation

Complete the sentences by translating into English the Chinese given in brackets.

1. Children are liable to _____（这儿秋季天气多变,孩子们易着凉）.

2. Unless economic conditions improve next year, _____（否则会有大面积的失业人员）.

3. Considerable evidence suggests that _____（学习好的往往是那些词汇量大的学生）.

4. Throughout the century, scientists have been engaged in the research to look for new sources of energy _____（来取代传统的能源形式）.

5. _____（如果我们答应立刻买车）, he would have knocked off the price another thousand dollars.

Translation Test Six

Part Ⅴ　Translation

Complete the sentences by translating into English the Chinese given in brackets.

1. _____（由于警方无法鉴定犯罪嫌疑人）, the criminal has gone unpunished as yet.

2. Without that temporary working site, the student _____（不可能按时完成设计）.

3. Sometimes we are asked _____（我们认为那样的行动可能带来什么样的后果）.

4. _____（要是你早点告诉我们他是谁）, we could have introduced him at the meeting.

5. Commercial banks make most of their income from interest _____（靠贷款获取的）and investments in stocks and bonds.

Translation Test Seven

Part Ⅴ　Translation

Complete the sentences by translating into English the Chinese given in brackets.

1. Sometimes children have trouble _____（把事实和虚构的区分开）.

2. Many a delegate was in favor of his proposal that _____（成立一个特别委员会负责调查这一事件）.

3. Things might have been much worse if _____（如果这位母亲坚持对孩子的抚养权）.

4. _____（考虑到他的能力和学识），they assign him to undertake the toughest job in this research work.

5. The traditional approach to _____（解决复杂问题）is to break them down into smaller，more easily managed problems.

Translation Test Eight
Part Ⅴ　Translation
Complete the sentences by translating into English the Chinese given in brackets.

1. In the Chinese household，grandparents and other relatives _____（起着不可缺少的作用）in raising children.

2. （这个计划成功的关键）_____ is good planning.

3. If you had _____（听从了我的劝告，你就不会陷入麻烦）.

4. Animal experiments will continue to be necessary to resolve existing medical problems _____（尽管一些人公开反对）.

5. The little boy next door has been beating his drum for a whole morning，which got on my nerves so much _____（以至于我无法集中注意力学习）.

Translation Test Nine
Part Ⅴ　Translation
Complete the sentences by translating into English the Chinese given in brackets.

1. During our first year of marriage _____（我和妻子遇到了意想不到的挑战）.

2. （应该特别强调宽容）_____ in the development of friendship.

3. This program _____（会允许你有更多的时间集中于设计技能）you will need and build a stronger foundation from which to begin your mechanical designing career.

4. （尽管日益上涨的材料成本可在很大程度上归因于）_____ natural disasters，the study nonetheless raises the prospect of broader inflation and higher interest rates.

5. IT workers also need to have business skills and experience，_____（这些技能和经验在许多方面都与其他服务行业所需的技能和经验相似）.

Translation Test Ten
Part Ⅴ　Translation
Complete the sentences by translating into English the Chinese given in brackets.

1. Only when I myself became a mother _____（我才意识到父母话中的含义）.

2. Now that you've passed the test，_____（你可以独自开车了）.

3. Soon after Susan started to work，_____（她发现自己面对大量困难）.

4. He took a thick coat with him for fear that _____（小孩会着凉）.

5. In his closing speech，the chairman expressed gratitude to all those _____（他们的工作为会议的成功做出了贡献）.

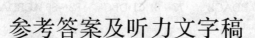

参考答案及听力文字稿

第一章 全真试题篇

2006年6月全国大学英语四级考试试卷

第一部分 参考答案

Part Ⅰ Writing（30 minutes）

On Students Choosing Lecturers

Nowadays，some universities give students the right to choose who teaches some of their classes. This has led to some debate over whether students should be allowed such freedom. Despite the disagreement，some universities take the initiative in providing chances for students to select the lecturers of some courses.

There are several factors that students often take into account when choosing a lecturer. Top priority is almost invariably given to the academic background of the lecturer，which reflects students' considerable emphasis on his or her expert knowledge. Second，students also attach greater importance to the teaching style of the lecturer. He who employs innovative teaching methods is usually applauded by students. In addition，research has shown that a lecturer who displays great personality in his or her teaching career often earns the greatest respect and admiration of students.

There are both positive and negative aspects to allowing students to choose their lecturers. On the one hand，giving students the choice to attend the possible courses they find most appealing and instructive encourages them to develop their own academic interests. On the other hand，efforts of this kind will put great pressure on teachers，as a result of which they will try their best to improve their teaching skills so that they can keep their students in class. However，the factors that students consider might not be the ones that lead to the highest quality of education. Schools might end up with lecturers who teach interesting classes without substantial content.

Part Ⅱ Reading comprehension（skimming and scanning）（15 minutes）

1. N 2. Y 3. Y 4. Y 5. N 6. NG 7. N

8. personal freedom of mobility 9. 75 percent 10. his vision and leadership

Part Ⅲ Listening comprehension（35 minutes）

11～15 AACDB 16～20 ABBBC 21～25 DDCBD 26～30 DABAC 31～35 BCDBA

36. future 37. trained 38. admire 39. schedule 40. considerate 41. waste

42. visible 43. necessarily

44. something that is simply there around them，not something they can use.

45. the fast food industry can be seen as a clear example of an American cultural product

46. spread around the world，they have been viewed as symbols of American society and culture

Part Ⅳ Reading Comprehension（Reading in Depth）（25 minutes）

47. F) phenomenon 48. B) strength 49. E) tropical 50. L) bringing 51. K) starvation

52. J) destructive 53. N) worth 54. A) estimate 55. O) strike 56. I) completely

57～61 DCABC 62～66 DBCBD

Part Ⅴ   Cloze（15 minutes）

67～71 CBAAD   72～76 BDACB   77～81 CDDBC   82～86 ACBDA

Part Ⅵ   Translation（5 minutes）

87. finding the way to the history museum

88. In order to support my university studies（to finance my education）

89. we should hand in our research report(s)

90. the more confused I am

91. he was fired/dismissed/discharged by the company

第二部分　听力文字稿

Part Ⅲ   Listening Comprehension

Section A   Short conversations

11. M：What would it be like working with those young stars?

    W：It was a great group. I always got mad when people said that we didn't get along, just because we were girls. There was never a fight. We had a great time.

    Q：What does the woman mean?（A）

12. M：Are you telling me you don't have a housekeeper?

    W：No, we don't. If you make a mess, you clean it up yourself.

    Q：What do we learn from this conversation?（A）

13. W：I hear that the Edwards are thinking of buying another house.

    M：Should they be doing that with all the other expenses they have to pay? Anyhow, they are over 70 now, and their present house is not too bad.

    Q：What does the man imply?（C）

14. M：You look like you are freezing to death. Why don't you put this on?

    W：Thank you, it was so warm at noon. I didn't expect the weather to change so quickly.

    Q：What do we learn from the conversation?（D）

15. M：I'll have the steak, French Fries, and let's see, chocolate ice cream for dessert.

    W：Oh, oh, you know these things will ruin your health, too much fat and sugar. How about ordering some vegetables and fruit instead?

    Q：Where did the conversation most probably take place?（B）

16. M：What was it like growing up in New York's Browns District? Was it safe?

    W：To me, it was. It was all I knew. My mom would send me to the shop and I'd go and buy things when I was about 8 years old.

    Q：What do we learn from the conversation?（A）

17. M：Nice weather, isn't it? Oh, I've seen you around the office, but I don't think we've met. I am Henry Smith. I work in the Market Research Section.

    W：Nice to meet you, Henry. I am Helen Grant. I am in the Advertising Section on the ninth floor.

    Q：What can we infer from the conversation?（B）

18. M：Ma'am, I hear you have an apartment for rent. Can I take a look at it?

    W：Sure, you're welcome any time by appointment, but I have to tell you the building is close to a railway with the noise. You might as well save the trip.

    Q：What do we learn from the conversation?（B）

Long conversations

Conversation 1

W：Please have a seat, Mr. Saunders. I received your resume last week, and was very impressed.

M: Thank you!

W: We are a small financial company trading mostly stocks and bonds. May I ask why you are interested in working for us?

M: Your company has an impressive reputation and I've always wanted to work for a smaller company.

W: That's good to hear. Would you mind telling me a little bit about your present job?

M: I'm currently working in a large international company in charge of a team of 8 brokers. We buy and sell stocks for major clients worldwide.

W: Why do you think you are the right candidate for this position?

M: As a head broker, I have a lot of experience in the stock market. I deal with clients on a daily basis, and I enjoy working with people.

W: Well, you might just be the person we've been looking for. Do you have any questions?

M: Uh-hum. If I were hired, how many accounts would I be handling?

W: You will be working with two other head brokers. In other words, you will be handling about a third of our clients.

M: And who would I report to?

W: Directly to me.

M: I see. What kind of benefits package do you offer?

W: Two weeks of paid vacation in your first year employment. You'll also be entitled to medical and dental insurance, but this is something you should discuss with our Personnel Department. Do you have any other questions?

M: No, not at the moment.

W: Well, I'll have to discuss your application with my colleagues and we'll get back to you early next week.

M: OK, thanks, it's been nice meeting you!

W: Nice meeting you too! And thanks for coming in today.

19. What's the purpose of Mr. Saunders' visit? (B)

20. What is Mr. Saunders' current job? (C)

21. What can we conclude from the conversation? (D)

Conversation 2:

M: Hey, Karen, you are not really reading it, are you?

W: Pardon?

M: The book! You haven't turned the page in the last ten minutes.

W: No, Jim, I suppose I haven't. I need to get through it though, but I keep drifting away.

M: So it doesn't really hold your interest?

W: No, not really. I wouldn't bother with it, to be honest, but I have to read it for a seminar. I'm at a university.

M: It's a labor of labor then rather than a labor of love.

W: I should say. I don't like Dickens at all really, the author. Indeed, I am starting to like the whole course less and less.

M: It's not just the book. It's the course as well?

W: Yeah, in a way, although the course itself isn't really that bad, a lot of it is pretty good, in fact, and lecturers are fine. It's me, I suppose. You see, I wanted to do philosophy rather than English, but my parents talked me out of it.

M: So the courses are OK as such. It's just that had it been left to you, you would have chosen a different one.

W: Oh, they had my best interest at heart, of course, my parents. They always do, don't they? They believe that my job prospects would've been pretty limited with the degree of philosophy. Plus, they give me a really generous allowance, but I am beginning to feel that I'm wasting my time and their money. They would be disappointed, though, if I told them I was quitting.

22. Why can't Karen concentrate on the book? (D)

23. Why is Karen starting to like the course less and less? (C)

24. Who thinks Philosophy graduates have limited job opportunities? (B)

25. What is Karen thinking of doing? (D)

Section B　Passages

Passage One

In Greece, only rich people will rest in peace forever when they die. Most of the population, however, will be undisturbed for only three years. Then they will be dug up, washed, compressed into a small tin box, and placed in a bone room. If the body has only partially decayed, it is reburied in a smaller, cheaper grave, but not for long. The body will be dug up again some time later when it has fully decayed. Buying a piece of land for a grave is the only way to avoid this process. The cost of the grave is so great that most people choose to rent a grave for three years and even after being dug up, lasting peace is still not guaranteed. If no one pays for renting space in the bone room, the skeleton is removed and stored in a building in a poor part of the town. Lack of space in Athens is the main reason why the dead are dug up after three years. The city is so overcrowded that sometimes dead bodies are kept in hospitals for over a week until a grave is found. Athens' city council wants to introduce cremation. That is, burning dead bodies as a means of dealing with the problem. But the Greek Church resists this practice. They believe the only place where people burn is hell, so burning dead bodies is against the Greek concept of life after death. To save space the church suggested burying the bodies standing up instead of lying down. Some people proposed building multi-storey underground graveyards.

26. What must Greeks do to keep the dead resting in everlasting peace? (D)

27. Why are most dead bodies in Athens dug up after three years? (A)

28. What suggestions does the church give about the burying of dead bodies? (B)

29. What practice does the Greek Church object to? (A)

Passage Two

If you visit a big city anywhere in the world, you will probably find a restaurant which serves the food of your native country. Most large cities in the United States offer an international sample of foods. Many people enjoy eating the food of other nations. This is probably one reason why there are as many different kinds of restaurants in the United States. A second reason is that many Americans come from other parts of the world. They enjoy tasting the foods of their native lands. In the city of Detroit, for example, there are many people from Western Europe, Greece, Latin America, and the Far East. There are many restaurants in Detroit which serve the foods of these areas. There are many other international restaurants too. Americans enjoy the foods in these restaurants as well as the opportunity to better understand the people and their way of life. One of the most common international restaurants to be found in the United States is the Italian restaurant. The restaurant may be a small business run by a single family. The mother of the family cooks all of the dishes, and the father and children serve the people who come to eat there. Or it may be a large restaurant owned by several different people who work together in the business. Many Italian dishes that Americans enjoy are made with meats, tomatoes and cheese. They are very delicious and tasty.

30. Why are there so many international restaurants in the United States? (C)

31. Why do Americans like to go to international restaurants apart from enjoying the foods there? (B)

32. How is the typical Italian family restaurant run in the United States? (C)

Passage Three

One winter day in 1891, a class at a training school in Massachusetts, USA, went into the gym for their daily exercises. Since the football season had ended, most of young men felt they were in for a boring time. But their teacher, James Nesmith, had other ideas. He had been working for a long time on the new game that would have the excitement of American football. Nesmith showed the men a basket he had hung at each end of the gym, and explained that they were going to use a round European football. At first everybody tried to throw the ball into the basket no matter where he was standing. "Pass! Pass!" Nesmith kept shouting, blowing his whistle to stop the excited layers. Slowly, they began to understand what was wanted of them. The problem with the new game which as soon called "basketball", was getting the ball out of the basket. They used ordinary food baskets with bottoms, and the ball, of course, stayed inside. At first, someone had to climb up every time a basket was scored. It was several years before someone came up with the idea of removing the bottom of the basket and letting the ball fall through. There have been many changes in the rules since then, and basketball has become one of the world's most popular sports.

33. What did Nesmith do to entertain his students one winter day? (D)

34. According to the speaker, what was the problem with the new game? (B)

35. How was the problem with the new game solved? (A)

Section C   Compound Dictation

For Americans, time is money. They say, "You only get so much time in this life; you'd better use it wisely." The (36) future will not be better than the past or present, as Americans are (37) trained to see things, unless people use their time for constructive activities. Thus, Americans (38) admire a "well-organized" person, one who has a written list of things to do and a (39) schedule for doing them. The ideal person is punctual and is (40) considerate of other people's time. They do not (41) waste people's time with conversation or other activity that has no (42) visible beneficial outcome.

The American attitude toward time is not (43) necessarily shared by others, especially non-Europeans. They are more likely to regard time as (44) something that is simply there around them, not something they can use. One of the more difficult things many students must adjust to in the States is the notion that time must be saved whenever possible and used wisely every day.

In this context, (45) the fast food industry can be seen as a clear example of American cultural product. Mc Donald's, KFC, and other fast food establishments are successful in a country where many people want to spend the least amount of time preparing and eating meals. As McDonald's restaurants (46) spread around the world, they have been viewed as symbols of American society and culture, bringing not just hamburgers but an emphasis on speed, efficiency, and shiny cleanliness.

2006 年 12 月全国大学英语四级考试试卷

第一部分　参考答案

Part Ⅰ　Writing（30 minutes）

Spring Festival Gala on CCTV

Many Chinese, whether at home or abroad, enjoy watching the Spring Festival Gala on CCTV on New Year' eve. As long as two decades ago, the Spring Festival Gala on CCTV became a household word in China. Even today, it is far from unusual to see the whole family gather in front of the TV to watch the program. For one thing, it provides a good chance for the whole family to get together and communicate with each other. For another, the songs, dances, cross-talk and short plays in the program, combined with the intimate chatting among family members, often provide good memories. That's why watching the Gala on CCTV is made a fashion to celebrate the most important festival of the year.

However, in recent years, some people have suggested that the Gala be cancelled for several reasons. For example, they think that such a big event costs too much and the money could be better spent on helping the poor. The program is also getting boring both in form and content, and the types of performances are found invariably similar to each other.

Maybe this makes sense. However, in my opinion, we cannot find a real substitute for the Gala. I hope that this TV program will continue and even flourish because the Gala is not merely a TV program, but the symbol of family reunion, harmony and peace. So, in this sense, the Spring Festival Gala on CCTV should be continued.

Part Ⅱ Reading comprehension（skimming and scanning）（15 minutes）

1. N   2. N   3. Y   4. N   5. Y   6. Y   7. NG

8. move forward   9. looking back   10 the more you get back

Part Ⅲ Listening comprehension（35 minutes）

11～15 BCACD   16～20 BDADC   21～25 BADBA   26～30 CBDCD   31～35 ABBDA

36. natural   37. usage   38. exception   39. particular   40. reference

41. essays   42. colleagues   43. personal

44. What we may find interesting is that it usually takes more words to be polite

45. but to a stranger, I probably would say "would you mind closing the door?"

46. There are bound to be some words and phrases that belong in formal language and others that are informal.

Part Ⅳ Reading Comprehension（Reading in Depth）（25 minutes）

47. O) primarily   48. K) voluntary   49. G) situation   50. J) gap   51. C) generate

52. N) purchase   53. M) insulted   54. I) potential   55. H) really   56. D) extreme

57～61 CBDAB   62～66 CADBC

Part Ⅴ Cloze（15 minutes）

67～71 ABDAC   72～76 DBACB   77～81 CABDC   82～86 DABDC

Part Ⅵ Translation（5 minutes）

87. adapt to the life in different cultures / adapt (oneself) to living in different cultures

88. nothing is more attractive / appealing to me than reading

89. would/might/could have a chance to survive might / would /could have survived / been alive

90. might feel lonely when they are away from home / might feel lonely when away from home

91. at the rate of 12 million people per year / at the speed of 12 million people every year

第二部分　听力文字稿

Part Ⅲ Listening Comprehension

Section A Short conversations

11. M: Christmas is around the corner. And I'm looking for a gift for my girlfriend. Any suggestions?

　　W: Well you have to tell me something about your girlfriend first. Also, what's your budget?

　　Q: What does the woman want the man to do? (B)

12. M: What would you like for dessert? I think I'll have apple pie and ice cream.

　　W: The chocolate cake looks great, but I have to watch my weight. You go ahead and get yours.

　　Q: What would the woman most probably do? (C)

13. W: Having visited so many countries, you must be able to speak several different languages.

M: I wish I could. But Japanese and, of course English are the only languages I can speak.

Q: What do we learn from the conversation? (A)

14. M: Professor Smith asked me to go to his office after class. So it's impossible for me to make it to the bar at ten.

W: Then it seems that we'll have to meet an hour later at the library.

Q: What will the man do first after class? (C)

15. M: It's already 11 now. Do you mean I ought to wait until Professor Bloom comes back from the class?

W: Not really. You can just leave a note. I'll give it to her later.

Q: What does the woman mean? (D)

16. M: How is John now? Is he feeling any better?

W: Not yet. It still seems impossible to make him smile. Talking to him is really difficult and he gets upset easily over little things.

Q: What do we learn about John from the conversation? (B)

17. M: Do we have to get the opera tickets in advance?

W: Certainly. Tickets at the door are usually sold at a higher price.

Q: What does the woman imply? (D)

18. M: The taxi driver must have been speeding.

W: Well, not really. He crashed into the tree because he was trying not to hit a box that had fallen off the truck ahead of him.

Q: What do we learn about the taxi driver? (A)

Long conversations

Conversation 1

W: Hey, Bob, guess what? I'm going to visit Quebec next summer. I'm invited to go to a friend's wedding. But while I'm there I'd also like to do some sightseeing.

M: That's nice, Shelly. But do you mean the province of Quebec, or Quebec City?

W: I mean the province. My friend's wedding is in Montreal. So I'm going there first. I'll stay for five days. Is Montreal the capital city of the province?

M: Well, Many people think so because it's the biggest city. But it's not the capital. Quebec City is. But Montreal is great. The Saint Royal River runs right through the middle of the city. It's beautiful in summer.

W: Wow, and do you think I can get by in English? My French is OK, but not that good. I know most people there speak French, but can I also use English?

M: Well, People speak both French and English there. But you'll hear French most of the time. And all the street signs are in French. In fact, Montreal is the third largest French speaking city in the world. So you'd better practice your French before you go.

W: Good advice. What about Quebec City? I'll visit a friend from college who lives there now. What's it like?

M: It's a beautiful city, very old. Many old buildings have been nicely restored. Some of them were built in the 17th or 18th centuries. You'll love there.

W: Fantastic. I can't wait to go.

19. What's the woman's main purpose of visiting Quebec? (D)

20. What does the man advise the woman to do before the trip? (C)

21. What does the man say about the Quebec City? (B)

Conversation 2:

M: Hi, Miss Rowling, how old were you when you started to write? And what was your first book?

W: I wrote my first finished story when I was about six. It was about a small animal, a rabbit, I mean. And I've been writing ever since.

M: Why did you choose to be an author?

W: If someone asked me how to achieve happiness. Step one would be finding out what you love doing most. Step two would be finding someone to pay you to do this. I consider myself very lucky indeed to be able to support myself by writing.

M: Do you have any plans to write books for adults?

W: My first two novels were for adults. I suppose I might write another one. But I never really imagine a target audience when I'm writing. The ideas come first. So it really depends on the ideas that grasp me next.

M: Where did the ideas for the "Harry Potter" books come from?

W: I've no ideas where the ideas came from. And I hope I'll never find out. It would spoil my excitement if it turned out I just have a funny wrinkle on the surface of my brain, which makes me think about the invisible train platform.

M: How did you come up with the names of your characters?

W: I invented some of them. But I also collected strange names. I've got one from ancient saints, maps, dictionaries, plants, war memoirs and people I met.

M: Oh, you are really resourceful.

22. What do we learn from the conversation about Miss Rowling's first book? (A)

23. Why does Miss Rowling consider her so very lucky? (D)

24. What dictates Miss Rowling's writing? (B)

25. According to Miss Rowling where did she get the ideas for the Harry Porter books? (A)

Section B   Passages

Passage One

Reducing the amount of sleep students get at night has a direct impact on their performance at school during the day. According to classroom teachers, elementary and middle school students who stay up late exhibit more learning and attention problems. This has been shown by Brown Medical School and Bradley Hospital research. In the study, teachers were not told the amount of sleep students received when completing weekly performance reports, yet they rated the students who had received eight hours or less as having the most trouble recalling all the material, learning new lessons and completing high-quality work. Teachers also reported that these students had more difficulty paying attention. The experiment is the first to ask teachers to report on the effects of sleep deficiency in children. Just staying up late can cause increased academic difficulty and attention problems for otherwise healthy, well-functioning kids, said Garharn Forlone, the study's lead author. So the results provide professionals and parents with a clear message: when a child is having learning and attention problems, the issue of sleep has to be taken into consideration. "If we don't ask about sleep, and try to improve sleep patterns in kids' struggling academically, then we aren't doing our job", Forlone said. For parents, he said, the message is simple, "getting kids to bed on time is as important as getting them to school on time".

26. What were teachers told to do in the experiment? (C)

27. According to the experiment, what problem can insufficient sleep cause in students? (B)

28. What message did the researcher intend to convey to parents? (D)

Passage Two

Patricia Pania never wanted to be a national public figure. All she wanted to be was a mother and home-maker. But her life was turned upside down when a motorist, distracted by his cell phone, ran a stop sign and crashed into the side of her car. The impact killed her 2-year-old daughter. Four months later, Pania reluctantly but courageously decided to try to educate the public and to fight for laws to ban drivers from using cell phones while a car is moving. She wanted to save other children from what happened to her daughter. In her first speech, Pania got off to a shaky start. She was visibly trembling and her voice was soft and uncertain. But as she got into her speech, a dramatic transformation took place. She stopped shaking and spoke with a strong voice. For the rest of her talk, she was a forceful and compelling speaker. She wanted everyone in the audience to know what she knew without having to learn it from a personal tragedy. Many in the audience were moved to tears and to action. In subsequent presentations, Pania gained reputation as a highly effective speaker. Her appearance on a talk show was broadcast three times, transmitting her message to over 40 million people. Her campaign increased public awareness of the problem, and prompted over 300 cities and several states to consider restrictions on cell phone use.

29. What was the significant change in Patricia Pania's life? (C)

30. What had led to Pania's personal tragedy? (D)

31. How did Pania feel when she began her first speech? (A)

32. What could be expected as a result of Pania's efforts? (B)

Passage Three

Many people catch a cold in the spring time or fall. It makes us wonder if scientists can send a man to the moon. Why can't they find a cure for the common cold? The answer is easy. There're actually hundreds of kinds of cold viruses out there. You never know which one you will get, so there isn't a cure for each one. When a virus attacks your body, your body works hard to get rid of it. Blood rushes to your nose and causes a blockade in it. You feel terrible because you can't breathe well, but your body is actually eating the virus. Your temperature rises and you get a fever, but the heat of your body is killing the virus. You also have a running nose to stop the virus from getting into your cells. You may feel miserable, but actually your wonderful body is doing everything it can to kill the cold. Different people have different remedies for colds. In the United States and some other countries, for example, people might eat chicken soup to feel better. Some people take hot bath and drink warm liquids. Other people take medicines to relieve various symptoms of colds. There was one interesting thing to note. Some scientists say taking medicines when you have a cold is actually bad for you. The virus stays in you longer, because your body doesn't develop a way to fight it and kill it.

33. According to the passage, why haven't scientists found a cure for the common cold? (B)

34. What does the speaker say about the symptoms of the common cold? (D)

35. What do some scientists say about taking medicines for the common cold, according to the passage? (A)

Section C   Compound Dictation

You probably have noticed that people express similar ideas in different ways depending on the situation they are in. This is very (36) natural. All languages have two general levels of (37) usage: a formal level and an informal level. English is no (38) exception. The difference in these two levels is the situation in which you use a (39) particular level. Formal language is the kind of language you find in textbooks, (40) reference books and in business letters. You would also use formal English in compositions and (41) essays that you write in school. Informal language is used in conversation with (42) colleagues, family members and friends, and when we write (43) personal notes or letters to close friends. Formal language is different from informal language in several ways. First, formal language tends to be more polite. (44) What we may find interesting is that it usually takes more words to be polite. For example, I might say to a friend or a family member "Close the door, please", (45) but to a stranger, I probably would say "would you mind closing the door?"

Another difference between formal and informal language is some of the vocabulary. (46) There are bound to be some words and phrases that belong in formal language and others that are informal. Let's say that I really like soccer. If I am talking to my friend, I might say "I am just crazy about soccer", but if I were talking to my boss, I would probably say "I really enjoy soccer".

2007 年 6 月全国大学英语四级考试试卷

第一部分　参考答案

Part Ⅰ　Writing（30 minutes）

Welcome to Our Club

If you feel that your spoken English is not so good and want to improve it, or you just long for a chance to help your fellow students with their oral English, please do not hesitate to join our Oral English Club. Our club aims to help you gain more confidence in your English ability. To reach this goal, it will provide you with a great variety of lively activities, such as English corner discussions, singing contests, English performances and so on. We will also show English films from America and Europe. Through these activities, you can practice your oral English and your listening skills.

By joining our club, you will acquire more than knowledge and skills. In the process of communicating with others, you will come to realize what your merits and shortcomings in English learning are. Moreover, it is a good opportunity for you to meet friends from different places. Perhaps what is most important is that you will be offered a chance to act as a leader of our club for a few weeks and take responsibility for the management of routine affairs, which is full of challenges and helps to boost your leadership qualities.

I hope everyone can seize this opportunity. Those who want to join us, please visit the Club Union or the club website to register your personal information. We are looking forward to meeting you.

Part Ⅱ　Reading comprehension（skimming and scanning）（15 minutes）

1. Y　　2. Y　　3. N.　　4. Y　　5. NG　　6. N　　7. Y

8. unwelcome emails　　9. names and contact information　　10. economic gain

Part Ⅲ　Listening comprehension（35 minutes）

11~15 CDBAC　　16~20 DDACB　　21~25 ACBAC　　26~30 CBDCA　　31~35 BDABD

36. meaning　　37. adjusting　　38. aware　　39. competition　　40. standards　　41. accustomed

42. semester　　43. inquire

44. at their worst, they may threaten to take their children out of college or cut off funds

45. think it only right and natural that they determine what their children do with their lives

46. who are now young adults must, be the ones responsible for what they do and what they are

Part Ⅳ　Reading Comprehension（Reading in Depth）（25 minutes）

47. L) complained　　48. G) seriously　　49. I) determining　　50. D) range　　51. O) specialize

52. F) issues　　53. B) involves　　54. M) respect　　55. J) limited　　56. C) significant

57~61 DBCBA　　62~66 BACDC

Part Ⅴ　Cloze（15 minutes）

67~71 ABDCB　　72~76 CDADB　　77~81 CABCD　　82~86 ACBDA

Part Ⅵ　Translation（5 minutes）

87. take people's sleep quality into account

88. the field (where) we can cooperate / the field in which we can cooperate

89. decided to quit the match

90. contact us at the following address

91. if it is convenient for you / at your convenience

第二部分 听力文字稿

Part Ⅲ Listening Comprehension

Section A Short conversations

11. W: Did you watch the 7 o'clock program on channel 2 yesterday evening? I was about to watch it when someone came to see me.

   M: Yeah! It reported some major breakthrough in cancer research. People over 40 would find a program worth watching.

   Q: What do we learn from the conversation about the TV program? (C)

12. W: I won a first prize in the National Writing Contest and I got this camera as an award!

   M: It's a good camera! You can take it when you travel. I had no idea you were a marvelous writer.

   Q: What do we learn from the conversation? (D)

13. M: I wish I hadn't thrown away that reading list!

   W: I thought you might regret it. That's why I picked it up from the waste paper basket and left it on the desk.

   Q: What do we learn from the conversation? (B)

14. W: Are you still teaching at the junior high school?

   M: Not since June. My brother and I opened a restaurant as soon as he got out of the army.

   Q: What do we learn about the man from the conversation? (A)

15. M: Hi, Susan! Have you finished reading the book Professor Johnson recommended?

   W: Oh, I haven't read it through the way I read a novel. I just read a few chapters which interested me.

   Q: What does the woman mean? (C)

16. M: Jane missed the class again, didn't she? I wonder why?

   W: Well, I knew she had been absent all week. So I called her this morning to see if she was sick. It turned out that her husband was badly injured in a car accident.

   Q: What does the woman say about Jane? (D)

17. W: I'm sure the Smiths' new house is somewhere on the street, but I don't know exactly where it is.

   M: But I'm told it's two blocks from their old home.

   Q: What do we learn from the conversation? (D)

18. W: I've been waiting here almost half an hour! How come it took you so long?

   M: Sorry, honey! I had to drive two blocks before I spotted a place to park the car.

   Q: What do we learn from the conversation? (A)

Long conversations

Conversation 1

M: Hello, I have a reservation for tonight.

W: Your name, please.

M: Nelson, Charles Nelson.

W: Ok, Mr. Nelson. That's a room for five and...

M: But excuse me, you mean a room for five pounds? I didn't know the special was so good.

W: No, no, no-according to our records, a room for 5 guests was booked under your name.

M: No, no—hold on. You must have two guests under the name.

W: Ok, let me check this again. Oh, here we are.

M: Yeah?

W: Charles Nelson, a room for one for the 19th...

M: Wait, wait. It's for tonight, not tomorrow night.

W: Em..., I don't think we have any rooms for tonight. There's a conference going on in town and— er, let's see...yeah, no rooms.

M: Oh, come on! You must have something, anything!

W: Well, let—let me check my computer here...Ah!

M: What?

W: There has been a cancellation for this evening. A honeymoon suite is now available.

M: Great, I'II take it.

W: But, I'II have to charge you 150 pounds for the night.

M: What? I should have a discount for the inconvenience!

W: Well, the best I can give you is a 10% discount plus a ticket for a free continent breakfast.

M: Hey, isn't the breakfast free anyway?

W: Well, only on weekends.

M: I want to talk to the manager.

W: Wait, wait, wait...Mr. Nelson, I think I can give you an additional 15% discount...

19. What's the man's problem? (C)

20. Why did the hotel clerk say they didn't have any rooms for that night? (B)

21. What did the clerk say about the breakfast in the hotel? (A)

22. What did the man imply he would do at the end of the conversation? (C)

Conversation 2

M: Sarah, you work in the admissions office, don't you?

W: Yes, I'm...I've been here ten years as assistant director.

M: Really? What does that involve?

W: Well, I'm in charge of all the admissions of postgraduate students in the university.

M: Only postgraduates?

W: Yes, postgraduates only. I have nothing at all to do with undergraduates.

M: Do you find that you get particular-sort of... different national groups? I mean, do you get large numbers from Latin America or...

W: Yes. Well, of all the students enrolled last year, nearly half were from overseas. They were from African countries, the Far East, the Middle East, and Latin America.

M: Em. But have you been doing just that for the last 10 years, or, have you done other things?

W: Well, I've been doing the same job. Er, before that, I was secretary of the medical school at Birmingham, and further back, I worked in the local government.

M: Oh, I see.

W: So I've done different types of things.

M: Yes, indeed. How do you imagine your job might develop in the future? Can you imagine shifting into a different kind of responsibility or doing something?

W: Oh, yeah, from October 1, I'll be doing an entirely different job. There's going to be more committee work. I mean, more policy work, and less dealing with students, unfortunately—I'll miss my contact with students.

23. What is the woman's present position? (B)

24. What do we learn about the postgraduates enrolled last year in the woman's university? (A)

25. What will the woman's new job be like? (C)

Section B   Passages

Passage One

My mother was born in a small town in northern Italy. She was three when her parents immigrated to America in 1926. They lived in Chicago when my grandfather worked making ice cream. Mama thrived in the urban environment. At 16, she graduated first in her high school class, went onto secretarial school, and finally worked as an executive secretary for a railroad company. She was beautiful too. When a local photographer used her pictures in his monthly window display, she felt pleased. Her favorite portrait showed her sitting by Lake Michigan, her hair went blown, her gaze reaching toward the horizon. My parents were married in 1944. Dad was a quiet and intelligent man. He was 17 when he left Italy. Soon after, a hit-and-run accident left him with a permanent limp. Dad worked hard selling candy to Chicago office workers on their break. He had little formal schooling. His English was self-taught. Yet he eventually built a small successful wholesale candy business. Dad was generous and handsome. Mama was devoted to him. After she married, my mother quit her job and gave herself to her family. In 1950, with three small children, dad moved the family to a farm 40 miles from Chicago. He worked hard and commuted to the city to run his business. Mama said goodbye to her parents and friends, and traded her busy city neighborhood for a more isolated life. But she never complained.

26. What does the speaker tell us about his mother's early childhood? (C)

27. What do we learn about the speaker's father? (B)

28. What does the speaker say about his mother? (D)

Passage Two

During a 1995 roof collapse, a firefighter named Donald Herbert was left brain damaged. For ten years, he was unable to speak. Then, one Saturday morning, he did something that shocked his family and doctors. He started speaking. "I want to talk to my wife." Donald Herbert said out of the blue. Staff members of the nursing home where he has lived for more than seven years, raced to get Linda Herbert on the telephone. "It was the first of many conversations the 44-year-old patient had with his family and friends during the 14 hour stretch." Herbert's uncle Simon Menka said. "How long have I been away?" Herbert asked. "We told him almost ten years," the uncle said, "he thought it was only three months." Herbert was fighting a house fire December 29, 1995 when the roof collapsed, burying him underneath. After going without air for several minutes, Herbert was unconscious for two and a half months and has undergone therapy ever since. News accounts in the days and years after his injury, described Herbert as blind and with little if any memory. A video shows him receiving physical therapy but apparently unable to communicate and with little awareness of his surroundings. Menka declined to discuss his nephew's current condition or whether the apparent progress is continuing. "The family was seeking privacy while doctors evaluated Herbert", he said. As word of Herbert's progress spread, visitors streamed into the nursing home. "He's resting comfortably," the uncle told them.

29. What happened to Herbert ten years ago? (C)

30. What surprised Donald Herbert's family and doctors one Saturday? (A)

31. How long did Herbert remain unconscious? (B)

32. How did Herbert's family react to the public attention? (D)

Passage Three

Almost all states in America have a state fair. They last for one, two or three weeks. The Indiana state fair is one of the largest and oldest state fairs in the United States. It is held every summer. It started in 1852. Its goals were to educate, share ideas, and present Indiana's best products. The cost of a single ticket to enter the fair was 20 cents. During the early 1930's, officials of the fair ruled that the people could attend by paying with something other than money. For example, farmers brought a bag of grain in exchange for a ticket. With the passage of time, the fair has grown and changed a lot, but it's still one of Indiana's most celebrated events. People from all over Indiana and from many other states attend the fair. They can do many things on the fair. They can watching the judging of the price cows, pigs, and other animals; they can see sheep getting their wool cut, and they can learn how that wool is made into clothing; they can watch cows giving birth. In fact, people can learn about the animals they would never see except at the fair. The fair provides a chance for the farming communities to show its skills and farm products. For example, visitors might see the world's largest apple, or the tallest sunflower plant. Today, children and adults at the fair can play new computer games, or attend more traditional games of skill. They can watch performances put on by famous entertainers. Experts say such fairs are important, because people need to remember that they're connected to the earth and its products, and they depend on animals for many things.

33. What were the main goals of the Indiana's state fair when it started? (A)

34. How did some farmers gain the entrance to the fair in the early 1930's? (B)

35. Why are state fairs important events in America? (D)

Section C   Compound Dictation

Students' pressure sometimes comes from their parents. Most parents are well (36) meaning, but some of them aren't very helpful with the problems their sons and daughters have in (37) adjusting to the college. And a few of them seem to go out of their way to add to their children's difficulties. For one thing, parents are often not (38) aware of the kinds of problems their children face. They don't realize that the (39) competition is keener, that the required (40) standards of work are higher, and that their children may not be prepared for the change. (41) Accustomed to seeing A's and B's on the high school report cards, they may be upset when their children's first (42) semester college grades are below that level.

At their kindest, they may gently (43) inquire why John or Mary isn't doing better, whether he or she is trying as hard as he or she should, and so on. (44) At their worst, they may threaten to take their children out of college or cut off funds.

Sometimes parents regard their children as extensions of themselves, and (45) think it only right and natural that they determine what their children do with their lives. In their involvement and identification with their children, they forget that everyone is different, and that each person must develop in his or her own way. They forget that their children, (46) who are now young adults, must be the ones responsible for what they do and what they are.

2007 年 12 月全国大学英语四级考试试卷

第一部分   参考答案

Part I   Writing (30 minutes)

What Electives to Choose

In recent years, universities and colleges offer a wide selection of electives, which are warmly applauded by students. These elective courses can meet students' needs either for future academic pursuits or for future career planning. At any rate, the courses can offer a variety of skills and abundant knowledge apart from what they learn in the usual school curriculum.

Students usually take several factors into account when they make a selection of optional courses. Most students choose elective courses with the aim to boost their competitive edge in the fierce job market. They believe an additional certificate or skill means more opportunities, which can partly account for the popularity of such courses as English interpretation, computer science, marketing and finance, etc. Others, however, make elective course selections purely for the sake of interest. They hold the university to be a place not only for learning survival skills, but also for developing analytical thinking and cultivating good taste. Still some others find it essential to choose electives as a significant way of boosting their intellectual capacity.

Personally, I prefer to select courses which can be a substantial boost to my academic pursuits. But with the gloomy job prospects, I also have to take courses which are of practical value in the hope that these courses may help stand me a better chance of landing a decent job after graduation. Whatever purposes make no big difference to me because I simply believe "To learn is fun".

Part Ⅱ   Reading comprehension（skimming and scanning）（15 minutes）

1～5 BCBDA   6～7 CB

8. changes in the visa process   9. take their knowledge and skills back home   10. strengthen the nation

Part Ⅲ   Listening comprehension（35 minutes）

11～15 CDBAD   16～20 BDCAC   21～25 CACAD   26～30 ABCDB   31～35 ADCAB

36. alarming   37. increased   38. sheer   39. disturbing   40. comparison

41. proportion   42. workforce   43. reverse

44. The percentage of people living in cities is much higher than the percentage working in industry.

45. There is not enough money to build adequate houses for the people that live there, let alone the new arrivals.

46. So the figures for the growth of towns and cities represent proportional growth of unemployment and underemployment

Part Ⅳ   Reading Comprehension（Reading in Depth）（25 minutes）

47. K) projects   48. M) role   49. A) acting   50. J) offers   51. D) cooperative

52. G) forward   53. F) especially   54. I) information   55. O) victims   56. E) entire

57～61 ACDCB   62～66 ABCCB

Part Ⅴ   Cloze（15 minutes）

67～71 ACDAC   72～76 BDBCA   77～81 DADCB   82～86 ADBDA

Part Ⅵ   Translation（5 minutes）

87. Thanks to a host of new inventions   88. I am more likely to get tired than before

89. whatever sacrifice I have to make   90. it is more convenient and less time-consuming

91. is measured by how many they can loan

第二部分   听力文字稿

Part Ⅲ   Listening Comprehension

Section A   Short conversations

11. W: I ran into Sally the other day. I could hardly recognize her. Do you remember her from high school?

    M: Yeah, she was a little out of shape back then. Well, has she lost a lot of weight?

    Q: What does the man remember of Sally? (C)

12. W: We don't seem to have a reservation for you, sir? I'm sorry.

    M: But my secretary said that she had reserved a room for me here. I phoned her from the airport this morning just before I got on board the plane.

    Q: Where does the conversation most probably take place? (D)

13. W: What would you do if you were in my place?

    M: If Paul were my son, I'd just not worry. Now that his teacher is giving him extra help and he is working hard himself, he's sure to do well in the next exam.

    Q: What's the man's suggestion to the woman? (B)

14. M: You've had your hands full and have been overworked during the last two weeks. I think you

really need to go out and get some fresh air and sunshine.

W: You are right. That's just what I'm thinking about.

Q: What's the woman most probably going to do? (A)

15. W: Hello, John. How are you feeling now? I hear you've been ill.

M: They must have confused me with my twin brother Rod. He's been sick all week, but I've never felt better in my life.

Q: What do we learn about the man? (D)

16. M: Did you really give away all your furniture when you moved into the new house last month?

W: Just the useless pieces, as I'm planning to purchase a new set from Italy for the sitting room only.

Q: What does the woman mean? (B)

17. M: I've brought back your Oxford Companion to English literature. I thought you might use it for your paper. Sorry not to have returned it earlier.

W: I was wondering where that book was.

Q: What can we infer from that conversation? (D)

18. W: To tell the truth, Tony, it never occurs to me that you are an athlete.

M: Oh, really? Most people who meet me, including some friends of mine, don't think so either.

Q: What do we learn from the conversation? (C)

Long conversations

Conversation 1

M: Mary, I hope you are packed and ready to leave.

W: Yes, I'm packed, but not quite ready. I can't find my passport.

M: Your passport? That's the one thing you mustn't leave behind.

W: I know. I haven't lost it. I've packed it, but I can't remember which bag it's in.

M: Well, you have to find it at the airport. Come on, the taxi is waiting.

W: Did you say taxi? I thought we were going in your car.

M: Yes, well, I have planned to, but I'll explain later. You've got to be there in an hour.

W: The plane doesn't leave for two hours. Anyway, I'm ready to go now.

M: Well, now you are taking just one case, is that right?

W: No, there is one in the hall as well.

M: Gosh, what a lot of stuff! You are taking enough for a month instead of a week.

W: Well, you can't depend on the weather. It might be cold.

M: It's never cold in Rome. Certainly not in May. Come on, we really must go.

W: Right, we are ready. We've got the bags, I'm sure there is no need to rush.

M: There is. I asked the taxi driver to wait two minutes, not twenty.

W: Look, I'm supposed to be going away to relax. You are making me nervous.

M: Well, I want you to relax on holidays, but you can't relax yet.

W: OK, I promise not to relax, at least not until we get to the airport and I find my passport.

19: What does the woman say about her passport? (A)

20: What do we know about the woman's trip? (C)

21: Why does the man urge the woman to hurry? (C)

22: Where does the conversation most probably take place? (A)

Conversation 2

W: Oh, I'm fed up with my job.

M: Hey, there is a perfect job for you in the paper today. You might be interested.

W: Oh, what is it? What do they want?

M: Wait a minute. Eh, here it is. The European Space Agency is recruiting translators.

W: The European Space Agency?

M: Well, that's what it says. They need an English translator to work from French or German.

W: So they need a degree in French or German, I suppose. Well, I've got that. What's more, I have plenty of experience. What else are they asking for?

M: Just that. A university degree and three or four years of experience as a translator in a professional environment. They also say the person should have a lively and enquiring mind, effective communication skills and the ability to work individually or as a part of the team.

W: Well, if I stay at my present job much longer, I won't have any mind or skills left. By the way, what about salary? I just hope it isn't lower than what I get now.

M: It's said to be negotiable. It depends on the applicant's education and experience. In addition to basic salary, there is a list of extra benefits. Have a look yourself.

W: Hm, travel and social security plus relocation expenses are paid. Hey, this isn't bad. I really want the job.

23. Why is the woman trying to find a new job? (C)

24. What position is being advertised in the paper? (A)

25. What are the key factors that determine the salary of the new position? (D)

Section B Passages

Passage One

When couples get married, they usually plan to have children. Sometimes, however, a couple can not have a child of their own. In this case, they may decide to adopt a child. In fact, adoption is very common today. There are about 60 thousand adoptions each year in the United States alone. Some people prefer to adopt infants, others to adopt older children, some couples adopt children from their own countries, others adopt children from foreign countries. In any case, they all adopt children for the same reason—they care about children and want to give their adopted child a happy life.

Most adopted children know that they are adopted. Psychologists and child-care experts generally think this is a good idea. However, many adopted children or adoptees have very little information about their biological parents. As a matter of fact, it is often very difficult for adoptees to find out about their birth parents because the birth records of most adoptees are usually sealed. The information is secret so no one can see it. Naturally, adopted children have different feelings about their birth parents. Many adoptees want to search for them, but others do not. The decision to search for birth parents is a difficult one to make. Most adoptees have mixed feelings about finding their biological parents. Even though adoptees do not know about their natural parents, they do know that their adopted parents want them, love them and will care for them.

26. According to the speaker, why do some couples adopt children? (A)

27. Why is it difficult for adoptees to find out about their birth parents? (B)

28. Why do many adoptees find it hard to make the decision to search for their birth parents? (C)

29. What can we infer from the passage? (D)

Passage Two

Catherine Gram graduated from the University of Chicago in 1938 and got a job as a news reporter in San Francisco. Catherine's father used to be a successful investment banker. In 1933, he bought a failing newspaper, the Washington Post.

Then Catherine returned to Washington and got a job, editing letters in her father's newspaper. She married Philip Gram, who took over his father-in-law's position shortly after and became a publisher of the Washington Post. But for many years, her husband suffered from mental illness and he killed himself in 1963. After her husband's death, Catherine operated the newspaper. In the 1970s, the newspaper became famous around the world and Catherine was also recognized as an important leader in newspaper publishing. She was the first woman to head a major American publishing company, the Washington Post company. In a few years, she successfully expanded the company to include newspaper, magazine, broadcast and cable companies.

She died of head injuries after a fall when she was 84. More than 3 thousand people attended her funeral including many government and business leaders. Her friends said she would be remembered as a woman who had an important influence on events in the United States and the world. Catherine once wrote, "The world without newspapers would not be the same kind of world". After her death, the employees of the Washington Post wrote, "The world without Catherine would not be the same at all."

30. What do we learn from the passage about Catherine's father? (B)

31. What does the speaker tell us about Catherine Gram? (A)

32. What does the comment by employees of the Washington Post suggest? (D)

Passage Three

Obtaining good health insurance is a real necessity while you are studying overseas. It protects you from minor and major medical expenses that can wipe out not only your savings but your dreams of an education abroad. There are often two different types of health insurance you can consider buying, international travel insurance and student insurance in the country where you will be going.

An international travel insurance policy is usually purchased in your home country before you go abroad. It generally covers a wide variety of medical services and you are often given a list of doctors in the area where you will travel who may even speak your native language. The drawback might be that you may not get your money back immediately, in other words, you may have to pay all you medical expenses and then later submit your receipt to the insurance company.

On the other hand, getting student heath insurance in the country where you will study might allow you to only pay a certain percentage of the medical cost at the time of the service and thus you don't have to have sufficient cash to pay the entire bill at once. Whatever you decide, obtaining some form of health insurance is something you should consider before you go overseas. You shouldn't wait until you are sick with a major medical bills to pay off.

33. Why does the speaker advice the overseas students to buy health insurance? (C)

34. What is the drawback of the students buying international travel insurance? (A)

35. What does the speaker say about students getting health insurance in the country where they will study? (B)

Section C   Compound Dictation

More and more of the world's population are living in towns or cities. The speed at which cities are growing in the less developed countries is (36) alarming. Between 1920 and 1960, big cities in developed countries (37) increased two and a half times in size, but in other parts of the world the growth was eight times their size.

The (38) sheer size of growth is bad enough, but there are now also very (39) disturbing signs of trouble in the (40) comparison of percentages of people living in towns and percentages of people working in industry. During the 19th century, cities grew as a result of the growth of industry. In Europe, the (41) proportion of people living in cities was always smaller than that of the (42) workforce working in factories. Now, however, the (43) reverse is almost always true in the newly industrialized world. (44) The percentage of people living in cities is much higher than the percentage working in industry.

Without a base of people working in industry, these cities cannot pay for their growth. (45) There is not enough money to build adequate houses for the people that live there, let alone the new arrivals.

There has been little opportunity to build water supplies or other facilities. （46）So the figures for the growth of towns and cities represent proportional growth of unemployment and underemployment，a growth in the number of hopeless and despairing parents and starving children.

2008 年 6 月全国大学英语四级考试试卷

第一部分　参考答案

Part Ⅰ　Writing（30 minutes）

Recreational Activities

Nowadays，there are a diverse range of recreational activities from traditional outdoor sports to all kinds of online entertainment have mushroomed all over the country. It is commonly accepted that recreational activities are as vital as air and water in that they can be a great supplement to both work and study.

Recreational activities can be either beneficial if managed sensibly or harmful if undertaken inappropriately. On the positive side, recreational activities can maintain physical fitness，ease stress and anxiety，aid relaxation，and are a great diversion from troubles and distress. For those who lack self-control，however，recreational activities can be hazardous，and even disastrous simply because these people would easily get lost and become addicted to them，which might seriously affect their life，work and interpersonal relationships.

As a college student，I think what really matters is to make better choice and exert more strict discipline. It is advisable to put recreational activities within certain limits and keep a proper balance between entertainment and study. Anyway，steering clear from those addictive，time-consuming and less meaningful activities is a wise decision.

Part Ⅱ　Reading comprehension（skimming and scanning）（15 minutes）

1～5 ADBCA　　6～7 BC

8. quite homogeneous，but small　　9. relationships with consumers　　10. the appropriate media

Part Ⅲ　Listening comprehension（35 minutes）

11～15 ACBDD　　16～20 BADCD　　21～25 CCADB　　26～30 AADBD

31～35 BBCCA

36. labor　　37. ingredients　　38. vital　　39. individuals　　40. engage　　41. figures

42. generating　　43. Currently

44. will be making decisions in such areas as product development，quality control，and customer satisfaction.

45. to acquire new skills that will help you keep up with improved technologies and procedures.

46. Don't expect the companies will provide you with a clearly defined career path.

Part Ⅳ　Reading Comprehension（Reading in Depth）（25 minutes）

47. D) claim　　48. H) limited　　49. O) totally　　50. G) interviews　　51. M) regret

52. J) moments　53. B) advanced　54. N) scary　　55. C) balloon　　56. A) accomplish

57～61 DCABB　62～66 ACBDD

Part Ⅴ　Cloze（15 minutes）

67～71 ADCBA　　72～76 ABCAB　　77～81 DACCA　　82～86 CDCAA

Part Ⅵ　Translation（5 minutes）

87. could be applied to the development of the new technology

88. must be out of control/wrong

89. no matter what kind of job it should be

90. Being compared with the place where I grow up

91. Not until he had finished his mission

第二部分　听力文字稿

Part Ⅲ　Listening Comprehension

Section A　Short conversations

11. M: Today's a bad day for me. I fell off a step and twisted my ankles.

    W: Don't worry. Usually ankle injuries heal quickly if you stop regular activities for a while.

    Q: What does the woman suggest the man do?（A）

12. W: May I see your ticket, please? I think you are sitting in my seat.

    M: Oh, you're right. My seat is in the balcony. I'm terribly sorry.

    Q: Where does the conversation most probably take place?（C）

13. W: Did you hear Jay Smith died in his sleep last night?

    M: Yes, it's very sad. Please let everybody know that whoever wants to may attend the funeral.

    Q: What are the speakers talking about?（B）

14. M: Have you taken Professor Young's exam before? I'm kind of nervous.

    W: Yes. Just concentrate on the important ideas she's talked about in the class, and ignore the details.

    Q: How does the woman suggest the man prepare for Professor Young's exam?（D）

15. W: I'm so sorry, sir. And you'll let me pay to have your jacket cleaned, won't you?

    M: That's all right. It could happen to anyone. And I'm sure that coffee doesn't leave lasting marks on clothing.

    Q: What can we infer from the conversation?（D）

16. W: Have you seen the movie "The Departed"? The plot is so complicated that I really got lost.

    M: Yeah. I felt the same. But after I saw it a second time, I could put all the pieces together.

    Q: How did the two speakers find the movie?（B）

17. M: I'm really surprised you got an A on the test. You didn't seem to have done a lot of reading.

    W: Now you know why I never miss a lecture.

    Q: What contributes to the woman's high score?（A）

18. W: Have you heard about the new digital television system? It lets people get about five hundred channels.

    M: Yeah, but I doubt that will have anything different from what we watch now.

    Q: What does the man mean?（D）

Long conversations

Conversation 1

W: Gosh, have you seen this, Richard?

M: See what?

W: In the paper, says there's a man going round pretending he is from the electricity board. He is been calling at people's homes, saying he's come to check that all their appliances are safe. Then he gets around them to make him a cup of tea, and while they are out of the room, he steals their money, handbag, whatever, and makes off with it.

M: But you know Jean, it's partly their own fault. They should never let anyone like that in unless you are expecting them.

W: It's all very well to say that, but someone comes to the door and says electricity or gas. And you automatically think they are ok. Especially if they flashed a card to you.

M: Does this man have an ID then?

W: Yes, that's just it. It seems he used to work for the electricity board at one time. According to the paper, the police are warning people especially pensioners not to admit anyone unless they have an appointment. It's a bit sad. One old lady told them, she's just been to the post office to draw her pension, when he called, she said he must follow her home. He stole the whole lot.

M: but, what does he look like. Surely they must have a description.

W: Oh, yes. They have. Let's see, in his 30s, tall, bushy dark hair, slight northern accent. Sounds a bit like you actually.

19. What does the woman want the man to read in the newspaper? (C)

20. How did the man mentioned in the newspaper try to win further trust from the victims? (D)

21. What is the warning from the police? (C)

22. What does the woman speaker tell us about the old lady? (C)

Conversation 2

M: Miss Jones, could you tell me more about your first job with hotel marketing concepts.

W: Yes, certainly. I was a marketing consultant responsible for marketing ten UK hotels. They were all luxury hotels in the leisure sector, all of very high standard.

M: Which markets were you responsible for?

W: For Europe and Japan.

M: I see from your resume that you speak Japanese. Have you ever been to Japan?

W: Yes, I have. I spent a month in Japan in 2006. I met all the key people in the tourist industry, the big tour operators, and the tourist organizations. As I speak Japanese, I had a very big advantage.

M: Yes, of course. Have you had any contact with Japan, in your present job?

W: Yes, I've had a lot. Cruises have become very popular with the Japanese both for holidays and for business conferences. In fact, the market for all types of luxury holidays for the Japanese has increased a lot recently.

M: Really? I'm interested to hear more about that. But first tell me, have ever traveled on a luxury train, the Orienting Express for example.

W: No, I haven't. But I've traveled on the Glacier Express to Switzerland, and I traveled across China by train about 8 years ago. I love train travel. That's why I am very interested in this job.

23. What did the woman do in her first job? (A)

24. What gave the woman an advantage during her business trip in Japan? (D)

25. Why is the woman applying for the new job? (B)

Section B   Passages

Passage One

Time

I think a lot about time and not just because it's the name of the news organization I work for. Like most working people, I find time or the lack of it, are never ending frustration and an unwinnable battle. My every day is a race against the clock that I never ever seem to win. This is hardly a lonesome complaint, according to the families and work institutes, national study of the changing work force, 55% of the employees say they don't have enough time for themselves, 63% don't have enough time for their spouses or partners, and 67% don't have enough time for their children. It's also not a new complaint. I bet our ancestors returned home from hunting wild animals and gathering nuts, and complained about how little time they had to paint battle scenes on their cave walls.

The difference is that the boss of the animal hunting and the head of nut gathering probably told them to "Shut up!" or "No survival for you!" Today's workers are still demanding control over their time, the difference is: today's bosses are listening. I've been reading a report issued today called *When Work Works*, produced jointly by 3 organizations. They set out to find and award the employers who employ the most creative and most effective ways to give their workers flexibility. I found this report worth reading and suggest every boss should read it for ideas.

26. What is the speaker complaining about? (A)

27. What does the speaker say about our ancestors? (A)

28. Why does the speaker suggest all bosses read the report by the 3 organizations? (D)

Passage Two

Loving a child is a circular business. The more you give, the more you get, the more you want to give, Penalapy Leach once said. What she said proves to be true of my blended family. I was born in 1931. As the youngest of six children, I learn to share my parents' love. Raising 6 children during the difficult times of the Great Depression took its toll on my parents' relationship and resulted in their divorce when I was 18 years old. Daddy never had very close relationships with his children and drifted even farther away from us after the divorce. Several years later, a wonderful woman came into his life, and they were married. She had two sons. One of them is still at home. Under her influence we became a blended family and a good relationship developed between the two families.

She always treated us as if we were her own children. It was because of our other mother, daddy's second wife, that he became closer to his own children. They shared over 25 years together before our father passed away. At the time of his death, the question came up of my mother, daddy's first wife, attending his funeral. I will never forget the unconditional love shown by my stepmother, when I asked her if she would object to mother attending daddy's funeral. Without giving it a second thought, she immediately replied, "Of course not, honey, she is the mother of my children."

29. According to the speaker, what contributed to her parents' divorce? (B)

30. What brought the father closer to his children? (D)

31. What message does the speaker want to convey in this talk? (B)

Passage Three

In February last year, my wife lost her job. Just as suddenly, the owner of the greenhouse where I worked as manager died of a heart attack. His family announced that they were going to close the business because no one in the family wanted to run it. Things looked pretty gloomy. My wife and I read the want-ads each day. Then one morning, as I was hanging out "Going out of Business" sign at the greenhouse, the door opened and in walked a customer. She was an office manager whose company has just moved into the new office park on the edge of town. She was looking for part of plants to place in the reception areas and offices. "I don't know anything about plants," she said. "I'm sure in a few weeks they'll all be dead." Why was I helping her select her purchases? My mind was racing.

Perhaps as many as a dozen firms have recently opened offices in the new office park, and there were several hundred more acres with construction under way. That afternoon, I drove out to the office park. By six o'clock that evening I had signed contracts with seven companies to rent plants from me and pay me a fee to maintain them. Within a week, I had worked out an agreement to lease the greenhouse from the owner's family. Business is now increasing rapidly. And one day, we hope to be the proud owners of the greenhouse.

32. What do we learn about the greenhouse? (B)

33. What was the speaker doing when the customer walked in one morning? (C)

34. What did the speaker think of when serving the office manager? (C)

35. What was the speaker's hope for the future?（A）

Section C   Compound Dictation

We are now witnessing the emergence of an advanced economy based on information and knowledge. Physical （36） labor, raw materials, and capital are no longer the key （37） ingredients in the creation of wealth. Now the （38） vital raw material in our economy is knowledge. Tomorrow's wealth depends on the development and exchange of knowledge. And （39） individuals entering the work force offer their knowledge not their muscles. Knowledge workers get paid for their education and their ability to learn. Knowledge workers （40） engage in mind work. They deal with symbols，words，（41） figures and data.

What does all this mean for you? As a future knowledge worker，you can expect to be （42） generating，processing，as well as exchanging information. （43） Currently，three out of four jobs involve some form of mind work，and that number will increase sharply in the future. Management and employees alike （44） will be making decisions in such areas as product development，quality control，and customer satisfaction. In the new world of work，you can look forward to being in constant training （45） to acquire new skills that will help you keep up with improved technologies and procedures. You can also expect to be taking greater control of your career. Gone are the nine-to-five jobs like time security，predictable promotions，and even the conventional work place as you are familiar with. （46） Don't expect the companies will provide you with a clearly defined career path，and don't wait for someone to empower you—you have to empower yourself.

第二章　实战模拟篇

New College English Model Test One

第一部分　参考答案

Part Ⅰ   Writing

Why Do College Students Take A Part-time Job?

In recent years，more and more college students choose to do part-time jobs in their spare time. Some students work as part-time family tutors，while others find part-time jobs in companies or joint ventures.

What encourages the students to take part-time jobs? This involves their diverse considerations，but the following are what they mention the most. For the large number of students from poor families，taking part-time jobs can partly ease/relieve their parents' financial burdens. Some students also list developing their independence as a primary motive for choosing to do part-time jobs. In addition，there are many others who believe taking part-time jobs can prepare them well for their future career development.

Whatever factors the students may take into account，several points deserve their attention in doing part-time jobs. Firstly，they should strike a proper balance between work and study so that in no case should part-time jobs interfere with their schoolwork. Besides，students should have a correct outlook on what' happening around them since their early contact with society may expose them to some social ills. If properly handled，doing part-time jobs can be a beneficial supplement to their college life.

Part Ⅱ   Reading Comprehension （Skimming and Scanning）

1. N   2. Y   3. N   4. N   5. NG   6. NG   7. Y

8. how the human body works   9. another even more vivid dream forms   10. reaching for the stars

Part Ⅲ   Listening Comprehension

Section A

11. B   12. A   13. A   14. D   15. C   16. D   17. C   18. D   19. D   20. C   21. A   22. B
23. C   24. C   25. A

Section B

26. C   27. D   28. C   29. B   30. D   31. D   32. C   33. D   34. B   35. B

Section C

36. satisfaction   37. particularly   38. assessment   39. crucial   40. matters

41. probably   42. sorted   43. procedures

44. Social meetings to be held and procedures set up, to say when, where, how and in what circumstances the employees can talk to the management.

45. Through the union all categories of employees can pass on the complaints they have and try to get things changed.

46. Instead of each employee trying to bargain alone with the company, the employees join together and collectively put forward their views.

Part Ⅳ   Reading Comprehension（Reading in Depth）

Section A

47. essentially   48. perceived   49. principle   50. minority   51. evident
52. confined   53. violate   54. subject   55. inspections   56. present

Section B

57. A   58. C   59. A   60. B   61. D   62. C   63. A   64. D   65. B   66. A

Part Ⅴ   Cloze

67. B   68. A   69. A   70. B   71. D   72. C   73. C   74. A   75. A   76. A   77. A   78. D
79. B   80. B   81. C   82. B   83. C   84. A   85. B   86. A

Part Ⅵ   Translation

87. the application forms (should) be sent back before the deadline

88. In the face of her serious illness

89. what she says makes sense

90. when the road is to be opened to traffic

91. to have been caused by the government's policy in housing

第二部分   听力文字稿

Section A

Short dialogues

11. M: I'm sorry, madam. The plane is somewhat behind the schedule. Take a seat. I'll inform you as soon as we know something definite.

    W: Thank you. I'd rather look around and I'll be back in several minutes.

    Q: What can be concluded about the plane?

12. W: What an accident! If you had been careful, things would not be as they are.

    M: What do you mean? It was my fault? If it were, surely I will take all responsibility for it.

    Q: What does the man mean?

13. M: I'm sorry to tell you that you needn't come next week. You know, sales of our company have been very poor recently.

    W: I've always worked hard. Would you be kind enough to give me a month's time so that I can find a new job?

Q: What has happened to the woman?

14. W: It's nearly ten o'clock. Let's listen to the weather forecast.

    M: Here's the weather forecast. Fog is spreading from the east and it'll affect all areas by mid-night. It'll be heavy in some places.

    Q: What's the weather forecast?

15. M: I forgot all about the two o'clock meeting. Tom's going to kill me!

    W: Oh, god. I can see why you're upset. It can be really annoying when something important sweeps your mind.

    Q: What's the woman's attitude towards the man's forgetfulness?

16. W: Do you know Jim works as a dishwasher at a restaurant around the corner?

    M: It isn't a bad job to start with. I wouldn't mind that job for the summer if no others are available.

    Q: What does the man mean?

17. M: John is certainly the funniest person in class. He can always make everyone laugh.

    W: I think I still have to get to used to his sense of humor.

    Q: What does the woman mean?

18. M: Where is Joan? She said she would be here at three, and now it's three thirty. She must have missed the train.

    W: I think so. But I hope she won't miss the next one. Otherwise she will be late for the opening address of the conference.

    Q: What's the woman worried about?

Long Conversations

Conversation One

M: Come on, Julia, how're we going to convince everybody that I'm the best candidate?

W: It won't be easy!

M: Thanks a lot!

W: Oh just kidding. Actually I think once we show everyone how well you did as junior class treasurer, you're sure to be elected president.

M: Well... What's your strategy?

W: One thing I was thinking of is to hang campaign posters in all the hallways...

M: But everybody puts up posters. We need to do something different.

W: Let me finish: The campus radio station is willing to let you have five minutes tomorrow morning at 7 to outline your plans for the year. Lots of students will hear you then.

M: Great idea!

W: I've also arranged for you to give a speech during dinner tomorrow. Over a hundred students will be there. And you can answer questions after you finish speaking.

M: That means I'd better come up with a speech pretty quickly. How about if I write it tonight and show it to you after chemistry class tomorrow?

W: Fine. I'll see you after class.

M: You're really good at this. I'm glad you agreed to help me out.

Questions 19 to 22 are based on the conversation you have just heard.

19. What election are the speakers discussing?

20. What is the relationship between the two speakers?

21. According to the conversation, what did the man do for the class?

22. What will the man do tonight?

Conversation Two

W: Now, please tell me something about the difference between American education and education in many other countries.

M: In many countries, children have a lot of homework in the lower and high school. But in the U. S. extracurricular activities such as sports, chorus, the student computer club, the military drill team, the student newspaper etc. All of them are important in high school. These activities give students valuable lessons in leadership, teamwork and effective communication, which are very useful in their future work.

W: Good. Now, why does the educational system in America attract so many foreigners?

M: Well, the U. S. system emphasizes individual choices. Many American high school students decide to take difficult classes in subjects they're interested in. And if they want to continue their education, it's easy to complete all the required courses and get enough credits to earn a bachelor's degree. In many other countries it's difficult to get into college, but once you're there, you can coast along and not work too hard.

W: You're right. American education begins to get very competitive in college.

M: And for foreign students, the huge amount of high-level reading and writing that is expected proves to be quite difficult. From all the research that's been done on how to learn a language, it's clear that most foreign students have never read enough English to develop a vocabulary equal to that of native speakers.

W: That's true enough! Many foreign students never get interested in reading English for fun. They are only interested in learning grammar. But tell me, why is your English so good?

M: Ever since I was a kid, I've read a lot of American storybooks. My mother worked in a library in Stockholm. She was always borrowing English books and magazines for my brother and me.

W: Well, that explains your excellent English. OK, let's go on. How long does it take for a college student to get a BA Or a BS?

M: After four years of study, students receive either a bachelor of arts or a bachelor of science degree. But just like high school, many students flunk out of college because of their poor grades.

W: And why de some students get poor grades?

M: Poor grades can be due to medical problems, too many hours spent working a part-time job, partying often, or simply not having the attitude and skills needed to perform well in a college classrooms.

W: Thank you, Victor, for your giving me so much information about the American education.

Questions 23 to 25 are based on the conversation you have just heard.

23. Why do students in American high schools pay a great attention to extracurricular activities?

24. What problem do most foreign students have in American colleges?

25. Which of the following isn't included in the reasons of poor grades of some students in America?

Section B

Passage One

Hollywood produces many different kinds of films, including mysteries, musicals, love stories, and horror films. As different as these films may be, they generally have one thing in common — conflict. The main character wants something very badly and will do anything to get it. The opponent tries to stop the main character from achieving his goal. This opposition creates conflict, and conflict is the heart of drama. To give an example, let's say the main character is a young man of humble origin who wants to marry the beautiful daughter of a rich banker. The father thinks the young man is unworthy of his daughter, and he does not allow her to see him. The young man, who's very much in love, refuses to give up without a fight. The conflict between the young man and the girl's father is what makes the story interesting; it forces the main character to take action, and through their actions we see them as they actually are. In a good story, the main character changes — he is not the same at the end of the story as he was at the beginning. He learns something from his experiences that make him a different, perhaps better person. And we learn something from watching him. Good movies not only entertain us, they also help us understand a little more about life.

Questions 26 to 28 are based on the passage you have just heard.

26. What is common to all the films produced in Hollywood?

27. What usually happens to the main character in a good story?

28. What can we learn from good movies?

Passage Two

Started in 1636, Harvard University is the oldest of all the colleges and universities in the United States. Yale, Princeton, and Dartmouth were opened soon after Harvard. They were all started before the American Revolution made the thirteen colonies into states.

In the early years, these schools were much alike. Only young men attended college. All the students studied the same subjects and everyone learned Latin and Greek. Little was known about science then, and one kind of school could teach everything that was known about the world. When the students graduated, most of them became ministers or teachers.

In 1782, Harvard started a medical school for young men who wanted to become doctors. Later, lawyers could receive their training in Harvard Law School. In 1825, Harvard began teaching modern languages, such as French and German, as well as Latin and Greek. Soon it began teaching American history.

As knowledge increased, Harvard and other colleges began to teach many new subjects. Students were allowed to choose the subjects that interested them.

Special colleges for women were started. New state universities began to teach such subjects as farming, engineering and business. Today, there are many different kinds of colleges and universities. Most of them are divided into smaller schools that deal with special fields of learning. There is so much to learn that on kind of school cannot offer it all.

Questions 29 to 32 are based on the passage you have just heard.

29. What is the passage talking about on the whole?

30. When did Harvard start a medical school?

31. What foreign languages did Harvard teach in 1825?

32. What can be inferred from the passage?

Passage Three

The Atlantic Ocean is one of the oceans that separate the old world from the new. For centuries it kept the Americas from being discovered by the people of Europe.

Many wrong ideas about the Atlantic made early sailors unwilling to sail far out into it. One idea was that it reached out to "the edge of the world". Sailors were afraid that they might sail right off the earth. Another idea was that at the equator the ocean would be boiling hot.

The Atlantic Ocean is only half as big as the Pacific, but it is still very large. It is more than 4,000 miles wide where Columbus crossed it. Even at its narrowest spot it is about 2,000 miles wide. This narrowest place is between South America and Africa.

Two things make the Atlantic Ocean rather unusual. For so large an ocean it has very few islands. Also, it is the world's saltiest ocean.

There is so much water in the Atlantic that it is hard to imagine how much there is. But suppose no more rain fell into it and no more water was brought to it by rivers, it would take the ocean about 4,000 years to dry up. On the average the water is a little more than two miles deep, but in some places it is much deeper. The deepest spot is near Buerto Rico. This "deep" measures 30,246 feet—almost six miles.

Questions 33 to 35 are based on the passage you have just heard.

33. What made early sailors unwilling to sail far out into the Atlantic?
34. Which of the following statements is true?
35. Which of the following is the best title for the passage?

Section C

Working relations with other people at the place of work include relationships with fellow employees, workers or colleagues. A major part of work or job **satisfaction** comes from 'getting on' with others at work. Work relations will also include those between the 'boss' and yourself: management-employee relations are not always straightforward, **particularly** as the management's **assessment** of your performance can be **crucial** to your future career

There will always be **matters** about which employees will want to talk to the management. In small businesses the 'boss' will **probably** work alongside his workers. Anything, which needs to be **sorted** out, will be done face-to-face as soon as a problem arises. There may be no formal meetings or **procedures**. The larger the business, the less direct contact there will be between employees and management. **Social meetings to be held and procedures set up, to say when, where, how and in what circumstances the employees can talk to the management.** Some companies have specially organized consultative committees for this purpose.

In many countries of the world today, especially in large firms, employees join a trade union and ask the union to represent them to the management. **Through the union all categories of employees can pass on the complaints they have and try to get things changed.** The process through which unions negotiate with management on behalf of their members is called 'collective bargaining'. **Instead of each employee trying to bargain alone with the company, the employees join together and collectively put forward their views.** Occasionally a firm will refuse to recognize the right of a union to negotiate for its members and a dispute over union recognition will arise.

New College English Model Test Two

第一部分 参考答案

Part Ⅰ Writing

Is Frustration a Bad Thing?

Since frustration is displeasing, some people tend to think that frustration is harmful and undesirable. They believe that constant frustration may cause serious mental health problems. People suffering from such psychological problems often resort to violence or suicide, which poses a big threat to the people around, thus causing instability to the whole society.

However, the majority hold a contrasting view. They maintain that it often goes side by side with opportunity and success since it can inspire people to overcome hardships and difficulties to achieve the final success. People with this view even go so far as to say that without frustration, there will be no sweet success. They often cite Thomas Edison as a case in point.

In my opinion, frustration itself can not be termed as good or bad. It is people's approach to it that matters a lot. Frustration is an inevitable part of our life experiences, a real test of our courage and determination. Numerous facts have shown that if we correctly view frustration and take it as a source of inspiration and motivation, we may ultimately enjoy the hard earned success. Therefore, it is safe to say that it is improper to view frustration as good or bad and that it is our attitude toward it that makes much difference.

Part Ⅱ   Reading Comprehension (Skimming and Scanning)

1. Y   2. N   3. N   4. NG   5. Y   6. N   7. NG

8. heart failure   9. smoker or drinker   10. surviving members of karoshi victims' families

Part Ⅲ   Listening Comprehension

Section A

11. A   12. B   13. A   14. D   15. A   16. B   17. B   18. C   19. A   20. B   21. D   22. C

23. B   24. A   25. B

Section B

26. D   27. B   28. A   29. B   30. B   31. A   32. C   33. B   34. A   35. B

Section C

36. buried   37. platform   38. Generations   39. clues   40. abandon

41. entire   42. creating   43. stirring

44. The palace — a three-story complex built around 11 courtyards — is the largest Mayan palace ever discovered.

45. Over the past decade, archaeologists have discovered numerous new sites, transforming our understanding of classic Mayan civilization.

46. the Mayan civilization may have been victims of their own success. Some estimates put the Mayan population in the lowland jungles at a surprising 200 people per square kilometer.

Part Ⅳ   Reading Comprehension (Reading in Depth)

Section A

47. strides   48. phenomena   49. scale   50. otherwise   51. dominant

52. fraction   53. incredible   54. separation   55. shrink   56. frontiers

Section B

57. D   58. A   59. B   60. C   61. D   62. C   63. A   64. D   65. D   66. C

Part Ⅴ   Cloze

67. C   68. B   69. D   70. A   71. B   72. A   73. D   74. D   75. C   76. B   77. B   78. A

79. C   80. D   81. A   82. A   83. D   84. C   85. B   86. C

Part Ⅵ   Translation

87. get in the way of your success

88. as much as one-third of the job hunters failed to find jobs

89. when it comes to computer repairing

90. might have chosen another career

91. what would be the outcome

第二部分   听力文字稿

Section A

Short dialogues

11. W: Have you heard about the plane crash yesterday? It caused a hundred and twenty deaths. I am never at ease when taking a flight.

    M: Though we often hear about air crashes and serious casualties, flying is one of the safest ways to travel.

    Q: What do we learn from this conversation?

12. W: I have a complaint to make, Sir. I had waited ten minutes at the table before the waiter showed up, and I finally got served. And I found it was not what I ordered.

    M: I am terribly sorry, madam. It's a bit unusually busy tonight. As a compensation, your meal will be free.

Q: Where does the conversation most probably take place?

13. M: I can't find my pen. I need to write a letter.

W: I'll look for it later. Right now I need you to help fix the shelf before paint it.

Q: What would they do first?

14. M: Mrs. Winter, I need your advice, I want to buy a dress for my wife, can you tell me where I can get one at a reasonable price?

W: Sure, go to Richard's. It has the latest styles and gives a 30% discount to husbands who shop alone.

Q: What do we know about Richard's shop?

15. M: My headaches are terribly. Maybe I need more sleep.

W: Actually, you need less sun and some aspirin. It would help if you wear a hat.

Q: What does the woman think is the cause of the man's headache?

16. M: Did you notice after almost ten years in the United States, Mr. Lee still speaks English with such a strong accent.

W: Yes, but he is proud of it. He says it is a part of his identity.

Q: What does the conversation tell us about Mr. Lee?

17. W: This is Mrs. Thatcher. My heater is not getting any power and weatherman says the temperature is going to fall below zero tonight. Could you get someone to come over and fix it?

M: This is the busiest time of the year, but I'll speak to one of our men about going over some time today.

Q: Whom did Mrs. Thatcher want to come over?

18. M: Though we didn't win the game, we were satisfied with our performance.

W: You did a great job. You almost beat the world's champions. It's a real surprise to many people.

Q: What do we learn from this conversation?

Long Conversations

Conversation One

M: Cindy! Have you heard the news?

W: No, Steve. What do you mean?

M: You know all the classes we've missed because of the snow?

W: Uh oh...

M: Yup—we're going to have to make them up and the dean says it will have to be during spring break.

W: Steve! We have our vacation all set! What are we going to do? Do the others know?

M: I don't know but I certainly can't afford to miss five days of classes this semester, with that week I was sick...

W: But I really don't want to cancel our trip. All of us have already made our plane reservations!

M: I can try to call the travel agency; maybe they can refund our money. But before we do anything we need to speak with our professors.

W: You think they'll excuse us from class?

M: Probably not. But I was talking to Kevin this morning and he said that one of his professors told him that they could make up the class at a different time.

W: Wow—that's great! Which professor was it?

M: I don't know. But we're going to have to speak to all of them anyway.

W: Why didn't they add extra days at the end of the semester before summer classes?

M: Because of the graduation date, which can't be changed.

W: Are other colleges around here doing the same thing?

M：I would imagine so—it's been such a bad winter and we've missed too many classes. We do really need to make them up.

W：I know, I know. I was just really looking forward to this vacation. The idea of the sun and the beach!

M：Oh look, there's Professor Hampton right now!

W：Come on, let's go talk to her!

Questions 19 to 22 are based on the conversation you have just heard.

19. Why are the man and woman upset?

20. What can be inferred about the man's and woman's vacation?

21. Why can't the semester be extended?

22. Why can't the man miss classes?

Conversation Two

M：Uh, could I borrow a few bucks until payday? I'm a little short of cash.

W：Uh, yeah, I guess, but I'm running out of money myself, and you still owe me $20 from last week. And Mom and your friend Bob said you borrowed money from them this past week. How are things going anyway?

M：Well, not very well. To be honest, I'm really in debt, and I can't seem to make ends meet these days.

W：What do you mean? I thought you found a great job recently.

M：Well, I do have a job, but I've used my credit cards to pay off a lot of things recently, but now, I can't seem to pay the money off.

W：Well, let me see if I can help you. How much money do you spend on your apartment?

M：Uh, I pay $890 on rent for the apartment downtown…not including utilities and cable TV. But the place has a wonderful view of the city.

W：Uh, $890! Why are you paying so much for such a small place when you could find a cheaper one somewhere outside of the downtown area?

M：Yeah, I guess.

W：Okay. How much money do you spend on food a month?

M：$600?!

W：And what about transportation?

M：Oh, I commute to work everyday in my new sports car, but I got a great deal, and my monthly payments are only $450. Come outside and take a look. We can go for drive!

W：No, I've heard enough. You've got to cut down on your spending, or you'll end up broke. I suggest you get rid of your credit cards, cut back on your entertainment expenses, and sell your car. Take public transportation from now on.

M：Sell my ear?! I can't date without a car. What am I going to say? "Uh, could you meet me downtown at the bus stop at 7:00? Come on!

W：And you need to create a budget for yourself and stick to it, and start with paying off your bills, starting with me. You owe me $50 dollars.

M：Fifty dollars! Wait, I only borrowed $20 from you last week. How did you come up with $50?

W：Financial consulting fees. My advice is worth at least $30!

Questions 23 to 25 are based on the conversation you have just heard.

23. To whom is the man speaking?

24. How would you describe the man's apartment?

25. What does the woman suggest the man do at the end of the conversation?

Section B
Passage One

In many places in the world today, the poor are getting poorer while the rich are getting richer, and the programs of development planning and foreign aid appear to be unable to reverse this trend. Nearly all the developing countries have a modern part, where the patterns of living and working are similar to those in developed countries. But they also have a non-modern part, where the patterns of living and working are not only unsatisfactory, but in many cases are even getting worse.

What is the typical condition of the poor in developing countries? Their work opportunities are so limited that they cannot work their way out of their situation. They are underemployed, or totally unemployed. Some of them have land, but often too little land.

Many have no land, and no prospect of ever getting any. There is no hope for them in the rural areas, and so they drift into the big cities. But there is no work for them in the big cities, of course no housing. All the same, they flock into the cities because their chances of finding some work appear to be greater there than in the villages. Rural unemployment then becomes urban unemployment.

Questions 26 to 28 are based on the passage you have just heard.

26. What is the trend in the world today?

27. Which of the following statements is not true?

28. What is the main reason that causes the poor to move into the big cities?

Passage Two

Until the twentieth century cigarettes were not an important threat to public health. Since the cigarette industry began in the 1870s, however cigarette manufacturing machines have developed rapidly. This made it possible to produce great numbers of cigarettes very quickly, and it reduced the price.

Today cigarette smoking is a widespread habit. About forty-three percent of the men and thirty-one percent of the adult women in the United States smoke cigarette regularly. It is encouraging to note, however, that millions of people have been giving up the smoking habit.

Income, education, and occupation all play a part in determining a person's smoking habits. City people smoke more than people living on farms. Well-educated men with high income are less likely to smoke cigarette than men with fewer years of schooling and lower incomes. On the other hand, if a well-educated man with a high income smokes at all, he is likely to smoke more packs of cigarettes per day. The situation is somewhat different for women. There are slightly more smokers among women with higher family income and higher education than among the lower income and lower educational groups. These more highly educated women tend to smoke more heavily.

Questions 29 to 32 are based on the passage you have just heard.

29. What reduced the price of cigarette?

30. What is the percentage of American adult women who smoke regularly?

31. What plays a part in determining a person's smoking habit?

32. Which of the following is true according to the passage?

Passage Three

One of New York's most beautiful and valuable buildings is in danger. The New York Public Library, in the heart of the city at 42nd Street and 5th Avenue, may have to close its doors.

The library is a very special place. Even though it is in the busiest part of the city, it has grass and trees around it, and benches for people to sit on.

And what books there are to work with. The library has over thirty million books and paintings. It owns one of the first copies of a Shakespeare play, a Bible printed by Gutenberg in the 15th century, and a letter written by Columbus in which he tells of finding the new world.

Every New Yorker can see and use the library's riches free. But the cost of running the library has risen rapidly in recent years, and the library does not have enough money to continue its work. In the past, it was open every evening and also on Saturdays and Sundays. Now it is closed at those times to save money.

The library is trying in every possible way to raise more money to meet its increasing costs. Well-known New York writers and artists are trying to help. So are the universities, whose students use the library, and the governments of New York City and New York States. But the problem remains serious.

Yet a way must be found to save the library because, as one writer said, "The Public Library is the most important building in New York City—it contains all our knowledge."

Questions 33 to 35 are based on the passage you have just heard.

33. What part of New York City is the Public Library at?

34. Which of the following statements is true?

35. Why is it important to save the library?

Section C

From the top of Temple IV, dense jungle *canopy*(遮篷) spreads to the horizon in every direction. Some 215 feet below lies Tikal, the greatest of the Mayan cities, much of it still **buried** by trees that have swallowed Temple IV up to the base of its **platform**.

Generations of archaeologists have worked to *excavate*(挖掘) this vast city since a Spanish governor rediscovered it in 1848. They're still at work today, clearing trees from nearby temples, searching for **clues** to how the ancient Maya lived and what caused them to **abandon** their great cities six centuries before the Spanish conquest. New inscriptions, villages, even **entire** cities are being discovered every year, **creating** great excitement among archaeologists.

The latest and most **stirring** find was announced on Sept. 8: the discovery of a nearly intact 170-room palace buried at Cancuen, 70 miles south of Tikal. **The palace — a three-story complex built around 11 courtyards — is the largest Mayan palace ever discovered.** It's so large, in fact, that previous expeditions to Cancuen mistook it for a great jungle-covered hill.

Over the past decade, archaeologists have discovered numerous new sites, transforming our understanding of classic Mayan civilization. But what to make of a city abandoned so swiftly? Dr. Hammond finds evidence that the city was in the midst of a massive expansion project when its inhabitants suddenly left. Hammond thinks **the Mayan civilization may have been victims of their own success. Some estimates put the Mayan population in the lowland jungles at a surprising 200 people per square kilometer.** "Just before the collapse, there are more Maya around than ever before, and they're packed into cities that are larger, more numerous, and more closely spaced," he says.

New College English Model Test Three

第一部分　参考答案

Part Ⅰ　Writing

Scholarship Budget

As can be seen from the table, the student spends most of his money on clothing, trip, get-togethers with friends, date and other entertainment, which cost 2500 RMB yuan in total. The money spent on daily necessities, books and VCDs accounts for less than 20 percent.

In my opinion, it is neither reasonable nor beneficial for students to make scholarship budgets like that. Managing money affairs properly can suggest a person's healthy living habit. Judging from this, it is obviously not reasonable for the student to make such an ill-advised budgets. In addition, such an ill-balanced budget will yield little benefit to his study as excessive entertainment costs a person's considerable energy and time.

If I were the student, I would budget my scholarship as follows. Firstly, I would put aside a third of the money in case of the rainy day. As a student, I clearly know the hardships paid for my scholarship. Therefore, I would set aside another big sum for books and instruments essential for my future study. As for the other expenses such as daily necessities, clothing, travel and so on, I would give due consideration within my budget. In the final analysis, every student should learn how to correctly judge his or her own demands for the hard-earned scholarships.

Part Ⅱ   Reading Comprehension（Skimming and Scanning）

1. N   2. Y   3. NG   4. Y   5. N   6. N   7. Y

8. communication /communicating   9. relieved   10. it is a crucial tool

Part Ⅲ   Listening Comprehension

Section A

11. B   12. D   13. A   14. B   15. B   16. C   17. A   18. D   19. B   20. A   21. A   22. D   23. A   24. D   25. C

Section B

26. B   27. C   28. D   29. C   30. C   31. D   32. D   33. D   34. D   35. B

Section C

36. records   37. relation   38. violent   39. addition   40. committed

41. December   42. statistic   43. Apparently

44. made a lot of studies to discover the seasons when people read serious books, attend scientific meetings, make the highest scores on examinations, and suggest the most changes to patents.

45. June is the peak month for suicides and for admitting patients to mental hospitals. June is also a peak month for marriages!

46. There is, of course, no proof of a relation between humidity and murder; why murder's high time should come in the summer time we really don't know

Part Ⅳ   Reading Comprehension（Reading in Depth）

Section A

47. pouring   48. really   49. chief   50. shock   51. occasions

52. despair   53. preliminary   54. worthwhile   55. enormously   56. exclusive

Section B

57. D   58. B   59. C   60. B   61. C   62. B   63. D   64. A   65. D   66. C

Part Ⅴ   Cloze

67. D   68. C   69. A   70. C   71. A   72. D   73. A   74. C   75. B   76. D   77. A   78. D   79. A   80. C   81. B   82. D   83. D   84. D   85. B   86. C

Part Ⅵ   Translation

87. only to show his ignorance of the subject

88. picked several persons at random from the audience

89. would do it in a different way

90. two-thirds of whom are women

91. There's no reason why you shouldn't tell them in advance

第二部分   听力文字稿

Section A

Short dialogues

11. W: I haven't had much exercise lately. My only recreation has been watching TV or going to the

movies. What do you do for recreation?

M: In summer I like playing tennis instead of swimming and boating, and my favorite sport in the winter is skating.

Q: What is the man's favorite sport in summer?

12. M: I'm sorry to have kept you waiting for such a long time. I didn't think the meeting would be so long.

W: That's all right, Dr, Green. I've got the data you required and a few reference books which I think may be useful to your representation at the conference.

Q: What's purpose of the woman's visit to the man?

13. W: Excuse me, Sir. I've been waiting here for nearly 20 minutes long just to pay my telephone bill.

M: I'm sorry about that. But the computer is down, and everybody has had to wait this afternoon.

Q: What's the woman complaining about?

14. M: I just got a statement from the bank. It says I've drawn $ 300 more than I have in my account.

W: Well, we did spend a lot on our vocation. In fact, we didn't know exactly how much was in our bank.

Q: What are they talking about?

15. W: Take a seat, Mr. Brown. Could you tell me which position you think most appeals to you?

M: Well, as for me, I prefer to take the post of sales manager if you think I'm qualified.

Q: What's the man's purpose in meeting the woman?

16. W: Billy, have you heard the latest news? It appears that we won't be laid off after all.

M: Oh, somewhat I'm tired of working here anyway.

Q: What's the man's reaction to the news the woman told him?

17. W: Your room is a mess. When is the last time you tidied your room?

M: It was when Linda came over. She is been so helpful that I simply can't do without her.

Q: What does the man mean?

18. M: I'm terribly sorry, Anna, I lost the magazine you lent me the other day.

W: It doesn't matter, It was a back number any way.

Q: Why doesn't the woman care about the lost magazine?

Long Conversations

Conversation One

Man: You know, Chris, my grandpa told me this story once about his dad. It's actually pretty sad.

Woman: What happened? Ryan.

Man: Well, my grandpa said that his father never hung out with him or played ball or anything because he was really old. I guess my grandpa was born when his dad was like 50 or something.

Woman: Right, so he was too old to play basketball and stuff.

Man: Yeah, and then when my grandpa was about 18 his dad died. The last thing his dad said to him was that he was sorry they could never play ball together.

Woman: Wow that's really sad.

Man: I know. So my grandpa decided he would never let that happen with his kids, and I think he probably told that same story to my dad so that he would remember too.

Woman: That's cool. I think it's so lame that my dad just doesn't get it. He's too busy thinking about work or whatever.

Man: Yeah, maybe you should tell him the story.

Woman: That's a good idea.

Man: Dads can be really thick-headed sometimes but if you tell them enough they will finally understand that you mean it.

Questions 19 to 22 are based on the conversation you have just heard.

19. What did Ryan's grandpa say about his father?

20. What was the last thing grandpa's dad said to him?

21. What does Chris think of Ryan's idea of telling the story to her dad?

22. Why does Ryan think Dads will make some change if children make efforts?

Conversation Two

W: John, have you chosen a physical education class yet for this semester?

M: No. Why?

W: You've got to take rock-climbing. We just had the first class and it looks like it's gonna to be great.

M: You think I should take rock-climbing? You've got to be kidding. Besides, how can they teach rock climbing when it's completely flat around here?

W: That's not important. You can't just start climbing without any training. You have to get in shape, learn how to use the ropes, the belts, there's a lot of preparation first.

M: You don't think it's just a little bit dangerous?

W: Not if you know how to use the safety equipment, which is, by the way, pretty hi-tech. The ropes are made of elastic fabrics that stretch a little, the shoes have special grapes on the bottom and the helmets are made of some kind of special plastic. You have to learn how to use all these before you do any real climbing.

M: Well, what's the appeal? We'll spend the whole semester studying something we don't actually get to do.

W: We will take a climbing trip during spring break. But that's not the point. Climbing is not the only goal. In preparing to climb you learn patience, mental discipline and you gain fantastic physical strength, especially in your hands. For the first few weeks we're going to concentrate entirely on hand and upper body exercises.

M: All that in one sport? Maybe you are right. Since it is not too late to join the class, maybe I will.

Questions 23 to 25 are based on the conversation you have just heard.

23. What is the woman trying to do?

24. What does the man imply about rock-climbing at their college?

25. What will the first few classes focus on?

Section B

Passage One

From the earliest times the sea has been a place of secrets—a place of mysteries hidden from us by thousands of kilograms of water. The early Greeks sailed the oceans. They wrote about the seas. But since they could not dive deep into the waters, they could not lay bare these secrets. And so the secrets remained.

But today we have more ways to study the sea than did the early Greeks. Scientists are learning about life in the sea, and how it may improve life on land.

The study of sea plants and animals may help us to learn new ways of getting food.

Scientists are searching the ocean floor for oil and gas deposits, to keep our world running smoothly. And they are also learning how not to pollute the oceans. For if the sea dies, so dies life on earth. The sea may even become our home someday. People are studying ways to build cities on the ocean, and make more room to live in an overcrowded world.

Modern study was done, at first, by divers. But it was too dangerous for divers to keep diving and coming to the surface.

So now, laboratories on the oceans floor are the homes for divers for months on end. Divers can work outside in the water and returned to the laboratory to eat and sleep.

Little by little we are solving the mysteries of the deep. Little by little the sea is showing us how we can live a better life on land.

Questions 26 to 28 are based on the passage you have just heard.

26. Who wrote about the seas in early times?

27. What kept early people from understanding the sea?

28. What happens if the sea dies?

Passage Two

Although we are told when young that honesty is the best policy, we are often taught the opposite by experience and observation. A child quickly learns that she cannot always tell the truth. For instance, the little girl who tells her great aunt that she's fat and ugly learns that honesty can have some unfortunate results. Similarly the five-year-old who admits to pinching the baby soon has ample evidence that dishonesty might be the real virtue. In addition to her own experience, the child also observes that adults don't practice what they preach about honesty. Any alert child knows by the age of eight that adults really employ the little white lie to serve their own purposes. For instance, a child may hear a parent explain on the phone that his family have a lot of company when the child knows that no one is there but family members. Another child may hear her mother insist that she's terribly glad to see an old friend who has dropped by and then, two hours later, hear her mother complain about her day being interrupted by the visit. As a result, the child learns from watching that dishonesty is the practice even when honesty is the stated policy.

Questions 29 to 32 are based on the passage you have just heard.

29. What does the child learn after he tells the truth according to the speaker?

30. What does the child learn by observing adults?

31. What does the speaker imply about the topic?

32. How is the passage organized?

Passage Three

Today I'd like to continue to talk about the reason why the United States developed at such a high speed in the past 400 years; there are many factors. The land has an abundance of natural resources and includes some of the best farmland in the world. People from many countries settled there, bringing with them a wealth of knowledge and skills. But in the last 100 years it has been the workingman that has been the backbone of the nation.

What is the American workingman? He's a worker in a shoe factory or a meat packing-house or a coal mine. But more than that, he's a husband and a father. He raised his children to understand the value of a day's work. He raised his children to respect the usefulness of cooperation. And he raised his children to help them better themselves. Seldom do their children forget the values they have learnt at home.

The workingman fought hard for almost all his life to achieve what he has, but today the workingman is faced with a new kind of struggle. Ever-advancing technology is taking his job. It's very probable that the workingman will be replaced by a machine.

Questions 33 to 35 are based on the passage you have just heard.

33. Which of the following is not mentioned in the passage?

34. What's the main reason why the United States developed so rapidly?

35. What is the workingman faced with now?

Section C

Crime has its own cycles, a magazine reported some years ago. Police **records** that were studied for five years from over 2 400 cities and towns show a surprising **relation** between changes in the season and crime patterns.

The pattern of crime has changed very little over a long period of years. Murder reaches its high during July and August, as do other **violent** attacks. Murder, in **addition**, is more than seasonal; it is a weekend crime. It is also a nighttime crime: 62 percent of murders are **committed** between 6 p. m. and 6 a. m.

Unlike the summer high in crimes of bodily harm, break and enter or "B and E" has a different cycle. You are most likely to be robbed between 6 p. m. and 2 a. m. on a Saturday night in **December**, January, or February. Which is the least criminal month of all? May—except for one strange **statistic**. More dog bites are reported in this month than in any other month of the year.

Apparently our intellectual seasonal cycles are completely different from our criminal patterns. Professor Huntington, of the Foundation for the Study of Cycles, **made a lot of studies to discover the seasons when people read serious books, attend scientific meetings, make the highest scores on examinations, and suggest the most changes to patents.** In all examples, he found a spring peak and an autumn peak separated by a summer low.

On the other hand, Professor Huntington's studies showed that **June is the peak month for suicides and for admitting patients to mental hospitals. June is also a peak month for marriages!** Possibly, high temperature and humidity bring on our strange and surprising summer actions, but police officers are not sure. **"There is, of course, no proof of a relation between humidity and murder; why murder's high time should come in the summer time we really don't know,"** they say.

New College English Model Test Four

第一部分　参考答案

Part Ⅰ　Writing

Student Use of the Internet

Students tend to use the Internet more and more frequently nowadays. The chart shows that the average number of hours a student spends on the Net per week has increased dramatically. For example, in 1995, it was less than 2 hours. In 2000, it increased to almost 4 hours, and in 2004, the number climbed to about 18 hours per week.

There are several reasons behind this phenomenon. First, easy access to the Net attracts more and more students. Obviously, the rapid spread of personal computers, telephones and Internet cafes make it easy to go online. In addition, the Internet facilitates many aspects of life such as communicating via E-mail and chat-room on line.

However, there still exist some problems. What troubles schools a lot is the harmful materials and false information, which will surely adversely affect students' healthy development. Besides, online charges may be too expensive for students to pay, adding great financial burden to their families. What's worse, some students indulge in computer games and the virtual world, resulting in their failure in the academic work.

My advice is to use the Internet but do it properly.

Part Ⅱ　Reading Comprehension (Skimming and Scanning)

1. Y　2. N　3. NG　4. Y　5. NG　6. N　7. Y

8. express themselves　9. talking openly about a problem　10. committing suicide

Part Ⅲ　Listening Comprehension

Section A

11. C　12. B　13. A　14. B　15. A　16. D　17. C　18. A　19. C　20. D　21. C　22. D

23. D 24. B 25. A

Section B

26. A 27. D 28. B 29. B 30. C 31. D 32. A 33. D 34. C 35. B

Section C

36. directed 37. efficient 38. totally 39. constantly 40. individuals

41. united 42. conduct 43. cooperation

44. Without clear guidelines mutually agreeable to students, teachers, and administration, the classroom can become chaotic.

45. No matter how skillful the teacher is in uniting students and establishing a positive atmosphere, the task is never complete.

46. Sometimes outside pressures such as holidays, upcoming tests or athletic contests, or family troubles cause stress in the classroom.

Part Ⅳ   Reading Comprehension（Reading in Depth）

Section A

47. permanent 48. sector 49. disabilities 50. circumstances 51. flexible

52. negotiate 53. package 54. committed 55. applicants 56. assess

Section B

57. C 58. C 59. A 60. D 61. A 62. D 63. C 64. C 65. A 66. C

Part Ⅴ   Cloze

67. D 68. A 69. C 70. B 71. B 72. C 73. D 74. D 75. A 76. B 77. C 78. C

79. A 80. B 81. A 82. A 83. D 84. B 85. A 86. C

Part Ⅵ   Translation

87. taking strict measures to control pollution

88. will have risen by about 10%

89. the new electronic instrument should be tested at once

90. regardless of the consequences

91. No sooner had we reached this conclusion

第二部分　听力文字稿

Section A

Short dialogues

11. W：It's a pity you missed the concert yesterday evening. It was wonderful!

    M：I didn't want to miss the football game. Well, I'm not a classical music fan anyway.

    Q：What do we learn from the conversation?

12. W：Hey! If you can't enjoy that at a sensible volume, please use earphones. I'm trying study.

    M：Oh! I'm sorry. I didn't realize it was bothering you.

    Q：What is the man probably doing?

13. M：Can I help you, Ms?

    W：Yes, I bought this telephone last week, and it works all right with out-going calls, but it doesn't ring for the incoming ones.

    Q：What's the problem with the woman's telephone?

14. W：I thought Tom said he got A's in all his tests.

    M：Mary, you should know better than to take Tom's words too seriously.

    Q：What does the man imply?

15. W：Can you show me how to use this, John?

M: It is fully automatic. All you have to do is focus on the scene and press the button here.

Q: What are they talking about?

16. M: I think we should move on to the next item.

W: Ok. But I'd like to take this matter up again at the end of the meeting.

Q: What does the woman imply?

17. W: You know, the Browns have invested all their money in stocks.

M: They may think that's a wise move, but that's the last thing I'd do.

Q: What's the man's opinion about the Browns' investment?

18. M: What is Mr. Peterson going to do with his old house on London Road? Rent it or sell it?

W: I heard he is thinking of turning it into a restaurant, which isn't a bad idea, because it's still a solid building.

Q: What will Mr. Peterson do with his old house?

Long Conversations

Conversation One

W: Hi, Li Hua. What are you doing this semester?

M: Oh, I'm still learning English. I have to do one more semester before I can start my real studies at the university.

W: You make it sound like prison. How are the classes?

M: They're all right, I guess. I don't know. It seems like they never tell us what we really need to know.

W: What do you mean?

M: Look, when I study mathematics, for instance, we start with definitions. Then we have problems and some equations and processes to learn. You go to class, you keep up, you do the homework, and you know it. You pass exams. But English class is quite different. First of all, they don't want to teach us all the rules. They tell us one rule. Fine. We use that rule, but soon it won't work. It's more complicated or there are a lot of exceptions or something. Sometimes I think the teachers don't know the rules either.

W: But you don't learn a language from the rules, anyway. You have to use it.

M: Yes. That's something else they tell us. But why can't we just go to class, study, and do our homework? That's what I know how to do.

W: Look at this way, can you learn to play soccer by sitting at home and reading about soccer?

M: No, of course not. Not if you want to play well.

W: But why not? You could understand the rules of strategy, the duties of each position, and all the special situations. You have to feel the ball, practice kicking it hundreds of times, practice running down the field, moving toward the goal, and centering the ball. No one can learn that by passively studying. Learning a language is more like learning to play soccer than learning mathematics. You have to ask a lot of questions and hear how the answers sound. You have to listen to how people indicate the important part of what they're saying. And then of course endless practice on all the details—spelling, "s" endings, articles. . . just like practice in simple dribbling and kicking.

M: But if it's a skill like soccer, not a science, why do they teach it in schools and universities, and give you diplomas and grades?

W: That's a good question. It is confusing, but languages are important and people do want to learn them. But the main thing is to practice the language a lot, just like soccer.

M: Maybe I'll join a soccer team and practice English and soccer at the same time. I can talk with people before and after the practice.

W: That's a good idea.

Questions 19 to 22 are based on the conversation you have just heard.

19. What is mainly discussed in the conversation?

20. What is the purpose of Li Hua's learning English?

21. Which of the following can describe the woman's opinion?

22. What can be inferred from the conversation?

Conversation Two

W: Dave. I'm going to the supermarket to pick up food and drink for Saturday's picnic. Any suggestions?

M: Well, everyone has been talking about having a barbecue down by the river, so why don't you pick up some hamburger and hot dogs?

W: Okay, but how much hamburger are we going to need? And hot dogs too?

M: Uh, I don't know. How about three pounds of hamburger and a couple packages of hot dogs?

W: Oh, that's not going to be enough. Do you remember the last picnic we went on? Your roommate, Jim, ate about ten hamburgers by himself!

M: You're right. Let's see. I'd better write this down. Uh, let's see about nine pounds of hamburger meat and, uh ..., seven packages of hot dogs.

W: And you'd better pick up some chicken for those who don't like hamburger or hot dogs.

M: Okay. How about five or six bags of potato chips?

W: Humm. Better make that eight or so.

M: All right. Oh, and we're gonna need some hamburger and hot dog buns, How about five packages a piece? I think that sounds about right.

W: Yeah, you'd better pick up some mustard, catchup, and mayonnaise too.

M: Okay. What else? Uh, we're gonna need some soft drinks. How about ten of those big 2-liter bottles?

W: Sounds fine, but be sure to buy a variety of drinks.

M: Okay. And what about dessert?

W: Well, maybe we could ask Kathy to make a few cherry pies like she did last time.

M: Well, I heard that she's been very busy working two jobs, so we'd better not ask her, uh ... Hey, why don't you whip up some of your oatmeal cookies? Hey, you could even ask, uh .... what's her name ...yeah that new girl, Susan, the one that moved in across the street! I bet she'd be willing to help you!

W: Nah, I don't think I could ask her, I haven't got a phone number. Anyway, I can try myself.

Questions 23 to 25 are based on the conversation you have just heard.

23. Where is the picnic being held?

24. How many packages of hot dogs do they decide to buy?

25. Why has Kathy been so busy lately?

Section B

Passage One

I'm Mr. Britain, the head librarian, and today I'd like to introduce you to the facilities in our university library and show you how to use them. The first room on your tour is the reference room, where you will find all sorts of materials: dictionaries, bibliographies, literature guides, even telephone books. You may use these books only in the reference room itself. The next room is the periodicals room, where you'll find various newspapers, magazines and academic journals. The current issues are usually directly available to you on the shelves. And you can get an older issue by filing out a slip for the librarian. These items must also be used in this room. This next room contains the card catalogs. All the library's books are listed here by title, by author and by topic. When you are looking for a book you must write the book's call number, title and author on these slips and present them with your library card at the desk. The books themselves are kept in the stacks, which are open only to graduate students, faculty members and library staff. Our library has over a million volumes in these stacks which cover five floors. If you have any further questions about using the library, I'd be glad to help you after the tour. Thank you for your attention.

Questions 26 to 28 are based on the passage you have just heard.

26. What is the main topic of this talk?

27. Who is probably listening to Mr. Britain?

28. Which people are usually not allowed to use the stacks?

Passage Two

Why do people smoke?

One reason is that people become addicted to cigarettes. The addictive substance in cigarettes is nicotine. When people smoke, the nicotine goes right into the blood stream and makes people feel relaxed. A smoker's body gets accustomed to the nicotine and if he stops smoking he feels nervous. Many smokers try to stop smoking but because of the addiction to nicotine they feel so uncomfortable that they often find it too difficult to stop.

Another reason is that people simply enjoy smoking. Having a cigarette for many people means taking a break. For some people smoking becomes part of their daily life. Many people enjoy smoking because it gives them something to do with their hands.

Many people also like the taste of tar in cigarettes. However, it is the tar that causes cancer. While governments and health experts have tried to get people to give up smoking entirely, cigarette manufacturers have tried to keep selling them by producing cigarettes with less tar. Many people in western countries have welcomed these cigarettes since they find it hard to stop smoking but they want to reduce the risk to their health.

Questions 29 to 32 are based on the passage you have just heard.

29. Why do so many people become addicted to cigarettes?

30. What is the substance in cigarettes that causes cancer?

31. What are health experts trying to persuade people to do?

32. Why do smokers welcome low—tar cigarettes?

Passage Three

Spacemen have to be specially trained for traveling in space. They should be in very good mental and physical health. Most of them are experienced pilots of very fast aeroplanes.

All spacemen have to do various space exercises before traveling to space. They have to be strong enough to bear the great pressures they will feel at launching and landing. When traveling in space or orbiting round a planet, spacemen have to become used to the weightless conditions and learn how to walk, eat, drink and sleep in a condition of weightlessness. They train for their space travels in model spacecraft, which are like the actual spacecraft. Spacemen also have to know all about the various parts of their spacecraft. They should be able to repair any part that is damaged while traveling.

When man goes into space he must take air, food and water. He must also get rid of bad air and waste matter. Food is prepared in a paste form and kept in tubes. Waste is stored in containers and got rid of when the spacecraft reaches the Earth. These problems have been solved for short space trips, but not for long trips.

Questions 33 to 35 are based on the passage you have just heard.

33. What do spacemen need for space traveling?

34. What do spacemen have to become used to?

35. Which of the following is not the necessary thing that spacemen must take?

Section C

Teaching involves more than leadership. Some of the teacher's time and effort is **directed** toward instruction, some toward evaluation. But it is the teacher as a group leader who creates an **efficient** organizational structure and good working environment so that instruction and evaluation activities can take place. A group that is **totally** disorganized, unclear about its goals, or constantly fighting among its members will not be a good learning group. The leadership pattern includes helping to form and maintain a positive learning environment so that instruction and evaluation activities can take place.

On the first day of class, the teacher faces a room filled with **individuals.** Perhaps a few closely **united** groups and friendships already exist. But there is no sense of group unity, no set of rules for **conduct** in the group, no feeling of belonging. If teachers are successful leaders, they will help students develop a system of relationships that encourages **cooperation.**

Standards and rules must be established that maintain order, ensure justice, and protect individual rights, but do not *contradict*（与…矛盾）school policy. What happens when one student hurts another's individual rights? **Without clear guidelines mutually agreeable to students, teachers, and administration, the classroom can become chaotic.** Students may break rules they did not know existed. If standards are set without input from the class, students may spend a great deal of creative energy in ruining the class environment, finding ways to break rules.

No matter how skillful the teacher is in uniting students and establishing a positive atmosphere, the task is never complete. Regular maintenance is necessary. Conflicts arise. The needs of individual members change. A new kind of learning task requires a new organizational structure. **Sometimes outside pressures such as holidays, upcoming tests or athletic contests, or family troubles cause stress in the classroom.** One task for the teacher is to restore a positive environment by helping students cope with conflict, change, and stress.

New College English Model Test Five

第一部分　参考答案

Part Ⅰ　Writing

A Letter to the Editor-in- chief about A Newly-Published English Magazine

Dear Editor-in-Chief,

My name is Li Ming, a regular reader of your English magazine. Young as it is, this magazine has grown in popularity among us students, which is mainly attributed to its outstanding characteristics.

Firstly, with quite a few exquisite illustrations, the magazine's new page layout so impresses me that I cannot help picking it up and looking it through. What's more important, your magazine offers a huge amount of valuable reading materials for readers at various levels. For example, "news channel" helps us keep track of what's happening around the world. "classical prose" and "corner of literature" turn out to be the best choice for literature lovers. "CET（Band 4 and 6）" offers practical guidance to prepare us well for the examination, which arouses much concern for many college students. By the way, the reasonable price distinguishes your magazine from others so that we college students can easily afford it.

May I put forward a suggestion? Would you mind providing cassettes for the articles of your magazine so that we can practise our listening and oral English as we appreciate the beautiful lines?

Wish your magazine a greater success in time to come.

Yours sincerely,

Li Ming

Part Ⅱ　Reading Comprehension（Skimming and Scanning）

1. NG　　2. N　　3. Y　　4. Y　　5. N　　6. N　　7. Y

8. genes　　9. lifestyle　　10. recess and physical education

Part Ⅲ　Listening Comprehension

Section A

11. C　12. A　13. A　14. C　15. C　16. D　17. C　18. A　19. A　20. C　21. A　22. B

23. B　24. C　25. B

Section B

26. C　27. A　28. A　29. B　30. D　31. B　32. D　33. B　34. D　35. A

Section C

36. pilots　　　　37. incidents　　38. unconfirmed　　39. blame　　40. mobile

41. recommended　42. stages　　43. total

44. although some airlines prohibit passengers from using such equipment during take-off and landing，most are reluctant to enforce a total ban

45. Experts know that portable devices emit radiation which affects those wavelengths which aircraft use for navigation and communication.

46. The fact that aircraft may be vulnerable to interference raises the risk that terrorists may use radio systems in order to damage navigation equipment.

Part Ⅳ　Reading Comprehension（Reading in Depth）

Section A

47. religious　　48. inconveniences　　49. resorts　　50. solid　　　51. attracts

52. handle　　53. garbage　　　　54. spoiling　　55. Obviously　　56. tolerate

Section B

57. B　58. D　59. C　60. B　61. D　62. A　63. D　64. D　65. D　66. A

Part Ⅴ　Cloze

67. D　68. A　69. D　70. A　71. C　72. A　73. C　74. D　75. B　76. C　77. A　78. D

79. C　80. B　81. A　82. D　83. A　84. A　85. D　86. C

Part Ⅵ　Translation

87. on condition that you don't lend it to others

88. a great weight taken off my mind

89. who wished to have more chance to speak English

90. many problems remain to be solved

91. (should) have failed to see her own shortcomings

第二部分　听力文字稿

Section A

Short dialogues

11. M：Could you please tell me what room Robert Davis is in?

　　W：Yes，he's in the intensive care unit on the fourth floor. I suggest that you check with the nurse's station before going in though.

　　Q：Where did this conversation most probably take place?

12. M：Why do you look so worried? Only one person finished ahead of you last time.

　　W：Well，this time I want to make sure I come in first.

　　Q：Why is the woman worried?

13. M：I went to New York yesterday but I forgot to call Barry.

W: Barry wouldn't have been there anyway. He's an economist in California now.

Q: What information does the man find out?

14. M: It only takes two hours to get to New York, but you'll have a six-hour layover between flights.

W: Oh, that's all right. I don't mind having the time in New York. I still have a few things to shop for.

Q: How many hours will the woman be in New York?

15. M: We don't have to start for the stadium yet. Wouldn't you like something else?

W: No, thanks. You'd better tell her to bring our check. It'll take a while to find a parking place, especially with so many star players involved.

Q: Where are the man and woman going?

16. M: I'd like to buy a ten-dollar ticket to Friday's concert.

W: That'll put you on the floor. The tickets in the lower balcony are five dollars while the upper balcony seats are two-fifty.

Q: What is the man's ticket for?

17. M: We'll have to hurry if we're going to be on time to the airport. It's already 8:30.

W: Well, it takes only half an hour to get to the airport, and the plane doesn't leave until 9:15. I think we'll make it all right if we leave immediately.

Q: How much time is the couple allowing once they get to the airport?

18. M: Your son is only badly bruised. In a couple of days he'll be well enough to go back to climbing trees.

W: He won't be climbing any more trees if I can help it. A fall like that could have killed him.

Q: What happened to the boy?

Long Conversations

Conversation One

M: Hi, Shelly! How was your vacation?

W: Great! I went to New Orleans.

M: Really? Why did you decide to go there?

W: Well, I have a cousin who lives there. She's been trying to get me to take a vacation down there for a long time, and so finally, she talked me into it.

M: How did you get there?

W: Well, at first 1 was going to drive, but my cousin said parking is a big problem there, so I flew. Once I was there, I took buses and taxis.

M: I've seen some pictures of New Orleans—the architecture there is really interesting, isn't it?

W: Yeah, it's incredible, especially in the French Quarter and in the Garden District where my cousin lives. And I love the spicy food there, and the music, of course. My cousin took me to some great little restaurants and jazz clubs.

M: How was the weather when you were there?

W: That's the only thing I didn't enjoy. It was really hot and sticky.

M: Wasn't New Orleans originally a French city?

W: Yes, the French founded it. And then the king of France gave it to the king of Spain, and later the French took it over again. And then the French sold it to the United States along with the rest of the Louisiana Purchase.

M: I remember reading in a history book about the battle of New Orleans. That was during the War of 1812, wasn't it?

W: Right. The Americans under Andrew Jackson fought a battle with the British near there. In fact, Jackson Square in the French Quarter is named after him.

M: Well, it sure sounds like you had a great time.

W: Oh, I sure did. And I plan to go back there next spring for my birthday.

Questions 19 to 22 are based on the conversation you've just heard.

19. What were the speakers primarily discussing?

20. How did the woman get to New Orleans?

21. What was the aspect of New Orleans that the woman didn't enjoy?

22. According to the woman, what role did Andrew Jackson play in the history of New Orleans?

Conversation Two

Man: Are you close to your parents?

Woman: Yeah, we're close. My father and I have always been close. Sometimes my mom and I don't really see eye to eye. What about you?

Man: Well, I think my parents definitely don't understand me. My mother always says I'm perfect while my father often criticizes me for doing things wrong.

Woman: That's interesting. Do you think that's just a generational thing?

Man: Well, I don't know. My parents grew up in the 60's. But they didn't seem to know much about their times.

Woman: So they were kept away from all the big social activities?

Man: Yeah. They grew up in a small town and neither of them knew anything about politics, even though my father's father was a local judge and lawyer.

Woman: My parents grew up in the 60's too, but my dad taught physics at the university and my mom ran a small bookstore in town. I guess they were the kind of people who were open to current events.

Man: I'm jealous. Sometimes I feel a lot more educated than my parents, which is fine, but also uncomfortable at times.

Woman: I can imagine.

Man: They just don't understand some things. They haven't experienced life in the same way I have.

Woman: You mean the traveling you've done?

Man: Yeah. My dad thinks I ran away from home because I hated him or something ridiculous like that. I just wanted to see the world.

Woman: I told my dad once that I'd find a way to study in America and then live there forever.

Man: My dad always tells me that I'd be really homesick if I studied at a European university.

Woman: And then you have to remind him that Europe is only 10 hours away by plane.

Questions 23 to 25 are based on the conversation you've just heard.

23. What are the two speakers are mainly talking about?

24. What does the man complain about?

25. What does the woman think of her parents?

Section B

Passage One

Last summer I was working in Washington, D. C., as an intern at the Armed Forces Institute of Pathology. In one way it was an awful job because the purpose was to figure out ways to identify dead people, like identifying the remains of soldiers in wars, or bodies after disasters such as plane crashes or earthquakes. But the exciting part was that I was working with a scientist who heads a program that is identifying bodies by their DNA structures. As you know, DNA is the name for the genetic material in our bodies. In the past, all soldiers had to wear a necklace and a metal tag with their names and identification numbers on the tag. But this method of identification was not very accurate because the tags could be lost or switched around. So in my job I worked at helping the Institute to set up a DNA file to store the genetic information for new soldiers. The armed forces will get a blood sample from each person in the military. Then, if the body of a military person cannot be identified by its tag, fingerprints, or dental records, the body tissue can be analyzed and matched with DNA records at the Institute.

Questions 26 to 28 are based on the passage you have just heard.

26. What is the purpose of the program the woman is discussing?

27. What did the speaker say was exciting about her work?

28. In what class would the students most likely be making this presentation?

Passage Two

In America, where labor costs are so high, "do it yourself" is a way of life. May people repair their own cars, build their own garages, even rebuild their own houses. Soon many of them will also be writing their own books. In Hollywood there is a company that publishes children's books with the help of computers. Although other book companies also publish that way, this company is not like the others. It allows the reader to become the leading character in the stories with the help of computers. Here is how they do it. Let us suppose the child is named Jenny. She lives in New York, and has a dog named Hody. The computer uses this information to make up a story with pictures. The story is then printed up. A child who receives such a book might say, "This book is about me," so the company calls itself the "Me-books Publishing Company."

Children like the me-books because they like to see their own names in print and the names of their friends and their pets. But more important, in this way, readers are much more interested in reading the stories. Me-books are helping a child to learn how to read.

Questions 29 to 31 are based on the passage you have just heard.

29. Why do Americans do most things themselves?

30. What distinguishes the company mentioned in the passage from the others?

31. What are the "Me-books"?

Passage Three

In today's class we'll be examining some nineteenth-century pattern books that were used for building houses. I think it's fair today that these pattern books were the most important influence on the design of North American houses during the nineteenth century.

This was because most people who wanted to build a house couldn't afford to hire an architect. Instead, they bought a pattern book, picked out a plan, and took it to the builder. The difference in cost was substantial. In 1870, for example, hiring an architect would have cost about a hundred dollars. At the same time, a pattern book written by an architect cost only five dollars.

At that price, it's easy to see why pattern books were so popular. Some are back in print again today, and of course they cost a lot more than they did a hundred years ago. But they're an invaluable resource for historians, and also for people who restore old houses. I have a modern reprint here that I'll be passing around the room in a moment so that everyone can have a look.

Questions 32 to 35 are based on the passage you have just heard.

32. What was in pattern books?

33. What course would this talk be most appropriate for?

34. According to the speaker, why were pattern books so popular?

35. According to the speaker, who uses pattern books today?

Section C

The biggest safety threat facing airlines today may not be a terrorist with a gun, but the man with the portable computer in business class. In the last 15 years, **pilots** have reported well over 100 **incidents** that could have been caused by electromagnetic interference. The source of this interference remains **unconfirmed**, but increasingly, experts are pointing the **blame** at portable electronic devices such as portable computers, radio and cassette players and **mobile** telephones.

RTCA, an organization which advises the aviation industry, has **recommended** that all airlines ban such devices from being used during "critical" **stages** of flight, particularly take-off and landing. Some experts have gone further, calling for a **total** ban during all flights. Currently, rules on using these devices are left up to individual airlines. And **although some airlines prohibit passengers from using such equipment during take-off and landing, most are reluctant to enforce a total ban**, given that many passengers want to work during flights.

The difficulty is predicting how electromagnetic fields might affect an aircraft's computers. **Experts know that portable devices emit radiation which affects those wavelengths which aircraft use for navigation and communication.** But, because they have not been able to reproduce these effects in a laboratory, they have no way of knowing whether the interference might be dangerous or not. **The fact that aircraft may be vulnerable to interference raises the risk that terrorists may use radio systems in order to damage navigation equipment.**

第三章　单项强化篇

第一节　阅读演练篇

Part Ⅰ　Reading Comprehension(Reading in Depth)

1~5 ADCBC	6~10 DACDB	11~15 ACDAC	16~20 BADBC	21~25 CBBAA
26~30 BDDCA	31~35 DACAD	36~40 BACAD	41~45 BCDDC	46~50 CBAAD
51~55 BBADB	56~60 ABCDC	61~65 DBCCA	66~70 DBADC	71~75 BBDCA
76~80 CADBC	81~85 CABDB	86~90 ACADD	91~95 ACBDD	96~100 ADBAB
101~105 ADCBA	106~110 CBDCD	111~115 DBDAC	116~120 BBBCD	121~125 CABCA
126~130 BDDAC	131~135 BDCBA	136~140 BACDD	141~145 DDABC	146~150 ACBAD
151~155 ABCBC	156~160 DBCBD			

Part Ⅱ　Reading Comprehension (Skimming and Scanning)

Passage 1

1. Y　2. NG　3. N　4. NG　5. Y　6. N　7. Y

8. matches the kind of person you are

9. what you can do and how well you are capable of performing/your talents and skills

10. 8

Passage 2

1. N　2. N　3. Y　4. Y　5. NG　6. Y　7. Y

8. burying and burning　9. natural resources　10. return to the soil safely or recycled indefinitely

Passage 3

1. N　2. Y　3. Y　4. Y　5. N　6. NG　7. Y　8. Parts of speech，8

9. Old English，Middle English and Modern English　10. coined new terms，borrowed words

Passage 4

1~5 BBCAD　6~7 CD　8. use our imaginations

9. create better public policies　10. the purchasing power of a person or a nation

Passage 5

1. N　2. Y　3. NG　4. N　5. NG　6. Y　7. NG

8. most of its refractive power　9. inner ears　10. touch sensor

Passage 6

1. Y　2. N　3. Y　4. Y　5. N　6. NG　7. NG　8. one-third

9. glaciers and ice caps　10. herbicides and pesticides, nitrates and nitrogen-rich fertilizer

Passage 7

1. Y　2. N　3. NG　4. N　5. Y　6. N　7. Y　8. complaint

9. Education Inspection and Review Request Form　10. height, weight, sport participation

Passage 8

1. N　2. N　3. Y　4. NG　5. Y　6. Y　7. N

8. more than half　9. being supervised　10. media influence

Part Ⅲ　Reading Comprehension(Blanks-Filling)

Passage 1

| 1. conduct | 2. hinders | 3. consist | 4. president | 5. discipline |
| 6. reliability | 7. dulls | 8. underlying | 9. acquisition | 10. occasions |

Passage 2

| 1. impression | 2. barrier | 3. automatically | 4. fundamental | 5. essentially |
| 6. concerned | 7. undergo | 8. sustain | 9. spectator | 10. devices |

Passage 3

| 1. considerably | 2. reared | 3. handicapped | 4. attain | 5. demonstrated |
| 6. processes | 7. foster | 8. isolated | 9. intellectually | 10. roughly |

Passage 4

| 1. unlikely | 2. charms | 3. accounts | 4. overseas | 5. scale |
| 6. identified | 7. innovative | 8. crucial | 9. facilitate | 10. enterprise |

Passage 5

| 1. abandoned | 2. authorities | 3. foreseeable | 4. undoubtedly | 5. economical |
| 6. automated | 7. attached | 8. monitor | 9. route | 10. handle |

第三节　翻译演练篇

Translation Test One

1. enter and edit your text more easily

2. on this happy occasion

3. why so many people in that region/area like to wear dresses of such dull/dark colors.

4. Were they to arrive before we depart/set off/out the day after tomorrow

5. took effective measures to control the increasing prices/ bring the increasing price under control

Translation Test Two

1. to acquire the skills they need to succeed/achieve success

2. they should be attacked by wild animals

3. passengers must have died at the very moment of the crash

4. at the expense/cost/price/sacrifice of the consumers' interests

5. whether it is worthwhile to make so much (painstaking) effort

Translation Test Three

1. devoted half as much money and effort to

2. Judging from In light of the number of cars

3. no matter what we may have done during the day

4. Whatever /What he saw and heard on /during his trip

5. making his own clothes

Translation Test Four

1. whether they are liquid or solid/be they liquid or solid

2. in harmony with all wildlife

3. it will have won twenty races in the past three years

4. that she will be disappointed if I don't

5. their making such buying decisions

Translation Test Five

1. (catch) cold because of the variable /changeable weather here in autumn

2. there will be widespread unemployment/ there will be huge number of people who are out of job/ employment/jobless

3. those who do well in school are those who have a large /sizable vocabulary

4. in place of /to replace /to take the place of the traditional /conventional energy forms

5. If we had agreed to buy the car right away/immediately/at once

Translation Test Six

1. Because the police couldn't identify who the criminal was

2. couldn't/wouldn't have finished the design on schedule /on time

3. what we think the likely result of the action will be

4. If you had told us earlier who he was /Had you told us earlier who he was

5. earned on loans

Translation Test Seven

1. separating fact from fiction

2. a special committee be set up to investigate the incident

3. the mother had insisted on her right to keep the baby/child

4. In view of/Considering his ability and competence

5. dealing with complex problems

Translation Test Eight

1. play essential /indispensable roles

2. The key to the success of this plan /project

3. followed my advice，you would not be in trouble/get into such trouble

4. even though some people object to/are against/are opposed to it openly/in public

5. that I cannot concentrate on my study

Translation Test Nine

1. my wife and I encountered an unexpected challenge

2. Special emphasis should be laid on tolerance

3. allows /enables you to have more time to focus on designing skills

4. Although the rising material costs can be mostly /to a large extent attributed to

5. which in many ways are similar to those needed by people in other service professions

Translation Test Ten

1. did I realize the meaning of my parents' words

2. you can drive on your own/by yourself

3. she found herself faced with a lot of difficulties

4. the child (should) catch cold

5. whose work had contributed /made contribution to the success of the meeting/conference